MARKED BY MASKS AND SECRETS

MAGGIE SUNSERI

CONTENT WARNINGS

For a list of content warnings please visit Maggie Sunseri's website: maggiesunseri.com.

For generational cycle breakers, shadow integrators, wounded healers, and those blessed with sensitive, intuitive hearts.

This world needs you.

1

KYLO

The first time I saw her, I thought she was an angel.

She was a celestial being of light, an innocent lamb dressed in a delicate white dress that gently billowed in the wind. A vulnerable, wide-eyed, tiny little creature.

She was everything that I was not.

She was everything I'd forsaken the day I turned.

And her scent—gods above and below—her *scent*. My fangs ached painfully in my gums. It was abnormal for a signature to be this potent from so far away.

I watched her from across the city square. Gentle rays of morning sun illuminated her long blonde hair. When she moved a piece out of her face, I held my breath, imagining how the feathery-soft strands would feel against my own calloused fingers.

She lugged an empty merchant's wagon behind her, as if she'd already sold all her goods for the day. Questions about what she sold and to whom burned in my mind. It was an unquenchable need to know exactly who she was and who'd sent her to ruin my perfect focus.

Her light pink wagon rattled against the cobblestone, and

1

she made an adorable little huff when the wheels caught in a dip, and she had to pull it free.

I rose to my feet, nostrils flaring and teeth grinding together. My gaze traced the delicate floral detailing on the skirt of her dress and the white sneakers stained green and brown as if she frequently traipsed through meadows.

When she weaved through a mass of people and crossed the street, this strange and uncharacteristic insanity didn't cease.

It multiplied.

I couldn't help but follow her—this vulnerable little forest nymph, oblivious to the predator who was homed in on her fluttering jugular.

I forgot about today's agenda. My careful strategizing could wait. Harmony had been scolding me for months about *balance* and *fun* and *taking time for myself.*

This was likely not what she'd had in mind, but progress was progress.

At least, this was the careful justification I was crafting about my current morally questionable behavior.

My delicate distraction moved through the streets with purpose, unaware of the beast stalking her from the shadows. She was lost in her own world, only looking up to sneak peeks at the colorful boutiques, flower and crystal shops, and storefronts decorated with blooming flowers and greenery. Her longest pause was in front of a bookstore, where she eyed one of the new fiction novels on display in the front window. I made a mental note of the title.

She didn't greet anyone, nor did she entertain the men who nodded or smiled or leered her way.

My lip curled into a snarl. Violence bubbled under my skin as I stared at one of those men who'd turned to his friend to whisper something vile.

It would be a shame if his tongue went missing.

When we reached a residential neighborhood, a few drops of

sanity finally penetrated through my primal need to hunt my blonde angel.

What the *fuck* was I doing?

That question rattled around in my immortal brain as I watched her climb a steep hill to an expansive, opulent estate. Marble columns lined the front, seating arranged on the vast front porch. Flowers bloomed in meticulous landscaping, and large oak and willow trees stood scattered around the property.

Of course, she was a wealthy little mortal princess.

It was strange—her blood was distinctively human, yet it was also stronger, like a witch's or shifter's. She smelled of morning dew and wildflowers, honey and springtime, with an elusive, darker note I couldn't quite place. Perhaps if I were closer to her, I'd be able to uncover all the fragments of her essence.

I should've stopped this madness when I watched her disappear around the back of the mansion.

But, I didn't.

I cloaked myself in shadow before climbing the cobblestone path. It was a skill I hadn't yet perfected, but I'd be able to hold the glamour for a short while.

As long as I was careful and kept my distance, I'd be fine. Then I could pretend this never happened, and I could go back to vastly more important matters.

That was all this was—a consequence of working too long of hours year after year, letting myself become consumed by my ambition without a single break in focus.

I'd always been prone to obsession. It was a predisposition that was often rewarded in games of power and domination.

Under the canopy of a massive willow tree, I watched the blonde princess read on a blanket in the center of a sprawling flower garden. Now I was certain she'd been sent from the heavens. Glimmering white statues of deities and mythical creatures, meticulously trimmed shrubs, and benches filled the space, along with fountains and bird baths gently flowing with fresh, cool water.

It was as though I'd entered Helia's domain, the goddess of the sun, humanity, and all things living and beautifully vulnerable.

When she popped a grape into her mouth, I had to suppress a groan. My cock swelled in my dark pants, my fangs throbbing now. I imagined those soft, pink lips on mine.

I wanted to corrupt her innocence, to stain her with my darkness.

A slight blush arose on her fair cheeks, and those full lips tipped up in a slight smirk. She was on her stomach, her feet kicking slightly as she flipped the page.

What the hell was she reading?

All of my muscles tightened, forcing myself to stay perfectly still as my predator's gaze narrowed and blood ran molten.

Her essence overpowered my judgment. When she rolled over on her back, and her dress hiked up to reveal her upper thighs, my jaw clenched hard.

So much of her was on display. A cool summer breeze pushed the skirt ever higher, and she was slow to pull the fabric back down as her eyes stayed glued to the page.

She suddenly laughed, and it was the first time I'd heard a sound leave those beautiful, plump lips.

Her giggle melted something hard and cold inside me. It shocked me out of my stupor, reminding me of a part of myself I'd lost long ago.

And I didn't like it. Not at all.

At the same time, my shadows threatened to leak as if to snatch her from this princess palace and drag her into my world of violence and depravity instead. My cock stood painfully alert to her every breath. What would she look like if I stole those breaths away?

As soon as my threads of control began to unravel irreversibly, I left without a trace.

She didn't leave *me*, though.

I wondered how far away I'd have to go to shake the haunting sound of her infectious laugh.

I wondered how much time would need to pass before I'd be free of her.

But I soon discovered that thoughts of my angel multiplied at a frightening rate the longer I stayed away.

2

EVIE

I sat in my favorite coffeeshop on Etherdale University's campus, lost in thought as I waited for my brother, Idris. A sudden shrill laugh made me jolt.

I'd been extra jumpy lately, plagued by the unreasonable delusion that I was being followed and watched.

Earlier this morning, Mena had reminded me that this was to be expected. *You say that every summer, doll,* she'd said while we drank our coffee. *It's normal. And it'll likely get worse the closer we get to... well, you know.*

She'd called it a trauma anniversary. One of her professor friends had told her about it. She said pain gets stored in the body on the cellular level, reminding us of all the bad shit that has happened to us during the same time of year it occurred. I didn't want to buy into all of that, or even *think* about it. Those painful experiences happened so many years ago, and I could hardly remember any of it anyway.

Life was good now. My childhood might as well have happened to a different person.

I'd changed the subject, expertly riling Mena up into a rant about the Donaldsons' run down and crumbling estate. Her gold bracelets jingled beneath flowy turquoise sleeves as she waved her arms animatedly. *It's a damn shame! That property deserves custodians who will tend to her beauty. How could they let it deteriorate to that point? They need to drop their pride and ask for help. It's a matter of historic preservation...*

She soon forgot about the matter of my paranoid delusions entirely.

I tried my hardest to follow suit.

Etherdale's sprawling university for mortals sat in the center of the city, boasting plentiful gardens, greenhouses, academic buildings, libraries, and even an observatory. It was the perfect place for ambitious mortals who reached for the stars.

Idris was one of them. Mena, our adoptive guardian, was a retired art history professor. I'd never seen her beam with brighter pride than when Idris announced he was beginning his studies last year. He was one of the youngest students in his architecture class. He'd turned eighteen only a few months ago.

"Hi, Evie," Idris said with a wide grin, sporting a casual black shirt and slacks.

My gaze snagged on the abundance of dark fabric and frowned on impulse.

He cleared his throat as he slid into the chair across from me in my favorite coffeeshop on campus. Our table was up against a window, the perfect location for people watching and daydreaming. The lazy trickle of rain outside was quickly evolving into a downpour, students giggling as they quickly walked or jogged to shelter.

I shook the frown away and mirrored Idris's smile. He was six years younger than me. I scanned his features, noting the slight puffiness and circles under his soft brown eyes.

"Having too much fun to sleep?" I asked.

Idris rolled his eyes, stealing my coffee and taking a generous swig. Then another.

"Hey!"

His smile was impish now. "You should be thanking me. I bet this is your third cup?"

My lips made a thin line.

"Fourth?" He shook his head. "Evie, that cannot be good for you."

"Way to evade the question."

He slid the mug back toward me. My *third* cup of the day, thank you. I was a *reasonable* half-witch.

"You worry too much," he said. His eyes flashed, and he ran a hand through his short, dirty blond hair.

He was hiding something. Call it an elder sister's intuition. Or perhaps a witch's.

"Are you okay?" I asked, hating that I was playing into the character flaw he'd just accused me of.

Idris's brows drew together, his features quick to offer reassurance. "I'm more than okay. I'm really happy here. Maybe the happiest I've ever been in my entire life."

I could see that truth plainly—the way he was laid back in his chair, his arms spread wide. My heart unclenched, and I sighed in relief.

"Like you said, it's probably the excitement of a new term keeping me up," he said. "I'll finally be able to join more of the clubs and organizations on campus, to shadow architects in the field, and to take classes outside of my specialty. You know, for fun."

His grin was almost disarming enough to rid me of my lingering anxiety. But I snagged on his admission that something was keeping him up at night.

"You're having nightmares again," I said softly, reaching for his hand.

He tensed beneath my touch. "I guess. I don't remember them. I wake up... panicked, that's all. I'm sure they're about being late for class or something."

I knew he wanted me to drop it. And it would be hypocritical of me not to acquiesce. I retracted my hand and took another sip from the ceramic mug.

He was an adult now. He could take care of himself. I wanted to tell him that he could always come to me if he was struggling. That I'd always be there for him. But he already knew it, and I didn't want to irritate him and drive him away.

"What kind of *fun* classes are you going to take?"

"Hey, Idris," a human girl said with a wave, holding a pastry as she walked arm-in-arm with her female friend.

Idris was human too. Sometimes witches were born from human-witch parents, like me, and other times their children were born fully human.

He smiled at the girl and waved back. "See you tonight!"

The mischief in his eyes was slow to fade as he focused back on me. "Some friends." He shrugged.

"Uh-huhhh," I said with a smirk.

He feigned innocence, stealing another sip of my coffee. "Well, okay, this may not help the over-worrying issue, but..."

I braced myself.

"I'm taking some weapons and fighting classes," he said. "You know, for self-defense."

My fists clenched as my stomach dropped. "Why? Etherdale is under mortal control. It's probably the safest city in Ravenia."

My mouth went dry, imagining Idris in harm's way. Something potent slithered around in my blood as memories threatened to surface, and I was quick to squash it down with the other ghosts.

"Etherdale might be safer than elsewhere, relatively speaking, but you know that argument is holding less weight with each passing day," Idris said gently. "Besides, nowhere in the realm is *truly* under mortal control. This is only going to keep me safer, Evie. Please don't be upset."

I chewed on my bottom lip and stared down at the table.

Idris sighed. "More and more students are getting attacked, murdered, or going missing. Mostly humans."

My fingernails dug into my palms.

"And our lords aren't doing anything about it. If anything, they're corrupt enough to be involved in the mortal slave trade themselves. The born have never liked Etherdale's progressiveness, nor our resistance to vampire influence. Their tolerance is growing thin. Especially now that the Masked Order is growing."

I shook my head. "*They're* the problem," I hissed, earning a glare from a nearby student with a high ponytail and sharp green eyes. It was clear I was the minority opinion on a university campus. I met Idris's frustrated gaze. "You can't fight violence with violence. The Order has only made matters worse."

Idris shook his head, and the condescension that oozed from his usually lighthearted features was a dagger to my heart.

"The Order is the future," he said. "They didn't start the violence. They rose up *because* of the unspeakable cruelty that had been steadily mounting, like all other turned clans. They are not the enemy. They are *protectors*."

The Order was a secret society of turned vampires—vampires that were once human—with demonic, shadowed powers. They were shrouded in mystery, only ever appearing to the public wearing inky black masks. They were unnatural, a blasphemy of Helia's will. They preyed on idealistic human students in Etherdale, recruiting them to throw their lives away to fight in some futile underground war against the natural-born vampires.

A war they would *never* win.

The bitter truth was, the born vampires—descendants from the Dark Goddess, Lillian—would always rule the kingdom of

Ravenia. They were immortal, their bodies reaching maturity in their mid-twenties, where they remained eternally youthful, cold, and soulless. The born lords ruled each region on behalf of King Earle and his council, and the wealth and power of the born elites was unchallengeable. The best we could do was avoid extremism, protect our own, and stick to mortal-dominant areas where we had safety in numbers. Witches, humans, and shifters protected each other, for the most part.

My stomach knotted, fighting against the past's phantom limbs. I focused back on the present—the only thing I could control.

"If they're such noble protectors, please do enlighten me on who the Order feeds from? They sustain themselves with mortal blood, do they not?" I hated the way my lip trembled, a flash of memory poking its jagged edge at my walls of denial.

"Willing volunteers," Idris said firmly, never once hesitating. "There are plenty of them."

I shut my eyes for a moment before opening them again.

"You've only been here a year, and you've already been radicalized with this nonsense," I said. "I thought you were more intelligent than to think like everybody else."

Idris's lips turned down. "You need to face reality. Your sensitivity is childish. Better to fight than to blindly allow mortal brothers and sisters to be picked off one by one to be sold as livestock."

The hairs on my neck stood straight up. His words cut deep, but my pain paled in comparison to the fear for my only living blood relative. The way Idris spoke... it was as though he more than admired the Order. It sounded like he wanted to *join them.*

"I love you, Idris. I'm happy you're thriving here," I bit out before taking my last sip of coffee and grabbing my bag.

"You can't run forever," he said, so quiet I almost didn't hear him as I pushed out the door.

Useless tears pooled in my eyes, covered by the pouring rain. I beelined for a campus building I knew would bring me comfort, somewhere I could get lost in for a while.

I was so blinded by my spinning thoughts and the bleeding, dark sky that I slammed right into a tall, firm body the moment I entered the library.

3

KYLO

T scented her before I saw her, positioning myself directly in front of the library entrance just as she pushed through the door.

I hadn't expected my angel to find me today before I could find *her*.

She was full of surprises. It was one of the things I loved most about her.

She gulped in a startled breath. "Oh," she said. "I'm sorry." She quickly backed up and wiped the rain off her face.

Rain and… Had she been crying?

Who the *fuck* had made her cry?

Her wide gray eyes scanned the imposing length of me, stopping when they found mine. I towered over her, eclipsing her with my size. And I enjoyed the way it made her little heart pick up speed, that delicious fear coating her intoxicating blood with every pump.

I wanted the only tears that slid down those rosy cheeks to be shed for *me*.

"No worries, angel," I said. "I'm sure you'll be more careful next time you run into me."

Confusion was soon replaced by irritation. "I—what?"

So flustered. It was crushingly adorable. I slid into an easy grin. "No jacket?" I nodded at her sodden pastel pink dress, the little bow at her neck all droopy and sad looking. She was soaked.

And not in the way I'd been envisioning.

She stared at me like I was an insane person.

Which was smart of her. Because I *was* an insane person.

My grin never faltered. "I thought little green witches could predict the rain," I said, my brows drawing in mock concern.

She crossed her arms. "How do you know I'm a witch? And what makes you think I'm a *green witch*?" She lifted her chin, showing she was fiery underneath the most innocent, cute exterior. It made my cock throb.

I shrugged. "Saw you in here earlier, reading about green witchery." My smile widened. "Just a wild guess…"

Her plump pink lips refused to budge from their skeptical frown. It made me want to bite them into submission.

"You're strange."

To my amusement, she simply stepped around me and walked away.

"Thank you, angel."

"Don't call me that," she said, her voice farther away now and clearly still flustered.

I took my time turning on my heel, watching her quickly take the steps ahead, never once looking back at me. The way the fabric of her dress clung to her perky breasts and round ass —droplets of water dripping down her legs—was an image I was sure I'd never forget.

Though I was calm and controlled on the outside, my heart pounded hard in my chest after our first encounter. Or at least, the first encounter in which she'd been aware of me.

I'd tried to stay away from her. But the truth was, I was more distracted from my work when I was avoiding her than when I allowed myself to watch her from afar. I called it my new hobby, in an effort to appease Harmony's demand that I strive toward a better work-life balance.

The trouble was, I didn't think most people's hobbies were nearly as consuming as mine. This was dangerous. *She* was dangerous.

And now that we'd finally met… gods help her pure, ethereal soul. Because I feared the level of insatiable addiction brewing in my cold, dead heart.

I had to drag myself away from her to the other side of the library where my favorite section on war and history lay. I sat in a leather chair as I re-read one of my favorite books on Valentin, the island now ruled by the turned vampire clan leader, Rune.

He was the historical figure I admired above all others. Although, I supposed that made it seem like he was dead. He was still alive and well, ruling the semi-autonomous island of Valentin with his clan after a bloody war centuries ago. The turned and mortal populations had allied to overthrow born leadership, eventually forcing King Earle of Ravenia to give his blessing for a transfer of power from the defeated born to the turned. It was masterful. I couldn't read enough about Rune or Valentin, soaking up all the wisdom I could glean from history and her crucial lessons.

History never stayed in the past. Great men studied history to gain control of the present and future.

The minutes ticked by. Students came and went, and only a few meandered close to my section.

When I heard the soft padding of approaching footsteps on the burgundy carpet, I didn't glance up.

"Let me guess," said a sweet voice tinged with derision.

My nostrils flared, the scent of springtime and innocence nearly too much to bear without ripping through my human glamour and pinning her to the nearest wall.

I lazily glanced up from my book to lock on those stormy gray eyes.

"You're just another human man who would do anything to ride the dick of Rune the Ruthless and thinks that useless displays of violence are the pinnacle of masculinity."

I feigned shock. "I did not expect such dirty words to leave that mouth." With a smirk I rose, once again towering over her. My gaze never once left her lips. "What's wrong with rugged masculinity, angel? Not to your taste?"

She faltered, and it was the most delicious victory to see pink stain her fair cheeks. Nearly the color of her dress.

"My tastes are none of your concern."

I pouted my lip mockingly. "I disagree."

She glanced at the book I'd left face-up on my chair. "We're not on some faraway, secluded island. You're all buying into delusions and fairy tales."

My angel was so fucking cute, waving those dainty hands around as she spoke. It was taking all of my self-restraint not to touch her, to resist finally feeling those silky strands of light blonde hair beneath my fingers.

"What's wrong with fairy tales, princess?"

At this, she scoffed, crossing her arms as if I'd called her something vile.

"I'm getting the sense that this unprovoked harassment has little to do with me," I said, biting on a smile.

I caught the momentary lapse in her irritation, revealing the truth. Whoever made her cry had set her off about the bad, scary vampires. How interesting.

What I found infinitely more interesting was how she'd come and found *me,* a perfect stranger, to use as her punching bag. From my weeks of watching her, she hardly seemed like a people-person. Certainly not one to take an interest in strangers.

Maybe she was just as drawn to me as I was to her. It was another maddening thought, a hope that was nearly *human.*

And that lingering shred of mortality had me walking off without even a glance over my shoulder, leaving her standing there all confused, angry, stunned, and alone. Maybe she was stomping her little feet in those beat-up sneakers.

It was, unfortunately, a rather sexy mental image.

NOTHING WAS MORE satisfying than a midnight hunt. It was nostalgic, reminding me of when I was merely human, hunting the vampires on campus who prowled for easy prey. It had been a far more dangerous pastime back then. I almost missed the perilousness, the threat of death pushing against me from all directions. It made each kill vastly more satisfying, knowing it could've so easily ended in my demise.

Now, I was more powerful than every lowlife born on my path.

I turned the chase into an art form, picking my prey meticulously before I stalked and toyed with them. I relished their confusion, so sweet on my hungry tongue.

Each turned clan was different. We were not a distinct race; we were monsters born of magick and blood. The chaos witch who created my comrades and me had built us with a very unique signature.

The Masked Order might've preferred mortal blood like any other vampire.

But we could also feed from the born, effectively giving them a taste of their own medicine. And gods, did they fucking *hate* that.

I grinned.

My prey turned a corner into a dark, quiet alley, following

an unsuspecting human woman. Entirely unaware that I was closing in on *him*.

The woman was clearly intoxicated. I could smell both alcohol and elixir in her veins. Not the wisest choice to pair with walking home alone late at night.

I hated that mortals had to be careful at all.

My dark tattoos tickled my skin, slightly burning. Magick awakened in my blood as my shadows gathered.

One day, mortals would be able to walk these streets as they pleased without fear of born cruelty. One day, I'd be able to bear my tattoos and fangs before the world, free from that accursed, uncomfortable human glamour that stuck to my skin like a film.

The born had no idea the reckoning slowly building against them and their incompetent rule. Their arrogance would spell their downfall.

Tonight, I had no need for my glamour. My mask was in place, a fluid film of shadow that covered most of my head, moving diagonally to leave my mouth and one side of my face partially exposed. I generally let it take a frightening onyx skull appearance.

The woman screamed, but she was quickly silenced to a muffled groan of protest.

"Shh," the man hissed. "Be a good little human whore and take it. You knew exactly what you were doing walking around alone dressed like this. Don't start playing coy now."

My lip curled, my tattoos scalding now, demanding a release of power. In a rush of shadow, I was behind the born scumbag before he could even react. His hand was over the brunette's mouth, his body pressed against hers as he flashed his fangs. I yanked him off her with ease, throwing him against the opposite building. His skull hit the dark stone with a resounding *crack.*

I whistled, alerting Harmony to the human woman in need of help. Meanwhile, I allowed my hungry shadows to wrap around the born man like hissing snakes. They coiled and coiled, restraining him as he flailed futilely. He conjured fire magick that was quickly extinguished by my void of onyx.

His venomous green eyes bulged as my shadows tightened around his form. His stringy auburn hair clung to his forehead.

"Abomination!" he screeched. "Lillian will scourge the earth of you blasphemous vermin."

A tendril of shadow wrapped around his mouth, gagging him.

I casually glanced over my shoulder, ensuring that Harmony had arrived. Even with her mask, she appeared bright and non-threatening, her smile warm and genuine. Her mask only covered the top half of her face, and it was considerably less frightening than mine. Her long black hair cascaded to her shoulders in loose curls. Her light brown skin was warm-toned in the moonlight, and the bright yellow dress cloaking her figure perfectly matched her personality.

She was a living embodiment of the sun itself. We stood in stark contrast.

"Hi, honey," she said sweetly. "Let's get you somewhere safe, okay?"

The woman was shaking, her teeth clattering violently. Her trembling palms pulled at the short skirt of her satin dress. At first, I feared she might not trust us enough to be escorted home.

But, like most everyone else, she decided Harmony was too genuine to resist—fangs and all. She avoided looking in my direction and let Harmony lead her away.

Now that she was out of eyesight, I slowly turned back to the panicking, hissing born man. I laughed at the cold shards of hatred in his eyes.

I stalked toward him. "Would you like to know how it feels? To fear death, to be trapped and helpless, your life force slowly drained from your veins..."

He let out a muffled growl against the shadow gag.

"I didn't quite hear you, but I'm going to assume you said *yes*. Why else would you be walking these streets all alone?" My eyes darkened, wrath building beneath my skin. I pushed his head to the side. "Be quiet and take it."

I ripped into his jugular. My jaw clamped down and fangs ripped through skin and muscle, with little concern for whether I might accidentally remove his head from his body.

I tasted defenseless humans in his blood, evidence of his long list of crimes.

As I fed, my power grew ever stronger.

Soon, these streets would be full of patrolling turned to keep the born in line. This low-level vigilante justice was nothing compared to what I had planned.

First, we'd take Etherdale.

Next, the turned would take this whole damned realm.

4

EVIE

I was slow to emerge from the cottage this morning. Idris wasn't the only one having nightmares again.

The smaller dwelling was across from the main house where Mena lived, the sprawling gardens separating the two buildings. My cottage had a large bedroom, a bathroom, a spare room I used for my magickal workings, a living area, and a tasteful kitchen. I'd taken great care in filling the place with warm lights, plush furniture, and personal touches that made the environment cozy and inviting. My space was an extension of myself, from the fresh springtime scented candles, the chunky throw blankets, the dried bunches of flowers and herbs, and the pops of soft pastels. I woke up every day grateful that the fates had been so extraordinarily generous with me. Even if I probably didn't deserve it.

It was just Mena and me now, as Idris had decided to live on campus. I admired his bravery. Change and I had a complicated relationship.

Mena came from a long line of human scholars, tracing back to co-founders of the university itself. She'd decided not to marry or have biological children of her own, much to her now-deceased parents' displeasure. She'd always been the type to shun tradition, preferring instead to live a life worthy of the most riveting stories and endless anecdotes, a different kind of eternal legacy.

Even still, it was clear that Mena had needed Idris and me as much as we'd needed her.

A memory flashed in my mind before I could stop it.

My limbs screamed in pain. Idris was in my arms, too tired to walk any longer. He was heavy, and I felt so weak. But we had to keep going. Had to keep moving. My black dress clung to my skin with sweat and—

The cottage door slammed shut behind me, and I cleared my head with a deep breath and a short chant for forgetting.

I was so disoriented that I nearly tripped over the package at my feet. It was a pretty blush color, similar to the dress I'd worn yesterday when I'd met that strange, tall man with black hair and deep blue eyes. His devastatingly beautiful, masculine features were imprinted in my mind, and that made me feel guilty as hell. I needed to stop thinking about that defined, wide jaw. Those taunting, smirking lips. The way his gaze pierced straight through me, as if we'd already met countless times before—as if I *meant something* to him, somehow. Men like him were dangerous, scheming creatures. Especially ones with a fixation on Rune and Valentin's war against the born.

I was glaring down at the package now, lost in a daze of irritation. How dare he call me *angel* or *princess* as if we were lovers. As if he even knew me. And worse than his teasing words and abrupt departure in the middle of our conversation —why in the hell had I initiated that second encounter in the first place?

Oh, gods. Maybe he was an incubus—a sex demon. Yep, that explanation made a whole lot of sense. Even more reason to hope I never saw him again.

I picked up the small package, fingering the pretty pink bow tied perfectly neat. I knew who it was from, and nervous butterflies bloomed in my stomach. It was strange for him to leave it outside the cottage rather than giving it to me in person, especially since he hadn't seen me in weeks. But he also never surprised me with gifts, so perhaps this was something special.

Maybe his travels had changed him. Maybe he'd missed me terribly, and he wanted to show me how much I meant to him with a series of romantic gestures and time together. That thought seeded beautiful, warm hope in my veins as I walked through the gardens.

I joined Mena for breakfast most mornings, except when I overslept and needed to rush to Celeste's with the new supply. Celeste's was a flower shop that doubled as a witch supply store—the biggest and most renowned in the city. I sold both floral and herbal goods from my garden, each with their own unique witchy twist.

Today was a crafting day for me, though, not a sales day. I might even take the day off. That way I could enjoy a long breakfast with Mena before my boyfriend, Jacob, made himself known.

Mena was already sitting at the head of the dining room table when I arrived at the main house. She was reading a local gossip pamphlet as she sipped on coffee and picked at a plate of toast and eggs.

"Evie, darling, did you know about this?" Mena asked without looking up.

Even in her late sixties, she was the most fashionable, chic woman I'd ever met. Today's outfit was a leopard print blouse, a chunky gold and ruby necklace, and dark pants. Her silver hair was pulled back with an ornate hair clip adorned with tiny golden butterflies.

"University administrators are in heated discussions with Lord Conrad about free speech ordinances in Etherdale. The born want to do away with all vampire-free zones on campus too, I'm afraid. There's talk of banning books, outlawing certain classes and discussion topics. It's madness. They'll never allow it."

My first thought was Idris as my stomach soured. My second thought was of that black-haired male sex demon reading a book that would most certainly be the first to burn.

When I said nothing, Mena looked up for the first time. Eyeing my mysterious package, she set down the pamphlet and clapped her hands together. "Oh! A gift! Please tell me it's from a *new*, exciting suitor."

I rolled my eyes. "I have a boyfriend, remember?"

Mena pursed her lips, brows raised high. "Hard to remember someone so dull."

"Everyone is dull to you," I muttered.

"No, only dull people are dull," she said. "High standards are not a flaw, my dear. They guarantee a life worth living." She spread her arms out wide before gesturing to the box again with a twirl of her wrist. "Come on, then. Let's see what's inside."

I laughed as I shook my head. I delicately untied the perfect pink bow, letting the ribbon fall to the sleek wooden table. Then, sliding a finger under the seam in the pretty pink paper, I removed the wrapping to reveal a book in perfect, new condition.

Not just any book. The new fantasy romance book I'd been eyeing for weeks.

I'd been spending all my spare earnings lately on more witchy supplies, as well as saving for a new dream project I'd yet to tell anyone about. I'd resigned to waiting a bit longer before I could splurge on new books for myself.

I grinned. I wondered how in the world Jacob knew I'd wanted this one so badly.

"Is there a note?" Mena asked, the same excitement in her voice as when she spilled juicy Etherdale gossip.

I flipped open the front cover and flipped through the first few pages, then glanced down at the wrapping, looking for any sign of a note I might have missed. "No," I said with a shrug before finally sitting next to her and taking a sip of the coffee Mena had already poured for me.

I knew coffee didn't work instantly, but gods, it felt like the warmest shot of happiness had already settled in my veins as soon as the divine liquid touched my tongue.

"No note makes it more mysterious, I suppose."

Mena lifted a single brow as she eyed me. "I'm unconvinced that man knows how to be *mysterious*."

As if on cue, a resounding knock sounded from the front door.

I gulped down more coffee before rising and going to the front door, ignoring Mena's typical anti-man rhetoric.

I opened the door to find Jacob with his hands in his pockets. He wore a cream button-down shirt and navy pants. His spiky blond hair was shorter than before, and the sprinkle of freckles around his strong nose a shade darker.

"I'm back," he said before leaning in and kissing me, the action brief and chaste.

As always, his handsomeness stunned me for a moment. His disarming grin was wide as ever.

To be honest, I'd been hurt when he'd announced his travel plans after he finished his university studies in business management. It was a sudden declaration, and he left a week later, even though he'd clearly been planning the adventure for a while. He never once asked if I wanted to join him.

I wouldn't have gone, but he didn't know that. There was a lot he didn't know about me. It was safer for everyone that way.

I smiled. Before I could speak, I heard Mena mutter, *"Clearly,"* from behind me.

"How was it?" I asked, ignoring Mena and hoping Jacob hadn't heard her. I reminded myself how lucky I was to have someone like Jacob in my life. How much I *wanted* him in my life.

He trailed a hand down my shoulder before waltzing inside. "It was a dream. I met the most interesting people. The food, the natural landscape… gods, the countryside was especially beautiful. Even if the people there were pretty backward." He scrunched up his face with derision as he joined us at the dining room table, as if remembering the people he'd found distasteful.

I swallowed. Hard. Yes, it would've been a terrible idea to have joined him.

Mena's reading glasses were low on her nose, her lips turned down as she leveled her narrowed gaze on Jacob.

I cringed when he barely greeted Mena, only continuing to speak without pause for several minutes.

I could sense Mena's patience wearing thin. I wished she saw the good parts of him, rather than his innocent character flaws. He didn't mean to be so un-self-aware. He was just excited about his adventures, always trying to prove to the world he was more than a cutthroat businessman born to a long line of the same. He wanted to show that he had depth, that there was meaning to his actions and dreams. I loved that about him. His insecurities and earnestness were beautifully human and pure.

My muscles were tense when he finally halted his animated recount of his journey and eyed the fantasy novel lying on top of the wrapping paper in the center of the table.

I opened my mouth to thank him, but he spoke before I could.

"What's this?" He grabbed the book and flipped it over, skimming the description. He shook his head and sighed. The curve of his smirk deflated something inside me. "Another pornographic faerie novel, I'm sure."

Mena's eyes darted to mine, her frown quickly transforming into the most mischievous of smiles.

She raised her coffee mug. "To a most joyous homecoming," she declared with a wink.

Jacob placed the novel back down and didn't mention it again, as if he didn't care enough about who had given it to me or why.

I sipped my coffee, attempting not to wear my mounting disappointment on my face. That would only irritate Jacob and make it all worse. I wanted things to be good between us. I wanted to feel what I'd felt before. I wanted to feel what the characters of my favorite novels felt—that undeniable soulmate love.

But maybe Idris was right, and that was just another childish yearning that didn't fit into reality.

I chased eggs around with my fork, distracting myself from the lump in my throat with a single burning question.

If Jacob hadn't gifted me the book, then who had?

5

EVIE

"Have you ever thought about doing something more? Like completing a course at university or getting trained in something?" Jacob asked as we strolled through the summer markets in the heart of Etherdale.

I paused for a moment, trying not to read into the negative implications of the question—the question he'd asked nearly a dozen times since we'd started dating. Instead, I leaned into the excitement bubbling in my chest. I hadn't told anyone about the secret project I'd been drafting the past couple months, squirreling away funds and ideas as I dreamed.

I began selling my goods to tiny merchants and shops before Celeste's made me a deal to sell exclusively to them. Ever since, demand for my products had steadily grown as word spread. I imbued each good with distinctive spells and magick, mostly for healing or protection. I guessed customers found them especially potent, and as my confidence in my abilities grew, so too did my desire to scale up.

After all, I was helping people. I'd never been more fulfilled and certain about my place in the world as when I was using my power for good.

"I actually think I want to open my own shop," I said. "You know, instead of selling my goods to others." I smiled, examining the beautiful pendant necklaces at one of the booths. They shimmered in the afternoon sunlight, and I was particularly attracted to the moonstone. As soon as my fingertips brushed the crystal, a flash of intuition about its magickal properties flooded my mind.

The merchants were helping a customer, clearly annoyed with his aggressive haggling.

Jacob's heavy sigh behind me made me tense up on instinct. "Evie, my love," he started, the condescension already sending a pool of disappointment to my guts. "How can you possibly open a shop of your own? You don't even like people."

My smile faded. "That's not true." Well, not entirely. It was more complicated than that. I wanted to like people. We just often didn't understand each other, and I found it hard to trust them. But I didn't need to be especially charismatic to own my own store; my goods would speak for themselves.

"And there are a million witchy stores in Etherdale already."

I deflated, the last puff of excitement leaving my lungs. "I know that. I'd have to be unique."

Jacob sighed again, and I couldn't bear to turn and see his irritated features. I kept thumbing the jewelry, reading each signature, busying myself with new spell ideas to distract from my boyfriend's doubts about my dreams.

"I'm not trying to be a downer. It's just reality."

There was that word again. *Reality.* I'd never been a fan of the notion. Perhaps why I spent so much time escaping to other worlds between the pages of a book.

Still, it stung just as much as when Idris had said it, along with his condemnation of my sensitivity and childishness. Predictably, my eyes pricked with tears. And I hated it.

Stop crying! a voice that didn't belong to me screeched. It was the voice of a ghost, one I tried desperately to forget—one who might haunt me forever.

Not that I wouldn't deserve it.

"No, it's fine," I said, hoping I sounded stronger than I felt. "You went to university, and I didn't."

It wasn't merely that I *didn't* go; I *couldn't*. That was what no one understood. To go to university as a witch studying magick, I'd have to be tested. Examined. Studied.

It wasn't an option. Not for me.

Jacob spun me around and kissed my forehead. "I didn't mean it like that. I push you because I think you're brilliant. You're unlike anyone I've ever met. I would hate to see you waste your potential." He paused. "And it's not just that I went to university—I actually studied *business*. I'm only trying to help you."

My vision blurred with tears, and I blinked them away, praying they didn't spill over.

Jacob scanned my eyes and let out yet another frustrated breath. "Gods, Evie. Not in public. You make me look like some kind of abusive dickhead."

He recoiled from me, anger flashing in his eyes.

Don't cry, don't cry, don't cry.

I forced a smile. "I'm sorry. I know you're just trying to help. I'm sorry," I repeated.

"I need to go soon," he said.

My heart dropped. Clearly, my vision for the day had been very different from… reality. I swallowed, but it didn't shift the mass in my throat. He'd been gone for so long, and he'd been too busy and nomadic to write to me. Or maybe he'd wanted to live in the moment. Either way, I hadn't heard anything from him in weeks after barely receiving notice of his departure.

I'd hoped we'd walk around the market longer, and I'd tell him all about my ideas for my future shop. All the new spells I'd been working on. The things I'd read lately about philosophy and mythology. And maybe we'd do something romantic like a picnic, or a romantic dinner in—

"I'll just go now, actually. I'm clearly not making you happy, and I want you to enjoy your day. I have to help out with preparation for the party tomorrow night."

My last thread of hope for a beautiful day together died. I wondered if what he'd said was even true. Who planned their own welcome-home party? Especially when you had a mother like his. It would be strange for Cindy to make her darling son lift even a finger for his own celebration. Or for anything at all, really.

I nodded. "Oh, okay. I understand. I'm sorry. I just..."

Wanted more from you. Wanted more for *us*.

"... haven't seen you in so long. I've missed you."

Jacob's eyes softened, pulling me in for a hug. "I'll see you at the party."

He pulled away with a smile that didn't reach his hazel eyes. Then, he left.

THERE WAS a place I retreated to in my mind in order to make this world less crushing or confusing or disappointing. It was a lens of fiction, a way to layer fantasy on top of the physical world. In this place inside my mind, I could fantasize that people were different. That my life was more exciting—that I hadn't been born terrified and alone.

Right after Jacob left, I retreated to that place. I came up with solid explanations for his behavior, ones that made his actions hurt a lot less. He was this way because his dad was so hard on him growing up. He learned to express love differently than what I wanted—with pushing and questioning and toughness—and that wasn't his fault. It wasn't his fault that he didn't understand gentle, thoughtful love, and my expectations were probably too high, anyway. Ruined by romance novels, like he always reminded me.

Besides, he was right. There were too many witchy shops in Etherdale. I wasn't ready. I needed to be more than just special. I needed to be the *best*. Maybe then I wouldn't be such an outsider, and Jacob would love me differently.

There was only one obstacle before me, and it was a rather large one.

There was nothing I feared more than the full brunt of power buried in my veins. Power I'd been blocking and avoiding for years now—power that I, frankly, wanted nothing to do with.

But enough time had passed, and the small amount of magick that I *was* currently tapping into was helping people. Jacob had been right: I needed to do something *more*.

And I knew Idris felt the same. *You need to face reality. Your sensitivity is childish.*

You can't run forever.

The truth was, I was being left behind by two of the only people who'd ever cared about me. And I couldn't bear to be any more alone than I already felt.

"What in the heavens are you thinking so hard about?" a deep, amused voice said from behind me.

I tensed, realizing I'd been staring at a shelf of magickal objects, motionless, for far too long.

A presence was at my back, accompanied by the scent of dark musk, leather, and fresh mint and berries.

"Let me guess: Pretty flowers and picnics in meadows?"

I swallowed and slowly turned. He was standing far too close, his body heat pressing against me. I had to lift my chin to stare into those dark blue eyes.

"Hilarious," I said. "You know green witches can specialize in poisons, right?" I smiled warmly.

His powerful jaw ticked, a strange intensity brewing in his eyes. Had that *turned him on?*

I tried to step back before I realized the shelves were behind me. I was trapped. He wore a dark blue shirt similar to the shade of his eyes and black pants. On his feet were heavy combat boots.

"Do you have a name, pretty little forest nymph?" he asked, his voice deceptively sweet.

My fists tightened. "Yes. Do you?"

He took a step closer to me, his body nearly brushing against mine. His gaze was intense enough that I could feel it in my stomach, a warmth that spread lower and lower…

The merchant at the counter cleared her throat.

The man didn't move at first, his eyes flitting from my eyes to my lips as his breathing quickened.

Electricity jolted through my system. Anticipation and confusion warred in my mind as the world slipped away.

"I'll tell you my name if you allow me to accompany you through the market," he said, low and commanding. "There are a lot of vampires here today."

I lifted a brow, struggling to concentrate as he overwhelmed all my senses with his proximity. "So?"

He bent down, his breath fanning over my face, our lips only inches apart. "*So*, angel, you're the most delicious looking prey for miles."

Something coiled inside me—heat and danger and desire.

"You're an incubus, aren't you?"

His brows drew together, the intensity in his eyes melting as he broke into a deep laugh that vibrated beneath my skin.

"If I was an incubus, you wouldn't suspect it. That's literally the entire point of their defensive glamour."

Oh, shit. He was right. Why did the idea of him *not* being a sex demon frighten me even more?

"Let me protect you," he said softly. "I can also offer charm, wit, and, dare I say, *fun*. It's a spectacular deal for you, truly."

No. Hell no. Also, I had a boyfriend.

I didn't realize I was chewing my bottom lip until he was glaring at it.

"You're arrogant," I said.

He lifted a brow. "I prefer *confident*. Arrogance is born of insecurity and a lack of humility. Confidence is knowing exactly who you are and taking pride in your particular skill sets and strengths. Such as protecting vulnerable little angels while they stroll through markets."

That fucking smile. It looked like he wanted to devour me whole. I opened my mouth to say no, but *"Fine,"* came out instead.

"Correct answer," he purred. "Very good girl."

The words shocked me, a confusing mix of yearning and shame swirling in my blood.

I scoffed. "I already regret my decision."

"No, you don't," he said, finally backing up and giving me space. "My name is Kylo."

"Well, Kylo, I'm going to poison the hell out of you with my pretty flowers."

He groaned. "Enough with the dirty talk. I'm trying to be a gentleman, and you're making it extraordinarily difficult."

I walked next to him, my stomach nervous with butterflies, as he moved even closer to me and scanned our surroundings as if for threats.

"My name is Evie, and this is platonic," I blurted.

"Of course, Evie. Wouldn't dream of anything more." Kylo slowly turned his head to side-eye me with a smirk.

He spoke as if he wasn't taking me seriously, and it was irritating. And once again I was confused by the effect it had on me.

I felt clunky and awkward walking next to him. He moved

with such fluid grace it was eerie—especially for someone so tall and scary-looking.

I knew rationally that his bravado and talk of protecting me was part of his game. He was only trying to seduce me. Even if I knew it was fake, the act produced very real palpitations in my chest.

Why had I agreed to this? This was a horrible idea.

When the third person waved *hello* to Kylo, I eyed him curiously. "You have a lot of friends."

"They're meticulously curated, I assure you."

I slowed my pace, eyeing a booth with rare and ancient books. Kylo noticed and immediately stopped moving. I felt the warmth of his hand near the small of my back, subtly guiding me toward the stall. He still hadn't touched me, and he made no move to.

"What are your friends like, angel?"

Friends. I was friendly with a lot of Jacob's friends. And with the owners and regulars of Celeste's—the people I helped with my spells. And, of course, Mena's circle found me *fascinating*. I'd always gotten along better with older humans than people my own age. I generally didn't even bother with witches, fearing they'd pity or distrust me for not belonging to a coven. Or worse, they'd immediately know how different I was and shun me.

I preferred to reject others before they could reject me.

And, *hey*, points for self-awareness.

"They're mostly human," I said blandly. I feared everything I said would end up shattering whatever fleeting fascination this man had with me. Though, shouldn't that have been what I wanted?

Entertaining him was a shitty thing to do to Jacob. The only person who would approve of this uncharacteristic behavior was Mena, and she was hardly trustworthy when it came to long-lasting romantic endeavors.

Perhaps I should be myself and let that scare him away.

"I'm closest to my brother. But he's living on the university's campus now. Studying architecture," I offered.

I examined the beautiful, ancient texts spread before me on one of the folding tables before the counter. There were a couple of other people browsing—a human woman and a shifter man. As soon as my fingers skimmed over a thick book with golden emboss detailing, a flicker of knowing infected my mind. It was a book on divination—the psychic art of telling the past, present, and future.

I hadn't realized how intently Kylo had been watching me until I focused back on the world around me. I quickly retracted my hand. I was sure I looked more than a little eccentric zoning out like that.

"What do you study?" I asked quickly.

"I'm not a student."

I glanced over at him. "Then what do you do?" He appeared to be in his mid-to-late-twenties, too young to be a professor—but perhaps he was training to be one.

"I'm a private tutor."

I narrowed my gaze. "Of what?"

"Philosophy," he said, studying the row of books before him. His eyes snagged on one that was black and nondescript, the title in tiny golden letters. *Diary of Theo Renee.*

"Of course, you're a *nihilist*," I said with a sigh, recognizing that philosopher's name.

Kylo's eyes flashed to mine, amusement ripe on his soft-looking lips. "Said with such venom." His grin spread as he leaned over the table between us and stared hard into my eyes. "Not a fan of nihilism, angel?"

The blue of his eyes was so deep, like the darkest depths of an ocean during a violent storm. "Nihilism is intellectually lazy."

Surprise colored his features for a moment before he

laughed, the sound of it stirring something potent in my stomach.

"Intellectually lazy," he repeated with another chuckle. He held my gaze intently, as if he saw something inside me that he wanted to drag out into the light.

I squirmed under his prying eyes, resisting the urge to back down and look away.

"It's easy to say it's all random, that none of it means anything at all. I feel like too many people use nihilism as an excuse to avoid being earnest."

Kylo's eyes softened.

"But maybe that's just me avoiding reality. Being childish and idealistic," I said quickly. I winced. Why the hell did I feel the need to say my inner monologue out loud? Gods.

Kylo frowned, not speaking for several moments. I was suddenly too hot and exposed, my skin itchy and uncomfortable. I finally broke our locked eyes to pretend to study the books again. My heart was beating hard and fast, his gaze a brand on my soul.

"I agree with you," he said softly. "Reality is malleable. If you don't like your current one, you can always surround yourself with those who dream of something more."

Whatever the opposite of disappointment was—that was the warm, surprised feeling that burrowed in my heart.

He was so… unexpected.

"Choosing meaning over meaninglessness is vulnerable, and vulnerability isn't wrong. It's beautiful and brave."

I slowly met his eyes again, the only part of him that was soft and open.

"It's not childish to be idealistic," he continued. "All the greats are."

6

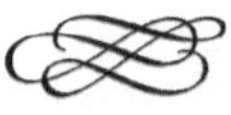

KYLO

Accusing me of being a sex demon was rather amusing. I was beginning to wonder the same about her. Was *she* a succubus designed to destroy me from within?

There was no other logical explanation for my inexplicable draw to her. Or the way it was only getting more and more undeniable and potent as more words spilled from her perfect pink lips.

Today's summer dress was faerie-like—a pastel blue that hung off her shoulders. A layer of wispy chiffon covered the satin material beneath. Combined with her black platform Mary Jane's and white frilly socks, her big gray eyes, and angelic blonde hair, I thought she was possibly the most enticing, vulnerable little creature I'd ever laid eyes on.

This meant she had a similar effect on others. That much I'd gleaned from men's lingering stares, my vampiric hearing capable of discerning all manner of lewd remarks. She was oblivious to all of it. The first born who passed us homed in on her immediately, nostrils flaring.

The glare I'd sent him was downright venomous. My

shadows stirred beneath my glamour and yearned to squeeze the life out of his beady, black eyes.

The desire to protect Evie was instinctual, as strong as my drive to protect my clan and my vision of a better world.

She was everything mortal and pure, a living embodiment of what the born desired most: blood rich with innocence and sunshine.

I wished it was only the thought of the born touching her that sent me spinning into violent, depraved thoughts. But I'd felt the same way when that human man had touched her—no doubt the reason for her declaration that our time together was *platonic*.

I'd heard the way he spoke to her. And whether the punishment fit the crime, his attitude made me want to pluck his undeserving eyes right from his skull.

He was a fucking idiot. He shouldn't have been allowed to breathe the same air as someone so open, excitable, and *good*.

I watched Evie run her fingers over a deck of tarot cards. They'd been taken out of the box to be displayed, and she eagerly leafed through each one. Every once in a while, her eyes grew glassy, as if she were staring into some other plane of existence. Sometimes, she'd frown at what she saw, or her brows would adorably furrow. Other times, she'd smile with pure delight.

What bothered me most about her was the ever-present note of fear in her veins. Vampires could sense fear and arousal in mortals—both sensations making their blood infinitely more delicious. Even better when they were combined, such as when I'd corned her in the booth of magickal objects with my large frame. Or when I called her a *very good girl*.

Fear wasn't supposed to be a constant state. It made me equal parts curious and livid, to know that someone or something had harmed her so irreversibly.

"Are you hungry?" I asked her.

"Sorry, I didn't mean to take so long," she said quickly, setting down the card she was examining.

"Don't apologize," I said. "You weren't taking long at all. I enjoy watching your mind work."

She stared at me like she didn't believe a word out of my mouth. It only made me want to earn her trust more—to prove to her that not every man was like the shitty one who'd pissed all over her ideas.

I had a feeling Evie was used to people walking all over her. The way she apologized was almost as if she were apologizing for even existing at all.

It made me want to murder someone.

"I wanted to make sure you ate."

Her stare only grew more confused and suspicious. "Why?"

Because I wanted to take care of her. Because I wanted to keep following this thread of obsession wherever it led.

And I knew how much of a problem that was. She was a liability I couldn't afford.

But the thought of walking away now was a stab of ice in my heart. There was too much I didn't understand about her—like that elusive note of darkness in her essence that reminded me of the deepest, coldest winter woods. It was in sharp juxtaposition with everything else about her.

A drop of poison in a field of wildflowers.

"Because you indulged me with your company, and I want to express my gratitude," I said.

"Oh." She hesitated, her cheeks flushing with my new favorite shade of pink. "Okay, sure. Something quick."

"Deal."

I eyed a booth selling quilts and blankets, perfect for an impromptu picnic. I wanted to pry more secrets from her depths. I wanted to ask her about her family and where she grew up.

"Kylo," a familiar voice called.

Fuck.

I halted, and Evie slammed into me, clearly lost in her own mysterious inner world again and not paying attention.

When her hand clutched my bicep, she gasped, her eyes getting that faraway look again. She quickly let go.

"Sorry," she said.

At the same time, Princeton, my maker, moved closer. His light brown, curly hair was past his shoulders, wild and untamed. His eyes quickly moved from me to Evie, sharpening with a ferocity that instantly put me on edge. I didn't like the shocked fascination that marked his features.

His stance alerted me to a certain severity, which meant my time with Evie had officially been cut short.

I nodded at him, silently communicating for him to wait a moment.

I turned to the blonde angel still staring up at me with her big doe eyes. "My sincerest apologies, Evie, but I'm afraid I forgot about a meeting with my very cranky and impatient mentor."

"No worries," she said with an understanding smile.

"I will make it up to you."

An inner war played out behind those mysterious gray irises.

Before she could decide on a response, I moved behind her. Around her delicate neck, I placed the moonstone pendant necklace she'd been eyeing when that insufferable man had made her feel so small. "A souvenir to remember our day," I whispered next to her ear.

I was careful not to touch her, no matter how badly I wanted to.

I stole a glimpse of her surprised features before grinning and walking away.

~

PRINCETON WORE a billowy white top and a series of amulets around his neck, some made of tiny bones, others of arcane, magickal materials. They rattled together as we moved away from the crowds of people around us.

He was a frighteningly powerful witch. If there was a living embodiment of the *fine line between genius and madness* phenomenon, it was him. He tended to jump back and forth over that line several times a day.

"What in the good gods did I just witness?" he asked in bewilderment. "Is that the *new hobby* Harmony was blabbering about? I'd hoped it was knitting."

"Drop it," I hissed.

Princeton smiled. "Sheesh. And touchy about it too. That makes sense, knowing you."

"Meaning?"

"That you aren't interested in anything casually. You want it all-consuming or not at all. I hope that witch knows what she's in for." He paused. "Do you know what *you're* in for?"

No. I had absolutely no idea. I didn't like that Princeton now knew about Evie, regardless of how much I trusted him. He was dangerous. He and Evie belonged to two completely different worlds.

"Her magickal signature, I mean," he continued.

I glanced over at him, noting the way his sharp features twisted in perplexity.

"That she's a green witch?" I asked. "Gifted in earth-based magick."

Princeton frowned. "Is that what she told you?"

I paused. Actually, Evie had never confirmed she was a green witch. She'd never corrected me, either.

"Bring her in if you're going to continue to pursue this new *hobby*. I need to examine her."

My teeth ground together. I couldn't do that to her. At least not yet.

Once Evie was mine, there was no going back.

7

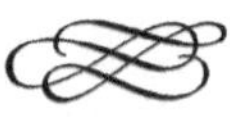

EVIE

When I'd stumbled and grabbed Kylo's arm, his skin had burned me. I'd let go immediately, as if I'd picked up a hot pan.

After he'd left, I examined my fingers, but they were unblemished. It was like I'd imagined the entire thing.

I couldn't make sense of it, other than that whatever I'd felt reminded me of the warmth that gathered in my stomach whenever our eyes locked. Or when he called me those pet names that I absolutely needed to put a stop to.

But the heat on his skin had been too much, too concentrated.

He wasn't a witch or a shifter—I would've been able to read that. The only explanation I could come up with was that it had been some kind of premonition or intuition about his future or his past, and I'd let go too quickly to fully understand the psychic message.

I needed to touch him again.

For scientific purposes.

"Please hurry up," Jacob groaned from my bed. He was

staring up at the ceiling, his features twisted with irritation as if he'd rather be anywhere else but here.

I thought it would be nice to spend some alone time together before the party. I imagined we could talk while I got ready, catching each other up on our inner worlds and lives since before his travels. But so far, he'd only been frustrated with my getting ready process, asking multiple times why he was even here.

I thumbed the moonstone pendant on a delicate golden chain around my neck. It resonated with feminine, sensitive energy—the domain of the goddess of witches, shifters, and the moon—Selena. It reminded me of myself. It was a declaration that softness and intuitiveness were just as powerful as masculine displays of strength.

But how had Kylo known I'd been drawn to this necklace? And why would he gift it to me, a stranger? It was too much. Yet, I couldn't take it off, and I wasn't ready to examine what that meant about me.

"You can go," I said to Jacob for a third time as I quickly applied the last of my makeup. I was careful to keep my tone cheerful and sweet. "I'll meet you there."

He sighed. "No. I just want you to consider my feelings, Evie, instead of making everything about you. I'm sacrificing time with my friends and family to be here. If I leave, you're just going to make me out to be the bad guy. It would be nice if how I feel gets considered for once."

The lump in my throat grew heavier. "How do you feel? What could I have done differently?"

Another huff. "I feel impatient. Why do I have to cater to your constant sad emotions, but you can't understand my frustration when you're taking forever to get ready?"

"I'm sorry you feel that way," I said calmly, trying to keep any amount of emotion from my voice. I couldn't let this escalate. I couldn't make it worse and ruin the entire night. "I wasn't sad until you said you didn't want to be here with me. I thought we could talk and catch up."

"I can't keep giving in to your every desire and whim, Evie. It's unreasonable. I have needs too. It can't be your way or no way."

Was that what I'd been doing? Maybe I *was* being unreasonable. Of course, he'd want to be with his friends and family after so much time away. I'd just hoped that… Honestly, the more I considered, I wasn't sure what I was even hoping for anymore.

I caught a glimpse of him massaging the bridge of his nose, eyes shut, in my vanity mirror. Embarrassment sunk low in my gut. I felt like a child begging for attention, irritating and stupid.

When I stood, I examined myself quickly in the full-length mirror. My blonde hair fell in full curls, partially pulled back with a jeweled pin, and my dress hugged my body in blush-colored satin and tulle.

"Finally," Jacob said.

He rose from the bed, and I watched him walk toward me in the mirror. He barely looked at me. He didn't move to touch me.

He didn't say anything at all before nodding toward the door.

My soft smile fell, and I followed him out.

THE WHITFIELD ESTATE was only a street over from Mena's, and it made our home look modest. Cindy and Roger Whitfield were some of the wealthiest mortals in the entire region.

When we entered the sprawling mansion, Jacob transformed into an entirely different person than the man who'd been glaring angrily at my ceiling.

He grabbed my hand and placed it on his arm. He smiled widely as dozens of people cheered in the wide foyer.

Cindy and Roger were quick to break apart from their huddle and greet us. Cindy's shimmering golden drink nearly sloshed over in the skinny glass flute. I wondered how many doses of elixir she'd already consumed. Elixir was a stronger drug than alcohol, forged by magick and designed to induce a relaxed, pleasurable, incapacitated state—tempered by a brutal comedown worse than any hangover. Though Cindy thoroughly enjoyed both vices.

"Well, don't you both look *dashing*," she said, raising her free arm wide. Her pink lipstick was a touch smudged, though her blond hair was meticulously straightened and immovable. "Evie, dear, so nice to see you again."

I smiled at her, moving quickly through the standard greetings and compliments. "And the witch lights display—how magickal."

"Just wait till you see the terrace and the gardens in the back!" Cindy exclaimed. "There are quite a few witches here, Evie. As you know, we enjoy diverse company."

She nodded enthusiastically, staring at me as if waiting for me to affirm her good natured-ness.

"That's wonderful. No one throws a party like you do," I said. More witch lights hovered above in shades of gold and silver, illuminating the opulent white and golden walls, the large crystal chandelier, the ornate furnishings, and double staircase. Chatter and laughter were uproarious all around us as people moved about.

Cindy beamed. Her soft blue eyes were glassy.

Roger clamped his hand down on Jacob's shoulder. "Your rascal friends are already up to no good."

Jacob grinned. "I expected nothing less."

Roger's eyes moved to mine then scanned the length of my body. His cocky smile didn't move an inch. "Evie," he greeted. "Darling as ever."

Jacob's arm flexed beneath my hold.

"You better be treating this one right," Roger said, speaking to Jacob but still looking at me. "Or I'm certain someone else will."

I tried not to squirm under this growing discomfort.

Jacob let out an irritated breath, though he maintained his air of joviality and pleasantness. He knew how to play the game. He'd had years of practice. "Of course."

Small talk exhausted me, especially the pleasantries of high society. It felt like wearing a heavy, ill-fitting glamour over my true self.

"You know women," Jacob continued. "If their expectations aren't met, they'll be sure to let you know."

Roger laughed, and Cindy joined, though her features twisted slightly as if she was still piecing together the joke.

Did I complain too much? I held fast to the smile I'd plastered on my lips. If I responded any other way, Jacob would be sure to tell me it had just been a joke.

Then I'd be playing into the very thing he was accusing me of: being... too much.

I could fix this. Tonight, I'd be the most carefree girlfriend in the world. I'd stop being so sensitive. I'd be absolutely perfect, like I belonged in this place and on the arm of a Whitfield.

Like I belonged in this *world*.

For a moment, I saw Kylo's face. I had the fleeting curiosity of where he was and what he was doing. What would he think of these high society party-goers?

Jacob dragged me forward. He greeted more of the older crowd—his parents' friends—and I increasingly felt like more of a showpiece than a person. At least that meant I was fulfilling my role. So long as I smiled and laughed at the same jokes or compliments on my appearance.

Mena had been invited, but I wouldn't find her here. We called it a *Valentin goodbye* when someone left a function without telling anyone, disappearing into the night without a trace. Mena had expanded on the term. She called it a *Valentin hello* when you simply never showed up at all.

I could see her now, smoking a secret cigarette in a lavish burgundy robe as she read a mystery novel over a glass of wine. Or maybe she had a suitor over.

Or two.

When we meandered into one of the dining rooms, Jacob was glowing, all evidence of his previous impatience gone without a trace.

The space was filled to the brim with platters and displays of food and cocktails. Guests filled tiny plates with a respectable amount of refreshments to nibble on as they mingled.

Jacob placed his hands on my waist, and I relished the rare soft touch. He used to touch me a lot more at the beginning of our relationship. We'd been dating for about four months now, and I supposed our honeymoon period was already over.

I looked up into his eyes, searching for that spark of chemistry that used to slam into my chest and warm my belly.

He let go of me.

"I'm going to go find some people," he said vaguely. "I'll be back soon. Help yourself." He gestured to the food and drink.

I nodded and murmured something warm and polite on autopilot.

I was slow to turn to the table of food. The atmosphere was suddenly twice as loud as it had been before. I busied myself with picking out a tiny sandwich and delicate pastry to place on the small white plate.

Next, I scanned the crowd, looking for any familiar, comforting faces. Everyone was paired or grouped up. I felt awkward and alone.

I pretended to walk with a purpose as I meandered through the space. A sudden bark of laughter to my right made me jump, and my cheeks instantly heated. I hoped no one had noticed.

When I finally reached the open backdoors and stepped out

onto the terrace, the fresh air instantly calmed me. Cindy hadn't been underselling the setup. Out on the back lawn was the most beautiful display of swirling lights, creating spiraling pathways for guests to follow. The trees were decorated with multicolored, glowing splendor, and tables and seating were interspersed throughout the property. In the distance were the looming Etherdale mountains.

They always brought me comfort, reminding me that Etherdale was in a valley, secure and protected by the natural landscape.

In the sea of people, I finally spotted a small group of familiar faces. They were a few of Jacob's friends, a man and two women he'd grown up with.

They were exiting the shimmering maze of light. As I approached, they moved behind one of the giant sculpted shrubs in the shape of a minor war deity with a drawn crossbow.

The hairs on the back of my neck stood straight up. A glaring shot of witchy intuition halted me in place.

The three friends were turned away from me, mostly obscured by the shrub. They watched a group of performing witches—women dressed in skin-tight outfits that barely covered their lithe forms. The thin fabric was adorned with hundreds of delicate jewels that glittered under the witch lights. More glowing orbs danced through the air in an orchestrated display as the performers twisted and contorted themselves.

"She's lasted longer than the others," Georgia said.

I stilled.

"Probably because she hasn't put out yet," the male friend, Farleigh, said.

The other woman, Mikki, gasped. "*What?* Are you serious? Wow."

Georgia laughed, and my heart sunk.

"I can't believe he invited Kailey too."

Kailey... she was one of Jacob's exes. It didn't exactly make me feel great that she was here, given Jacob had described her as *literally crazy*. But it was a huge party. I was sure it was impossible to avoid.

But how did I explain away the nausea now stuck in my gut like glue? How did I excuse the fact that Jacob had divulged the details of our sex life to his friends? Or, rather, our lack of one.

We'd done other things. I tried my best to make him happy. I'd just never had sex before. It wasn't like I thought sex was wrong or bad or terribly special; I wasn't so naive.

It was... complicated.

If you're impure, you're worthless, that cruel ghost whispered, her voice cutting and final.

Anger heated my neck, and I shoved those reaching, creeping memories back into the abyss.

The truth was, I wanted to lose my virginity as quickly as humanly possible. It was Jacob who was being so strange about it, as if it didn't really interest him. I was so inexperienced that I wasn't sure exactly what was normal. All I knew was that occasionally, he would kiss me and trace my body with his big hands and make me feel so special and loved. Then he would ask me to pleasure him with my mouth. He'd finish, kiss my forehead, and hold me. I liked being held.

The characters in my novels did things very differently. But Jacob always told me that fictional sex and romance were irresponsibly unrealistic. I'd asked him a couple times if we could do something more, if he could touch me and bring me pleasure. But he'd always made me feel embarrassed about it, like it was too exhausting or strange for me to ask.

You're so innocent. We should just take things slow, okay?

The only relief I found was when I took care of things myself.

His friends' voices rattled around in my skull, my eyes burning and throat constricting. *She's lasted longer than the others.*

As if I was merely a temporary, pretty object. If his friends thought that, what must he have said to them about me?

I backed up, trying to slow my breathing. I forced myself to remember all the good parts about us. Jacob had made me feel so pursued when we first met, like I was worth being courted and won. He'd taken an interest in me and brought me into his world. He made me believe I could have the romance and normal life I'd always fantasized about.

I took another step back, and a hand clasped around my arm as I bumped into someone's chest.

8

EVIE

"Evie," Jacob muttered. "What are you doing?"

"Oh, um, I was just going to set my plate down somewhere..." I said lamely.

Jacob stared down at my untouched miniature sandwich and pastry. He grabbed the plate and snapped his fingers at a meandering attendant. He wordlessly handed the plate to the stone-faced man dressed in server attire before walking with me to his group of friends.

"There he is!" Farleigh said, pulling Jacob in for a hug and clapping his back.

I waved hello to Georgia and Mikki, pretending as though I hadn't overheard their hurtful conversation about me. I worried my back was too stiff, my smile too forced.

"Hi Evie," Georgia said cheerfully, her auburn hair glowing red under the glimmering orbs above. "How are you? Still selling those flowers?"

A flicker of annoyance scorched my stomach at the sound of her condescension.

Jacob scratched his head. "She sells more than just flowers, Georgia."

53

My smile transformed into something more genuine, grateful he was sticking up for me.

"What else do you sell?" Mikki offered, her smile not quite reaching her dark brown eyes. Her long black hair was in dozens of braids, and she twisted one around her finger as she stared at me intently.

I shifted on my feet. "Herb bundles, oils, candles, teas…" I trailed off, struggling to remember what I'd already mentioned.

My crafting was a creative, intuitive process, and I was grateful to the owners of Celeste's for allowing me to follow where the magick led me. I brought entirely new products each time, and it apparently only bolstered the hype around my mysterious, potent magick.

"And they're all enchanted. Word around town is that her shit is powerful, too," Jacob said, words slightly slurred, as if he was already tipsy.

Still, his praise warmed my skin. My lips crept into a smile.

"Jacob said you were a chaos witch," Mikki said.

Georgia's eyes widened, and Farleigh's narrowed.

My stomach dropped. My smile evaporated. Everyone went silent. All eyes landed heavily on me.

I felt the color drain from my skin. I'd asked Jacob to keep that fact to himself. It wasn't something I advertised, especially as a witch without a coven. Chaos witches were met with a great deal of suspicion, even more so if they were solitary practitioners.

Chaos witches weren't gifted in one particular form of magick. Witches like me had all available currents open to us. We were in tune with the flow of the universe, connected to the spirit realm and the world of the gods, pulling from this natural order to concoct our own spells and magickal creations. We were necessary. We were the reason for innovation and change, new grimoires and covens, the keeping of balance and the communication with the powerful forces that ruled us all.

But we were also volatile. Powerful. Unpredictable. Some of us got lost along the way if we didn't have a moral compass and greater purpose to focus and ground our workings.

As more and more turned vampires appeared all over the realm, it was clear that chaos witches were responsible.

Who else could birth an entirely new species?

In my blood was the potential for blasphemy and destruction, chaos and catastrophe, monsters and plagues.

I'd made a vow long ago to only use my gift of creation for good. Just as many other chaos witches had pledged before me. I was a creator. An artist. A healer.

I was *good*.

I repeated that familiar mantra over and over, stunned and hurt by Jacob's breach of trust. On multiple counts, now.

"You better be careful, my friend. Looks like she's scheming ways to hex you as we speak," Farleigh joked, breaking the awkward silence as everyone burst into laughter.

Jacob slung his arm around me, and I stumbled with the sudden weight of him leaning against me.

He waved his other hand dismissively. "Evie sticks to her little earth spells and flower-picking. She's only a half-witch. She's basically harmless."

I deflated. Stupid, useless tears threatened to form.

They were just joking. It was fine. At least they knew I wasn't dangerous.

Like Jacob said, I was only half a witch. Too witch to fit in with humans, and too different to fit in with my fellow witches.

I had a foot in every door of the cosmos, and yet I belonged nowhere at all.

Something vicious flitted over Mikki's features. "I think I figured it out." Everyone looked at her with anticipation, as if hungry for the next dose of cruelty. She twirled a braid around her finger as her eyes found mine. "What do you know about love spells, Evie?"

Georgia smiled at first and then shook her head. "Mikki..."

I stared up at Jacob, who bit his lip as if holding back laughter. He looked nearly flattered by the suggestion that someone would go to such lengths to be with him.

"Clearly not much," I said.

I thought it would come out venomous and strong, like a dose of their own medicine. But instead of being a poisoned dart, my words came out all sad and puny.

I shrugged out of Jacob's hold and walked away, listening to Georgia quietly tell Mikki she'd gone too far.

As I walked back to the house, a pretty blonde woman approached, tall and thin. She moved with grace, her black dress mature and oozing old money. When she saw me, her eyes hardened to the coldest, meanest ice.

Kailey, Jacob's ex, stared forward, toward Jacob and his friends.

While her eyes remained cruel and calculated, a smile formed on her red lips as she brushed past me.

For a moment, I stood in the entrance hall, half out of my body as all of my repressed emotions rose to the surface. I'd wanted to be the perfect girlfriend tonight. Cool and unbothered, perfectly happy and agreeable.

That vision had been robbed from me. I'd been set up to fail.

I stood there motionless under another grand crystal chandelier. People laughed all around me, and I couldn't help but feel like I was the punchline of everyone's joke.

When, in reality, it was more likely that no one noticed me standing there at all.

"I heard the entire administration condones the masked thugs," a voice said loudly. "And there are *feeding* and *sex clubs* on campus now for these heretical abominations."

"There have always been salacious clubs on campus, Randall. You just weren't cool enough to be invited."

More uproarious laughter echoed through the hall.

I didn't have the bandwidth to process this loud political discussion as I waited for Jacob to catch up with me. I didn't even search for the source of these commanding voices.

"This is serious. They're a criminal organization preying off our youth. Etherdale University has officially gone to shit. They've given in to extremist propaganda. Something must be done."

I slowly turned to look out at the back lawn. I couldn't see the group I'd just escaped, as they stood too far in the distance.

But it was clear Jacob wasn't coming to find me, as he was nowhere in sight.

Kailey would keep him company.

Disoriented and far too raw, rare anger coiled up my spine like a snake. This was not a safe emotion for me to feel. I had to get out of here. The lights above flickered, and I held my breath.

I walked quickly through the house, terror pounding in my blood. Whispers tickled my eardrums, quiet enough for me to convince myself they were imagined.

When I was almost to the front foyer, a hand shot out and stopped me.

"Are you all right, dear?"

Roger Whitfield looked exactly like his son, but older. His blond hair was shorter and thinner, but his hazel eyes and strong nose were replicas. The smile lines around his lips made him appear more genuine, even as my witchy senses recoiled.

"I'm fine," I said. "Just need to get some air."

A lie. I was about to pull the Valentin goodbye of the century. Mena would be proud.

"He's young," Roger said, speaking low as he stepped away from the group at his back and looked down at me intently. "He'll be a good man one day. But right now, he's a boy. Boys are easily distracted and don't know what's good for them. They don't know what they want, and they're too busy figuring themselves out to realize the consequences of their actions."

Roger sipped from his whiskey, taking another step toward me so that we were uncomfortably close.

"Why don't we go somewhere private, so you can compose yourself, hmm?"

His smile was disarming, all warmth and paternal care.

I wanted to believe the surface, but when his hand brushed mine, the jolt of intuition was too strong to ignore.

This man wanted me alone with him for far different reasons than comfort.

Horror and disgust were rancid poisons in my gut. And the sudden disillusionment slammed into me from all directions, all at once.

This place was filled with sparkles and light and money and magick.

But underneath the glamorous façade was a sinister darkness that was all too familiar.

"Thank you, Roger," I forced out. "I'm going to use the bathroom first," I lied. Anything to get him to let me go.

"I'll find you after."

I wasn't sure if I smiled or not. I didn't care anymore about politeness. This time, when I made my dash to the door, I didn't stop for anything. Not when the lights flickered again, or when people stared at me like I was some kind of strange bird in an exhibit.

I didn't stop until I was off the property and onto the cobblestone street, my lungs tight, my hands shaking. I rushed to the nearest shrub. I threw up water and stomach acid from my empty, sickened gut.

I wiped a stray tear from my face as emotions spilled from the cracks of my mental dams, untethered and volatile.

"No, no, no."

I stumbled back as the shrub shriveled like I'd sucked the life out of it. The bright green leaves darkened and then fell to the ground, dry and lifeless.

I blinked once before turning away and slipping out of my shoes. I didn't walk.

I fucking ran.

There was something rotten inside me. If I stopped running from it for even a second, I knew in my bones it would swallow me whole.

9

KYLO

Evie wasn't where she was supposed to be tonight, safe in her princess palace. I tracked her by her scent all the way to her boyfriend's estate.

I had half a mind to claim her in front of all of them. I wanted to force my blood down her delicate little throat so I would know where she was at all times.

And if that was my desire before I'd seen her hurry from the mansion, clearly shaken and disturbed, her blood drenched in fear, I was downright fucking wrathful now.

I watched as she threw up into a shrub, her small body trembling with terror. I had to squash the urge to hold her hair, to rub soothing circles on her back. Scenario after scenario ran through my mind, envisioning all the ways someone could have harmed her.

It had likely been her shitty, undeserving child of a boyfriend, who was, unsurprisingly, nowhere to be found.

If mistreating her wasn't horrible enough, there was no damn excuse for allowing her to walk home alone at this hour. He was failing even the most basic tests of chivalry and competency, and in my world, those acts were punishable by death.

Cloaked in shadow and fuming, I had to force myself to stop imagining a scenario where I wasn't here to protect her.

My eyes widened. The shrub in front of Evie started to shrivel and decay at a rapid pace.

While I was shocked by the sight, Evie appeared horrified, quickly turning and running. It was as though her magick had a mind of its own, and she was petrified by it.

Who was this strange little creature full of mysteries and secrets?

She was clearly not a green witch. That much was apparent.

She also belonged to no coven, with no one around to help with her powers, whatever they may be. Where had she come from? Why was she surrounded by humans?

I followed her carefully. Her blood was so fearful that it had my cock hardened and alert, my fangs throbbing in my gums.

It didn't help matters that I was hunting her like a wolf chasing a vulnerably unaware rabbit.

The moon was bright and half-full in the sky, giving her hair a silvery and luminous sheen. She was a mythological temptress dressed in blush satin and tulle, offering merely a tease of her sinful curves.

She was so fucking pretty. How any man saw her looking like this and let her out of his sight was a baffling, nonsensical notion.

Yet, I was grateful for it. Because I didn't want my perfect angel anywhere near another man.

Evie stopped running when she reached the steep path up to her estate. Her breathing was heavy, fear still a steady pulse in her fluttering mortal heart.

For a moment, she just stood there, staring up at the looming two-story home. She hesitated. Then, she swayed.

A whispered curse escaped my lips.

I had two seconds to decide whether to catch Evie before she collapsed to the cobblestone and cracked open her skull.

My shadow glamour evaporated. In a rush of vampire speed, I scooped her into my arms as she fell.

Her eyes fluttered rapidly beneath her eyelids. Her soft pink lips tugged down, and her face went slack.

She was so warm in my arms. Her addictive, sweet scent overwhelmed my senses. I had to force myself to stop staring at her delicate features, almost in disbelief that someone this perfect existed.

This fallen angel was severing every last thread of my restraint.

She had no idea the monster she'd ensnared. This precious girl had not a clue the lengths her hunter would go to get exactly what he wanted.

I was a man of obsessions and fixations. I exerted control with ease. I did not hesitate, and I felt no remorse for the atrocities I committed for the greater good.

I brushed a stray strand of silvery blond from her cheek, my fingertips trailing along her smooth skin.

Snapping out of my stunned stupor, I held Evie tight to my chest as I carried her to the cottage.

When I set her down in the grass just before the porch, with extreme care and gentleness, she didn't stir. It was nearly concerning.

I fished for the key under a small flower pot by the door, where I'd seen her retrieve it before. After pushing the door open, I scooped her back into my arms and carried her to her bedroom. Her breathing was slow and measured. When I laid her down and pulled the covers up around her, she let out the cutest, breathiest moan that did ungodly things to my body.

I was rigid as I stared down at her, my jaw clenched tight. I wanted to touch her. My disobedient shadows escaped my skin, crawling all over her body above the covers in tendrils of smoke.

It took immeasurable effort to pull them back.

I stood there, watching her, for far too long. My bullshit justification was that I needed to make sure she was medically safe, but I could hear the steady, normal cadence of her heart and the gentle pump of blood. I knew she was fine.

I closed my eyes and shook my head, slowly backing away from her.

"Mama," she whined, the sound of her voice jolting me as if it were a strike of lightning.

I halted by the door, holding my breath.

"Hurts," she whimpered. "*Mama.*"

My heart cracked at the desperation in her voice. The raw pain. The steady course of fear in her blood that didn't stop even in her sleep.

"Just a... baby. Child. So small. Hurts," she mumbled, her speech fragmented and hard to discern.

My voyeurism was suddenly far too intrusive. This felt *wrong.* I shouldn't have been bearing witness to this state of raw vulnerability, the deep pain of a wounded subconscious.

Yet something about her childlike vulnerability triggered the deepest, darkest need to protect her. To take all her pain away and make sure no one ever harmed her again. To destroy all those who had ever hurt her, to make them suffer brutally, mercilessly.

It was perverse, this compulsion to mark and claim her, to spoil and care for her, to shield her from all darkness and violence.

When I was the most violent and dark being there was.

"Please," she begged.

A low growl built in my chest. Whoever had denied her pleas and harmed her had performed an act of depravity against humanity itself.

I forced myself to leave before I lost control and did something I couldn't take back.

One day, I would hold her while she slept. My shadows would coil around her small body and drive away all nightmares. I would be the only monster allowed to haunt her dreams.

The next time I touched her, she'd be conscious and aware of every second of it.

10

EVIE

"**M**ama, please!" I screamed.

Where was Idris? I had to find Idris. No one was coming to save us. No one was going to protect us.

It was all up to me.

I heard Idris screaming. The walls of the house were crumbling and rotting, and my vision was going in and out.

"I can't see!" I wailed. "Mama!"

They were laughing at me. The whole room of them. Cloaked in black, their prayers echoed through the disintegrating house. My mother and father, the entire coven… and, oh Lillian… *they* were here too.

My black dress was stifling. I couldn't make sense of the dreamlike warping of time and jagged memories and metaphors. The only thing I understood was that I needed to find my brother.

He was so small, still a child. I heard him scream again. Was he still a baby? He was just a baby.

We had to go.

I climbed the staircase, but it kept growing taller and steeper, and Idris's screams farther and farther away.

I couldn't—I couldn't—

I screamed, and the darkness consumed us all. As our flesh was pulled from bone and our souls scrambled, all I could think was: *I bet my family's last thought was how much of an endless source of shame and disappointment I was.*

~

I AWOKE with a scream lodged in my throat, but the memories of my nightmares were hazy and hard to understand.

As always, the prevailing feeling was an overwhelming terror for my brother's safety.

I used to rush to his room across the hall after these dreams, back when we both lived upstairs in the main house. I would have to make sure he was safe in his bed. I was only soothed when I saw the steady rise and fall of his chest. Even then, sometimes I'd have to stay with him until morning, just to be sure.

I'd tried to stop the habit as we got older. It became less frequent as the years passed. The compulsion always grew stronger in the spring, reaching its peak late summer.

This morning, I had that familiar urge. But Idris was at university, and I hadn't seen him since that day at the coffeeshop. He'd be home tomorrow night for dinner.

I could wait until then. He would hate if I showed up unannounced in this state of mind.

My lip was sore from how hard I was chewing on it. I took deep breaths, reminding myself that the paranoid thoughts dominating my mind weren't true.

We weren't in danger. No one was coming for us. No one was watching our every move.

We were safe. We'd been safe for over a decade.

I was so disoriented that the memories from last night were slow to surface.

Why couldn't I remember getting into bed? I rose, staring down at my blush pink dress in confusion. I'd been sober, as always. I remembered running all the way home. But I couldn't recall anything else.

I shut my eyes tight. *Calm the hell down, Evie,* I scolded myself. It was probably just stress. I'd clearly been too exhausted and emotional to change clothes before sleeping.

Everything was okay. I had it all under control.

I got ready for my day, sliding into the soft, oversized light-blue shirt I wore as a casual dress. Then I got to work, refusing to even think about last night until I'd created at least two new products and drank two cups of coffee.

My crafting and spell room was my haven. When I entered the space, I already felt ten times lighter. Flowers and herbs hung from lines of string strung along the walls to dry, while others were kept alive in pots and vases, depending on their intended usage. There were countless shelves of crystals, candle holders, vials, glass bottles, and other tools or adornments. I liked to grow or collect my own materials as much as possible, keeping the magickal energy pure to ward against contagion.

Magick was both an art and a science. While some rules could be bent or manipulated, others remained rigid, and it was all dependent on the particular witch, spirits, and energies involved at any given time.

Witchcraft was best thought of as an ecosystem. Witches who ignored basic tenets of reciprocity, harmony, and balance would be continually frustrated by their lack of results.

In the center of the space was my altar, where I visioned, made offerings or sacrifices to the spirit world, used divination tools like tarot or pendulums, and created new spells and sigils. It was a wide standing altar, with shelves and storage underneath and hand-drawn white sigils all over its surface for power and protection. The altar itself was painted pastel pink.

Because fuck the color black.

My magick was pretty and pink.

While I sipped coffee and nibbled on a piece of toast, I selected a purifying bundle of herbs to burn. The energy in the cottage was tense and heavy, a reflection of the inner chaos of my mind. I couldn't have any of that mental clutter affecting my magick.

I snapped my fingers, lighting the bundle with a touch of conjured fire. I let the flame glow for a few seconds before I blew it out. I then allowed the herbs to smolder and release a steady billow of smoke. I took soothing inhales as I moved about, thanking the spirits of the land for their aid and protection. I fed the spirits of the doorways and windows, asking them to banish all negative influences from my space. I asked Selena for clarity and wisdom. I asked Helia for the ability to heal and help all those who found my products.

I didn't ask the Dark Goddess for anything. Lillian and I were not on speaking terms.

I called to the four cardinal directions and their corresponding influences and elements, then to the worlds above and below.

I made an offering of fresh berries and roses at my altar. I offered the sustenance not only to spirits who already supported me but also to those who might stand down and out of my way for a seat at the offering table.

Let there be harmony between us for all of our days.

As I entered into the ideal headspace for witchery, my head cleared, my lungs released deep, soothing breaths, and my heart was filled with gratitude and excitement.

The world around me became brighter, and I knew I was no longer alone.

I smiled. "What are we making today?"

IT WAS a day of creativity and breakthroughs. Not only had I been called to create a healing salve for one of my regular buyers, but I'd also devised a new spell to invoke and feed the muses for artists who need a boost. The spirits were particularly jazzed about this one, insisting that it was going to help the right people at the exact right time. I crafted a sigil and consecrated three candles with the correct corresponding herbs, oils, and crystal fragments. Then I wrote down instructions for proper usage and tied the papers to each candle with a sparkly golden ribbon.

I'd ended up becoming so absorbed in my work that I forgot to feed myself lunch. I was woozy, glowing, and beaming with pride when I finally exited the cottage.

As I approached the main house, I could see Mena bustling about in her art studio on the second floor. She turned and caught sight of me through the tall, arched window. She waved a paint brush in greeting before moving away from the window.

In the kitchen, I made Mena and myself lavender and lemon tea as I soothed my stomach with a chicken sandwich.

"Darling," she exclaimed as she entered. "Whatever magick you're cooking up today, keep it coming!"

I grinned as I passed her a mug and stood opposite her at the marble counter while I finished eating.

She was in a floor-length, billowy, tunic-style magenta dress embellished with brown vines. Her glasses today were large, leopard print ovals.

"I was struck, as if by lightning!" She continued, raising her arms in a grand gesture as if opening herself up to the gods. "And I knew I must paint right away. Who was I to deny such a call?"

She sipped her tea, staining the yellow mug's rim with the burnt red shade of her lipstick. "How was the party?"

I swallowed. Ignoring what had happened last night had allowed me to enjoy my day immensely.

"You made the right call pulling a Valentin hello," I said.

She tilted her head back with laughter. "I'm never wrong about these things."

I sighed. "I'm starting to believe you about that." I quickly changed the subject. "What did you do last night?"

"Well, I went into town to dance," she said, her lips shifting into something mischievous. "Evie, I swear I don't know how these things happen to me, but I ended up at the most marvelous party with the most interesting and strange people. It was only when everyone began to undress that I realized it was an orgy!"

I almost spit out my tea. I shook my head. I was already keenly aware of how much cooler Mena was than me. Than any of us, really. She still managed to shock me with it at least twice a week.

"You know me," she continued. "Orgies are a perfectly acceptable way to spend your Tuesday evening. But with strangers? Not at my age. That's a young person's game of roulette."

She paused, one of her well-manicured dark brows lifting. She shook a finger at me. "You evaded the question." Her eyes narrowed before she let out a sigh. "That whiny man child ruined your night, didn't he?"

"Mena," I said, but it was a feeble protest, given that she was right.

Why hadn't Jacob come to see me today? Did he think it was my fault—that I was being too sensitive? Or was he too drunk to notice how hurt I was?

Or, the worst, most nagging possibility—perhaps he'd simply let Kailey take my place.

"I'm glad you've finally heeded my wisdom," she said, the mischief in her eyes back to its enthusiastic dance.

"What wisdom, specifically?"

"That two boyfriends are better than one, of course," she said.

She was talking about the case of the mysterious gifted book that still hadn't been solved. The most plausible explanation I'd come up with was that it had been from one of my friends from Celeste's or a grateful client, but the anonymity was strange. I figured someone would own up to it eventually.

"That way, when one boyfriend is dragging you down, you can merely focus on the second. And if the first never shapes up, replace him."

"Thank you, Mena," I said with a roll of my eyes. "Sound advice."

After Mena and I finished lunch, I set up camp in the gardens to escape into a fantasy world. Though my focus kept drifting away from the pages and back to my worries.

During my workings this morning, I'd pulled tarot cards for my relationship with Jacob, against my better judgment. I pulled Death and the Three of Swords. The Death card was self-explanatory. Something was ending, and a necessary rebirth loomed. The Three of Swords was an image of three swords piercing a wounded heart, the most classic depiction of heartbreak and loss there was.

In other words, it was over. We were breaking up.

I didn't read any more cards after that.

Most of me was heartbroken, but the strongest part of me was relieved. Jacob had betrayed me. And if that wasn't enough, I certainly couldn't be with someone who put my safety at risk. No matter how badly I'd wanted to feel special and chosen, like a grand romance was within reach and not merely a lofty fantasy.

But, later that evening, when Jacob finally showed up on my doorstep with a bouquet of pink snapdragons and a box of fine, dark chocolates—that strong, knowing part of me went quiet.

I accepted the gifts, and I let him apologize and shower me with the softest touches and kisses. I let him convince me that he was not only willing to change, but that he was capable of it too.

"Get dressed for dinner, my love. I'm taking you somewhere special," he said. "I have a whole night planned for us."

Here was the effort I'd been hoping for, that romantic show of appreciation. Maybe he really did understand what I wanted. Maybe the thought of losing me was enough to motivate him to treat me the way he knew I deserved.

11

EVIE

The restaurant was dimly lit and screamed wealth. White candles were placed on each table and set strategically across the dark wood furnishings to establish a cozy, relaxing ambiance. Waiters were attentive and serious, and the menu was brimming with delicacies.

As we ate, we spoke about Jacob's travels and goals for the future. He talked about starting his own business—though he wasn't sure exactly what kind of business—and building an *empire*. He mentioned his desire for marriage and children, and my stomach somersaulted.

Did he see those things with me?

"I crafted a new spell today," I said. "For artists."

Jacob smiled, swallowing his bite of steak. "That's lovely, Evie."

I waited for him to ask me about it, but he didn't.

"Do you want to travel again in the future?" I asked.

Jacob's eyes lit up. "Desperately. In fact, I'm considering going back to the countryside soon. For a month or two, maybe. I made some friends there. And I'm still brainstorming ideas for my business. The fresh farming air was doing wonders for my inspiration and focus."

My stomach dropped. Jacob continued to eat, staring off into space at times. I waited for him to ask me how I felt about him leaving again or ask me if I wanted to join him.

He didn't do either.

This relationship was making me feel insane. Was it really so normal to not consider your partner at all before you left them for weeks? To not want to bring them along?

Maybe if I had more experience, or more friends, I'd be able to understand if my disappointment was as irrational as Jacob always told me it was.

Not that I would ever return to the countryside. I'd likely never leave Etherdale.

After a long spell of silence, I spoke again. "I woke up from nightmares this morning."

"I'm sorry to hear that," Jacob said. "They're probably from all that worrying you do." He smiled teasingly, tearing off a piece of bread and popping it into his mouth.

"I do worry about Idris. Maybe too much," I admitted. "I just want him to be safe. And happy. I'm already concerned about him being on campus during times like these, but then to hear that he's going to take fighting classes, idolizes the Masked Order—a clan of literal violent criminals—"

"Evie," Jacob said, cutting me off. "Idris is an adult. He'll be fine. You're catastrophizing. I've heard about this every single time we've hung out."

"I'm sorry," I said. I shouldn't have said anything about the nightmares or worries. I shouldn't have changed the subject to something so negative.

"I'm not your emotional healer, you know? These are things you should talk about with a professional."

I shrunk back in my chair. "I'm sorry."

"You have to consider my feelings, too. You can't keep hogging all the emotional space. It's exhausting. I'm politely telling you that I'm at my limit. I have my own problems to worry about."

He was at his limit. I took note of the arrogant tilt to his head. He was looking at me as if he expected even more of a reaction —a stronger apology, maybe.

I suddenly remembered the tarot reading from earlier today and the clear message that our relationship was dead.

An uneasy feeling stirred somewhere deep inside my gut.

This relationship was *not* normal.

Or maybe normalcy had nothing to with it.

This relationship wasn't good for me. In fact, I realized it was slowly killing me inside.

The growing feeling inside my stomach continued to churn. It was becoming more than unease. That strong, angry part of me was waking from her slumber.

A witchy wind blew through the air, as if the spirits were affirming this sudden breakthrough in clarity—the shattering of my current reality in favor of a new one.

"Why did you invite your ex last night?" I asked, my heart pounding in my chest as defiance lit up my nerves.

"Evie," Jacob said, anger flitting in his eyes as his lips turned down. "Don't do this." He glanced sideways in both directions to see if people were staring.

"Why did you invite her?" I asked again.

Jacob rolled his eyes. "She's friends with my friends. It would've been weird if I hadn't invited her. Plus, I didn't send out invites. My mom did."

His answer confused me, as it seemed to be both a justification for his actions and a denial of responsibility rolled into one.

When he'd brought me gifts earlier today, he'd only apologized for letting me leave the party upset, as well as the cruel things his friends had said to me in front of him. I hadn't brought up his breaches in trust, or what I'd overheard.

"Why did you tell your friends that I was a chaos witch, when I specifically asked you not to?"

His lip twitched, something cruel entering his hazel irises even as his face appeared stoic and immovable.

"You never told me not to tell anyone," he said, suddenly shifting into a look of confusion.

All manner of warning bells rang in a cacophony.

He watched my face carefully, then continued. "Even if you did tell me not to, which is doubtful since I don't remember it, it's really not that big of a deal."

"What about our sex life? Why did they know we've never had sex?"

Jacob lowered his voice. "We're in public," he hissed. "But you never told me not to tell anyone *that* either. Besides, you tell Mena what a horrible boyfriend I am all the time. You think I haven't noticed how she looks at me, but I have."

I shook my head. "Jacob, I have never told Mena you're horrible. I—"

"How could I believe that? When you're hurling accusation after accusation at me? What is this incessant need to always make me the bad guy? You have your fair share of flaws, too, Evie, *believe me*. But here you go, painting your subjective view of reality as if it's fact. When really, your version of events is completely skewed. I pity living in a mind like yours, where everyone else is a mean evil villain and you're just a perfect little angel who could do no wrong."

For a moment, I was stunned. I tended to freeze during conflicts, no doubt a trauma response from my childhood, or whatever Mena's psychology professor friend had called it.

I could feel the weight of multiple pairs of eyes that had strayed our way toward Jacob's raised, emotional voice.

Angel.

For whatever reason, my brain snagged on that word, used it as a springboard for action. I thought of that mysterious man who'd treated me with such patience and care, who'd peppered me with meaningful questions and looked at me like I was something rare and priceless.

I might never see Kylo again, but whatever it was that he made me feel, that was what I wanted. That was what I deserved.

I stood up from the table.

"Sit. Back. Down." Jacob's eyes were pure venom. "People are staring." For a moment, I saw a wounded little boy, terrified of abandonment and on the verge of a tantrum.

When I placed my napkin on the table, he grabbed my trembling hand.

A flash of intuition flooded my mind from the channel he opened with his touch—the smell of perfume, a woman's laughter, red lips on his neck.

Weaker individuals tended to be the easiest to read.

Tears stung my eyes. I yanked my hand free, and after one last hard stare, I turned on my heel and walked away. Several candles snuffed out as I passed.

I walked as slowly and calmly as I could manage until I exited the restaurant. Once outside, I quickly made my way to a side street. It was only then that I finally allowed the broken sob to leave my lips. At this point, I wasn't even sure which part of that dinner from hell hurt the worst. The realization that he'd cheated on me was strangely low on the pain scale. The attacks on my character and the way he made me question my sense of reality were far worse.

Hysterical, inappropriate laughter spilled out of me.

The cards never lied.

"What are we laughing about, little human?"

I stiffened, then spun toward the voice. The vampire was in front of me in a flash. Only two feet of space stood between us.

Vampires often confused me for a human, given I had a human father.

Your blood smells unique. Delicious. Perfect, a ghost from the past whispered, turning my insides rancid.

I stood perfectly still, assessing my options quickly.

I'd never been fed from before, and that was *not* a form of virginity I had any desire to lose. Panic seized me, and a buried power promised protection.

But I stamped it down.

It wasn't that late. Surely there were vampire hunters around, or anyone at all who could help me. I opened my mouth.

"If you scream, I'll kill you. I will snap your little neck before anyone can hear it. Is that understood?"

My focus sharpened on the vampire before me. His rancid, copper breath fanned across my face. His red hair brushed his shoulders, and his suit was flashy yet ill-fitted. The bright crimson fabric made my heart skip a beat, reminding me that I might only be seconds away from death.

His cruel, near-black eyes were devoid of empathy—two deep, cold voids that sent a shiver straight to my soul.

Those voids sharpened to slits. "Is that *understood?*" he repeated.

I nodded. My heart hammered. Buried power roared to life in my bones, like a feral, caged animal.

The cage remained locked tight. I'd find another way to survive. I had to.

He grabbed me by the hair, jerking my head backwards and exposing my neck, and I winced, fighting against the instinctive urge to yelp.

"You smell so fucking good," he groaned, his lips nearly brushing my ear. His breath was hot against my cheek. "You may look sweet and pure, but I can scent the naughty truth."

His manic laughter twisted my guts into knots. In a flash of movement, he grabbed me and shoved me against a boarded-up door in a narrow alley so that we were completely obscured from sight.

Pure.

If you're impure, you're worthless.

My skin seared with heat.

"Ow, fuck," the vampire screamed, letting go of me and rearing back.

His eyes grew crazed, and I knew he was on the verge of bloodlust. Once he entered that wild, feral state, my demise was guaranteed. A vampire in bloodlust lost all control. They fed on their prey with no restraint, tearing them apart until they were nothing but ruined flesh.

He snarled. "Are you a fucking witch?"

It was already starting to leak out of me—this poison, this darkness that might swallow Etherdale whole. I couldn't hurt anyone with my magick.

I'd rather die.

When he grabbed my throat, I felt useless and weak. I couldn't scream. I couldn't fight. I was yet another innocent lost to pointless, disgusting violence. It was a vat of pain we were all drowning in, heaving lungs and flailing limbs, victims to a sickness that spread endlessly.

His grip tightened in response to my silence, and a cloud of darkness eclipsed my vision. I writhed and clawed at his arm, but he only flashed his fangs and squeezed harder.

I saw my mother's face. I searched her eyes for warmth, for comfort. Two empty voids stared back.

"Your body is going to be covered with my bites. Every single part of you."

I shut my eyes. I ignored the survival instincts begging me to fight. Begging me to grow the fuck up—to stop being childish and weak.

A growl tore through the night. The hand on my throat receded, and oxygen flooded my lungs.

I coughed, sucking in air and slumping against the door. I opened my eyes.

A man wearing a frightening, deep black skull mask that covered most of his face stood before me. His black shirt was rolled up, revealing elaborate onyx tattoos on his fair skin. Symbols, patterns, and sigil-like structures that I might've wanted to inspect closer under different circumstances.

Shadows crawled from him, tendrils of smoke and clouds of darkness. All that I ran from, all that I feared.

Those familiar whispers tickled my eardrums.

I flattened myself against the structure at my back. My chest rose and fell rapidly. The man's lips were uncovered and stained crimson. At his feet was the born vampire, crumpled and motionless in a pool of blood.

I was slow to move my eyes back up to the masked vampire before me. The vampire who was once human—a blasphemy of Helia's creation, an obscene mockery of Lillian's demon spawn.

His diagonally carved mask covered his eyes, obscuring any evidence of that lingering humanity. It was a strange opaque material, churning slightly as if made of the same inky shadow as his powers.

He was tall and muscular, a finely tuned weapon whose focus was trained entirely on me.

I swallowed. "Thank you." I rubbed at my burning, sore throat. "You saved me, right?" That was *supposed* to be the Masked Order's purpose—to defend mortals against the born. "Or are you going to hurt me, too?"

He shook his head. When he stepped over the dead born's body, I realized I'd been trembling. When his hand slowly reached toward me, those trembles turned violent.

His fingers brushed against my cheek. The touch was so

gentle that it made me shiver, goosebumps erupting over my exposed arms.

I held my breath, disoriented, confused, terrified, and yet...

There was something inside of him that called to me. The dark stillness around us was comforting. Familiar.

A drop of blood trickled down the corner of his mouth.

He was a fucking monster. A monster who ate other monsters.

There was something familiar about his smirk, but before I could place it, the mask itself shifted to cover his entire face.

"I will never hurt you," he said.

His words came out deep and powerful, yet muffled, as if the shadows were disguising his true voice.

"Unless you ask very politely."

A startled, surprised noise escaped me as I tripped over my words.

He cocked his head, as if amused. A sly cat toying with a mouse.

"Please let me go."

The tattooed, masked vampire towered over me. Even if I couldn't see his eyes, I could feel their scorch on every inch of my skin.

My body had never been more confused, caught between intrigue, comfort, terror, and the strangest, most dangerous curiosity.

He stepped back. "Go straight home."

I gritted my teeth. "I'm not one of your brainwashed henchmen. You can't order me around."

"Mm," he rumbled, his chest shaking slightly with a low chuckle. He took more steps back, utterly ignoring the dead and mangled born at our feet. "You're right. You're far too adorable to be one of my henchmen."

I scoffed, my brows shooting up.

"You're going to do what you're told because you're my good girl."

I'd stopped shaking at some point. My panic had dissipated. Those ghoulish hands from the past stopped their reaching.

All I felt was flustered irritation.

I didn't look at my attacker's body on the ground as I delicately stepped around his crumpled form.

"You're disgusting."

He shrugged, stepping back onto the side street. "Do you need a healer?"

I exited the alley slowly and cautiously, half afraid he was about to snatch me up and hurt me after all.

Did I need a healer? What a bizarre question from a violent street thug who was brazenly flirting with a stranger who'd just been attacked.

He was insane. No need to overanalyze.

It was hard to look away from this masked vigilante. Shadows circled him like he was some kind of dark god of the underworld. The power he radiated could be felt viscerally, emitting a forceful hum that rang through the air.

"I—no. I don't need a healer," I mumbled. I heard voices in the distance. The man shrouded in violent magick didn't move. He only stared at me from behind his impenetrable mask.

I backed up from him slowly and walked in the opposite direction. Away from the restaurant where my boyfriend was likely finishing his glass of red wine, oblivious to the fact that I'd nearly had my throat ripped out.

Away from this man with poison coursing through his veins. The darkness that whispered to me—the darkness I'd shunned long ago, in some nowhere village amid the rolling hills of the countryside.

12

KYLO

I didn't let Evie out of my fucking sight the whole way home. I'd kept calm in front of her, carefully tucking my true identity away.

The truth was, I'd never been more enraged.

Not only because she'd been attacked—a born vampire had laid hands on my perfect angel—but also because of what I'd witnessed just before the born had dragged her back into that enclave.

That sorry excuse for a man, Evie's incompetent, selfish boyfriend, had seen the vampire confront her.

He'd stood there, peeking around the street corner after following her out of the restaurant. He'd seen the vampire threaten her, and at the first hint that he'd been spotted by the born man, he took off in the other direction.

Like a pathetic, sniveling coward.

It was more than likely he'd gone in search of help. But he'd done it quietly. Carefully. He'd chosen to prioritize self-preservation over helping Evie immediately, by whatever means necessary. Lest he stain his finely tailored suit.

Little did he know, it was failing to protect Evie that had truly sealed his fate.

It wasn't until Evie was back to her princess estate that I felt my chest begin to untighten. From behind a shadow glamour and an impressive willow, I watched her collapse in her garden. She sunk to the grass, surrounded by flowers and herbs, a stone bird bath to her left and hovering witch lights above.

One of her light blue sleeves slipped off her shoulder as she cried. Her shoulders shook. Sobs escaped her, a cacophony of emotions spilling from some dammed up, secret place. In the sounds of her whimpers, I heard my own pain. My family's pain. My clan's. This city's. This entire damned realm's.

I wanted to scoop her into my arms and hold her tight to my chest. I wanted to taste the saltiness of her tears on my tongue. I wanted to shove my blood down her petite throat so I would know exactly where she was at all times. I wanted to mark and claim her, to prevent her from ever being touched by another man again.

I was unraveling. Possessed. Consumed.

It was a sickness, a deep obsession that had me pierced between its talons.

I would know her. Every part of her. The secrets she'd buried, the dreams she feared were too big for this world, every last yearning and desire hidden beneath her angelic mask. I would pry each piece of her out into the open. I would consume every last drop of her the way she fucking consumed *me.*

But first, I had an execution to attend to.

~

I FOUND Evie's ex-boyfriend halfway between her estate and downtown Etherdale. He was running his hands through his hair, visibly shaken. I imagined that by the time he'd found and brought back reinforcements, Evie had already been on her way home.

Perhaps he thought she was dead.

To be perfectly honest, I didn't much care what he thought or what had happened after he'd abandoned Evie.

Nothing about this person mattered. Not anymore.

It took little effort to flex just a drop of my rage, snatching him off the street, stuffing shadow in his mouth to gag him, and dragging him into the cemetery to the left. I threw him roughly against a tomb, letting his head smack into the stone.

His confusion transformed into terror, now facing Etherdale's judge and executioner.

I was the clan leader of the Masked Order, shrouded in shadows that hungered for righteous violence.

My mask was in place, my tattoos proudly displayed.

The man—Jonathon? Jeffrey? Jason?

Fuck knew what his name was.

The man stared up at me in utter horror, shaking as he writhed against my shadows holding him in place.

"Would you like to know a secret?"

The boring narcissist stared up at me in nearly a glare, but not quite, as he seemed too terrified to display anger. His lip wobbled.

Sure would be nice if someone heroic was around to help him.

I casually reached for my favorite dagger, a beautiful silver blade with an onyx hilt connected to my magick. Tiny sigils glowed under the moonlight.

I spun it around in my hand as if it were a toy. I let the silence stretch, listening to his heart hammer fast and hard.

When Evie had been attacked, her heart had sounded similar, at first. Then it had slowed, as if she'd given up. As if she'd lost all hope of being protected long ago.

It snapped something inside of me.

I crouched down in front of him. My shadows were still gagging him and holding him down as he squirmed. He was the perfect captive audience.

"My secret is that I wanted to kill you from the moment I laid eyes on you," I said casually, as if discussing my favorite way to prepare steak. I dragged the blade up his chest to the center of his sternum with feather-light pressure. When he whimpered like a child, I grinned. "I resisted the urge, of course. Because I'm a *man*, not a boy wearing a man's suit."

Beautiful anger flashed in his eyes, for the briefest moment, as I took a swipe at his comically fragile ego.

"I could say that it was because I knew immediately you weren't good for Evie, due to my keen judge of character. And that would be true. But it is equally true that I wanted to kill you merely for touching her. For speaking to her. For thinking you have even the tiniest of claim on her body, her heart, her soul."

His words were muffled nonsense against the gag, but I knew instinctively that he'd finally started to plead. To barter. He was likely offering Evie up on a silver platter and vowing never to touch her again, so long as I let him live.

"The thing about me is…"

In a flash of movement, I had the blade pressed up against his throat. He went perfectly still, and the smell of piss filled the air.

"…I don't mind being unhinged. In fact," I said, drawing the words out as if I were savoring a fine meal. I dragged my eyes down to his damp black pants and back up to his eyes. I jutted out my bottom lip, as if with pity. "I'm really rather fond of my insanity."

My shadows pressed up against his chest and neck now, starving him for air as he gasped violently. Just like Evie had struggled to breathe when the born had his grimy hands around her throat.

Rage tore through me at that mental image. My jaw ticked.

"You can afford a touch of madness when you're also highly effective. And rest assured, when it comes to taking care of what belongs to me, there is no one more attentive, focused, and thorough."

I let the gag drop, if only out of curiosity.

The fragile man's lip curled. "King Earle is going to obliterate your kind from the realm. As soon as you come out from your cowardly hiding, you will be annihilated. You're nothing but rebellious adolescents," he stammered as his voice shook with fear and his lungs screamed for air. "You're a delusional fucking *freak!*"

When a droplet of his spit landed on my cheek, my grin turned vicious.

I laughed. "You are very bold for a man who just pissed himself."

Rage twisted his ugly face into something uglier. "If you want Evie, you can have her. I'm no longer interested in her, anyway. Your band of criminals needs resources, no? Well, I have plenty. Spare me, and you can have whatever you want."

"Johnny, you have not been listening to a word I've said, have you? Which tracks, given what I've observed about you."

"Johnny? My name is—"

I slit his throat. Blood sprayed and then ran down his neck and chest in a flood.

"Don't care."

Refusing to waste blood, no matter how unappetizing, I pulled back my shadows and fed.

When I was finished, I stood. I wiped the blood from my mouth and stared at the blood-and-piss-soaked man at my feet. "I don't need weaker men to give me what I want. I am perfectly capable of taking it myself."

A pleasurable, satisfied feeling washed over me. I flexed my hands and inhaled deeply.

Blood not only sustained vampires and kept us from

mummifying, but it also fueled our power and magick. And given my station, I needed more blood than most.

I was the most powerful vampire I'd ever encountered. Princeton, my maker, wasn't sure why some turned were born more powerful than others, or why certain gifts appeared. He frequently experimented with different sigils and spells in attempts to control how new recruits developed after the turning ritual.

But in the end, it was ultimately up to the gods and the spirit dimension how each individual was reborn.

Something inside me had found a home in the shadows—and the shadows had made a home in me. It was a symbiotic relationship built on a mutual desire for power and supremacy. A thirst for creation and destruction, two sides of the same coin.

Now, my shadows and I wanted *her*.

My little blonde angel.

Who was I to question such an undeniable, inexplicable gravitational pull? My intuition was never wrong. That was something my clan was keenly aware of.

Protecting Evie meant I needed to dispose of this body carefully. I was going to make it seem like he'd left Etherdale. I had no interest in unnecessarily harming her.

The threat to Evie's safety had been eliminated. The fact that a man could no longer touch what belonged to me was merely an added bonus.

I DESCENDED THE STEEP, spiral stairs bathed in darkness to the underground. Beneath the bustling streets of Etherdale lay a sprawling, hidden world.

To the mortals and the born, only a dangerous labyrinth of catacombs—mass graves from a failed mortal uprising hundreds of years ago—lay under city center. Tales of the harm that befell any soul who entered the catacombs were useful to ward off curious eyes.

Then, of course, our actual wards, spells, traps, and protections were added barriers. Because beyond the catacombs lay a system of hidden libraries, studies, training rooms, and social clubs.

The mortal loyalists and born were under the false impression my clan was merely a nuisance, a small collection of disorganized, impassioned flies buzzing in their ears.

Jonathon had summarized it well. We were viewed as adolescents. Merely a secret society of youth on Etherdale University's campus, another failed uprising in the making.

Those outside of the Masked Order had no idea the numbers we'd amassed, nor how many years we'd been steadily building, planning, and plotting. They were unaware of the allies we'd secured in Etherdale and beyond. They were blissfully ignorant about the parts of the city we controlled above ground, nor did they know of the city we'd built beneath.

They had not a single. Fucking. Clue.

And that would remain true until the moment I decided otherwise.

At the bottom of the stairs, a long hallway came to life. An onyx sigil on my upper biceps burned, and torches erupted with white flame on both walls. As I passed through the wards, my essence was recognized, my presence welcomed by the magick of the underground.

Through the door at the end of the next hall, a din of chatter and laughter could be heard.

I pushed into the room, where my inner circle and several high-ranking officials were gathered for a debrief. Witch lights bathed us in warm light. To distract from the eerie nature of existing so far beneath ground, the space was adorned with tasteful décor, potted plants, plush furnishings. Thorny vines with blooming purple and black flowers that crawled up the stone walls.

The group went silent when I strode into the room and walked straight for the small dais in the center.

Harmony stood to my right, and my scariest comrade, Blade, stood to my left. Blade was easily the largest among us, both in height and in width. His bulging muscles stretched every article of clothing to its limit. His beard was light brown with auburn notes, the same as his cropped hair. He winked at me with a roguish grin before crossing his arms, accentuating his size even further, and putting on his mask of pure intimidation.

Harmony raised a dark brow with a smirk and pointed at her cheek. I lifted a hand to my own cheek, finding a dried speck of blood I'd missed during cleanup. Oops.

Blade and Harmony were my two closest and oldest friends. They'd been with me since the beginning, when we were merely human vampire hunters.

My entire clan was loyal, but there was something transcendent about the bond I shared with the first round of turned. They were the humans who courageously took the plunge with me, allowing Princeton to rebirth them into vampires with no guarantee he would be successful. We'd essentially been his test subjects, and it was a miracle we survived the initial torturous iteration of the turning ritual before it had been perfected.

I looked out over my most effective, powerful vampires, and they stared back with equal respect.

"Before we go through regional updates and discuss the matter of the new recruitment curriculum, I wanted to deliver news from Zander in the Isolde region," I said, my voice ringing with power as tendrils of shadow circled my feet. "The Servants of Lillian cult is growing. This is no longer an issue of fanatical, brainwashed witches in rural areas. The ethos is evolving into something infinitely more dangerous, and it's crucial to the growing slave trade."

Servants of Lillian was a religious movement that had gone in and out of fashion over the centuries. At its core, it was a cult masterfully created by the born in order to justify mortal slaves and the marriage of mortals, often children, to wealthy born elites. These witches shunned their goddess Selena, choosing instead to dedicate themselves to the Dark Goddess, Lillian, from whom the born vampires, succubi, and incubi were descended.

Their myths and traditions were a vile justification and methodology for grooming innocents to serve their born vampire masters. There was even word from Valentin that Rune and his clan might be facing a similar resurgence among the born side of Aristelle.

"There are whispers of migration and infiltration. This city is full of young, idealistic mortals from rural lands. They're the most coveted meal for born scum. If these blasphemous witches don't already lurk among us, they will soon. We must prioritize their total elimination."

13

EVIE

"I think we broke up," I said to Idris at family dinner when he asked about Jacob.

It had been one night since I was attacked. No word from my boyfriend. I knew that he wasn't aware I'd been harmed by a vampire, but his absence still cut deep. At the very least, I'd hoped maybe he would apologize for the way he spoke to me at dinner. But the harsh reality was that Jacob didn't believe he'd done anything wrong.

Underneath my anger, I was heartbroken. But I'd survive. I was more than well-versed in comforting and caring for myself at this point.

"You *think*?" Idris asked, settling in the chair across from me. "Well… good. I'm sorry, Evie, but that guy sucked." His eyes went straight to my neck. "Why are you wearing a scarf? It's summer, and you hate scarves."

"She doesn't hate *my* beautiful scarves," Mena scoffed, her glasses low on her nose as she sipped white wine at the head of the table.

One of my summery flower arrangements sat in the center

92

of the dining table, imbuing the air with soothing celebratory energy to facilitate harmonious conversations.

"Yeah," I said with an enthusiastic nod. "I love Mena's scarves. Plus, it's pink. It's a summer scarf."

Idris's face scrunched. "You're full of shit. What are you hiding?"

I flattened my lips. "I wasn't fed on by one of your idols, if that's what you're thinking."

"Ew," he retorted. "That is not an image I care to imagine. Gods."

My cheeks heated. Somehow, that sounded like an easier lie to sell than the truth of the bruises on my neck. Because if I told Idris the truth, I'd not only worry Mena, but I'd also encourage his hatred of the born and his adoration of the Masked Order.

It wasn't as if I didn't *also* hate the born. I hated all perpetrators of violence. The turned weren't the solution—they were only dragging more mortals into futile, circular bloodshed.

"Evie, you couldn't lie if your life depended on it. You're clearly withholding something that you don't want to tell us." His eyes narrowed. "Did Jacob hurt you?" he spat, his fist clenching where it rested on the table.

Mena's eyes darted to mine, and she set down her glass.

"No," I said quickly. "Well, not physically." I stared down at my plate of potatoes, chicken, and asparagus.

I'd cried myself to sleep last night. When I woke up, I took my goods to Celeste's. I squashed what had happened down with the other hidden, secret wounds. I laughed with the owners. I received a big hug from my elderly regular Cecil for the healing salve I'd made for him. He tipped me generously and whispered that I should open my own shop.

I'd smiled wider than I had in days.

But Idris had been right. I couldn't run from everything forever.

"I was attacked by a vampire," I said, meeting Idris's soft brown eyes.

"Evie," Mena exclaimed, covering her mouth with her hand as her face fell. "Helia above, why on earth didn't you say anything?" She looked at Idris as her voice cracked. "She just carried on with life like nothing happened."

"That's the Evie way," Idris said quietly.

The words sounded like an insult, but his voice was soft and wounded. Idris stared at me, his lips turned down.

"Are you okay?" he asked.

"He didn't—he didn't feed from me," I said hurriedly, the words clawing out of my chest.

For a moment, I saw our mother and her soulless gray eyes.

Idris swallowed and reached for my hand. He looked at me in silent understanding, and for a moment, I wasn't alone when the past reached with her icy cold hands into the present. I wasn't alone when I heard the words, *if you're impure, you're worthless.*

A scratchy, hot sensation of discomfort spread over every inch of my skin. All I wanted was to lean into Idris's comfort, his unspoken solidarity. But there was this shameful, sticky nausea in my gut at the thought of offloading any of this pain onto someone else.

I didn't want Idris to know my suffering. I wanted him to be free from all of this. From our violent past, this tumultuous present, and the uncertain future. I wanted him to live a life liberated from all pain. I never wanted to see him hurt again.

"Are you okay?" he repeated. "I can move back home for a while."

"No." I shook my head. "I mean, yes, I'm okay. And no, please don't move back. I want you to keep thriving and living the life you deserve."

Idris studied my face. His lip twitched, and for a moment,

his eyes glassed over as if remembering something. When he came back to himself, the pain transformed to anger.

"Did someone give your attacker what he deserved?"

I swallowed, slowly retracting my hand from his. "Yes, someone did."

A masked god of vengeance and shadow cloaked in black. Something dangerous surged inside me. The more I remembered about his smirk and his filthy words, the angrier I became. I wanted to study those damn sigils on his arms, to uncover the origins of his unholy magick.

Idris nodded. "Good."

I took a bite of food, refusing to discuss this further.

After a few beats, I changed the subject. "How's campus life?"

Idris was slow to transition back to his normal disposition, but thankfully, he yielded. As he spoke about mundane things, like his new friends and trivia nights and athletic competitions, I relaxed.

We would be okay. All three of us.

I peeked at Mena, who'd been watching our conversation in a contemplative, observant silence. She met my eyes, immediately standing from the table and rubbing a soothing circle on my shoulder.

"I'm going to fetch dessert. You're getting extra whipped cream, doll."

TWO THINGS BECAME PAINFULLY clear over the next week.

First, Jacob must have returned to the countryside as promised, without so much as a goodbye. That was that, I supposed. I should've known a normal, healthy romantic relationship was far too big of an ask when I was... well, *me.*

Second, I was being watched.

I kept that second piece of intuition to myself, as I knew that

Mena and Idris would both attribute it to the upcoming trauma anniversary.

But I knew. I could feel it. They hadn't hurt me, at least not yet. But something had its eyes on me, for unknown, terrifying reasons. Did they know who I was? My magick? My past?

Each time I lost myself to a paranoid spiral, I pulled myself back out by focusing on what was directly in front of me.

Fuck Jacob's business degree. Now that he was gone, I decided to ignore all of his warnings and rededicate myself to opening up my own shop. It was going to take a lot of work and far more savings than I currently had at my disposal, but I'd make it happen.

I could feel it buzzing under my skin—this greater purpose, the promise of a new, better reality than my current fear-based, comfortable normalcy. I wanted a challenge. I wanted to help as many people as I could in this world teeming with violence and apathy.

This time when I entered the library, I didn't go to my usual, safe sections on herbalism and green witchcraft.

I went to the hidden, obscure section that only a particular kind of witch could sense and access. Witches like *me*.

In an unassuming, unmarked section upstairs, I found a bookcase of texts in various shapes and sizes, varying from ancient to modern. Some of them were made from scratch, with handwritten and hand-drawn pages, while others were clearly collaborative works created by covens or printed by scholars.

I closed my eyes and held out my palm. *Show me what I need to read right now.*

When I opened my eyes again, I had half a second to dodge a book flying through the air before it smacked into my face and broke my nose.

I squealed and ducked.

A deep rumble of laughter erupted from behind me.

When I turned, Kylo was leaning against a bookcase. In his broad hand, he held the book that had attempted to assault me.

"Up to no good, are we, angel?"

His voice and body were far more attractive than I remembered. It had perhaps been an act of self-preservation to downplay his beauty before. But now that he was here, in the flesh, there was no hope for curbing his ungodly effect on my insides.

My skin tingled as if all of my nerve endings had come alive all at once. Heat burrowed deep in my belly.

He was so tall that I'd have to leap for my book if I wanted to snatch it back from him.

And his smirk told me he was well aware of that reality. He followed my enraged gaze to the book he held high above me. "I believe the words you're looking for are *thank you.*"

"How long have you been standing there?" I asked, acutely conscious of the paranoia creeping from the periphery of my mind and into my tone.

"A few seconds before I caught you trying to damage university property with your witchy telekinesis tricks."

"I wasn't—urgh—Can you please give me back that *university property?*"

"Aw, well, since you asked so nicely," he purred.

A flush crawled over my chest, my heart beating erratically. He glanced down, as if he could sense it too.

Or maybe he was checking out my breasts. That made more sense.

He lowered the book and stepped toward me. Those perfect lips curved into something dangerous.

I snatched it from his hands with an exhale.

"That's a very sweet dress, angel," he said, only moving closer until my back hit the bookcase behind me.

The dress was white with blue, purple, and pink floral patterns and a corset top. I didn't usually show this much cleavage, but it was too pretty of a piece to resist. Besides, this was my era of evolution. Trying new things. Growing out of old, childish behaviors and tastes.

If anyone was a better embodiment of everything I'd once avoided, it was this tall, frightening man with a heart-melting grin.

"We're going to have to work on your manners, aren't we?" he said with a mocking pout. "That's two missed opportunities to say *thank you, Kylo.*"

"Fu—"

Before I could utter the next syllable, Kylo's hand was over my mouth.

"Uh-uh," he said, pressing his body against mine. "Be a good girl and watch your mouth."

What the hell was wrong with me? I glared at him with nothing but fury, but my body only flushed with more heat, more confusing yearning. Everywhere he touched, I felt alive—more alive than I'd ever felt beneath a man's touch before.

Jacob had never made me feel this way. As if my body answered to his command, like I wanted to be consumed by this maddening, uncontrollable draw to his powerful presence.

You're my good girl.

That was what the masked vampire had said to me. Right after he'd flashed that wicked smirk.

Wait.

I writhed under Kylo's hold. I carefully placed my book on the shelf next to me. I reached for his arm and pushed up his long, midnight blue sleeves.

"This is a bizarre way to try to undress me, princess."

His skin was bare. No tattoos. No sigils. No shocking heat under my touch.

He was human. Yet that didn't solve the confusion and murky, twisted intuition in my bones. I was more perplexed than ever.

A strand of his black hair dipped onto his forehead, and I had the fleeting curiosity about how soft it might feel under my fingertips. I lowered my hands to my sides and kept them glued there.

He removed his hand from my mouth, but his gaze remained on my lips. Intense, nearly angry, his deep blue eyes a stormy sea.

"Behave for me, please," he said, low and commanding. The edge in his voice was wicked, his breath warm against my cheek as he leaned forward. "Libraries are excellent places to teach ornery little princesses harsh lessons."

My brows scrunched, staring at him in utter shock.

I wanted to be angry. Gods, I wanted to be so fucking mad at him for speaking to me like this.

But the truth was, Kylo spoke to me like the men from my romance novels spoke to the main characters. The confidence, the danger, the focused attention. I wanted to run, but I couldn't. I was a fly caught in his honey trap, and it was terrifying. Because I knew it wasn't real. I knew he was going to hurt me.

Yet all I could do was inhale the scent of fresh mint and dark musk, with hints of leather and fresh berries. All I could do was try to slow my heart as he held his face inches from mine.

When he stroked my cheek, I inhaled sharply as if he'd shocked me. It was the slightest brush across my cheekbone, over too soon.

"Tell me what you're thinking," he said.

Hell no. The mere thought of this near-stranger knowing that he reminded me of my favorite romantic leads was utterly mortifying.

I shook my head.

"My new favorite shade of pink," he whispered, touching my cheek again.

I shuddered, squirming under his scrutiny.

He pressed into me, and I nearly gasped at the hard bulge now resting against my stomach.

When Kylo chuckled, I was certain my blush had turned cherry red.

He was hard from this? From pinning me to a bookcase?

And gods, why was *it* so big? Were they supposed to be that big?

"What's that they say? A closed mouth doesn't get fed?" He dragged his thumb down my lips, making them part. "Tell me what you want, Evie."

My eyes blew wide. "I—this isn't platonic," I said, a touch too loudly. They were the only words I could think of, the place between my thighs aching as tingles cascaded over my skin.

There was a tiny dimple in his cheek when he grinned, the only piece of him that wasn't devastatingly ruthless.

"Is that what you want?" he asked, staring at my lips like they held the answers to life's greatest mysteries.

When his hand moved to the base of my neck, his thumb tracing circles on my sensitive flesh, I nearly melted into a puddle at his feet.

"*Platonic?*"

KYLO

If I was any other man, my self-control would've crumbled long ago. My blonde angel stood perfectly still, as if she were petrified of revealing her desire.

Unfortunately for her, I could smell every last drop of it. Her lust intertwined with the sinfully sweet scent of her blood, making it so intoxicating it physically hurt my nostrils. I'd never wanted to sink my fangs into someone's throat more desperately than this moment.

Thank the gods I'd fed generously before I'd found her. I always had to feed before I saw Evie. And after.

She was driving me fucking crazy. And I wanted to punish her for this obsession just as much as I wanted to protect her vulnerable, fearful heart like it was the precious gift that it was.

I didn't know where to look. Those pretty pink lips, those big gray eyes, the perky tits pushed up by the corset of her darling little floral dress…

As I waited for her to answer me, I settled on her lips. If I so much as attempted to capture them with mine, I was fully convinced I'd rip a hole in my glamour and dig my fangs into her sensitive flesh.

Her pulse fluttered beneath my hand on her delicate throat. When she opened her mouth, it was as if I'd been awaiting the judgment of Helia herself.

"No, I don't want *platonic*," she said.

My heart hadn't felt this vulnerably human in years, and I couldn't help but smile at the adorable hesitation in her voice. As if she'd mustered all of her courage to be this forward and truthful. A skittish rabbit in the jaws of a wolf.

"But that doesn't matter," she continued. "You're going to hurt me."

She looked embarrassed. She thought I was playing boyish games, that my confidence was a weapon. She had no idea how special she was to me. She had no idea the true depths of my preoccupation.

"How about we slow down, then, angel?" I asked, slowly pulling my body from hers. It took every ounce of my restraint to move away from her body heat, to pull my hand off her throat.

Trust issues weren't surprising, given how men in general behaved, let alone her recently deceased ex-boyfriend.

"Come read with me," I said, tilting my head toward the nook I'd been studying in.

She grabbed her book back from the shelf, and she stared at me for several beats. I could see the distrust in every twitch of her features.

I could also still scent her overpowering, mouthwatering arousal.

"Okay."

Good girl. Good fucking girl.

I would earn my angel's trust. She was smart not to trust a man's words. Actions were the only thing in this world that mattered.

She walked a few steps behind me, following me like a hesitant baby duck. It was irritatingly adorable.

We settled into my favorite corner of the library, where a small couch rested against the back wall, and a wooden table with high-back chairs sat on a green rug.

My books were already spread out across the table, including several notebooks protected by magick from prying eyes.

"Let me clear a space for you."

She removed her small leather crossbody purse and patiently waited for me to tidy up. I moved my things to the head of the table, smiling when she chose to sit at the opposite end—the farthest seat from me.

That was for the best, seeing as I couldn't have her peeking at anything I was plotting. But when she pulled out her own notebook and pen, and I took a better look at the mysterious black book that had flown from the shelf, I had a sudden realization.

She didn't want *me* to know what she was reading or writing, either.

The book was unmarked, clearly of magickal origins. And it had come from an unlabeled section that seemed not only random but also dispelled all interest as if warded against non-witches.

"Whatcha working on?" I asked her.

She sat down, immediately tensing and showing the truth on her face. I liked that Evie couldn't keep anything to herself if she tried. Her lack of subtlety was as endearing as it was incredibly dangerous for her.

It meant she was frighteningly easy to manipulate and take advantage of.

"Witch business," she said, cagey as ever. "What are *you* working on?"

"Curriculum to effectively radicalize the youth."

Her gaze turned to ice. "That is not a funny joke."

I chuckled. It wasn't a joke.

"I bet you're reading about effective incubus seduction tactics," she muttered.

I pinned her with a stare from across the table, both of us opening our notebooks at the same time.

"You're a fiery, suspicious little creature, aren't you?"

She made a soft noise of derision that made my cock strain in my pants. She had no fucking idea what I would do to her for being such an incorrigible brat—once she was *all mine*.

She'd better enjoy her freedom while it lasted.

Evie quickly focused on the text before her, chewing on her lip as her brows furrowed.

What *was* that book? And why had it made such a bold attempt to break her nose?

Every once in a while, fear would spike in her blood as she read. Her face would pale, and she would tap her fingers nervously on the table. It made absolutely no sense.

I remembered the way she'd stared at the wilting, dying shrub in utter horror.

Was she afraid of her own magick?

Fuck. This precious girl had no one in her life to mentor her, to help her understand herself or her powers. Before me, she'd had no one to protect her, no one to look out for her.

It was all so irritating.

My angel needed me.

She just didn't know it yet.

When I had her pinned to the bookcase, she'd rolled up my sleeve to search for my tattoos. She didn't know for sure who I was, but she was intelligent enough to suspect it. Probably because I couldn't help but tease her in my vampire form just as I did while glamoured.

In a strange, nonsensical way, I was almost angry that both versions of me turned her on. Even if *I* knew we were one and the same, *she* didn't.

I was self-aware enough to recognize the insanity of letting my violent possessiveness get triggered by another version of *myself*.

"What are you smiling about?" Evie asked.

"Am I not allowed to experience pleasure and amusement, Evie darling?"

She made a face. "No."

Gods, she was such a brat right now. And I knew she was only this prickly as a defense mechanism. She was testing me. She could sense I was different from any other man she'd met before, and she wanted to ensure her intuition was real. That I truly did possess the bare minimum of patience, respect, and chivalry.

Her pen hovered over the page, unmoving.

"I'm not sure men deserve to experience pleasure and amusement," she said.

I laughed, and a cheeky smile broke through her icy façade. She met my eyes, almost appearing pleasantly surprised to have made me laugh.

That was a good sign. I wanted her to feel satisfaction when she pleased me.

"Some don't," I agreed. I let my smile fade, showing her a more serious expression. "Not everyone will disappoint you, Evie. If you hide from the world, the world will hide from you."

She crossed her arms, and I had to suppress a groan at what it did for those perfect breasts spilling out of her top.

"Here I thought you were lying about your philosophy tutoring gig. That was a good line," she said indignantly. "But you don't know me."

"I want to know you."

"Why?"

I shook my head, my lips unable to stop themselves from tipping up. "Why is that so hard for you to believe? You fascinate me. You're an intriguing rarity in a world that tends to churn out the exact copies and archetypes every generation."

"*Every generation* makes you sound a lot older than you look."

"You already know my penchant for history."

She squirmed in her seat. She had no idea of her own uniqueness. The genuine passion ripe in her blood, the idealistic dreaming that most people exorcise from their souls out of fear. I knew her depth was likely an unfortunate by-product of past suffering, but she had no idea how refreshing it was all the same.

"Most people think and talk and move through life exactly as their parents had," I said.

I didn't miss the way she flinched slightly.

"They fit into a role that feels safe. They don't challenge themselves. They don't grow. They cower from greater purpose or meaning. They run from the terrifying and beautiful art of being seen and understood, or, gods forbid, the heavy responsibility of truly seeing and understanding another. They live for comfort, and then they die. Maybe they leave behind the exact same sort of person who will take their place before they go."

"That's bleak," Evie said with a frown.

"I don't think so," I said. "They live and love in the way they've chosen, and that's still worthy of respect and empathy. Life is hard and grueling, and I do not blame them for prioritizing safety over uncertainty." I paused. "But it does make those with the bravery and gall to stand out from the crowd that much more delightfully unexpected."

I could see the unmistakable gleam of excitement in those big gray eyes. She opened her mouth and then closed it, as if she wanted desperately to say something but wouldn't allow herself to say it.

"I fear I'm going to disappoint you. I'm not as interesting as you're making me seem," she said finally, unable to hide the way her hopeful features betrayed her.

"I highly doubt that."

She thought she could conceal her beautiful, leaping heart from me, but I heard every beat of intrigue against her ribcage.

Even still, she focused back on her book. She jotted down notes that disappeared as soon as they were scribbled. It appeared she wasn't the only one who used magick to hide her work.

I could sense a low buzz of power from her, but I couldn't read its exact frequency.

Just when I thought she was done talking to me, she spoke without looking up from her notes.

"I want to open my own shop. That's what I'm working on—new spells and more information about my particular gifts. I know it sounds stupid in a city already saturated with magickal goods. But my clients believe my products are unique and potent, and I do too. I want to help as many people as I can."

I couldn't stop my grin, a kind of warmth infecting my heart that I hadn't felt consistently in years.

"That's not stupid, Evie," I said. "That's brave. You deserve to feel proud. You deserve to believe you can accomplish exactly what you desire. That's the only way to conquer anything worthy of being conquered."

I watched those full pink lips curve. It was as though the whole room lit up as she did, the lights around us growing warmer.

She would conquer her big, magickal dreams. And I would conquer her.

Loud shouts erupted from beyond the bookcases. A woman screamed just as I sensed the magick of Lillian's demon spawn flood the air.

15

EVIE

I had to hide what I was reading from Kylo, from *anyone*, at all costs.

The book that had jumped out at me was a chaos magick text on a chthonic goddess the author called Hekate. She was a minor deity I'd never heard of before, but her resemblance to Lillian instantly put me on edge. Though, unlike Lillian, she clearly served witches and other mortals above all others.

I'd asked the spirit realm for guidance, and here Hekate was, making herself known. Gods and spirits tended to be that way. If they had something to say, they'd be sure to let you know.

I could ignore them, if I wanted to. But the more powerful the call, the more persistent they were in getting a witch's attention.

It was also in bad manners to ask the otherworld for help and then blatantly shun what I received.

But the more I read about these encounters with Hekate, and the rituals and spells concocted with her aid, the more wary I became.

This was powerful work. Beyond a healing herbal salve or a candle spell for inspiration.

This book was everything my fellow witches feared about chaos workers like me. To some, the rituals described might be viewed as disruptive to the natural flow of the universe.

And I hated how alive it made me feel, the way these handwritten pages called to the deepest, most buried parts of me.

Almost as much as I hated the way Kylo stirred those hidden depths too.

I tried to focus back on the text, still swimming with warmth and intrigue from Kylo's assessment of me and this confusing world.

It was terrifying how his words seemed to come from my own unspoken thoughts. Did he feel as lonely as I did? Did he feel different from everyone else too?

I remembered all those humans who'd greeted him in the market. He said his friends were meticulously curated. Did that mean they were as special as he made me feel?

I burned with curiosity, with strange obsession. I wanted to know if this was all a trap. I wanted to know this man and why he made me feel like he might actually understand me.

He hadn't thought my idea was stupid. He—

A scream rang through the space, cutting through my racing thoughts.

The text beneath my palm seared in warning. In a flash of intuition, I grabbed the book and shoved it in my purse with my notebook.

Kylo was already on his feet. I thought he might leave in search of whoever screamed, but he moved in front of me instead.

He was a wall of muscle, and something about the fact that his first instinct was to protect me made my heart pang.

I stepped closer to him, and he peeked down at me. His eyes

darted back and forth as if he were thinking rapidly, making quick assessments.

He cursed. "There's a private study room nearby. We're going to take shelter there, understood?"

I nodded, watching his sharp jaw tick.

"Let's go, angel," he said softly, guiding me with a hand on my lower back.

But when we passed by the first bookcase, another jolt of intuition shot down my spine, halting me in place.

"Evie—"

"By order of Lord Conrad, we will not harm any mortals so long as you stand out of our way."

The voice boomed, and I knew instantly it was a born vampire speaking. But there was another presence, a familiar energy, just a few rows away.

My head swiveled. As humans escaped past us to the lower level, I homed in on where the commotion was coming from. I ignored Kylo's sharp commands and grip on my arm, shrugging free to turn a corner and gain a vantage point of the section with the authoritative voice.

The section we were just in—the shelves of books created by and for fellow chaos witches.

"You can't do this," a woman wailed from the ground, as if she'd been shoved there. "University buildings are vampire-free zones—"

"Bullshit," the man from before snarled, a tiny red flame in his palm. "This university is overrun with blasphemies of Lillian's will. You may shun natural-born vampires, but you allow bastard ones to roam free."

My stomach turned over.

They were going to burn those books. Those handwritten gifts from one witch to the next, witches like *me*. Powerful, feared, beloved, despised.

Innovators, artists, healers, destroyers.

"No," I said, before I could stop myself.

Kylo was glued to my side, his fists clenching and unclenching as he stared between the born and me.

I spotted a third body—an older woman in all black—standing next to the vampire. She was a witch, and her role was clear. The vampire turned toward the shelves.

But the witch who'd betrayed her own kind to lead a vampire to our ancient texts stared straight ahead. Her eyes found mine, and they instantly narrowed.

I could hear my heart beating hard and fast in my ears as my blood rushed to my head. Black. She wore all black.

A witch who served Lillian. A witch who served bloodthirsty, soulless demons.

Two opposing urges battled in my system.

First, to fucking *run*.

Second, to stop them from burning those books.

Buried anger surged in my blood. Dangerous, forbidden. I couldn't let them know what I was or what I carried in my purse. I couldn't accidentally harm anyone, especially humans like Kylo.

"We have to do something," I said, even as I trembled, even as buried memories assailed my mind's eye.

Witches in black, gathered with *them*. Idris screaming somewhere I couldn't reach.

Kylo stared down at me, those deep, dark blue eyes at war. "Fuck. I—"

He shook his head, looking from them to me. "I can't. There are more downstairs. Let me get you somewhere safe first. I'm sorry, Evie, I…" He trailed off, as if thinking hard as he spoke.

I didn't understand what he was saying or why he was apologizing. I knew logically there was nothing he could do.

I glanced at him, that nagging intuition still lodged somewhere in my gut. Unless he *could* do something…

When I looked back at the witch, she was still staring at me.

"What's in your bag?" she hissed.

I heard a child scream, and tears burned my eyes.

I took a step back, my muscles locking up even as my mind yelled, *Run, run, run!*

The vampire flung a ball of deep red fire at the bookcase. I screamed. The room went completely black. Kylo shoved me to the ground. Something exploded against the wall behind us.

Had *I* made the lights go out? Magick surged in my blood, angry and vengeful, and I resisted its pull to surge from my fingertips.

But even if the lights were off, I wasn't powerful enough to extinguish the sun. And it wasn't merely dark in this room, it was *onyx*. Impenetrable, as if subdued by a field of shadow.

I heard a loud crack, like bones snapping. The smell of smoke filled the air, and it broke my heart. Those were pages and pages of love and dedication, scorched and destroyed in an instant.

Where was Kylo? I swung out my arms wildly. It was so quiet for a moment, the briefest of seconds. I stood.

A body slammed into mine.

Sour breath flooded my nostrils. "What's in the bag, *witch*?"

The voice was a grating screech. I heaved as I recovered from having the wind knocked out of my lungs.

Hands reached for my purse, clawing at my arm. I saw my mother's cold eyes. I heard Idris's voice, so small. Only a child, hands so tiny. Reaching, trusting, hoping.

No one protected us. It was up to me.

Something feral left my lips as I grabbed the woman by the throat. Magick leaked from my fingertips, and my head swam with delirious pleasure.

I'd finally let the poison buried inside me out of its cage.

The woman gurgled, and something hot sprayed across my face. Suddenly she flew off me, and I was being lifted in the air.

"Kylo?"

The room flickered from darkness to light and back again. The strobing made me want to vomit. From strong arms and a sturdy chest, I caught a glimpse of the witch who'd attacked me lying on the floor. Her eyes had popped out of her skull, and sticky black goo marred her flesh.

I shut my eyes.

I did that. I killed her.

I hadn't realized I'd been repeating those words until a deep voice spoke.

"Shhh. It's okay," he whispered. "If you hadn't, I was about to."

Idris. I had to get to Idris. I was going to be sick. I knew we were moving, but all I could focus on was not throwing up or passing out. I kept my eyes squeezed shut until I was certain we were on the lower floor.

The lights continued to strobe, and I clung to Kylo as more commotion erupted all around us. Turned vampires in masks, humans running, born fangs flashing.

I searched the crowd for Idris, for any more witches dressed in black. And it wasn't until we were outside that I realized I was in a masked man's arms.

I screamed. He set me down as more bodies ran in all directions around us.

"Shhh, baby," he said softly, his voice unmistakably distorted. "Behave. No screaming."

Behave.

Where was Kylo?

Splotches erupted in my vision, and I felt my blood pressure tank.

Oh fuck. I was going to pass out. Idris. Idris…

The last thing I heard was a sigh. "I'm going to take your swooning as a compliment."

16

KYLO

"This is the new hobby?" Harmony squealed. She stared down at the blonde mystery in my arms.

My hand was buried in her hair, slowly combing through her impossibly soft tresses. I'd wanted to do this for a very long time. Pity she was unconscious for it, but it did make for easy access and pliability.

I was sitting up against a tree in a nearby university park. My clan had made quick work of the born in the library. I'd snapped the neck of the vampire leading the charge—the one who'd managed to burn a handful of witch texts.

Chaos witch texts. The books that Evie had been perusing. I'd already tried to open the book in her bag, and it had shocked the fuck out of me as if charged with lightning.

"She's... very pretty," Harmony said. She crossed her arms and tapped her foot. "They're after witches like her now, aren't they?"

"It would appear so," I said through a clenched jaw. I'd already filled Harmony in on the basics of the situation. I didn't like that more people knew about Evie, regardless of if I trusted Harmony absolutely.

That was how ruthlessly protective I'd become.

Had Princeton detected that Evie was a chaos witch at first glance? Was that why he'd asked me if I knew *what I was in for?* If so, that meant my maker had placed loyalty to a fellow chaos witch above informing me of pertinent information. And I wasn't sure how to feel about that possibility.

"They're looking for makers," I said. "They know chaos witches had to be involved in our turning rituals. And I'm not sure the born will care whether individual witches are actually guilty. Any powerful, solitary chaos practitioner is now in grave danger."

"I hate to say this," Harmony said with a sigh.

I nodded. "I know. This is good for us."

"They're only going to radicalize more beings capable of destroying them. You don't fuck with powerful chaos witches. Anyone with half a brain knows that."

I looked down at my perfect angel. Her features were deliciously vulnerable. She'd clearly channeled her power out of fear, and that loss of control had cost her. She was terrified of her own power, her own darkness—and that was hurting her.

I, on the other hand, wanted to lap up every last drop of her buried violence.

"Attacking a university library does not bode well for their public image in a mortal-run city," I said. "They are blatantly spitting in the face of the codes of conduct that have maintained peace for centuries."

Harmony rubbed her mouth. The orange hues of the falling sun made her light brown skin glow with warmth. "The loyalists will still find a way to blame us."

I shrugged. "Let them. This is a pivotal moment for mortals on the fence, not those with hands over their eyes and ears."

Harmony glanced at Evie again, and I had to squash the primal possessiveness it spiked in my blood.

"Are you... what are your plans with her?"

I must've been glaring, because Harmony immediately raised her hands.

"Sheesh, Kylo, gods. It's *me*."

I brushed my broad hand over Evie's cheek. I listened carefully for any change in her heart rate or breathing.

I sighed and met Harmony's concerned dark eyes. "My interest in her is not clan-related."

Harmony beamed, and I rolled my eyes.

"You really did listen to me about work-life balance!" She pushed her long, glossy black waves behind her shoulders. "Good, you deserve it. You've been working for the clan without a single break in focus for decades. You deserve a bit of fun and relaxation."

I shook my head, slowly starting to untense. At least Harmony knowing about Evie meant more protection for her.

I snorted. "I wouldn't call my new hobby *relaxing*. Though it has indeed been fun."

And it would only get better from here. Once I earned her trust, I would claim her. Evie had no idea the depths of pleasure that were about to torment her every waking moment.

Harmony was nearly bouncing up and down with excitement. "Can I meet her? In my human glamour, of course."

I ran a hand through my hair. "Soon," I promised.

She looked off into the distance for a moment, her forehead creasing. "You need to be careful, Kylo. You know what it means if you bring someone into our world. As soon as she knows more than she should, it's going to change her life forever."

My muscles tightened, my lips turning down.

"And, well, if she's a chaos witch... I just hope you're thinking about all potential dangers and consequences, that's all. Especially for the clan."

"Always."

We held each other's gazes for a moment, an unspoken push

and pull of power, loyalty, and a shared vision melding in the space between us.

Harmony knew me. She knew I was already staring into the future, weighing all considerations.

She also knew that once I set my sights on something, you could only pull that obsession out of my cold, lifeless hands.

"I'm going to head to the debrief. Anything else you want me to say that we haven't already discussed?"

I shook my head. "I'll be in later tonight."

Harmony nodded, all business again as she gave me a lazy, half-serious salute and jogged off.

After fifteen minutes of staring into the sunset, clutching Evie to my chest and resisting my shadows' urge to crawl all over her, she finally stirred.

Her heart picked up speed. Her usual dose of fear spiked in her blood. Her breathing became shallower.

When she opened her eyes, they found mine and widened.

She made a startled yelp and wiggled in my hold.

"Settle down," I whispered with a smirk. "You're safe."

"Let go of me."

"No."

My arms flexed around her shoulders and legs where they held her.

"If I let you go, you're going to stand too quickly and fall right back down."

She glowered. Slowly, her neurons started firing again one by one. She went from survival mode to deeper thinking. *Remembering.*

Her fair skin paled to a sickly pallor. Tears pricked her eyes. She went utterly limp in my arms yet remained keenly awake.

"I don't understand what happened," she said. She searched my eyes, her heart slamming against her ribs in a distracting cacophony.

I gave her nothing but resounding certainty and authority—

something to anchor herself to amid her ocean of fear and panic.

"The library was attacked, and the Masked Order came to our aid," I explained. "The room was pitch-black, but based on what I heard, that witch attacked you. A turned vampire came to your rescue and helped you to safety. I found you unconscious outside the library in the garden just a few moments later."

She blinked. Those concerned brows furrowed deep.

She knew she'd killed the witch. She'd repeated it over and over when I was carrying her. It broke my damn heart to see her so horrified.

Evie hated who she was.

"Are you hurt?" I asked.

She shook her head, beginning to squirm again. I let her escape my hold, watching her slowly move to sit across from me in the bright green grass.

"You—you took me here? Did you see the masked man who'd been carrying me?"

I cocked my head. "Yes, and I don't think so. No one was with you when I found you. Why? Did he make you uncomfortable?"

Her eyes snapped to mine, her cheeks flushing. "No. Yes. I don't know."

My cock twitched in my dark pants. I loved tormenting her like this. I could just barely make out the hardened peaks of her nipples beneath her corset.

I wanted to torment those, too.

"Evie? Are you okay, angel?" I showed her only concern, and she stared at me as if she were working through a puzzle.

She still suspected the masked man was me. Maybe even more than ever before. But she couldn't prove it. She didn't *want* to believe it.

Even if both versions of me made her panties slick.

At that mental image, I nearly cracked my teeth grinding them together. My hands were glued to the ground, so I wouldn't do something regrettable. Not for my sake, but for hers. She needed slow. She needed to trust.

"I'm fine," she lied. "Why did you take me here?"

"Where else was I supposed to take you? You weren't conscious to tell me where home was," I said, tactically evading a lie. Because of course I knew where her princess palace was. "I wanted to get you away from the fighting."

She got up suddenly, and I followed her just as quick. She reached a hand to her forehead, but she didn't sway.

"There's still fighting? I need to go find my brother."

"No, the fighting is over."

For now.

"Were any mortals harmed?"

"A few librarians were injured, but only one student was killed. She was a first year," I said bitterly.

I knew what her brother looked like, of course, and I'd already ensured that he hadn't been involved in the violence.

A powerful chaos witch with a human brother was a perplexing anomaly indeed.

She sighed in relief, but her lips trembled. I wanted to pull her back to my chest. I wanted her tears to fall so I could kiss them away, syphon her sadness from her soul and hide it within my churning darkness.

"I hate vampires," she said, venom on her tongue.

Her little fists clenched at her side.

I watched her with a perfect mask of control, not letting a single emotion slip. "Even the one who saved your life?"

"Especially him," she mumbled under her breath.

She stared into my eyes so deeply that it was nearly terrifying—if such an adorable little creature was capable of frightening me.

"I know you all think that the turned are protecting us," she said, an accusatory tone in her steadily climbing voice. "But it was only because of the turned that the born infiltrated the library in the first place. The masked criminals are provoking powerful forces like Lord Conrad. *He* is who rules over this region, on behalf of the king. If the lords decide to crack down and make our lives a living hell, regardless of this being a mortal-run city, then they will do so. And there's nothing we can do to stop them."

Her anger was turning, the fear in her blood reaching new heights. "They're ruining everything. The turned—they are *ruining* a city that was once a safe haven."

Evie's voice cracked on the word *safe*, once again inadvertently revealing all of her cards. I was the snake in her garden, the monster infiltrating all the hidden, locked away corners and crevices of her mind.

I understood her more and more every day. I got high off it —off knowing her, deeply knowing her, more than any man before me. Any being. One day, I would know her better than she even knew herself.

And I would cherish that responsibility just as I cherished this city I would one day claim as my own.

"What do you need right now to feel safe, Evie?" I asked her.

She crossed her arms, making herself smaller as she looked away. She wanted to hide from me. But she couldn't. She would never be able to hide from me again.

Those soft pink lips trembled, as if the question had rocked her to her very core. "I don't know."

"That's okay," I said. "Let me take care of you."

I approached her slowly, as if she were a skittish firebird. She frowned, still refusing to meet my eyes.

Every single piece of her body language told the exact same message.

Evie wanted to run.

"You *deserve* to be taken care of," I said.

She tilted her head up with a sudden swiftness, inhaling sharply. Those words shocked her most of all.

I could see the deep sense of unworthiness embedded in her soul, something she'd been taught over and over since birth. It was something I understood more than she knew.

"You don't have to say anything," I said softly. "You don't even have to think."

I gently took her small hand and placed it on my arm, guiding her to walk with me without another word.

Startled and deeply, heartbreakingly triggered, Evie was slow to relax beside me. When she finally released her stiffness and fell into a normal pace, her hand relaxing around my arm, I exhaled deeply.

Her obedience was as deeply satisfying as it was maddeningly erotic. Evie wanted to be my good girl. She wanted to listen and submit. She just didn't feel safe enough yet to fully let go.

I was a patient man.

Or, rather, a patient monster.

17

KYLO

e walked in silence until we made it to the nearest café. I guided Evie to a booth close to an exit, but also tucked into a corner. She visibly relaxed, staring at me imploringly as she slid onto the wooden seat across from me.

She wondered how I knew what would make her feel safest.

When the waiter approached, his eyes flashed. One of my sigils tingled in recognition, and we exchanged a silent exchange—his head bowing slightly with respect.

"Water, please," I said to him. "And she'll have the fruit platter and the egg and cheese sandwich."

The man nodded. Evie's rain cloud eyes locked on mine.

"Did you just order my food for me?" she asked, incredulous.

"I'll be paying for it too."

The man quickly returned with a carafe of water and two glasses. I filled one of them and passed it to Evie.

"Drink."

Evie blushed furiously. "You can't order me around."

"Why not?"

"Because it's weird and—I don't know. I can order and pay for my own food. I can take care of myself," she protested.

I shrugged. "*Weird* doesn't bother me. And I know you can. But I enjoy doing it for you, and so do you."

I could see it in her face. The relief, just as potent as her ripe suspicion. Evie had been desperately trying to make herself feel safe for a very long time.

But she was tired of running.

She wanted to be caught for once.

"Do you want something different from what I ordered?" I asked her.

She didn't even glance at the menu, her eyes going in and out of focus. When nearby laughter boomed suddenly, the sound startled her.

"No, thank you," she said, answering on autopilot, as if she hadn't even heard the question.

When the food came, she slid back into herself.

"Are you not eating?" she asked.

"I've already had my fill."

She squinted at me, slowly lifting a fork.

I smiled, training my gaze beyond her, on the painting of Etherdale's cityscape hanging on the deep blue wall. "I've been thinking about what you said."

When she sipped her water and swallowed her first bite of food, the tightness in my muscles began to unwind. *Good girl.*

"About nihilism being intellectually lazy. What a funny thing to say," I said.

Evie's lips curved, her eyes going soft and docile as if she was now hanging on my every word. She picked up her sandwich.

"Some nihilists write that meaninglessness only took root when the gods left our plane to rule the heavens and the underworld. They see nihilism as a punishment, as if the gods left us because they deemed us unworthy of meaning and purpose," I said.

Evie's shoulders relaxed. Her eyes, once on the verge of dissociation, sharpened again as she ate and listened.

"Instead of seeing magick and art as evidence of the gods' presence in our lives, they see these expressions as beautiful distractions—a mirage to cover the unpleasant truth."

"What truth?" she asked.

"That fate doesn't exist. That the world and its magicks are ruled by power and illusion. That witchcraft and visioning are futile attempts to add color to a dismal reality of chaos and nothingness." I paused. "The truth that we live and die alone."

Evie blinked. Once. Twice.

Then she rolled her damn eyes.

"Yawn," she said.

I laughed. "Yawn? Is that your final rebuttal?"

She nodded with a heart-melting grin. It was a victory that I felt in the deepest part of me.

"There is no objective reality. If you want to live in *that one,* be my guest," she said, lifting her chin. "But you're not going to infect me with that edgy, pessimistic nonsense."

"No objective reality?"

She nodded. "When you commune with the spirit world—" She paused, quickly shutting her mouth as if she'd revealed something she shouldn't have.

"Hey," I said softly. "I know you're not a green witch. You're safe with me. You're special, Evie."

She took another sip of her water. Her eyes flashed on the words *special,* but her body language was protective, nervous. When she next spoke, it came out less fiery than before. "When you commune with the otherworld, you see it—that reality is ever-shifting. It's not static. It's not set. *We* decide reality. Everything is always in flux. The ether responds to us, and we respond to it; it's an ecosystem of influence. If you believe the world has no meaning except power, the world—both in the spirit and physical dimensions—will respond and interact with you in accordance with that belief. You should never put such stringent limits on yourself. You talk, and the gods listen. You are the arbiter of your own destiny."

She focused back on my eyes, quickly squirming in her seat and returning her focus to her food.

I watched her like I was seeing a flower bloom for the very first time.

"I'm sorry," she said. "I know that probably sounded like nonsense. Maybe I don't know anything. But that's *my* reality."

"I already told you that I believe reality is malleable," I said gently. "It's no wonder that the most famous nihilists were human. It's easier to shun what you cannot perceive with your own physical senses."

Evie nodded. Her features relaxed slightly.

"Don't ever apologize for that beautiful mind of yours, angel," I said. "Or the consequences will be grave."

Her mouth parted, mind whirring. "Are you threatening me? For *apologizing*?"

"Correct. You're such a good listener," I praised, leaning forward as my gaze snagged on her perfect lips.

I wanted to lick that tiny droplet of water that stuck to her cupid's bow. When her own tongue darted out to snatch it, I had the ungodly urge to pull her into my lap and suck that pretty pink tongue into my mouth.

I wanted to more than taste her. I wanted to devour her.

I wanted to take her sweetness, her innocence, and forever taint it with my unholy marks of depravity.

I was going to *ruin her* for all other men.

And if my possessiveness was unhinged now... I knew that when I finally claimed Evie, no man would so much as breathe in her direction in a way I didn't like without finding his hands removed from his body.

Who was I kidding? That was already true.

"Thank you," Evie said after I'd paid for her meal. Her voice was tinged with discomfort, as if I'd bought her an entire house.

"You can thank me by letting me take you out. Properly, next time," I said. It wasn't a question. It wasn't even a request.

Evie nodded like my perfect, good girl. "Okay."

We both knew she had no other choice. She'd never met someone like me. I was the antidote to her deepest, most painful wounds and yearnings. I was everything she feared. Everything she *despised*.

Everything she needed to finally feel safe and protected.

She would never be alone again.

18

EVIE

When I was finally alone again, I felt Kylo's absence in the lack of warmth in my stomach, the hollowness in my chest.

I immediately went to my altar and confirmed Idris was safe. Even though I knew that he was already—based on my intuition and Kylo's confirmation that the only person who'd died was a female first year. I hated the way my mind ruminated, got caught on a worry and couldn't let it go until I'd disproved it seven different ways. I'd been careful not to let this neurosis slip in front of Kylo. I knew how irritating I could be when I got caught in an irrational loop of fear. It used to drive Jacob insane.

After I woke up in Kylo's arms in the park, I wanted to run. I knew what I'd done, the violence that had leaked from my palms.

I had killed someone today.

And the only thing I could do was frantically bury that secret in a hole with all the others. Because if I dwelled on it, I'd be back to square one. I would hide from the world, from my plans to open my own shop. I would slide back into my comfortable solitude.

If you hide from the world, the world will hide from you.

How did Kylo know me? How did he make me stay, when with anyone else, I would've run and never looked back?

And how could I reconcile the sense of safety he evoked with the harsh, loud warning bells that went off every time he was near? It was maddening, the intensity of my attraction to him, knowing without a sliver of a doubt that he couldn't be trusted.

He was a poison I couldn't stop drinking, the same as the magick I'd locked away long ago. He was a contradiction, an anomaly.

Just like me.

The story didn't make sense. Where had he gone after the lights went out? Where was he when the masked man scooped me into his arms? I thought for sure it had been Kylo speaking to me. How did he get to safety? Why did the exact same masked man save me both in the alley and in the library? I recognized his mannerisms and build, the frightening shadow skull mask. His *flirtation.*

I knew that he made me feel the same way that Kylo did.

Alive. So fucking alive.

My tarot cards burned my hands when I touched them, alerting me to the fact that the spirits were tired of my shit. I was asking too many questions. They wanted me to live, to learn the lessons I needed to learn by experience.

Fuck *that.* I needed certainty. I needed to protect myself.

I pulled The Devil card. *Addiction, sensual pleasures, control and domination.*

Then The Lovers. *Two souls intertwined. Romance. Difficult choices.*

Wheel of Fortune. *Fate. You cannot be certain of the future. You must* live!

Seven of Swords. *Betrayal. Deception. Secrecy.*

Everything I feared.

Just one more… this time, the cards shocked me so hard I dropped the deck.

"Urgh," I grunted. "*Fine.*"

I thanked the spirits for their aid, albeit grumpily. I immediately sunk into a fantasy romance novel before another round of ruminations could take hold.

And as I read in my living room, curled into the blue fabric sofa, I felt that unmistakable warmth trail down my spine. The knowledge I was being watched.

By the man who was going to steal my heart and betray me.

The monster who hid behind a mask of shadows.

The Devil.

I rose from the couch. My nightgown skimmed my upper thighs, my nipples hardened peaks beneath the thin white fabric. I stood in front of the windows, staring into the dark night.

Something wild and unrestrained beat against the cage of my ribs. Foreign, beautifully wicked thoughts plagued me.

I didn't want to live in my old reality, where the only exciting fantasies existed between the pages of a novel. I didn't want to face the pain, the guilt, the horror always haunting me from the periphery.

I wanted to keep feeling *alive.*

I didn't stop to worry or dissect what I did next. I merely acted, following the thrill of danger and pleasure in my core.

My fingers skimmed up my gown to the right strap, and with a sharp movement, I pushed it off my shoulder.

I *wanted* him to see. I wanted him to know that I knew he was out there, watching me.

And I couldn't explain why. These acts were the exact opposite of everything I thought I was. Everything I thought I was *before him.*

Despite the fear and the danger, for the first time in my life, *I didn't know what came next.*

And I wanted to find out.

I pushed the second strip of fabric off my left shoulder, but before the gown could fall and exposed my breasts, I snapped my fingers. The curtains drew shut.

My heart was thunderous in my chest. My mind floated. I was flooded with heat and adrenaline, keenly aware of my own mortality.

I pulled my straps back up with a smug smile.

But when I headed to my bedroom and found that the window was wide-open, that smile evaporated with a sudden swiftness.

Cool air teased my skin as the adrenaline transformed instantaneously to fear.

I'd barely lifted my foot to step toward the window before strong hands grabbed me and pulled me back into a broad, hard chest.

I screamed. A hand covered my mouth, muffling the noise.

"What did I say about screaming, baby?" a deep, distorted voice asked in my ear.

I shuddered at the tickle of his breath. Flailing and kicking wildly, more limbs wrapped around me. Too many to count.

With my heart in my throat, I stared down at the thick shadows coiling around me like snakes.

"I thought we were playing games?"

His mouth brushed the shell of my ear, and full-body tingles swept down my skin.

"You made your first move. You thought I wouldn't respond?" He paused, his chest vibrating against my back with a chuckle. "It's like you don't even know me at all."

Motherfucker.

I couldn't move, bound to him with magick that whispered to my own.

His mouth moved lower, and I made a muffled sound of protest into his hand when his lips skimmed my shoulder. He kissed the strap I'd teased him with, pulling it between his teeth before letting it fall back in place.

My mind and body were at war. I wanted his lips on my skin. The place between my thighs pulsated with need unlike any I'd felt before.

I shifted my thighs together, and the masked vampire fucking inhaled. Audibly.

"Isn't that something?" he whispered cruelly. "You're more aroused than frightened. I can smell it in your blood."

My blood.

A wave of terror and heady desire ran through my body in waves. Something big and hard twitched against my back, just above my ass.

My blood.

This wasn't a romance novel. I was being tormented by a *vampire* who I knew—without a sliver of a doubt—had been watching me for weeks now.

And I knew who he was. Of course, I did. I wasn't stupid.

I shut my eyes tight. What if I was wrong? I wanted to be wrong.

Angel. Special. Safe.

Safe, safe, safe.

"How does it feel, little witch? To gain pleasure from your fear?" he asked.

Liberating.

Horrifying.

He removed his hand from my mouth.

"I hate you," I said, but it unfortunately came out as more of a needy whimper.

The masked vampire made a dissatisfied sigh. "Is that so?"

He dragged me backward, and before I knew it my back was

pressed up against the wall. The only light came from a lamp out in the hallway. In the dim glow, I faced him.

The Devil.

His mask of shadow covered almost all of his face but his lips, moving diagonally to expose part of his left jaw and cheek. And when he opened his mouth, I homed in on those razor-sharp elongated canines.

Shadows bound my wrists above my head, but my legs were free where I stood. I kicked at him. To my surprise, he allowed it.

He watched my legs swing, my feet delivering blows to his shins and knees.

Then, he laughed.

He *laughed at me*.

The shadow mask moved over his mouth to distort his voice. Which was nonsensical when I already knew who the fuck he was. And I knew he knew it too.

"Baby, please," he said, still laughing at my expense. "As if you weren't already infuriatingly adorable enough. If you keep kicking those little feet, I'm going to have to leave bites all over your thighs."

I stopped kicking. I tested the restraints around my wrists. The shadows were strangely smooth, almost like skin, when they solidified. They didn't give an inch. If anything, they tightened the more I wiggled.

My breathing was shallow, my head spinning. I was angry. Blisteringly angry. Because why was the first man I felt this attracted to, this safe with—this intrigued, seen, and understood by—a fucking *psychopath*?

A frustrated tear slid down my cheek. My masked stalker easily shoved my legs to the side and placed his thigh between mine, pressing against the sensitive, needy core of me.

"Why are you crying, angel?"

"They're tears of hatred," I said, a humiliating tremor in my voice.

The mask shifted, revealing his mouth again. To my horror, he leaned in close, and in a quick burst of movement his tongue was on my cheek.

He caught the tear on the tip of his tongue and slowly followed its trail upward before pulling back to stare hard into my eyes.

Or at least, I assumed he was staring behind his mask.

I was speechless. My lips parted as I stared into the abyss of slowly churning shadow. The void I'd been running from since I was a child, forsaken by parents who refused to protect their own children.

Did this man even have a soul? Was he feeding from *mine*?

His thigh pressed harder against my center, and I gasped. Tears burned my eyes, anger a bitter lump in my throat. Yet I slowly began to shift my hips, lightly grinding against his leg.

"Good girl," he cooed.

One of his hands was pressed against the wall. The other slowly skimmed across my chest. When it circled an erect nipple, I bucked against him.

"Uh-huh. That's it, angel," he praised. "Such a good girl. Show me how much you hate me."

He was making fun of me. Toying with me like a cat with a mouse between his paws. Yet I couldn't stop. I couldn't escape the pleasure coursing under my skin in waves, the delirious quiet that was starting to overtake my over-worked and exhausted mind.

"Mmhmm. You're being so good for me. Good girls get rewarded."

I felt his voice as a vibration moving up my body.

"What do you want, Evie?"

I wanted to tell him to go. I wanted to tell him to leave me alone forever. To take his darkness and violence and never come near me or Idris or Mena ever again.

Another tear fell, and I couldn't stop, couldn't stop chasing the pleasure a touch out of reach. I clenched around his thigh, and his accompanying groan filled me with equal measures of satisfaction and shame.

"I can't—I've never…" I trailed off.

The masked vampire stiffened. "You've never what, angel?"

My cheeks grew hot. I shook my head.

He grabbed my cheeks between his thumb and forefinger. "Use your words, baby."

He removed his grip, lightly tucking a strand of hair behind my ears. The acts of tenderness juxtaposed with his violations only drove my desire deeper, needier.

I wasn't even looking at his face, only an inhuman black mask, and that was still too much. I had to close my eyes.

"I haven't done… most things," I said. "I've never, um, come… with someone else. Only myself."

When the vampire removed his thigh from between my legs, I had to suppress a frustrated gasp.

"I wish I could say this was a surprise, but I know the caliber of men who came before me. And nope, doesn't shock me at all, really."

My eyes flew back open.

"You—what?" I stammered, dissecting his words. I knew he'd been watching me, but his blatant admission of it was a shockwave of horrifying reality to my system.

Kylo had come to my rescue the minute Jacob abandoned me at the markets. He'd positioned himself as everything Jacob wasn't.

Suspicion, distrust, and paranoia ripened in my veins.

This was wrong. All of it. What was I doing?

I opened my mouth to tell him to leave and never come back, but he spoke first.

"What else?"

I glared at him, and his hand was around my throat in an instant.

"What. Else. Have. You. Never. Done."

"Why does it matter?" I asked. That locked away, forbidden anger hissed in my ear. "Of course, a vampire freak like you would be perversely attracted to my *purity*."

He stood perfectly still. Watching. Waiting. Withholding his touch as my nerves screamed for him.

"I bet you think that *you* will be the one to take all of my firsts, is that right?" I spat.

The deep, distorted laugh that filled the room was devoid of all humor. The lamp in the hall switched off. Deathly potent power engulfed the space.

"I see we're done being my perfect good girl, hmm?" he asked, his voice eerily cold as wrath trembled beneath the surface. "Because *that…*"

The shadows around my wrists suddenly released me. I didn't think.

I ran.

A gust of wind shut the bedroom door in an instant. Strong arms yanked me back.

"… was the *wrong. Fucking. Answer.*"

19

KYLO

I threw Evie onto her light blue comforter. My shadows made quick work of binding her wrists together again, looping around the bed posts so she couldn't wiggle too far away.

I left her legs unbound merely because it was adorable to watch them flail and kick helplessly.

She couldn't see my smile behind my mask, as I watched her tire herself out and succumb to her bondage.

Rage was hot and slick in my blood. She'd been toeing the line with her bratty tendencies before, but insinuating that another man would *ever* lay a hand on her again was not something I'd tolerate.

Evie was mine.

And she was starting to understand that now too. Hence the futile attempts to lash out and cling to her lingering independence.

She hated how much she wanted me. She hated what I did to her mind even more than what I did to her body. Because I was challenging all of her faulty beliefs. I was both the embodiment of and the antidote to her every last nightmare.

Her anger wasn't about me. She'd been harmed long ago, and now she lived inside a cage of her own fear.

I was going to set her free.

She finally stopped writhing, her chest rising and falling as she let out a frustrated, high-pitched noise in the dark.

All of Evie's noises were maddeningly sexy.

I slowly stalked toward her.

Her arousal was still the most overpowering scent in the room, eclipsing her fear by miles.

I casually sat at the edge of the bed. I took my time lifting my hand, trailing down the center of her darling white nightgown. When I reached her navel, Evie bucked and let out a noise equally cute and feral.

"Did you just growl at me?" I laughed.

"No," she said harshly. "I don't *growl*." She huffed. "Why are you doing this?"

"Because you love it," I said.

"I do *not!*"

I made a soft tsking noise, wordlessly conveying my displeasure with her lies.

I kept my hand on her navel, slowly making a circle with my fingertip. That was all she was going to get until she begged for more.

The most primal, instinctual thought infected my mind as I stared at her stomach beneath the layer of thin white fabric. Evie would look so fucking perfect carrying our children. Our *powerful* children.

I didn't think I'd ever seriously thought about procreating before this moment.

Evie made another frustrated sound, twisting under my soft, teasing touch inches away from where she wanted me most.

"I said only good girls get rewarded," I said. "But if you *use your words* to tell me what you want, I will grant it."

She glared up at me with precious rage.

"You have twenty seconds."

I continued to lightly trace the same circle around her bellybutton. When I dipped lower than before, almost to her pubic bone, she gasped. But I was quick to trail back up.

"Ten seconds."

She stared up at the ceiling as if she wanted it to collapse and crush us both beneath the rubble. She tried to move her thighs together to give herself relief, and I let two tendrils of shadow yank her legs apart.

"I hate you," she repeated, shutting her eyes.

So vulnerable, so embarrassed. It made my cock painfully hard.

"Three seconds."

I yanked my hand back. Evie let out a frustrated, high-pitched noise of defeat.

"I want you to make me come," she said, as if the words were nails scraping out of her throat.

"Much better. Thank you for telling me the truth, angel."

In a burst of movement, I had Evie pulled up against my chest as I rested against the headboard. I kept her legs spread wide and let her bound wrists fall down to her stomach.

When my lips brushed the side of her head, I relished her shudder of pleasure.

"If you want me to stop, tell me. And I will," I whispered.

"Oh, good. I'm so glad the vampire who's been obsessively stalking me and broke into my home to attack me cares about consent."

I reached between her legs, and a deep groan escaped my lips at what I found.

"Shhh, baby. Or I'll take away your talking privileges."

Evie was fucking soaking wet. Slick and ready for me just like I knew she would be. I could feel it even over her cotton panties.

At my touch, she went beautifully quiet and still. Her breathing turned shallower. Her heart stuttered.

Fuck, it did ungodly things to me knowing I would be the first to make her come undone like this—knowing no man had ever satisfied her the way I would.

I was going to ruin her, but not because I gave a damn about *purity*.

But because I wanted to flood this precious girl with all the pleasure she didn't believe she deserved. I wanted to be everything she wanted and needed until she felt in her bones just how special, perfect, and worthy she was, and had always been.

I slipped my fingers under the fabric. Her legs were already trembling at the barest of touches.

This poor, needy girl. Deprived for too long.

I teased her sensitive clit slowly at first, testing and learning from her reactions. She moaned, breathy and desperate.

"How in the fuck has no one made you come before?" I asked, angry and raw. "You are my new favorite toy. I fear I won't be able to *stop* playing with you once I start."

I circled her with more pressure now, feeling the way her legs shook, and her breathing shifted. She arched her back, and I held her tighter against me.

"Good girl, angel," I said.

I fucking loved the way she melted against me when I praised her, already finding comfort in pleasing me.

"I'm scared," she mumbled, panting, her skin heating as she climbed closer to release.

She was scared to let go. She'd spent her whole life running. Of course she was terrified of ever being so vulnerable.

I knew the approach she needed.

"You will come for me," I said. I closed my hand around her throat with only faint pressure. "You don't have a choice."

Her moans grew louder, more violent, and I didn't relent. I

didn't let her escape my touch as it quickened with increasing pressure.

I didn't know if my fangs or straining cock had it worse. Her blood was rich with arousal, and I could scent the moment she reached the point of no return.

I kept steady, driving her over the edge as she whimpered.

And the moment she came, I pulled back all of my shadows and flipped to pin her underneath me.

I retracted the lower part of my mask, and I finally captured those perfect pink lips with mine. In the aftermath of her release, she was endearingly pliable. I conquered her with ease, finally teasing that bratty tongue with my own as I invaded her mouth and claimed every inch. I tugged her bottom lip with my teeth, letting my fangs lightly scrape.

It wasn't nearly enough. If I was a weaker man, bloodlust would've overtaken me the moment her timid lips began to move with equal desperation. Her tongue tentatively traced the outline of my lips before going in search of mine.

She moaned contentedly into my mouth, and it made me lightly grind my hips against her core.

Evie was done for. She might fight me for a while longer as she learned to trust me. But I knew her threats were empty. Her resistance was futile.

I finally broke away to stare into her wide gray eyes.

Her cheeks were flushed, her forehead dewy. She felt my lips with the pad of her finger, and when she traced my jaw, it was as if she were mourning something.

She knew who I was. She just didn't want to admit it out loud. She didn't want to make it true. She wasn't ready to fully leave her blissful ignorance.

I didn't blame her.

I would be the monster under her bed for as long as she needed.

"I'm going to hold you, and you're going to fall asleep."

She furrowed her brows, as if the words were spoken in a different language. "Why?"

"Because in my arms is the safest place you will ever be."

She continued to stare at me as if none of my words made sense to her. Like I was a figment of her imagination that might disappear any second.

I shuddered to think of what her recently deceased child of a boyfriend had conditioned her to believe about pleasure, sex, and expectations.

Her distrust melted into something else when I stroked her cheek with my knuckles.

Beautiful, innocent curiosity.

It might've even been hope that flashed in those stormy gray depths, for the briefest of moments.

I pulled her under the covers and into my hold. My shadows slithered blissfully around her form in wisps of smoke, satisfied to finally be so close.

Evie was slow to relax as always. Waiting for me to reveal some unspoken motive or deception or trick.

Instead, I let my breathing deepen, and I slowly ran my fingers through her angelic blonde hair.

At this, Evie finally let go. Her tension melted away. My good girl enjoyed when I played with hair just as much as I enjoyed doing it.

I loved making her feel safe.

When her heart decidedly calmed, mine followed. I inhaled the scent of her floral shampoo, remembering the first time I saw her in the square, lugging an empty wagon behind her.

No, I wasn't a nihilist.

I knew the world was a place of hidden meaning, inexplicable magick, and intertwining fates, because I knew Evie was mine the moment I laid eyes on her.

20

EVIE

It was rare these days for me to wake up from a slumber without nightmares. This morning was one of those blissful rarities.

I groggily opened my eyes and stretched, feeling more restful than I had in days.

The sun was bright, a cool, fresh air rolling over my body from the—

I stiffened.

My head snapped to the side to stare at the gently billowing white curtains. My feet hit the ground in the next breath, quickly pulling the window shut.

I stared at my empty bed for two beats before quickly walking through the rest of the cottage. He wouldn't have been able to access my spell room, thankfully. Everywhere else was clear.

And while I should've been glad for that, I felt something entirely inappropriate instead.

Disappointment rooted in my belly.

It was silly and childish and frankly, insane. I mean, *what?* Did I expect the masked vampire who'd been stalking me for weeks to be wearing an apron and cooking me pancakes in the kitchen?

The thought of that tall, muscular, tattooed body in only an apron was both strangely sexy and ridiculously absurd.

I ran a hand over my face. The only thing I could do was pad into the kitchen to get rid of my coffee withdrawal headache. As I poured the hot, bitter goodness into my tallest mug, my insides squirmed.

Because now I was remembering how that unhinged psycho touched me. That broad hand around my throat... The way he wouldn't let me run from him, his shadows holding me in place, the ecstasy that had coursed through my veins when I finally, *finally*—

Overflowing coffee splattered onto the counter and my arm, scalding my skin. I yelped. I set the coffee press down and quickly ran cool water over my burns at the sink.

And that was when I noticed where the hands rested on my pastel pink clock on the counter.

I cursed.

I didn't have time to spare, but I chugged my coffee, anyway.

THE STOREFRONT of Celeste's was an ancient building painted black, with flowers blooming in the upstairs windows and ferns and vines draping down the sides. More potted plants, herbs, garden decor, and faerie gardens were displayed out front. There were also a few giant amethyst slabs and geodes to indicate the witchy goods inside.

The energy of the trinkets and plants called to me. Some of the energies were intrigued, while others wanted to communicate with me or advance their own personal agendas. The spirit of a red rose bush was especially mouthy, for reasons I couldn't begin to imagine.

"I'm not currently available, but thank you for your interest," I said curtly as I passed, fortifying my own energy and closing out the barrage of spirit communication.

Inside the shop, the general aura was as usual. Tables and shelves of goods were dispersed throughout the space. Natural light streamed through the windows, and arrangements of flowers reached toward the sun.

The only hint of distress in the energetic field came from the counter in the back, where one of my regulars, Cecil, talked to a co-owner, Marietta.

"Look—she's here," Marietta said, clearly trying to keep a calm, easy demeanor in the face of Cecil's chronically perturbed one.

His energy changed the moment he turned and saw me. His wrinkled, human features shifted into relief. When he smiled, I couldn't help but smile too.

"Evie!" he exclaimed, facing me. His white hair was wispy and cloud-like, his eyes a murky hazel. "I was so worried. I know how much you love the university libraries. When I heard the news, I prayed to Helia, and Selena too, that you weren't caught up in the violence."

Marietta shook her head. "Fucking born," she muttered under her breath.

Ugly, prickly guilt crept up my spine. I hated that I'd endangered mortals by using that wretched, violent magick inside me.

However, I didn't regret killing that blasphemous witch. I was glad for it, even. She'd been too close to Idris.

And I wasn't ready to examine what that truth meant about who I really was, at my core.

My smile faltered, but I was well-versed in hiding from ghosts. "Thank you, Cecil," I said quickly. I grounded myself in his genuine show of paternal care, the way it touched my frightened, wounded heart. "How are you doing? How's the neck?"

The healing salve I'd made for him was crafted to ease his chronic pain, no doubt from years spent hunched over a desk studying religious texts. He was a scholar of Helianic mysticism.

"It's just wonderful," he said. "Feels better than it has in decades. Not to mention, you've provided me an excellent excuse to ask Jill for massages." He winked.

I laughed. Jill was his wife. I loved watching them together— the way she seemed both hopelessly in love and endlessly annoyed with Cecil both at the same time. It was a comforting, uniquely human depiction of devotion.

"Did you need anything else from me?" I asked.

I hadn't been called to make anything specifically for Cecil this week, but he was remarkably good at coming up with various mental and physical ailments that warranted special orders. It was flattering, and I loved being of service to good, hard-working humans trying to live meaningful lives surrounded by senseless violence.

He shook his head. "No, no. Was just curious about what you'd cooked up this week! And I'm buying flowers for Jill, on account of all the massages..." He scratched his chin, his grin impish.

Marietta and one of the meandering workers approached to help me unload my wagon. Bundles of herbs, special floral arrangements, a few satchels of tea, and a collection of anointed candles were packed with care.

"The candles are for protection," I said to Quill, a short man with tan skin and thick black hair.

He lazily saluted me with a flirtatious grin, reaching for my candles to stock the shelves. "I keep waiting for you to bring goods for evil and mischief. Still only doing pretty faerie magick for love and light?" he teased.

"I only do evil mischievous magick for you, Quill," I said

with a smile. "Why do you think you have such horrid luck with women?"

Quill clutched his chest. "Oh, thank the gods. I thought that was because of my personality."

Marietta snorted. "No, it definitely is." She eyed the plants I'd brought. "Those are gorgeous, Evie. Great condition. Have you ever thought of buying some land to produce more?"

I shrugged. I kept my schemes close to my chest. I had a feeling Marietta was fishing, just like the other owners, about my future plans. It was no secret that my products sold instantly, developing their own cult following that was only growing stronger.

"It's the magick that's special," Cecil said. "Everything else is a prop."

Cecil knew more than what was good for him.

I shifted under their curiosity and intrigue, quickly changing the subject to explanations on the goods I'd brought.

Marietta eyed me after we were done. I watched several humans and witches rush into the shop, all searching for the new stock. I needed to start coming in on different days each week. They'd learned my schedule.

I slowly met the shop owner's gaze.

Her curly brown hair was in a loose bun, her rich brown eyes sharp. "You seem different."

"Different how?"

"Hey, Evie!" someone called, interrupting us.

I tentatively waved to the teenage witch who'd snatched up one of my candles. She was just starting to develop divinatory powers.

"Last year, you would've shriveled away from all of this attention," Marietta said, her lips quirking up. "You're coming into yourself, I think. It's a joy to see."

I still didn't particularly love all the eyes on me. Standing out meant I was more visible. And being visible meant I wasn't safe.

But I was fulfilling my purpose, and I was proud of my work in a way that trumped all fear. I *had* to use my magick for good. Or else I'd fade away.

I blushed under Marietta's scrutiny. "I was recently relieved of some dead weight."

Her smile widened. She knew exactly what I meant. Like everyone else who cared about me, she was not Jacob's biggest fan.

"Thank the gods," she said, lightly bumping my shoulders. "Was wondering when you were going to kick that weasel to the curb."

I giggled. The afternoon light warmed my face, and for a moment, I felt peaceful. Like I was standing exactly where I needed to be, in perfect alignment with the flow of the universe.

"He was a small man, Evie. That was why he was so determined to make you even smaller than he felt inside," Marietta said softly. "You have to be more discerning in the future. Just because someone is drawn to your light, doesn't mean they're made of light themselves. Some recognize that you hold something they will never have, and they will do anything, anything at all, to try to starve that radiance until it dies. Because they'd rather you both live in darkness than for you to be the only one to shine."

Those words slammed into me as full-body chills swept over my skin. The spirits made it clear when it was time to listen with an open heart. This was one of those moments.

The truth was often just as painful as it was useful. Liberation was only possible after total destruction of everything we once thought we knew.

I looked down at my Mary Jane's, the frilly socks that came to my ankles. The lump in my throat grew until I finally accepted and integrated Marietta's words into my soul.

"Thank you, Marietta," I whispered. "You were right about

him. I don't regret any of it. People are messengers, even when the lessons they teach us are brutal and unforgiving."

The lump dissolved. I wiped away a stray tear.

Marietta smiled knowingly and rubbed my shoulder. "You're brilliant, Evie. You're going to be something. Don't you ever let a *man* hold you back from your destiny." She wrinkled her nose.

"If you ever see me repeating the same pattern, please spray me with that water bottle you use on Prince Worthington."

Prince Worthington was the little black cat that roamed Celeste's, causing all manner of mischief and mayhem in his wake.

Marietta threw her head back with a cackle. "Deal. Just remember that's what you asked for." She raised her hands in the air and waggled a finger before leaving me to help a customer.

I thought of my masked vampire stalker and frowned. How could the embodiment of shadow and death ever do anything but drain the light from my soul?

I begged my body to feel hatred or fear—to lean into this feral paranoia trying desperately to protect me from oblivion.

But all I felt was stubborn, childish euphoria. Hope. A flutter in my stomach, a course of sharp desire in my blood that swelled between my thighs.

I wondered if he was close by, watching me from the shadows. More heat flooded my system, my nipples pebbling under my pastel pink dress.

Would I find liberation when that weaponized, tattooed body devoured me whole?

21

EVIE

In a deep trance, my head dipped, my body grew heavy, and my soul lifted free like a feather in the wind.

I was searching for something, but I couldn't remember what it was. The smell of burning cedar provided almost enough clarity to recall why I was spirit walking, but as soon as I picked up the reins of awareness, they were yanked out of my grasp again.

My vision cleared, and I saw myself in my crafting room. I was sitting cross-legged, palms resting on my knees, facing up. My head was tilted down, a veil of blonde hair eclipsing my features. The fabric of my pink dress pooled around me.

I approached my body in my spirit form, my feet hovering above the ground. When I trained my gaze on my physical self, I could see a field of color and etheric matter crawling over every inch. There were so many murky gray attachments clinging to my aura, blocking my energy pathways.

In my periphery, glowing balls of light danced around. I felt multiple presences at my back, and I knew that they were protectors and guides. No negative force could enter the sanctity of my spell room.

My instinct was to remove the etheric burrs lodged in my body, to ask my guides for help. The one at my throat was the biggest, with grotesque appendages that reached to my heart and even lower, down to my sacral and root centers.

So much fear. So much pain.

Who had stolen my voice?

I reached with fingertips made of transparent etheric matter, channeling a frequency of healing from the world around me. But as soon as I brushed the ugly gray mass, I was yanked from the room.

Things worked differently in the otherworld. Fear was more a vibration than a scream.

My surroundings slowly took back shape.

No. No, no, no.

I was back in my childhood bedroom. I stood in front of the windows overlooking the farm. Other homes loomed in the distance. I could just barely make out Tilly and Melody playing on the small playground the coven had built a few years ago.

Our home was the biggest, maybe because Lillian had blessed my mother with a human son and a half-witch daughter with humanlike blood.

She was a powerful witch and the closest to the Dark Goddess, the coven said. Next in line to be our High Priestess.

No!

Someone inside my mind was screaming. I pressed my hands over my ears as my head pounded.

The door behind me flew open.

"Evelynn Lockwood," my mother bellowed.

At the tone of her voice, I stilled and went quiet, my hands going back to my sides. I slowly turned to face her.

Idris was on her hip, hands so small, just a baby—reaching, reaching, reaching.

His blond hair made golden ringlets, and his fair skin was rosy as he wailed and reached for me.

I walked forward, extending my arms toward Idris, but as soon as my fingers brushed his, Mama yanked him back and out of my reach.

"What is wrong with you? I told you we had to leave in an hour, and you are in the same clothes, your hair is a mess, and you're *filthy.*"

Tears pricked my eyes, and I followed her gaze to my feet, streaked with dirt and grass from playing outside with the other children.

"I'm sorry," I said. I didn't realize time had passed. I couldn't even remember what I'd been doing for the past hour. My head was empty and useless.

Idris continued to wail. He looked at our mother, and she ignored him. She didn't bounce him, didn't soothe him. She didn't even acknowledge his existence.

A lump formed in my throat, this desperation that had no end.

I had something to say. But I didn't know how to say it.

With a flick of her wrist, my knees hit the hardwood floor with a thud. A piercing throb echoed through my bones, but I knew better than to make a sound as tears streamed down my face.

"Recite three prayers to Lillian. May she have mercy on your soul," Mama spat.

I stared at the floor as my mouth moved, and that lump grew heavier and heavier.

Whispers spoke to me from the corners of the room, and something inside my blood felt strange, like a low buzz.

Idris continued to cry, and it reminded me of all the times I had cried for my mother and father. I'd wailed just like him, my hands reaching for something that I didn't understand, something I never received.

Idris hadn't learned yet that crying didn't work. Only being *good* worked, though I could never really get that right. The rules were always changing, and I could never keep up. Everything inside me was bad and useless and wrong.

"When we go into the village, you are not to speak a word to anyone. Do you understand me?"

Don't cry.

A trembling sob wanted to escape, and I squashed it back down. My eyes betrayed me, tears slipping free.

"Yes, Mama."

Don't speak. Don't argue. Don't fight. Don't question.

Mama watched my lip tremble with irritation. "Why are you *crying*? What is *wrong with you*? The world doesn't revolve around you, Evelynn. Have you ever once considered anyone else's feelings but your own indulgent ones?"

She huffed. Idris sobbed and then hiccupped.

"We don't have time for the Evelynn production today. If you don't shape up, I'll be telling the entire coven about what an ungrateful, disrespectful daughter you are."

I studied my hands. So small. Just a child.

The voice in my head screamed, and the world split open. Time sped up. The last thing I smelled was smoke. The last thing I felt was a heavy weight in my arms as I ran.

I RE-ENTERED my physical body violently. My breathing was shallow, an unmovable mass in my throat. It had been there for so long. No matter how far away I ran, no matter how good I was, these remnants of the past tormented me. Punished me.

I curled into a ball and cried until I felt numb.

Then I sat up, cleaned up my altar, closed my circle of protection, and tried my hardest to forget about the experience and move on with my day.

The past no longer existed. There was no use dwelling on

things that would never change. I'd rather look to the future—or literally anywhere else.

In a haze, I drank my coffee, slipped on my not-so-white-anymore sneakers, and made the thirty-minute trek to campus.

There were far more born in the streets than usual, no doubt a reaction to what had happened at the library a few days ago. Through magickally delivered notes, I'd learned from Idris that one shelf of books had been completely destroyed, with the rows above and below partially impacted. Whatever Ky—*the masked vampire* had done when the lights went out had saved countless books from destruction.

I kept my head down each time I passed a vampire, absently rubbing the obsidian protection ring on my right ring finger.

The moonstone pendant necklace Kylo gave me still rested around my neck.

Because why let a pretty thing go to waste? I loved pretty things.

I came to a halt as I turned a corner and entered the safety of the campus's vampire-free zone. I suddenly remembered the book that had been gifted to me weeks ago.

Of course, it had been *him*.

Which meant… gods, I'd only met Kylo once when that had happened. Yet he knew exactly which book to buy me, as if he'd seen me eyeing it on one of my walks through town.

How fucking long had he been stalking me?

My stomach rolled over. Fate had nothing to do with our meeting. I might've first run into Kylo in that library, but that was only because he'd planted himself directly in my path.

I was already on edge when I found Idris in the courtyard between four academic buildings. I tried my best to table my feelings for when I could unleash them on my stalker, but after this morning's disturbing visioning session, it was hard to reorient myself to normalcy.

Idris was lying on his back, his head cushioned by a backpack as he read one of his architecture textbooks.

"Not the best position for taking notes," I called.

When he spotted me, he smiled and pointed to his forehead. "Don't need notes. It's all up here."

I sat down on the quilted blanket he'd laid on the grass. Students milled about, some faster than others as if late to classes or meetings. Others sat on benches or in the grass like us.

"Did you bring snacks?" Idris asked.

I rolled my eyes. "Is that all I'm good for to you?"

He sat up and shrugged a shoulder. "On occasion, you say something surprisingly witty. And some of those times, you even *meant* to be funny."

"You're my harshest critic," I muttered, reaching into my satchel for the jars of berries and biscuits I brought.

"That's what brothers are for." He smiled. "I keep you honest. It's my way of motivating you to be your best self."

"Uh-huh," I said, throwing a strawberry at his head.

He swatted it away in record speed before it could hit his cheek.

"Hey, hey, hey," Idris said, raising his hands up in a silent truce. "I thought you were a pacifist."

I shook my head, glaring at him only half-heartedly. I popped a biscuit in my mouth, deeply inhaling the fresh air. Across the yard, a bush of pink flowers emitted a glowing aura, alerting me to the presence of active plant spirits. I tucked away a half-formed spell idea for later.

"It used to freak me out when you did that in the middle of conversations."

My gaze snapped back to Idris, who was shoveling raspberries into his mouth.

I scratched my neck. "I'm sorry."

He shook his head, brows furrowing. "No need to apologize.

I don't find it spooky anymore. You wouldn't be Evie if you didn't randomly space out and gaze into the great beyond." He paused. "How are you? I feel like you've had to deal with a lot lately. Jacob, then the vampire attack, then what happened at the library…"

Some might call a collection of undesirable events happening in quick succession bad luck.

But I was beginning to suspect a different explanation—one with a distinctive four-letter name.

"I'm okay," I said. "I just hate what's happening to Etherdale. This city used to be the safest in the realm."

"If you keep talking like that, people are going to assume you're a loyalist," Idris said, voice low as he scanned our surroundings.

Frustration coiled up my spine. "You know more than anyone that I hold nothing but hatred for the born."

Idris swallowed, his face dropping. A faraway sadness bled into his soft brown eyes, gone in the next blink.

"Yet you'd rather they terrorize us, traffic and kill us without repercussion, than do anything at all to fight back." He shook his head. "Evie, they killed my classmate last semester. One day she was sitting next to me, talking about her family in Morha—how they wrote to her constantly and sent her care packages they couldn't afford. How they couldn't wait until she came back and used her studies to uplift her whole community. She was bright. I'd never seen someone that excited about even the most boring parts of studies. One day, she was sitting there, laughing and taking way too many notes. The next, we were at her memorial."

My stomach sunk. That familiar lump in my throat arose, and this time, I recognized it. This bundle of my deepest pain, the trauma that had taken my voice. The only time I had power was when it was spilling out of me beyond my control.

I could feel it now, building.

"We are *always*," Idris said, his voice low yet strong, "at *memorials*."

Through the pain and anger in his eyes, I saw a mirror, a window into the past. And I wanted to run. Gods above and below, I wanted to fucking run.

"I'm sorry," I said. I'd failed him long ago, and now he didn't trust me to protect him.

"For what?" he asked, searching my eyes. He was always looking for something there, something we both lost in some nowhere village in the hills.

Idris said he didn't remember much of our childhood. He said he didn't remember that night—the night we ran. But there were dark circles under his eyes, evidence of the same nightmares that happened year after year.

Hide under the bed and don't come out until I come back for you, the ghost of myself whispered.

I remembered the way Idris had looked when I said it. Those wide, frightened brown eyes had stared up at me with a buried strength.

He'd believed in me. I was his guardian angel, the only source of light in a world of darkness.

Now, he just looked disappointed.

"I'm sorry you're surrounded by incredible violence and grief," I said. "And I'm sorry I failed to protect you from all of it. I'm sorry you think I'm so weak."

"Is that what you think?" Idris's face twisted. "Evie, you have it all wrong," he said, shaking his head. "I want to protect *you*. Not because I think you're weak. I want to help protect this city we both love—the one that welcomed us with open arms." He stared down at the blanket. "How could you think that you failed me?"

I shook my head. I could hear it—the meaning between the words, the culmination of my every doubt and fear.

"Idris, please, don't," I said, my voice breaking.

Don't cry. Don't you fucking cry.

He refused to meet my eyes, only confirming the truth I'd foreseen weeks ago in the coffee shop.

"Please don't turn your back on Helia," I begged. "You're eighteen—you're still a ch—"

"I am not a child," he snapped. "I won't be turning any time soon. They wouldn't allow it. But I want to start the process. I want to serve something greater than myself. Like you do—with your magick."

I couldn't think straight anymore. One of my feet was in the past, remembering how it felt to run up those steps, searching for Idris as he screamed. The other was in the future, imagining my brother as a bloodthirsty monster, always in danger from forces infinitely stronger than him.

"I'm not a kid anymore," he said again. "You can't control everything. You can't shut your eyes and dream reality away. All we can do is clean up our little space in this world. Everything else is out of our hands."

Like hell it was.

I trembled with rage. I suddenly remembered what Kylo had said in the library, when I'd asked him what he'd been working on.

Curriculum to effectively radicalize the youth.

I was such an idiot. And Kylo knew it—he'd been laughing at me, feeding off my naivety and ignorance.

To think I'd allowed him to *touch me.* To make me feel so delusionally safe.

"Evie," Idris said, his eyes wide.

I snapped back to myself. I followed his eyes to the slowly spreading black rot extending from underneath our blanket.

My anger had me bleeding death from my palms. Sowing destruction.

I was no angel.

"I'm sorry," I said, quickly rising to my feet. I stared at Idris in horror. He blinked quickly, and I didn't miss the flash of fear in his eyes.

"You need to go," he said. "It's not safe for you here."

I knew he was talking about the fact that the born were hunting for powerful witches. *Chaos witches.*

But all I heard was rejection.

I wasn't good enough for him. That was why he wanted to kill his humanity, our link by blood, and join a new family entirely.

The sky rumbled. Rain began to pour, as if Helia were mourning with me. A student yelped at a resounding boom of thunder that had seemingly come from nowhere.

The moment I felt eyes on me, I snatched up my things and ran.

22

EVIE

Out of breath and panting, I reached an arched brick tunnel under a bridge and collapsed against the curved wall inside. Students passed overhead, chatting about revolution and young love and the strange weather, oblivious to the deadly witch beneath them.

"It's no good that you're always on the run, baby," a distorted voice spoke.

I whipped my head to the side. My guts turned inside out at the vision of him standing there at the entrance to the tunnel, masked and hemorrhaging darkness.

"It makes me fucking crazy, in fact," the vampire said as he stalked forward. Behind him, rain and harsh gusts of wind rocked against the brick foundation. "Because I'm a hunter. When I see vulnerable little meadow nymphs on the run, I'm going to chase them."

I hoped my glare really was deadly.

"You've seen my magick," I said, my rage multiplying as I stared at the cause of all my grief, all my despair.

I pushed off the wall and faced him, refusing to cower and

get his cock hard from my fear. My fists clenched as I stared into that impassive mask of onyx.

"You know that I'm not a meadow nymph or an angel. I'm not a green witch. I'm not innocent or light or *pure* or fucking *harmless.*"

As my voice rose, lightning struck the earth in a violent crack nearby, briefly illuminating the walls of the tunnel. It reminded me of the library and those strobing lights.

A tremor rolled through me. My vampire hunter stood stock still, watching me in silence.

"You know what I did to that witch—you saw it." My voice steadily rose.

I remembered how the witch's eyes had popped out of her skull, and I wanted to vomit.

"I'm a plague on this world!" I screamed.

My voice crashed in a boom of thunder, like the violence in my veins that I couldn't run from.

I couldn't run from myself.

Shadows circled the vampire's feet, and I heard their whispers, heard the way they wanted me.

When they reached for my ankles, I didn't move. I let them tickle my skin, coil around me like snakes made of smoke.

"Take off your mask!" I yelled. "Take it *off!*" I took another step forward. "I know who you are, K—"

His hand covered my mouth before I could finish his name. "Uh-uh," he scolded. "You can throw your scary tantrum, my *innocent, adorable* little angel. But let's be careful with our words, hmm? Some things cannot be taken back."

I tried to bite his palm, and he pushed me back against the wall. His hand went around my throat next.

"There are a lot less dramatic ways to ask me to take you over my knee, baby," he cooed, the condescending note in his voice making me want to attack him with everything I had. "If you want to be punished for your wicked ways, you need only ask."

I could hear the grin in his voice, as if he wasn't taking me seriously.

The pressure had built up too much, for too long. I had to release something. All I could think of was Idris in harm's way, leaving me behind for good.

Alone. I was about to be all alone.

Because of *him.*

A feral noise escaped from my throat. Waves and waves of panic and anger and burning wrath spilled from my lips and fingertips, my throat and my heart and my solar plexus.

A wave of darkness rippled outward, an ear-splitting explosion ringing through the world.

Kylo flew back against the other side of the tunnel.

If not for his helmet of shadow, he might've split open his skull.

I could hear every single beat of my heart as blood rushed to my head. Water streamed into the tunnel along the cracks in the dirt path. The wind was impossibly loud, and for a moment, I worried I'd conjured a cyclone.

Kylo was motionless for two long seconds before he peeled himself off the wall and tackled me to the earth.

Mud was thick and sticky beneath me, and flood water splashed from the impact.

He straddled me as I writhed, his shadows suddenly suffocating, obscuring my access to my own power as I flailed and panicked.

I knew he was powerful, that he'd been hiding the sheer magnitude of his magick by keeping it carefully tucked away.

But gods above, I didn't realize he was *this* powerful.

My bones quaked, fighting his shadows' call for me to submit. Limbs held me down, too many to count, and a strong hand closed around my throat.

The mask was two inches above my face. *"Yield,"* the voice boomed, and my blood recoiled, nausea and heat turning me inside out.

"No," I said, my voice a hollow rasp. "Promise me. You have to promise me not to let him join."

Laughter rumbled through his chest. "I don't think you understand how leverage works, angel. But I'll give you a hint: You currently have none."

Suddenly, the water was so high that it was threatening to submerge my body.

"Promise me!" I cried. "You can have whatever you want. Just please, please don't let my brother join your clan. Put him on a blacklist, ask your leader for a favor, whatever you have to do."

As I writhed, water splashed, and soon it was up to my face. I could only lift my head a few inches. The hand around my neck was unrelenting, unyielding.

That same laughter echoed against the walls. "Evie, my sweet, pure, harmless little flower petal..."

He was going to let me drown.

"I have no leader. There is no greater authority in Etherdale than my own."

The water overtook my head, and I was too panicked, too emotional to fight through this wall of power. He held me under as I thrashed.

As soon as a trickle of water entered my lungs, I was pulled back up.

A bare face greeted me. I stared into Kylo's deep blue eyes. I was lost in them, the way they swam with yearning and reverence and rage and awe.

I sucked in deep breath after breath. I had to get out of this ravine. I had to stop leaking power, or I was going to drown the whole world.

"Promise me," I begged. *"Please."*

That was when I noticed that although his mask was off, his

fangs were bared, his tattoos crawling up his neck and down his arms. He was in his true form.

Kylo. The first man who'd made me feel like maybe, just maybe, I wasn't so alone. That I deserved someone who saw me, understood me, and adored all the parts of me that others had shunned.

But he wasn't a man at all.

I shut my eyes.

"Open those pretty, storm-cloud-colored eyes, Evie," he said, and his voice was his own. No distortions. No masks. "*Open.*"

When I refused, he shoved me back underwater.

My lungs burned, shadows continued to coil around every inch of me. And the most fucked-up part of all of this was that for some demented, nonsensical reason, my body was reacting to Kylo's murder attempts with *arousal.*

The place between my thighs was raw and aching as I struggled for air. The more helpless, disoriented, and heartbroken I became, the more desperate for his touch.

Kylo yanked me back up. My eyes flew open. He still bared those fangs like a feral beast as he trembled with dark, godly magick.

"Do as you're told," he growled. "You commanded me to take off my mask. You attacked me. Your words and actions have consequences, angel. Even when you're upset. *Especially* when you're upset."

The way he scolded me like I was a child didn't only enrage me, humiliate me. It also spread that wicked, forbidden heat through my core. I stared at his mouth, those fangs that I hated with all the marrow in my bones.

Those beautiful lips rose into a smirk. "Because your God is gracious, and you are so cute, I will allow a deal to be struck. The terms you offered were incredibly stupid, on your part, but I will take advantage of them as I see fit."

The rain outside continued, but the wind was less violent, and the thunder had ceded.

"Your brother will be blacklisted from clan recruitment," he said.

An exhale of relief escaped me. My magick slowly gave in, submitting to his power.

"And you will go out on dates with me, anytime and anywhere, so long as it doesn't interfere with your witchy business schemes. I also have full rein to pick out your adorable outfits."

I stared at him. "You—I—*what?*"

I offered him anything at all. He told me he was going to take advantage of that. And *this* was what he wanted?

"Additionally," he said, staring down at my lips.

A shadow teased one of my nipples, and I squirmed.

"If you ever try to hide from me, I will ensure you are never able to try it again," he snarled.

Another shadow dipped between my legs, brushing over my soaked panties.

"Tell me you understand."

In the aftermath of my magickal and emotional explosion, my shell-shocked body began to tremble. My teeth chattered. I was helpless and overpowered beneath Kylo's hold.

He could kill me in an instant. He clearly knew who my brother was. He knew where Mena and I lived. He knew everything about me.

"I understand," I whispered.

My life was in his hands. His identity was now in mine.

He watched my trembling jaw for two beats before lifting me into his arms. "Good girl." He kissed my forehead.

The most confusing mix of pleasure, relief, and anger warred in my blood. But I was also enormously depleted. My limbs were heavy, my once activated mind growing dim.

"I'm going to clean you up," he said softly. "You are now under my protection and care."

23

KYLO

I n an instant, everything had changed irreversibly. I wasn't sure Evie truly understood the predicament she was now in. And perhaps it was better that way, for the time being.

So long as she kept that pretty little mouth shut about what I'd revealed, she could remain in denial about who she'd just sold her soul to.

She would never betray me that way. She would never endanger her loved ones, for starters. But I also simply didn't think that was who Evie was. She thought she hated me, that I was the reason for all of her sorrows, but deep down, she knew the truth.

I was not the one who'd harmed her. I was not the reason she was always on the run.

I loved that Evie was violently protective of the people in her life. It was a quality I adored—one that reminded me of myself. It only made me that much more territorial over my angel, knowing that while she was the fiercest defender of her family —she had no one to truly care for *her*.

Not like I could.

She was so small right now as she walked next to me. She'd

eventually jolted from her state of shock and demanded I set her down.

I took her to my neighborhood off campus, where we were surrounded by the clan. My estate was covered by tall trees for privacy, on a small piece of land on the outskirts of the residential area. It was dark and regal, with castle-like spires and arched doors and windows. A large, circular stained-glass window stood on the second floor, detailed with bright, luminescent colors and a sacred geometric patterned frame. A path of stone led to the front steps, with black lamp posts dispersed on either side.

"Is there a sigil in your tattoos that corresponds with your glamour?" she asked me, staring at my bare arms with a furrowed brow.

I shook my head. Yes, Evie was far from stupid—too intelligent for her own good, honestly. But gods above, she was oblivious to the sheer amount of danger she was in right now.

"Baby, please," I warned. "Let's keep those questions at bay for now."

She was absolutely drenched and covered in mud, her arms tight around her body as her teeth chattered. It was one of the most precious sights I'd ever seen.

She frowned and returned to giving me the silent treatment as we approached my estate.

A smirk tugged at my lips. I deserved a medal for the self-restraint I'd exercised in that tunnel. There was something about Evie finally unraveling—displaying raw, unbridled power in her pink-rose-colored dress with frilly details and a bow around her neck—that had made me unquenchably ravenous. Desperate to taste her, to bite her, to sink into her, and to finally show her what it was like to be with a man. *Helia, Selena, and Lillian too.* I'd never been so painfully aroused.

Her anger was a drug. Everything about Evie was my new favorite addiction. The salt of her tears, the sinfully sweet smell of her arousal, the way she'd struggled and fought for air as I held her underwater, the most delicious relief of her submission when she finally yielded to my power.

I'd wanted to fuck her, right there in the rain and mud. I wanted to drive into her as she nearly drowned, force her to offer herself to me with her desperate bargaining over and over again.

Gods, the way she'd begged. I could listen to her plead for my mercy for an eternity.

Her deal was easy to accept, given that I had already been planning on taking Evie however and whenever I wanted until the end of time.

And if she wanted me to keep her brother away from the clan, there was no need for the drama. I would've agreed if only she'd asked nicely.

Not that I was complaining. Our explosive, dangerous power struggle was the far sexier option.

"Are you going to—"

Evie cut herself off when we reached the steps to my front porch, and she noticed we weren't alone.

I waved at the clan members gathered on my secluded porch, sitting around a table reading and playing cards.

When their eyes landed decisively on Evie, my fangs ached. A primal urge to claim her in front of my guards pressed against the walls of my mind. Even more so when she instinctively stayed a step behind me, recognizing me as her protector.

Good girl. Good fucking girl.

At my hardened stare, each of my guards averted their eyes in subservience.

"Good evening, gentlemen. You all may take your leave," I said.

They wouldn't go far. Just to the outskirts of the property or across the street, far enough away to give us privacy.

When I led her inside, Evie's mouth dropped open. She

stared at the double staircases weaving to the second floor, then peeked to the right where one of my libraries showcased row after row of ancient texts. To the left, the dining room, with a long wooden table and high-back chairs cushioned in green velvet. The color scheme was a mix of burgundy, black, forest green, and navy. Wooden furniture predominated, giving the atmosphere a studious, yet inviting energy. I made sure to hang plenty of art, mostly pieces that showcased Ravenia's natural beauty. The occasional moody, abstract piece could be found— generally creations that made me feel something deep and unnamable.

"What were you saying, angel?" I asked Evie as she gawked.

Her eyes were slow to find mine, still churning with unspoken heartbreak, ire, and distrust. She looked at me like I'd betrayed her.

And I fucking hated it.

She cleared her throat, still shaking and chilled to the bone. "You said that the deal was for dates..." She stared uncomfortably at the floor.

My hand lifted, my instinct to comfort her and make her feel safer. But when I reached to stroke her cheek, she flinched and recoiled.

I swallowed and retracted my hand.

"And now I'm in your home," she continued. "Are you going to take advantage of me? Did I agree to be your—"

"*No.*"

Rage cut through me like a knife, and Evie stared nervously into my eyes.

"Angel, gods, no. You're not a prisoner. You did not sell me your body. If you tell me you never want me to lay a hand on you again, I won't."

We both knew she would never utter those words. No matter how much false hatred coated that bratty tongue. But it was true. If Evie wasn't interested in me, if she told me in earnest that she never wanted to see me again, I would leave her alone.

But she wouldn't. She *couldn't.* Just like I couldn't stay away from her, couldn't stop winning her over until she'd yielded me all of herself and more.

"Is it about my power? Is that why you've stalked me and tricked and lied your way into my life?" she asked.

I lifted a brow. "I didn't even know you were a witch when I decided I was going to be in your life."

Evie's lips turned down, deeply exhaling and avoiding my eyes.

"*You*, Evie. That's the *why* you're searching for."

I took off my own shoes first, and then I reached for Evie's ruined sneakers. They'd already been beat-up, but now... they were trash.

I'd buy her new ones.

"You don't have to—"

"Hush, baby," I said, helping her out of each one before standing again to tower over her.

She was chewing on that abused bottom lip. "I'm going to get your house dirty."

"I have a cleaner. You're not the only one who's filthy."

I glanced down at my dark, muddy clothes. I took her small hand in mine and led her up the steps.

I wanted to take her to my own bathroom off my bedroom, but I took her to a separate bath attached to a guest bedroom instead.

"I want to care for you by bathing you," I said, and she stiffened. "But you aren't ready for that."

Evie visibly relaxed.

I nodded toward the door. "You should have everything you need, but if you don't, let me know. When you're finished, I'll make you dinner."

I studied her for a moment. Her power had gone completely

dormant, not only depleted but also buried deep inside herself. It was clear Evie had been shunning the most powerful side of her magick her whole life, which meant it only came out in uncontrollable, emotional bursts.

We were going to have to work on that.

"Okay, angel?"

She nodded, wordlessly turning away from me and slipping into the bathroom.

I didn't want her out of my sight for even a moment while she was this triggered. The idea of her accidentally harming herself with her wild, misunderstood magick haunted me as I walked to my bedroom.

Who was I kidding? I hated being apart from Evie under normal circumstances. Especially when I didn't know exactly where she was or who she was with.

As the water cascaded over my body in the shower, I closed my eyes. Vision upon vision tormented me. Evie soaked and flailing, my shadows teasing her nipples and the bud between her thighs, the way her arousal amplified the more I cut off her air supply with my hand around her throat.

I loved that she was capable of putting up a fight, that she held the most delicious violence in her soul. It made it all the more satisfying to overpower her, to dominate her into total submission.

The more I learned about Evie, the more I understood why my attraction to her had been so instant and overwhelming. My clan knew my instincts were never wrong. I was born with an intuition, a deep-seated knowledge of the world I was born to build and the beings who were meant to help me build it.

I wasn't drawn to Evie because she was a pawn on my board. I was drawn to Evie because she reminded me of my own soul, the humanity buried beneath the shadows, the loneliness I'd felt as a child. My family, peers, and community didn't know what to do with the ambitious boy who pored over historical and philosophical texts in his free time, who spoke like he was much older than he was, who brimmed with strange, fantastical dreams.

I might've been surrounded by a legion of comrades, mentors, students, and friends now, but for most of my human life, I might as well have been utterly alone.

Showering away the rain and dirt was a quick and unceremonious process. The mere thought of Evie doing the same had my cock straining all over again. My tongue flicked over the sharpened tips of my canines as I stood in my bedroom.

I eyed the painting of the Etherdale mountains that hung over the bed. The walls were navy blue with black vine patterns, my bed a mess of blankets and pillows of the same colors. A bookcase stood by the windows, with low, plush chairs around a small coffee table. I imagined my angel sitting there, gazing over Etherdale with one of her smutty fantasy novels in her lap.

I was once again grateful I'd fed generously before laying eyes on her today. I would never put Evie in danger, and that meant taking every precaution against bloodlust.

At the next throb of my fangs, I busied myself with dressing in a casual black shirt and slacks before picking out clothes for Evie.

I wanted her in one of my shirts and nothing else. One of the many ways I wished to mark her as *mine*.

Instead, I reached for one of the dresses I'd bought Evie in the past week. I skimmed the sky-blue, soft fabric absentmindedly before halting at the sound of footsteps.

In the hall, Evie looked like a frightened doe who'd just heard an approaching hunter. I couldn't help but grin at her endearing discomfort as she glanced around her unfamiliar surroundings. Her blonde hair was wet and messy, a long blue-gray towel wrapped around her—almost the color of those stormy eyes.

Her irises were quick to latch onto mine. "I need clothes."

She tried to sound strong, holding tight to that bitter feeling of betrayal. She looked me up and down, her lips forming a deep frown.

I followed her gaze curiously to my simple black outfit. "Not to your tastes?"

"A lot of black," she muttered.

Strange intuition crawled down my spine. Had I *ever* seen Evie in dark colors? Certainly never black, as if it didn't even exist in her wardrobe.

Interesting.

I tore my shirt off in one fluid movement before handing Evie her dress.

"Better?" I asked.

I tried not to smirk as Evie's eyes blew wide, one hand holding tight to her towel and the other now clutching the dress in a death grip.

Her eyes quickly flitted over my elaborate onyx tattoos, some tinged with midnight purple and blue shimmers. Her gaze fell downward for the briefest moment before snapping right back up.

In an instant, her cheeks had turned my favorite shade of pink.

"I need..." She swallowed, avoiding looking anywhere but my eyes. "I need a brush."

"I'll fetch you one. Get dressed."

"Stop ordering me around."

I stepped closer to her, watching as she continued to fluster as I eclipsed her with my size. My fingers skimmed her shoulders, and I heard her inhale shakily as her heart erratically jumped.

I placed my fingers under her chin, offering only the gentlest of touch. "*No.*"

"You said there was no greater authority in Etherdale than

your own," she said, staring into my eyes angrily. "Is that why you're like this? Are you—oh gods…"

Fear surged in her blood. She yanked herself away from me.

"I am not your enemy, angel. I am the monster that will tear your enemies limb from limb."

She made no response. She escaped back into the bathroom and slammed the door behind her.

If my task of earning her trust was arduous before, it would seem my unmasking had raised the difficulty by leaps and bounds.

Thankfully, I adored a challenge. And I couldn't imagine a sweeter reward.

When she reemerged, I was back against the wall with my arms crossed over my chest.

Her damp blonde strands were still in disarray. I appraised my good taste on her even better form, admiring the tulle sleeves that hung off her shoulders, the pastel blue fabric that curved around her breasts and ass and fell to her lower thighs.

"I don't see a brush," she snapped.

I chuckled darkly. "You are exceptionally bratty for someone who just got everything she asked for despite her painfully stark disadvantage." I pushed off the wall. "Be a good girl and follow me, please."

I didn't hear any footsteps at first. I had to stop myself from laughing again at the huff of air that left Evie's lips, nearly another growl.

When she finally recognized what was good for her, I smiled with satisfaction at the sound of her following me to one of my libraries.

The pattern of her heartbeat changed when we entered, as if the atmosphere had stunned her out of her façade of hatred.

I glanced back at her. She stood on the center of the rug, staring at the large stained-glass window on the far wall. Its floral frame was intricately detailed, dividing the bright colors into petals that illuminated the space with multicolored light. She was slow to take in the rest of the room. A circular lower level in the center had a space for reading, complete with a loveseat, chairs, a couch, and a glass coffee table.

She took in the shelves that surrounded us, the inside of a spire above our heads.

"Sit, please," I instructed. I picked up the brush I'd retrieved while she'd been changing, resting on a corner table next to the couch.

I pointed to the stool in front of the loveseat.

Indignation was ripe in her adorable features.

"Now, Evie."

She slowly sat down, but her glare remained.

I slid onto the loveseat behind her.

When she caught on to what was happening, she attempted to get up. My shadows were quicker. Tendrils yanked her back down.

"Baby, please," I murmured. "Settle down and stop squirming. Ask your burning questions, if you wish."

Evie gave up and went still. Her arousal was doing ungodly things to my body already pushed to its absolute limits. My shadows fought me as I pulled them back beneath my skin.

I gritted my teeth. "Just be my perfect angel and let me brush your hair."

EVIE

Kylo's touch was so gentle that it made me shudder. Pleasurable tingles slid down my spine and radiated outward.

"Good girl," he praised.

Something inside me melted against my will: this cloying, desperate part of me—the part that had only ever wanted one thing out of life.

Safety.

And deeper than that was my need for this other, related feeling—a four-letter word I tried not to think about. It was the deepest expression of safety that I could ever fathom.

It was what my parents withheld from me. What I tried desperately to give Idris, so he'd never feel as alone and broken as I did.

After pulling my hair behind my shoulders, Kylo slowly pulled the brush down a section closest to my face. He took great care not to pull on my scalp, using his other hand as a buffer as he smoothed through tangles.

It was subconscious and unavoidable, the way such an intimate, soothing act calmed my entire nervous system. He didn't need to hold me in place anymore. I was captive to the comfort sweeping through my body.

The strangest tears pooled in my eyes. Flashes of memory assailed my mind's eye—careless, impatient hands yanking a brush through my mess of windswept hair, my scalp searing with pain as I wailed. A voice yelling, asking me why I had to make everything so difficult, why I couldn't just be grateful.

I thought of the way Idris's hands had reached. The way they'd reached for love and comfort and received nothing at all.

I could think of no greater cruelty to a child.

To be deprived of something that appeared so simple, so instinctual.

Why had it been so hard for them?

Maybe that was why I was now rooted in place with tears pooling in my eyes. My parents, people like Jacob and his cruel friends—they'd made it seem as if protecting me and my sensitive feelings was an impossible, indulgent ask.

And even if the man behind me was an unhinged, deviant vampire stalker, Kylo made caring for me seem like the easiest thing in the world.

He made it seem like he couldn't *stop* caring about me, as if it consumed all of his attention and energy.

When his fingers brushed over my cheek, I shuddered and leaned into his touch.

"How are you doing angel?" he asked softly.

I didn't know how to answer that question, so I refused. "You lied. You said you were a philosophy tutor," I said, but my words were less accusatory and more curious now that he'd turned me into this useless puddle of warmth.

"I tried my best not to lie to you," he said with a slow exhale. "I may have abstained from telling you the truth. Which is something you might understand, my terrifying little chaos witch."

There was no disgust in his tone. No fear. No paranoia. Just humor and understanding.

Kylo knew what I was... and he seemed to actually *like* that part of me—the part I'd come to hate the most.

"I do tutor members of my clan in philosophy, just as I did when I was human. You'll find I'm an excellent teacher," he said, his voice skating over my neck and making me shiver.

Something in my belly tightened. Kylo continued to work the brush through my hair, slowly and meticulously.

I glanced down at my lap, the unfamiliar dress, and the strangest feeling tightened in my chest.

"Whose dress is this?" I asked, bracing myself. I remembered what I'd seen when I touched Jacob's hand at the restaurant, the red lips on his neck.

And Kylo was a vampire. Which meant he had to *feed*.

My muscles tensed, and my guts turned over.

Kylo paused behind me, the brush halting in place. "It's yours. I've been waiting very patiently to spoil you with everything I've bought over the past weeks."

The answer surprised me. I should've been disturbed, should've tried to get up and run again. He'd been not only following me for weeks but also buying me clothes? As if I was a foregone conclusion?

The *arrogance*.

"Who do you feed from?" I asked, staring at the floor.

Kylo was on his last section of hair. When the pleasurable tingles rippled through my scalp at his touch, I had to fight to hold on to my distrust.

"Willing mortal donors, mostly. But I avoid drinking straight from the tap unless I'm feeding from the born. I prefer to exercise and strengthen my muscles of restraint around blood."

My eyes widened, and my mouth fell open. "You can actually feed from other vampires?"

He'd torn into the born's flesh when he'd saved me in the alley, but I hadn't realized he could sustain himself on vampire blood. I'd heard rumors—we all had—but the born seemed to keep that fact quiet. I'd imagine it was humiliating for them.

I couldn't lie—the prospect of the born suffering in that way did trigger a degree of smugness in my heart.

"From the born, specifically, yes," Kylo said. "It's a kind of secondhand feeding, pulling from the life force they've syphoned from others. A redistribution of stolen blood, if you will."

I'd been so shocked that I nearly missed the phrase *from the tap.* The objectification of mortals irritated me.

"What's going on in that beautifully vast mind of yours, angel?" he asked. "If you're worried about my attention and devotion, you can rest assured you own every last drop."

His words did soothe me, even if my rational brain resisted the urge to believe them. I didn't want to find comfort in his insanity and obsession.

"How could there possibly be willing mortal donors?" I hissed.

Kylo set the brush down. I turned on the stool to face him, once again losing my train of thought as I took in his bare, tattooed chest. His body was a finely tuned weapon. He shifted forward, his legs planted on either side of me as I looked up into the darkness of his deep blue eyes.

The hint of a smirk ghosted across his lips. I was shocked by the intensity in his gaze—the rawness, like I'd split him wide-open the same as he'd done to me.

"Not everyone is so vampire-averse, Evie," Kylo said, leaning forward. His strong arms flexed, as if he was resisting the urge to reach for me. "There are plenty of mortals who enjoy giving themselves to the born, too. Hence the feeding clubs. It's the borns' greed and corruption that is now turning their own food supply against them. They've been spitting on the norms that have maintained peace between vampires and mortals in Ravenia for centuries. As a witch, you should understand that the balance of the universe must be maintained."

He looked down at the complex sigil markings on his arm. "So here I am."

"A bit grandiose," I muttered, remembering when he'd called himself my God.

Kylo grinned. "Grandiosity is only a problem if it's delusional."

His grin slowly faded, a serious expression replacing it instead. His fingers brushed a damp strand of hair behind my ear.

"Your heart rate, your breathing, the fear in your blood… it all slowed for me while I took care of you, angel. You have no idea what a relief that was," he whispered.

The words hit me somewhere deep—far too deep.

"I don't know your story yet," Kylo said. "But I do know you're unbelievably, admirably strong. I see the way you fight for the people you love. I know your distrust is born of deep wounding, and yet you're bright, warm, and open despite it all. You are a defiant streak of light in a world ruled by shadow."

I swallowed, my lip trembling. I averted my eyes.

"You were born worthy, Evie. You were born worthy of all the love in the world," he said. "You—"

"Stop," I said suddenly, cutting him off. "Please stop."

The sick and needy part of me wanted to crawl into his lap, to feel those strong arms around me.

The safest place you'll ever be.

The rest of me, predictably, wanted to bolt.

I stayed perfectly still instead.

"Come on," he said. "I'll make you dinner. Then you can run all the way home, if you wish."

THE KITCHEN WAS as grand as the rest of the home, with black cabinets, dark marble, and an arched window over the sink overlooking the property. Splashes of color came from the green barstools and the floral arrangement on the counter.

My eyes narrowed. *My* floral arrangement, purchased from Celeste's. It was spelled with healing, clarifying energy.

Maybe I wasn't such a powerful witch after all, given Kylo remained as psychotic as ever.

"How old are you?" I asked as I slid onto one of the barstools.

If not for our bargain, I would've already been as far away from this evil, deceitful man as possible.

"Do you really want to know?" Kylo asked with an amused grin.

I'd forced him to put on a shirt. It was white and short-sleeved, showing off his bulging, tattooed arms as he chopped vegetables.

The way he'd abided by my aversion to all-black clothing without so much as a question soothed something inside of me. I'd expected exasperated irritation at the very least, if not downright flippant refusal. Jacob had trained me well.

"Oh gods, you're old enough to be my father, aren't you?" I asked. I stared at his beautiful, youthful features, his body clearly halted in its late twenties.

"Try grandfather, angel," he said softly, his gaze flicking up to lock on mine. He watched my face, waiting for my reaction.

It was hard to feel disgusted while looking at his exterior. Could you be disgusted with someone for having an elderly soul?

"If I thought all of this couldn't possibly be more fucked-up," I mumbled.

Kylo chuckled. "Silly girl." He lifted the kitchen knife and leaned forward, his predator gaze narrowing on me. "This is only the beginning. It's only going to get so, so much better from here."

I leaned back as he tipped forward, even though my body was behaving in very irregular ways to his raised knife.

My eyes sharpened. "I think you're grossly misunderstanding the term *fucked-up.* It's not meant to be a positive descriptor."

Kylo smiled as he returned his attention to his zucchini and yellow squash. "I suppose we hear what we want to hear, don't we, baby?"

I made a disgruntled sound as I crossed my arms, and Kylo only laughed at me.

The sound of a dainty, melodic knock on the door made me jump. I'd nearly forgotten that while Kylo pretended to be some kind of god of domesticity, his dangerous, criminal vampire clan surrounded us.

Kylo seemed more irritated than concerned. "Come in," he called.

A woman with long black waves of hair bounced into the kitchen with glee. She was displaying her esoteric clan tattoos beneath her orange dress, her fangs visible when she smiled.

"Harmony," Kylo said, his tone clipped. "Is there a reason for this unprompted and unwelcome visit?"

"Harsh," I said, before I could stop myself.

Harmony's warm gaze never left me, like she was seeing a kitten for the first time. "Agreed," she said, clutching her chest as if wounded. The hand fell back to her side as she stepped forward. "Hello, Evie. I'm Harmony. It's so nice to finally meet you!"

I eyed her with suspicion, even as every single part of her aura screamed sunshine and genuineness. How was that possible for a monster who blasphemed Helia's perfect gift of humanity?

"Hi, I guess you already know who I am," I said nervously. I stayed still, watching the two vampires with focused attention.

Harmony looked to Kylo. "Why is she shaking like a leaf, Kylo? You're not holding her here against her will, are you?"

"Yes," I said, at the same time as Kylo said, "No."

Kylo sighed. "Evie is merely... cautious. She's still getting acclimated." He pointed the knife at me with a slowly creeping grin. "Isn't that right, angel? Tell my very sensible and empathetic comrade how much fun we're having."

I shut my lips tight.

Harmony's eyes widened as she stared at the knife. "This is not inspiring confidence, boss."

"And you didn't answer my original question," Kylo snapped.

Harmony shifted on her feet. "I'm sorry, but you're going to want to come in. The events you foretold did in fact transpire. We caught a big fish."

Kylo snorted. "Excellent use of coded language, Harmony."

Her smile was infectious, far too beautiful and *real.*

My gaze swept back and forth between the two vampires with rising curiosity. How in the hell did their interactions seem so normal?

Endearing, even?

"You're so fucking cute when you're thinking," Kylo said.

"I'm going to hex you," I bit out.

"No, you're not."

"Ohhh," Harmony said, interrupting us. "All the violent threats are foreplay. I get it. I *sooo* get it."

I scoffed, shaking my head.

Kylo's eyes flickered with something close to anger for a moment as he watched the vampire woman. Then he glanced at me, and I felt the emotion on his face like a brand on my skin. Hot, consuming.

Not anger. *Possessiveness.*

"Here's what's going to happen," Kylo said calmly. "Harmony, please fetch Allie." He never once broke eye contact with me. "Angel, after you eat, one of my guards will see that you get home safely."

When he lifted the knife again, he flipped it around in his hand with eerie gracefulness. "I'll see you soon. No funny business. *Behave.*"

25

KYLO

Etherdale's underground had two different kinds of dungeons. Both were immensely fun for me, in their own ways. But the variation that I entered this evening was filled with screams of agony rather than pleasure.

Born spies were getting bolder. As my clan tactically infiltrated channels of the slave trade, assassinated born elites, and rooted out members of the Servants of Lillian cult, the born were starting to suspect that we weren't as disorganized, youthful, and clueless as they'd originally assumed.

Turned clans in other regions tended to be severely politically and geographically disadvantaged. Etherdale was a university city positioned in a secluded valley with a long history of mortal-centric values. Along with our powerful witch covens, shifter packs, and vampire hunters and wards around campus, it was far harder for Lord Conrad to make moves against us.

Flooding the city with born would piss off the witches and shifters and turn mortals against the born even more decisively. And now that they were suspecting the clan's true power and numbers, they had the fear of provoking a major uprising to consider.

Mortal uprisings meant a severe drop in the vampire food supply. This was why there were checks and balances in the kingdom of Ravenia. Born nobility, along with King Earle's council, were supposed to work with mortal leaders to maintain basic codes of conduct and peaceful, reciprocal communities.

But now that a growing wave of born were chasing power and wealth through their hateful Servants of Lillian cult, the slave trade, and forced marriage rituals, the tides were turning. Mortals were looking to Valentin's war for guidance—taking note of the way that Rune and his clan had united with mortals to overthrow the born from power.

The born spy chained to the wall in front of me was a man with black shoulder-length hair. He was already roughed up by the clan members who'd discovered him lurking somewhere he shouldn't have been—on university campus, rooting out mortal sympathizers of the clan.

The worries that the clan controlled Etherdale's university were, of course, entirely warranted. I smirked.

Surrounding me were dozens of clan members. Some were advisors, and others were onlookers who simply wished to see a born dickhead suffer.

Blade stood to my right, hunger swarming in his warm brown eyes as he grinned. He'd cut off the sleeves of his black top, exposing the massive shoulders and biceps capable of crushing a skull with ease.

To my left was one of my eyes, Phineas. He was a gifted wielder of invisibility glamours, floating around the city from the shadows, collecting secrets and watching for irregularities.

He was the one who trained me to use my shadows to conceal my presence, which had been a useful asset in stalking my vulnerable little fallen angel.

"Which building?" I asked Phineas.

"One of the witches' academic buildings," he said.

I kept my rage carefully concealed, refusing to show a single change in my facial expression. I didn't want to give the bruised and bloodied spy an ounce of satisfaction before his demise.

In my hands was a plier forged with flecks of blood onyx, a poisonous, paralytic material to vampires. It was what the borns' chains were made of, to subdue his magick.

Inside my veins, fury steadily rose. Because the borns' persistent targeting of powerful witches—chaos witches—put my angel at risk. Even more so when she clearly had no control over her magick.

I fucking hated how far away from me she was right now. Even if this was no place for her. I almost prayed she stepped out of line, so I could finally mark her with my blood and be a part of her forever.

"What lovely fingers you have," I said, letting my feral protectiveness leak into my voice, my demeanor.

The born's eyes darted from my eyes to the pliers as he snarled. His black hair dipped forward, his hands limp where they hung, spread out on the stone wall.

I allowed myself to twist, to appear as something psychotic. Deranged. A creature of darkness without mercy, without even an ounce of sanity.

He was looking for *her*. They wanted to take her from me.

I cut off one of his fingers as he writhed uselessly, merely to show him how easy and quick it was to commit acts of violence. His appendage fell to the ground, and blood sprayed as the crowd laughed and made humorous, insulting remarks at his expense.

Next, Phineas and I repeated the same questions over and over. His refusal to answer was typical and expected. They trained their spies well. At the end of the day, the born were immortal demons. It was easy for them to reject all semblance of humanity and honor their sociopathic soullessness instead.

"Strange weather we had earlier today," the born scum spat, missing several of his teeth now as blood spilled from his mouth.

I stared at him, unmoving, as the words pierced straight to my soul.

Animalistic, vengeful rage consumed me, even as I kept every feature the same as it had been before he spoke.

"Aw, do you want to take a brief intermission for small talk?" I asked with deceptive sweetness, grinning widely.

The born's eyes flashed with satisfying alarm at my increasingly inconsistent displays of emotion and speech. I loved fucking with them psychologically even more than physically, to get inside their puny little brains and squeeze, poke, prod, utterly shatter them at their core.

Lillian's demon spawn were addicted to sensibilities, to social rules and customs. They acted predictably, with an eye on tradition. They were disturbed by displays of erraticism and disarray. They fucking hated it.

And I got high off their hatred like it was my second-favorite drug.

My first being Evie, of course.

"A witch-conjured storm is a curious thing," he continued, speech slurred. "But why? Such a strange, nonsensical display of raw power... *Rare* power."

He was delirious from the blood onyx, spilling his unfiltered thoughts. It was the perfect time to question him again, yet all I wanted to do was tear off his arms and legs and stuff them down his undeserving throat.

Evie had put herself on the map with her outburst. All manner of magick-sensing powers would be hunting for her now.

I warred with my primal rage to defend what was mine against all threats. I released a breath, and I pushed my all-consuming obsession with Evie to the side.

My clan needed my effectiveness. I could not falter. I could not hesitate. I could not slip.

I feigned disinterest. I buried my need to tear out his tongue somewhere deep.

I continued the physical and psychological dance with Blade and Phineas, destroying the born from within and extracting all available intel. I riled up my clan, showcased my shadowed power, my skill.

All the while, I saw her face in the back of my mind. I remembered the way her heart had slowed as I ran the brush through her hair, each little sigh of contentment, the way she'd leaned into my touch instead of pulling away.

For my clan, I was impenetrable, violent—all sharp edges, brutality, and razored, competent logic.

For her, only for her, I was anything she needed me to be.

26

EVIE

The hairs on the back of my neck stood in high alert as I entered Celeste's four days after my magickal explosion. A distinctive wave of warning washed over me from the otherworld, a disturbance in the field of the unseen.

I paused in the doorway, ears straining, eyes tracking for movement amid the tables and shelves of goods and plants.

"Evie," someone hissed from behind me.

I turned just as a hand clamped down on my shoulder and pulled me back outside the shop.

Cecil released me. His wife Jill held his arm with a worried expression. He placed a finger to his lips and pointed to the left with a jerk of his head. I followed them around the corner.

"There's a born vampire in there, dear, speaking with Marietta," Jill explained from the side of the building.

Cecil eyed me carefully.

"Marietta won't tell them shit. But if they come for you, just explain that you're a green witch with the gift of healing, okay?" Jill said with a tight smile.

The blood drained from my face as her words sunk in.

"I need to go make sure Marietta is okay—" I said.

"No," Cecil said. "You need to go home." Pity swam in his wrinkled features. "In fact, I no longer think it's safe for you to be selling anything more than plants and natural healing medicines. Some of the spells… they're attracting too much attention. Green witches shouldn't be able to affect the world like you do."

Jill nervously looked at me, quickly shushing Cecil.

Something inside me broke. My face heated with shame, a sickening feeling twisting my guts. The morning light was suddenly too revealing, leaving me vulnerable and exposed.

These dreams and aspirations that had been propelling me forward the past months were crashing down all around me.

I was growing. I was getting better, more comfortable in myself and my destiny.

The thought of being left without a purpose—without a way to prove to the world that I was a force for good—was like a knife straight to the gut.

"I'm sorry, Evie," Cecil said. "You're still welcome at our home, always. Please be careful. These are strange times." He paused, mumbling something to Jill, who now pulled on his arm. "But the world has a way of finding balance again. The same push and pull, the same shifts and patterns, repeating over and over again throughout the centuries. The world will right itself again, by Helia's grace."

Balance.

I thought of *him.*

Grief had my heart in a death grip as I walked in the opposite direction of my ex-client and my ex-employer.

A sharp pain drove into my chest over and over. Inside my head was this terrifying nothingness, with only the cruel, haunting whispers from the past to keep me company.

In a span of a month, nearly everything I loved had been stolen from me, piece by piece. Everything I thought I knew was wrong—about myself, about my future, about Etherdale, my home.

The only certainty now was the monster who followed me from the shadows.

I'd never despised anything more.

∾

MENA MADE me tea as I stared numbly out the kitchen window.

"This world hates strong, powerful women," Mena said, raising her fist as she spoke.

She wore a flowy, tunic-style leopard print dress with the brightest red lipstick. She wasn't going out—she merely believed that she wasn't her best self without color on her lips.

The late morning sunlight illuminated the space in a white glow. The smell of bread and herbs tickled my nostrils. By all appearances, it was a lovely summer day.

I crossed my arms. I was having none of it.

"None more so than witches." She slid me a mug of lemon balm and elderberry tea. At the look on my face, her theatrical display of anti-masculinity fizzled into something more somber. "I'm terribly sorry, Evie. I know how much your craft means to you. Our work is our lifeblood."

She reached for my hand on the marble countertop, her touch soft.

My lip trembled. "I keep waiting to hear word that it was all a misunderstanding. I can't—" My voice cracked, and I faltered. "I can't let this go. I *won't*."

Mena lifted my hand in both of hers, her amber eyes sparking. "Then you will find a way." A wave of emotion fell over her features before they tightened back up. Her smile was sad, soft, and wise. "There was a time I was much too protective of you and your brother."

She released my hand and sipped her tea, staring off into the past.

"My friends thought it most peculiar," she continued. "No one believed I had a single maternal bone in my body—*I* didn't think I had a single maternal bone in my body—until you showed up on my doorstep with Idris."

I seized up, my heart pounding.

"And when I saw..." Mena trailed off, shaking her head as water pooled in her eyes. "Well, from then on, I was ready to bludgeon anyone at all for you kids."

The idea of Mena committing acts of violence allowed the tiniest relief to my tense muscles and tight chest. I might've smiled if I wasn't still stuck—stuck on what Mena saw when I knocked on her door.

"You weren't the only one deathly afraid of leaving the house, you know," she said. "Any time we went to visit Wendy in those early days..."

I thought of Wendy's kind, knowing face—the eyes that saw too much of me, the voice that made me want to run. Wendy was Mena's friend, the retired psychology professor and part-time emotional healer I'd begged to stop seeing until Mena finally relented.

"... or even when you two would go outside to play, in the gardens or, gods forbid, at one of those spoiled brat neighbors' homes, I felt the most awful dread. It consumed me. When you were out of my sight, that was the worst. I feared you wouldn't come home. That my life would be forever dimmer without the beautiful light of your bravery and resilience."

A tear slid down my cheek, and Mena wiped at her own eyes.

"Gah!" she exclaimed. "You know I hate to cry." She took a dramatic breath and grinned. "The point of that sappy love fest is that my protectiveness reached a limit. And that limit was the desire to see you and Idris in full bloom. When Idris flew the nest to study at university, my soul knew peace. You coming into acceptance with your gifts and becoming a fierce little businesswoman… that growth became so much more important to me than my selfish fears."

"You've never been selfish with us," I said. "Never."

A warmth spread through my chest, this beautiful maternal connection that I'd been starved of for half my life. What a gift to have found it in someone who was once a stranger.

I savored another sip of tea. "We owe you everything."

Mena waved a hand dismissively. "Pshaw." She looked at me with a certain ferocity now. "Don't you dare give up on your life's work, my dear. It would break my heart."

"Mine too," I murmured. Anger simmered beneath the surface every time I thought of that beautiful, dangerous vampire's stupid face. The man who was taking everything I loved away from me.

"You must find a way," Mena said. "Even if your dreams must take new form, do not let them die. Don't close yourself back up just when those petals were finally beginning to unfurl."

Whispers tickled my ear drums, a low buzzing sensation at my throat and heart centers.

But I didn't—*couldn't* lean in. I couldn't bask in the sunlight and believe that everything was going to be okay.

"It's more complicated than that," I whispered. I studied Mena's face, her regally beautiful features accented with tasteful makeup and glasses low on her nose. "If I'm not careful, I'm not the only one at risk."

Mena had dedicated over a decade to us—these wounded, fearful children she'd never asked for. I would never put her in danger. Just as I would never draw attention to Idris while he lived his beautifully human life studying architecture.

I could never be so selfish.

They were already at risk enough. Because of *him*.

Because of *me*.

Mena rubbed my shoulder, her reassurances doing nothing to penetrate my walls—not when my selfish, naive actions had endangered my family.

And when I made it back to the cottage and saw the note left on my door, it was a combination of guilt and anger that propelled me forward.

Kylo was claiming his first coerced date. He wanted me to wear the dress he left in a box inside—a reminder that I was his pretty little doll to dress and order around, that he could enter my home whenever he wished. I was merely a silly mortal for him to torment and entertain himself with until he inevitably grew bored.

I put on the wispy, faerie-like lilac dress and laced up the shiny new white sneakers. And when I made it to the exact spot in the sprawling city gardens he'd requested, a presence at my back sent a wave of shivers down my spine. Hands reached for my waist.

I didn't hesitate. I spun around and threw a punch.

27

EVIE

Kylo, in his deceptive human form, caught my fist with ease before it clipped his jaw.

"Good afternoon to you too, baby," he said gruffly, his blue eyes flashing as a muscle in his jaw feathered.

He grabbed my other fist before I could lift it, snaking his fingers to circle around my wrists as he stared down at me. He studied my features, and it only made me angrier.

He was looking for more weaknesses to exploit.

"My guard said there was a born vampire at Celeste's," Kylo murmured. "And that you went home before selling the goods in your backpack."

"Excellent sleuthing skills," I spat with venom. "Do you also know what I ate for breakfast this morning?"

I closed my eyes and took a deep breath. I had to keep a short leash on my anger, to not let it rise and spill over like it had the day of the storm. When I opened my eyes again, I focused on the vivid colors of flowers surrounding us, the trees with bright green leaves gently turning in the wind. Besides the rich tapestry of energies and spirits of the otherworld, we were

196

alone. The air was quiet and serene in the vastness of Etherdale's largest gardens.

Kylo didn't answer that last question. He merely sighed. "Did they let you go because of the born's inquiries? If they did, then they're cowards, Evie."

I shook my head, contempt curling my lip. "No, that would make them *intelligent*. My goods don't matter more than other people's lives." I couldn't look at his face, the fake empathy softening those deadly, conniving features. "I'm removing myself from the equation. I know the owners protected me, because they're good people. So now I'm going to protect them."

"By giving up on your dreams," Kylo said softly, a tinge of irritation in his tone.

My eyes snapped to his. "I'm not *giving up*. Everything that has happened since you entered my life has been against my will!"

I snagged on the momentary lapse in Kylo's impenetrable mask, the flash of guilt.

He dropped my wrists. "If blaming me for everything actually helps you, then fine. I'll take it. But your refusal to accept reality is holding you back."

The words triggered something small and wounded inside of me, melting my anger into something more pathetic.

"Why don't you want to blame the born?" he asked, his gaze so imploring that it felt like the harshest, most exposing rays of the sun. "I know it's not because you're a loyalist."

"Of course not," I said, urging my lips not to wobble.

I wasn't loyal to King Earle or Lord Conrad or any of Lillian's soulless demons. I was loyal to Idris. I was loyal to Mena. And I wanted all of this violence to just *stop*.

"Then why?" he asked. "Why can't you see that the born are the reason you're unsafe—the reason, I suspect, that you've been unsafe for a long time? You were attacked by a born vampire only weeks ago, a man who was merely bored and thought you looked like a tasty meal."

I shuddered. Kylo lifted his hands, but he seemed to think better of reaching for me.

He swallowed. "When the demons in power are allowed to do as they please, unchecked and without consequence, they will only become crueler, greedier, and more soulless and depraved. You are not choosing *safety* when you choose not to fight. You are choosing the comfort of the danger to which you've grown accustomed. This only works in their favor."

I hated that he lectured me like I was a child, as if my reasoning and actions were nonsensical compared to his supreme logic.

"Why can't you see that the reason your brother has an interest in joining the clan is because he's tired of watching the born murder, torture, and kidnap mortals? He's not being brainwashed. He simply sees what's happening in this city—this realm—with his own two eyes."

Rage took hold with a sudden swiftness. Violence gathered in my palms. Kylo sensed it, and in a matter of seconds I was, once again, on my back while he straddled me. Surrounding us was a semi-translucent, strange wall of shadow. Grass tickled my ears.

Kylo pinned my wrists above my head as he stared hard into my eyes. My chest rose and fell rapidly.

"You are not defenseless, Evie," he said, his voice slightly strained. "Far from it. It is your refusal to accept who you are that has landed you in the most danger."

"You don't know him," I hissed, writhing beneath him as he leaned in close. "Don't talk about my brother. You have no idea who he is or—" I blinked, quickly censoring myself. "You don't know anything about us."

"I. Want. To." His eyes darkened, then dropped to my lips. "I *want to know you*, Evie. I want to help you understand your magick. I want to see you follow through on your every last dream. I want to show you that after years of keeping everyone safely behind those tall, impenetrable walls, you can finally let someone through."

I shook my head. My power deflated underneath him. The more he spoke, the more he cut through my addiction to my own denial.

"You are the most frighteningly complex creature I have ever encountered. It will be my greatest honor to earn your faith and trust. To help, protect, and care for you in all the ways you deserve."

I stared at him, feeling the weight of his hold on my wrists, the heaviness of his dark, hungry gaze on my body.

The shadow glamour evaporated, like clouds receding from the sun.

The only thing more loathsome than Kylo's decimation of my cherished, avoidant sense of reality was the fact that he and his sneaky shadows had *already* snuck past my walls.

I wanted to tell him I hated him. But it would be a lie. The truth was that I was terrified of him. Terrified of the way he was yanking me out of my tower, crumbling it from within, and forcing me to live out in this wide-open field, where nothing was safe, nothing was certain or predictable.

The world had opened to me. Irreversibly. And it gave me nowhere to run.

Even as he pinned me beneath him, there was tenderness in his deep irises. "I fucking adore you, Evie. I have since the moment I first saw you."

I closed my eyes, yearning to curl up in a defensive position as if he were stabbing me.

All of this anger and confusion and fear and yearning coalesced into heat that moved low, pooling in my lower stomach.

Rage burned behind my eyelids. Desire stoked my blood.

When I opened my eyes again, I anchored myself in the certainty of his gaze.

"There's my sweet, docile angel," he murmured, releasing wrists.

I wanted to punch him.

I kissed him instead.

My hands tangled in his black hair. His held my face as he consumed me, leaving me no room to breathe or think.

His tongue chased mine. This kiss felt like war. Like we couldn't get enough of each other—and maybe we never would.

Kylo won. He destroyed my defenses, just as I always knew he would. His tongue invaded my mouth. His lips overpowered mine. When his teeth teased my lower lip, I felt his fangs as if they'd escaped his glamour.

Then he moved to my neck, sucking at my skin in a way that made my heart flutter. Pleasure was a gentle wave that radiated outward, draining me of all semblance of self-preservation.

"Sweet girl," he hummed against my neck, inhaling deeply. "I already know you're going to be my new favorite taste."

Delirious from his touch, I was slow to tense underneath him. "You want to feed from me," I said. With his lips on my collarbone, my voice came out as more of a moan.

I wanted to be horrified.

When the familiar voice whispered about the importance of keeping my blood pure, it had the opposite effect. My curiosity was a dark desire, indicative of the dangerous way my body responded to his deceptive, vampiric tricks.

Kylo smirked, raising up and lightly stroking my cheek. "Baby, what makes you think I was talking about your blood?"

When his finger traced my jugular, I squirmed. My thighs pressed together, his words shocking me as soon as I put together what he meant.

"Men actually enjoy... doing that?" I asked.

Kylo frowned, his eyes darkening a shade. "Gods above, Evie. I am simultaneously infuriated by and grateful for your past partner's inadequacies." He glared at my lips. "Because on the one hand, the thought of anyone else tasting you makes me feel…"

I gasped when his hand slipped under my dress, his touch brushing against the most sensitive part of me.

"… *violent*," he growled, and I sensed that violence in his flare of power. "On the other hand, what useless waste of a human could ever let you believe that you don't deserve to be devoured at every opportunity?"

He found my clit, teasing before applying steady pressure and friction.

"He, um," I stuttered. Gods, I couldn't think straight anymore. "He said that things like that were only pleasurable for women. Only—" I lost my train of thought as Kylo tormented me. "Only normal in romance novels."

Kylo laughed, but it contained no humor. His gaze tore straight through me, his lip curling.

"We're, oh gods," I moaned. "We're in public, Kylo."

"Shh, angel," he whispered, kissing me briefly on my lips and then next to my mouth. "My needy, desperate, good girl," he said, equal parts degradation and praise.

It only drove these waves of pleasure to new heights. My legs shook violently, noises I didn't recognize leaving my lips— breathy and high-pitched.

"My name on your lips *nearly* made up for you talking about another man while I'm playing with your pretty little pussy," he growled. "But the dissatisfaction you suffered before you became mine seems like more than enough punishment."

"I'm not—" I cursed, and Kylo grinned. "I'm not *yours*."

"Aw," he said, pouting his lip. "Are you sure about that, baby?"

He yanked his hand away.

I made a frustrated noise of utter betrayal, and he only laughed at me.

His grin didn't shift as he grabbed my throat and squeezed. "Your body knows who the fuck it belongs to."

I glared.

"I wonder what consequences such a bold, bratty look warrants," he said. He sighed, glancing up at the shrubs mostly enclosing us from prying eyes. "We're alone by my design, you know. I have a couple of guards fielding people away from this part of the gardens. They're saying there was an altercation with vampire hunters and the area should be avoided."

That was a relief.

"All this power isn't good for your already over-inflated ego," I said as he squeezed at my airways.

I was lightheaded, frustrated, and swimming with pleasure.

"It wasn't a power flex. It was merely a kindness, a small reassurance for your precious, fearful heart."

I didn't understand what he meant until his shadows began to leak from his glamour, pinning my arms above my head.

"I hope you don't mind, angel, but I *will* need to be masked for this next part. Out of an abundance of caution."

His tattoos came into focus, and smoky shadows reached for his face, melding into a solid skull mask. It was diagonally jagged, once again leaving part of the left side of his face and his mouth exposed.

"Let me go," I spat.

"Don't you understand, sweet girl?" he said with a smile, lording over my body like a demonic prince of Lillian's underworld. "*I will never let you go.*"

Another shadow reached up my body. As soon as I opened my mouth to protest again, its tip crawled across my mouth and solidified into a gag.

"Hmph!" My voice was pitiful and muffled.

Kylo groaned. "Your sexiest noise yet." His fingers circled my right nipple once before squeezing it.

A burst of pain shot through my system before it landed in my core as a pool of strange, surprising pleasure.

"Brats get gagged, baby," Kylo said. "Actions have consequences. Be grateful I'm going easy on you. There are much larger things I could shove into that testy little mouth to pacify you."

He squeezed my second nipple. "If you ever *actually* want me to stop, simply kick me three times in quick succession. Understood?"

I said *fuck you* into my gag, but it came out as mush.

"I'm going to assume that was a polite, adorable, *yes, Kylo.*"

The impersonality of his mask, the show of his power, the bondage of his shadows—it all made me melt beneath him. My brain was being shut off against my will, and all I could do was lean into the blissful thoughtlessness.

Kylo pushed up my dress.

No. Not like this. I didn't want my first time to be like this.

I prepared to kick him three times. But I halted when I realized he made no move to unclothe himself. He wasn't trying to take my virginity. Instead, he moved lower, his face now between my thighs.

This felt wrong in a completely different way. I'd been *taught* that it was wrong. Why did he care so much about my pleasure when I gave him little in return? It didn't make any sense.

"Do not move," Kylo warned.

My eyes widened as I saw what he now held in his hand. Sunlight reflected off the pristine metal of a dagger. The hilt was made of onyx, inscribed with barely perceptible sigils.

He lowered the blade between my legs. I went utterly still. Panic was a volatile force in my veins.

Kylo suddenly inhaled, exposing his fangs. He almost looked pained. "Gods above, baby, please. The scent of your blood was already powerful enough. The fear and arousal make it maddening."

In a quick movement, he cut away my panties with the blade. His mask of shadow slipped for only a few short seconds. And as I stared down at him, wrists still bound and mouth gagged with shadow, I lost my ability to breathe.

Because the look on his face was like nothing I'd expected.

It was *reverent.*

As if he was in worship. In devotion. In awe.

His mask restructured. His thumb gently rubbed my clit before passing through my folds. "Evie darling, I'm going to feast on you now. Be a good girl and come on my tongue as many times as you can."

28

KYLO

I could gaze between Evie's thighs for an eternity. At her impossibly pretty pussy, but also at her shocked, adorable face staring down at me. The sight of her gagged and bound had my cock straining in my pants.

I wanted to bury myself inside her until I saw those beautiful, delicious tears fall down her rosy cheeks. I wanted to overwhelm her with pain and pleasure until she was nothing but putty in my hands—a messy, needy puddle kneeling at my feet.

When my lips brushed just above her clit, she shuddered. Those usually feisty legs were perfectly still and spread, almost as if she feared accidentally using her safe word by kicking me.

So fucking cute.

So fucking *mine*.

My mouth closed over her bud, and she moaned into her shadow gag. I gently sucked, and the taste of her had me both drunk and starving at the same time.

She was perfect, everything I'd ever wanted—but there wasn't nearly enough of her inside me, nor enough of me inside her.

I wouldn't stop breaking Evie's defenses until I was burrowed so deeply inside her walls that she had no hope of ever escaping my hold over her body, mind, and soul.

My tongue swirled over her clit before sliding down her seam to taste her center. I circled that tight little hole, savoring every inch of her.

"Your pussy is perfect," I said, and she shuddered. "And I was right. I fear I've already lost my appetite for any other taste than *you* for the rest of eternity."

I let my words hum against her sensitive flesh. I hoped they penetrated her protective fortress. I wanted to undo everything men had taught her before me. I needed her to understand how addictive she was, how worthy of pleasure and adoration. It turned me on to know I'd be the first and only man to satisfy her, that I would ruin her for all others.

This time when my mouth closed over her bud, those legs started to shake again for me—overcome with pleasure. I sucked and pulsed in a way that had her unraveling against me. Evie's arousal coated my mouth, my face, and I wouldn't have it any other way. Drowning in her would be an honor.

I knew that my mask had turned her on, but even more surprising was the way my dagger had a similar effect on her heart and breathing. It had been the same when I'd threatened her with the kitchen knife.

Though, it shouldn't have surprised me at all, really. Because my perfect, innocent little angel was made for me. And that meant that no matter what lies dripped from her tongue, her pussy would always tell me the truth.

She loved my violence.

My power, my shadows, my depraved games and wickedness —they made her feel alive after a lifetime of hiding.

I worshipped her pussy the way it deserved, reveling in the way she finally let go. She came on my tongue violently, as if against her will. But I didn't relent, even as she cried into her gag and struggled beneath me. I extracted another orgasm from her, and then another, and I didn't stop until she was limp and useless, and I was drenched in her.

"Good girl," I praised, kissing her clit and laughing when she made a muffled shriek of protest. "Calm down, baby. I'm finished playing with you."

I withdrew my shadows from her wrists and mouth.

"For now," I amended.

I watched her flushed face, the way she stared up at me in wonder.

I let my mask recede, concentrating my power on the correct sigil to activate my human glamour.

Evie slowly pulled her wrists back down to her side as she gazed into my eyes, her breathing beginning to even out.

"Well?" I asked.

She was still deep in a submissive headspace, likely struggling to form words. Which made it even more fun to force her to speak.

"I didn't know that anything could... feel that way," she mumbled.

I smiled with satisfaction, then slid her dress back into place before laying on my back and guiding Evie to rest her head on my chest.

"To think that was only a drop in the ocean of pleasure that awaits you," I murmured. "Thank you for trusting me enough to be so vulnerable."

"I don't trust you," she whispered, but it came out endearingly small and unconvincing.

"Whatever you say."

In direct opposition to her claims, Evie nestled her leg between mine, relaxing into my hold as she wrapped herself around me. The move did something to my heart that I didn't think was possible, not since I'd forsaken my humanity.

I kissed the top of her head before staring back up at the clear blue sky.

"Tell me about your world, Evie," I whispered.

I said it evenly, like a calm command. But beneath my layers of impenetrability, I was desperate.

"Don't you already know everything about my world?" she muttered.

"I only know the surface, what I can understand with my physical senses." I slowly ran my hand through her soft blonde hair. When she relaxed deeper, I felt like I was fulfilling my deepest purpose. "I want to hear about the other world—the one I can't see. The world of your mind, the world of your magick."

Her heart picked up slightly.

I didn't realize I'd been holding my breath until she finally spoke.

"Okay."

I smiled, staying silent as she decided what and how much to tell me.

"This layer of reality is only the surface, like you said," she began. She cleared her throat, her nervous heart pounding now. "The otherworld is vast, too multifaceted to fully comprehend, even as a witch. Everything in the physical has its corresponding spirits, entities, and energies attached. It's like a field with all these overlapping webs. I think most beings assume that a witch's job is to harness power from these sources and use them to exert our will, but that's a very ineffective way to practice witchcraft."

The more she spoke, the more she relaxed, as if she were floating out of her fear and into the realm of inspiration and purpose. It warmed my heart. I continued to offer her gentle, reassuring touch.

"The most powerful magick is a collaboration. It's not about *taking* power, it's about *asking* for it. I don't strong-arm spirits and energies into helping me. I give offerings, I forge relationships, and I'm intentional about who I ask to sit at my table. Just like in business and politics, the most long-lasting and impactful sources of influence are the kind gained from time, experience, and most importantly, *allies*. Without reciprocal relationships built from care and respect, we're swimming upstream."

The frightened girl on the run had receded. And in her place was this intelligent, thoughtful woman who talked about magick like it was her home, her family.

"Magick is falling in love," she said softly, "with this unseen world and its inhabitants. Most witches only interact with certain powers, unable to see the entirety of the spiritual field. Chaos witches are lucky. We can see it all. We can choose which relationships to forge, and we're—" She cleared her throat. "We're never alone."

My hand halted in her hair. I could listen to her speak for hours.

"Kiss me, please," I said.

Evie slowly raised her head up. As soon as she hovered over me, I grabbed her face and locked my lips with hers. I wanted to taste that sense of love and wonder on her tongue. I wanted to feel her mortal devotion to the ethereal, to beauty and truth and powers greater than herself.

What fierce bravery.

I released her and stared into those wide gray eyes. "You are incredible, and you should be proud of the person you have become. I know that being this unique has come at a price. I'm sure it's made you feel terribly lonely."

Evie's face fell. She was vulnerable, unsure. Yet those eyes sparked with hope—like she recognized me as the mirror of her own soul.

"But I hope you can one day look back on that loneliness with gratitude. Because without it, you wouldn't have fallen so deeply in love with your magick. You wouldn't have read so much, learned so much, evolved into the perfect expression of divinity that you are."

Her lip trembled, and I kissed her again, soft and brief.

"You wouldn't be this bright, powerful, indescribable force in a world that tries very hard to kill off anything different, anything special."

"I'm not special," she protested, even as those hopeful eyes betrayed her.

"Be grateful for the loneliness that has made you who you are," I said, ignoring her lie. "But know that you don't have to live in solitude anymore. There are others who see the world as you do. There are others who stood at the crossroads of greatness and mediocrity and made their necessary sacrifices."

I stroked her cheek, watching her process my words. "I know you have your otherworld for company, but you're not alone in *this* world, either."

She examined me as if scanning for threats, her angelic features raw with emotion. "You were once lonely?"

"Of course," I whispered. "I was lonely for a long time."

We were both silent for a moment. Birds chirped, and the wind feathered against our skin. A strand of Evie's hair swept into her face, and I carefully tucked it back behind her ear.

She lay back down on my chest. "Do you have a family?"

"Yes, I do. The family I was born to is dead," I said. "I loved my parents, but they were distant. They wanted me to be someone I wasn't, and they never cared to learn who I truly was. We never shared a deep emotional bond. We stayed at the surface, where they were most comfortable." I paused. "I have a new family now."

I could feel Evie tightening back up. But she made no move to take off. "Does your new family love you the way your parents' couldn't?"

My lips curved. This precious girl. I wanted to kiss her

again, to keep cracking through her shield until she was bare and exposed before me.

"Yes," I said. "I now have bonds that run deeper than blood. We cannot love and be loved by everyone, not in that deep, enduring way. But there are a few I've let completely in, and those are friendships I will nurture until the end."

I listened to the sound of her breathing. I could nearly hear her thoughts milling about, bumping into each other, growing so adorably tangled.

"My work abides by the same philosophy as yours, little witch," I murmured. "Reciprocity, mutual respect, strong alliances. Violence is necessary, but violence alone did not get me where I am today. And it sure as hell isn't what earns me the respect of my city."

"Your city," she scoffed. "Don't you mean your clan?"

"Nope."

She huffed. "The *ego*."

"You love my ego."

Her fist clenched where it rested on my torso. Her heart stuttered, and I relished the effect I had on her. Only twenty-four years old. She was so young—so beautifully idealistic no matter how hard she'd tried to stamp that quality out.

"I love nothing about you," she stammered.

I imagined how red her cheeks were right now. I needed to see them.

"Hush, angel. I hate when you lie to me." I quickly pinned her underneath me and kissed each of her flushed cheeks. "Time to get up. Our date has only just begun."

29

EVIE

Kylo couldn't keep his hands off me the entirety of our date. And not even in a sexual way, but in this affectionate, possessive way that made my toes curl against my will.

The differences between Kylo and my first relationship couldn't have been starker, not that I had any desire to reveal those differences to him and let his head inflate bigger than it already was. The pleasure, the attention, the patience, the intellectual and spiritual stimulation... It was as if I'd manifested this man out of one of my books, and I hated it. I hated how easy it was for him to worm his way inside my heart and mind.

Because I still hated his guts, too.

We talked more about philosophy and magick and power as we walked through the gardens. We ignored the topics that still weighed me down, that still made me want to throttle him.

I needed the escape. And Kylo knew it.

He made good on his promise for a picnic, watching me eat and staring at me as if I was a mythical creature from another realm.

As if I really were an angel. And not a confused and paranoid girl with poison in her veins.

~

LATER THAT NIGHT as I lay in bed, I thought of his strong jaw, his powerful muscles, the way his black hair brushed the top of his forehead, and those deep blue eyes that pierced straight through me. I thought of the time I'd seen him shirtless, those dangerous tattoos and the thin trail of hair that receded below his waistband.

What did he look like? I knew it was big. Frighteningly big. Would sex feel as pleasurable as his hands and tongue?

I pictured him in his mask, his shadows gagging, teasing, and binding me, leaving me exposed and helpless as he had his way.

My body flushed with heat, my core suddenly aching all over again, no matter how many times I'd come undone on his tongue earlier today.

I'd never touched myself while consumed by my own thoughts. While reading books, sure, but this was different. Kylo was changing everything—disrupting all that I once knew.

I reached between my thighs. A small moan escaped my lips as I began to move my fingers in circles.

The sound of the door creaking and a sudden heat on the back of my neck had me going still.

The room was dark. I shot up, but strong arms were quick to shove me back down. Before I could scream, a large hand covered my mouth.

"Naughty girl," a deep voice admonished. "Touching what belongs to me."

The weight at my core moved, hips rocking against mine.

I knew him by his scent—the fresh mint and woodsy musk, the slightest tinges of leather and berries.

He removed his hand, but before I could speak, two fingers were shoved inside my mouth.

"*Suck.*"

Another hand stroked the side of my head. I tentatively swirled my tongue, disoriented and burning with need.

"Good girl."

The fingers went deeper, and I gagged.

Kylo chuckled, as if delighting in my discomfort and humiliation like the sadistic freak that he was.

He slowly eased out of my mouth.

"You can't just break into my house—my bedroom—and—"

"I can, and I did."

The tone in his voice was nothing like the attentive, nurturing man who walked with me through the gardens. The man who ran a brush through my hair with such tenderness that tears had pooled in my eyes.

And gods above if this version of Kylo didn't make me burn with desire—a desire I had no idea existed before him.

"Keep that pretty mouth open."

I shut my lips tight. I wanted to test him. That rush of raw aliveness lit up my every nerve, goading me, propelling me straight into the darkness I ran from.

The dark laugh that filled the room rose the hairs on the back of my neck.

Strong hands manhandled my face, prying my jaw open.

Then, he fucking *spit.*

His saliva hit my tongue, and he removed his grip from my face. I swallowed.

"Now thank me," he growled.

I was still in stunned disbelief when he reached under my strappy nightgown and found my bare pussy. His fingers were still coated with my saliva as they skated over my folds before cupping my flesh possessively.

"Evie," he warned, and something about the tone of his voice penetrated deep.

It reminded me of who this man was, the countless born he'd likely slaughtered or tortured to be where he was today.

Why did I so naively think he wouldn't hurt me?

As if answering my question, he raised up and slapped my inner thigh.

I cried out. The sting shot up my body and then back down, gathering between my thighs were he still cupped.

"Thank you, Kylo," I whimpered.

"Good fucking girl."

All I saw was his imposing body lording over me, and I knew he was in his vampire form even in the dim lighting.

"Has *my* pussy ever been fucked with fingers before, angel?" he asked.

I had to stop myself from rocking my hips and grinding against his touch.

I nodded, finding my courage in this growing wave of anticipation and yearning. "I tried once myself, but it didn't feel very good. Then, um, someone else did another time. I don't remember it that well, only that I didn't understand the allure."

Kylo chuckled darkly, his fingers circling my opening now. "Say please."

He was giving me an out. He was taking all of my firsts one by one, rewriting every single lackluster experience, and I was *letting him*. I knew in my bones he would leave me alone if I asked.

But the bastard knew I wouldn't—that I *couldn't*.

Fear used to be something that only harmed me. Now it was something I craved, something I found myself leaning into the same as I would pleasure.

For him. Only for him.

"Please," I rasped.

One of Kylo's long, thick fingers plunged inside my opening.

The stretching feeling, the fullness, the way the appendage hit against this pleasurable center inside of me—it had my eyes rolling back.

"Good girl," he praised, and this time his voice was softer, more like the man beneath the mask. "What a perfect angel, clenching around her owner's finger."

"You are not my—"

The hand was back over my mouth. "Evie darling, I'm going to need you to be quiet and take what I give you with gratitude now, okay?"

His finger moved in and out, slowly at first as I spasmed around him. Then it began to pulse, hitting that sensitive spot inside me over and over again.

I moaned into his hand, losing all sense of myself in this rising tide of pleasure.

Could I come this way? Something was building, but it felt different—more powerful than previous orgasms. More frightening.

"Uh-huh. Perfect," he crooned. "Let go. My perfect good girl doesn't have to think. She trusts *me* to think for her."

Such a degrading notion should've insulted me, but it didn't. Just like when he'd spit in my mouth, all I wanted was more. More of him, more of this violence, more of this sickness. I was the prey that walked willingly into the hunter's trap. Over and over again.

Caught between those powerful iron clamps, I'd never experienced such liberation.

"You're going to take another," he said softly. "Let's not forget our manners, angel. Say *thank you*."

When a second finger slowly eased into me, I groaned, feeling fuller than ever before.

His hand on my mouth didn't move, so I said the words *thank you* muffled against his skin as he chuckled at my expense. He'd turned me into his cherished possession, a toy, a doll, to watch and dress and play with wherever and whenever he chose.

And gods, I... I liked it. I loved the way it all made me feel.

I whimpered as he pumped, angling against that place of pleasure until I was shaking and squirming beneath him. As my whimpers grew louder, he continued to praise me, to tell me I was his perfect good girl.

"If you can't take my fingers, however will you take my cock, princess?" he asked me, the condescension stirring more tightness in my belly.

I was riding higher and higher to a release that felt too big, too much. I was terrified of falling over such a steep edge.

And he knew it. Just like he somehow knew everything about me, seen and unseen.

"Don't be scared, baby." He finally removed the hand over my mouth. "Let go."

He freed my breasts from the top of my nightgown, teasing my nipples with his fingers before pulling one into his mouth. He sucked, and as soon as I felt his fangs skate across my sensitive flesh, I trembled.

His laughter rumbled through my chest. He continued to fuck me with his large fingers, to kiss, suck, and nearly bite my nipples.

And the most fucked-up part of all was that when I finally bared down and exploded in a violent, uncontrollable release, the only thing on my mind was one disastrous, forbidden question.

What would it feel like for Kylo to feed from me?

I knew what vampire venom did—the way it worked as an aphrodisiac, a powerful drug that rendered mortals into pliable, vulnerable vampire-pleasing puppets.

I rode wave after wave of my orgasm, imagining Kylo's fangs biting into my skin the same as his words had already burrowed deep in my soul.

He was slow to remove his fingers, continuing to pet my head and praise me. He kissed my forehead.

"Why—why haven't you fed from me?" The words tumbled from my lips, unfiltered in the aftermath of my release.

Kylo went utterly rigid. "Gods, Evie, please," he said, more strained than I'd ever heard before. His hips met mine, and I felt the swell of his cock underneath his pants. "As if you don't already have my self-control on its last thin thread."

Oh. My heart skipped a beat. I fought to catch my breath. Kylo had always appeared so in control. I hadn't even considered that the draw to my blood was difficult for him.

"Is it painful?" I asked.

Kylo moved away from me, and I wasn't prepared for what the absence of his touch would do to me in my vulnerable state. I was suddenly empty, disappointed—perhaps the first time I'd ever felt that way in his presence.

I swallowed, a lump forming in my throat as he moved to the edge of the bed, his back to me.

"Yes," he hissed, as if clenching his jaw. "My fangs ache, no matter how much I feed. You're all I can think about. Your scent is everywhere, taunting me. I'm already addicted to you. And I fear what will happen when I finally taste your blood. I'm terrified of what it will do to me—to *us*."

"Why?" I asked. "Because you're afraid of hurting me?"

His laugh was dry, flirting with unhinged. I could feel his shadows bleed into the room, darkening it a shade.

"No," he said. "I can't fucking wait to hurt you."

I held my breath. I sat up to stare at his back as my thighs finally stopped their shaking.

"Your tears, your pain, your pleasure, the dew between your thighs… your irresistible, otherworldly blood that's unlike any I've ever scented before," he said, the words seeming to claw their way out of his throat. "I'm obsessed with all of it. You already have too much of a hold over me. When I can no longer stomach feeding from anyone but you, when your life force is inside of me, fueling my power—I can't imagine the level of insanity that will root itself in my mind. I will *need* you. And that should terrify us both."

It did scare me. As much as it intrigued me, satisfied some deep, wounded need to matter that much to someone.

Our connection was too much too fast. It couldn't be trusted.

I couldn't be trusted. Not when my worst enemy had just admitted he couldn't wait to cause me more pain, and all I wanted to do was ask him to hold me until I fell asleep.

Instead of asking for what I needed, I sunk under the covers and curled in on myself. My eyes stayed trained on his broad, rigid back.

"I'm sorry, Evie," Kylo whispered.

Then he was gone.

30

KYLO

I had to get the hell away from her. Something about the sweetness, the innocent curiosity in her voice when she'd asked me why I'd never fed from her had triggered my most base, predator instincts.

The entire conversation that followed was beginning to split my mind in two. My conscious mind held the reins. But that animalistic, starving part of me was two seconds away from holding her down and biting her all over, pulling her blood inside me until I was sated.

The trouble was, I didn't think I'd ever be sated when it came to my Evie.

So I left. I left her even though I knew she needed me. She'd needed soothing touch, reassuring words, to be held until she drifted into the dreams that so often left her shaken and disturbed.

I knew what she needed most was for me to protect her from harm. And in that moment, I no longer trusted myself not to harm her, to ruin our tenuous trust forever.

She would forgive me for leaving. But she would never forgive me for breaching her boundaries.

And I sure as hell would never forgive *myself.*

~

THE NEXT FEW days I was too busy with clan matters to see Evie. I always had a guard posted near her estate. I was simultaneously relieved and disappointed to hear that she barely left her princess palace.

Was she still creating spells and goods with her beautiful magick? Was she still reading? Dreaming?

I had to let it go. My angel needed me, but Etherdale needed me more at the moment. I couldn't let my obsession with her put the world at risk.

When I could finally, officially claim her, things would be different. Maybe then I could relax.

It was a nice, helpful delusion, even if I knew it wasn't true.

As soon as I finished the paperwork that had gathered into a much-too-tall pile on my desk—correspondences from near and distant allies, initiatives from my commanders that needed my stamp of approval, new policies for recruitment—I was free to head to one of the underground training facilities.

New and old recruits alike were practicing and learning combat and magick together. It was a sight that warmed my heart—watching elder vampires mentor the young and the more powerful ones lend a hand to those reborn with less magick.

My clan was a perfect system, a web of reciprocal influence led by a shared dedication to something greater than ourselves. It bore a striking resemblance to Evie's magickal philosophy.

Witch lights above mimicked the natural light of the sun, giving the plants that ran down the stone walls much-needed nourishment.

Princeton snuck up on me as I watched a sparring match, giving instruction as I saw fit.

I gave him a side-eye. "How in the hell do you do that?" I muttered.

"Magick," he said with a grin.

I looked up at the ceiling, shaking my head. "I assume your network of weasels has already alerted you to the witch-conjured storm?"

"Of course," he said slyly. "Then I put two-and-two together."

"How bad is it?" I asked, turning to face him. "The witch hunt?"

Today's outfit was a billowy white tunic and wide, forest green pants. Bone amulets and other esoteric trinkets hung around his neck and wrists and dangled from his ears.

His light brown, curly hair cascaded past his shoulders, slightly windswept.

He crossed his arms. "It's not ideal. But those who are facing the most harm and danger are the witches without nearly as much power as I have—as *she* has. Born alley cats care more about the fresh kills and captives they bring to their masters than what is just or true."

In other words, born underlings were flexing their muscles with witches that had nothing to do with the clan. Harming innocents was, of course, their favorite pastime.

I massaged the bridge of my nose. "Funny that the loyalists keep calling us propagandists. If only they could see that the born simply *being the born* is the greatest recruitment tactic at our disposal."

"Hard to see anything with their heads stuck up their asses. Or, in this case, up the asses of Ravenia's benevolent, merciful demon rulers."

I read the glimpse of truth beneath the humor—the tinge of anger, the fear of grief.

"I'm sorry, brother," I said. "I know you still have friends in those communities. I hope they're staying safe."

"They'll be safer if I stay away for a while," Princeton said, shrugging a shoulder.

I thought of Evie, the similar choices she was being forced to make in order to protect her family.

Princeton's gaze unfocused for a lapse before driving into me like a psychic knife to scan my aura. Those bright, light brown irises darted around my face, then my chest, and then the space between my eyes.

He was motionless for two beats before grinning like a mad man.

"I hate when you do that," I muttered. "Even more than when you sneak up on me like the slithering, devious snake that you are."

Princeton laughed heartily, the most evil, sneaky gleam in his eyes. "You love me and my slithering ways, dearest Kylo."

The sound of a collision momentarily shifted our gazes to the left, where a nasty fight had broken out. Fire magick flared. A shield was erected around the sparring mat. I watched as a commander stepped in, the tenor of her voice sending both women to their knees as they worked to soothe themselves. I sensed they were newly turned just by the crazed looks in their eyes.

New recruits were a testy, hungry bunch. That was why we worked hard to temper their proclivity for bloodlust, territorialism, and base instincts. We taught them to channel their primal desires and violence into fuel for the good of the clan, for the protection of mortals and the annihilation of the born.

My focus swept back to Princeton.

"Did you sense Evie's power the moment you saw her?" I asked.

Princeton's face didn't move an inch. He let nothing slip. Just that infuriating little half-smirk on his lips.

"I could sense a buried power," he mused. "A very curious power. Blocked and denied, but hungry nonetheless."

"What if she had been a threat?" I asked, my jaw flexing with irritation.

"My loyalty is and shall always be to Spirit. I am not one of them," Princeton said with eerie calmness, gesturing to the turned surrounding us. Light caught the metal of his many rings. "There was nothing you needed to know at that time."

My anger was useless. Princeton did what Princeton wanted to do, nothing more and nothing less. He was a genius, a powerful chaos witch, and a major pain in my ass, but without him we were nothing.

"She hates the color black," I said. "Specifically all-black clothing."

Princeton's lips curved ever-so-slightly. "Interesting."

"Her blood..." I had to stop myself from grinding my teeth into dust. "Smells deceptively human, but stronger. She's a half-witch. Her brother is human."

"The boy you blacklisted?" Princeton asked. "My network of rodents was most perplexed."

I made no response. What was the use when Princeton already knew the truth?

He lowered his voice. "You think she was caught up with the Servants of Lillian?"

I frowned. Every time I ran through the possibilities of Evie's backstory, the reason for her nightmares, her trauma, her innocence, and her ever-present fear... I wanted to go on a born-killing rampage.

"She's been on the run for a long time," I said. "It's what makes the most sense."

He lifted a brow. "Have you considered asking her?"

Prick. My jaw tightened. "We're working through some trust issues at the moment."

Princeton chuckled. He twirled one of his curly strands

around his finger, gazing off into space. "I see." He sighed. "Well, if she was indeed a survivor of such a nasty cult, I'd imagine that would be a reason for her to fear and suppress her power. To despise violence. To despise *us*."

I'd suspected these things for a while, yet it still felt like I was grasping for answers in the dark. Exactly where Evie wanted me.

How could I protect her when I didn't know who she was hiding from?

"I know you're protective of this woman," Princeton said.

The tone instantly put me on edge as I waited for the *but*.

My eyes narrowed.

"But," he continued with a grin. "It is time to bring her in. She is too enmeshed in your aura now, her fate intertwined with the clan's. I did not glimpse all of her mysteries that day in the market. I only saw she was like me. That she could be *useful* like me."

A strange mix of guilt, dread, and territorialism sparked in my blood as I watched Princeton's eyes light up. I didn't want to bring Evie into my world, even if I knew it was what was best for her and for the clan. I hated that I had to be selfish with her after whatever horrors she'd endured as a child.

I hated that the *right thing* felt so wrong.

The moment I set my sights on her, our fates had become forever bound. Against her will. And some days, it felt like it had been against mine too. Our connection had throttled me, shaken me out of a decades-long haze, and now she had me dangerously consumed.

"I'm not interested in Evie for her *usefulness*," I said. "I will bring her in for her own safety and for that of the clan's. Not to be assessed for any other purpose."

Princeton lifted his hands in a position of surrender. His cheeky grin told a different story.

"She has no one," I said bitterly. "No teachers. No mentors.

Not even fellow witch *friends*, from what I have seen. Yet she grows more powerful by the day—her deepest, most hidden magick only coming out in fits of emotion."

Princeton nodded in understanding, but that hungry little smirk remained.

"I swear to the gods, Princeton," I hissed. "You and Spirit will become one if you so much as *attempt* to recruit her for clan purposes. Is that understood?"

Princeton's smile widened, his eyes growing hooded. "Mm, you're so fucking sexy when you threaten me. More please?"

I rolled my eyes and turned back to the sparring match. "You were the worst mistake of my career."

"And you were the worst mistake of mine."

31

EVIE

I should've been gleeful that the monster who'd ruined my life no longer wanted anything to do with me, but I felt something rather pathetic instead.

Heartbroken.

Not only had he abandoned me after burrowing inside me deeper than anyone else ever had—*literally*—but he'd also completely disappeared for five days.

It wasn't as if there'd never been gaps in our communication before, but I thought… I didn't know what I thought.

Other than, my feelings were, once again, painfully naive. Either he was busy being a wannabe criminal warlord, or he was ghosting me the same as Jacob did in lieu of an actual breakup.

This ghosting was a far more brutal blow.

Maybe because he'd promised to protect me and care for me, and those vows hurt the worst when broken. Idris and I had learned that lesson long ago.

Inside the main house, Mena was running around, frazzled and waving her arms with an increasingly dramatic flair.

Idris laughed, shrugging off his backpack as we watched Mena direct festivity planners and decorators.

She was hosting a soiree, inviting her vast and eclectic network of friends and colleagues for an evening of revelry and stimulating conversations.

Unlike the Whitfield's parties, Mena's were not ones to *Valentin hello*. Valentin goodbyes, however, were not only permitted, but enthusiastically encouraged.

Idris and I locked eyes, and he offered a hesitant smile. "Hi, Evie."

"Hi, Idris."

We both burst into laughter at the stilted, awkward formality. The break in tension was welcome, and my heart warmed.

He followed me into the kitchen, where I made us soothing chamomile tea amid Mena's chaotic storm of preparations.

"I'm glad you came," I said. "I'm sure it's a busy night for parties on campus."

Idris waved a hand dismissively. "Those parties are all the same. Mena's are one of a kind."

I snorted. "Do you remember when she invited that hypnotist?"

Idris laughed again, perching on a barstool as I heated the kettle. "Oh, gods, yes. The one who literally tried to rob everyone."

"But failed, because Mena couldn't stop asking questions to save her life and foiled his plans," I added through fits of laughter.

We composed ourselves just in time for another classic Mena story to rise to the surface, only to lose ourselves all over again.

"Or the time those weirdos showed up to the murder mystery party in robes and animal masks because they thought it was a sex party," Idris said with a guffaw.

I anchored myself to his crinkled features, his sparkling brown eyes. When Idris was happy, my soul was lighter.

His dirty blond hair was a touch shorter than when I'd last seen him, his shirt a soft blue.

Mena swept into the bright kitchen, her hair messily thrown back into a hair clip, her glasses low on her nose as she eyed us.

"There's no need for judgment, children. Those dearest friends weren't weirdos; they were merely confused. Happens to the best of us." She shook a scolding finger.

"Apologies," Idris said, biting back more laughter. "I assume that tonight's soiree is not, in fact, a sex party?"

Mena sighed dramatically. "If it were one of my sex parties, neither of you would know about it."

Idris and I exchanged a look.

Mena threw her hands up. "Oh, gods, I forgot about my sunshine cake."

"The hell is a sunshine cake?" Idris asked.

"A cake for happiness and sunshine, you silly egg!" Mena exclaimed, as if we were the strange ones for asking questions.

Idris tapped his head and made a faux look of realization. "Oh, duh, of course."

I giggled. "It's like you don't even understand tonight's theme."

Mena nodded enthusiastically before rubbing Idris's hair and then turning on her heel. Her fluffy black slippers click-clacked loudly against the wood floors.

Idris smoothed down his hair with an eye roll. "Hate when she does that." He paused. "What in the realm is tonight's theme?"

I smiled bashfully, knowing that all this fuss was for me—though Mena would never admit it aloud. Which was yet another act of kindness.

I passed Idris a mug of chamomile. "Hope."

~

THE SOIREE WAS JUST GETTING STARTED, with music, dancing, and drinking on one side of the vast house, and conversation, food, and games on the other.

Idris and I were mingling in the dining room, picking at the eclectic sweets and traditional snacks from every region of Ravenia. Neither of us had spoken of our conversation in the courtyard, and I preferred it that way. After all, I'd guaranteed his safety. There was no reason to stir up more conflict. We both needed this return to normalcy for a while.

Mena was a genius in the art of socializing, creating the most enticing environments for people to be their most authentic selves. It was a quality I greatly admired, as someone who generally felt clunky and out of place. I'd never once felt that way at one of her parties; she would never allow it.

Mena could make friends with anyone, though there were, of course, those she avoided by choice, like the Whitfields. She fed from the energy of others—their minds, their gifts, their dreams and fears. Instead of an art history professor, she could've easily been a private investigator with her ability to read people and pull out their darkest secrets with ease.

"Is there elixir somewhere, Mena?" an older gentleman asked as Mena waltzed into the space.

Mena's floor-length cherry red gown matched her lipstick and circular glasses. She took a bite of a chocolate-covered strawberry as she casually swept her attention to the man. "No, darling. You don't need to be drugged to enjoy my company. I can assure you tonight will be more than intriguing and mystifying stone cold sober." She lifted her hands and let her fingers dance like flickering stars.

The man smiled sheepishly. Idris and I exchanged an amused grin, enjoying watching Mena in full form.

"Alcohol can be found, but it is optional," she added before finding more chocolate to concern herself with. After a bite of a truffle, she suddenly paused. Her eyes found mine. "Silly me, I nearly forgot why I came in here!"

That was when I felt it—the hot sear on the back of my neck, the unmistakable hum of power somewhere close.

Mena grinned mischievously. "Your boyfriend has arrived, Evie."

Idris groaned from next to me. "Seriously?" he whispered low to my ear. "I thought you and Jacob broke up. Better yet, I thought he was halfway across the kingdom."

A presence behind me made me straighten my spine. A hand skated across my lower back.

"Oh good, you found her," Mena said. Her eyes sparkled, very noticeably scanning the man by my side up and down.

I, on the other hand, merely glared up at the tall vampire in a human disguise. His jacket and pants were black, but his shirt was a midnight blue.

Idris lifted a brow. "That was quick," he said under his breath, taking a step away so he could face both of us.

"Hi, I'm Kylo." Kylo extended a hand to Idris.

The moment their hands met, I saw red. Rage flooded my system, and the lights flickered. As soon as Idris shot me a look of concern, I squashed the emotion.

This was no place to unleash my poisonous magick. I took deep breath after breath, fear of harming the surrounding mortals forcing me to calm down.

"I took a look around," Kylo said, regarding Mena. "And I have to say that you have the loveliest taste. In décor, art, food, and, most importantly, in people. I've been to many events over the years, and this one feels unlike any before." His hand gripped my waist. "The energy is magnetic. You should be so proud."

I waited for Mena to put Kylo on trial like she did with any unfamiliar man, to show him prickliness or coldness to see how he stood up.

Instead, her smile was genuine, her eyes alight. She clutched her heart and batted her eyelashes. "You are a most charming young man!"

What? Fucking *what?*

I stared at Mena incredulously, the most famously anti-man woman I knew.

Then I looked to Idris, scanning his face for the derision and contempt he wore for Jacob. Not that Jacob ever noticed, far too concerned with himself.

But Idris's features were mostly curious, only slightly distrustful. "Where did you two meet?"

Most of the room was now watching us as they nibbled on their food and pretended to still be talking to each other. The older gentleman who'd asked about elixir had stopped mid-conversation to give Kylo a once-over. His eyes swam with the same lust that shone in the eyes of the woman next to him.

You've got *to be kidding me.*

"In a library," Kylo said, as I made no move to answer Idris's question. "She was slow to return my affections. But I'm a man of patience."

Idris snorted. "Perfect. Evie needs plenty of it."

"Hey!" I said, narrowing my eyes.

Idris smiled. "Just fulfilling my brotherly duties."

"I'm glad she has someone to look out for her," Kylo said. "She speaks so highly of you."

Idris stood a little taller, his face relaxing an inch. "She's said absolutely nothing about *you.*"

Kylo grinned. When his eyes met mine, even my own body betrayed me, my stomach fluttering and my mind scrambling.

"That's okay," Kylo said. "I'm still winning her over. She has every right to be cautious."

Idris nodded. "Good answer."

I opened my mouth to correct the narrative that Kylo was in any way, shape, or form my *boyfriend*, but Mena spoke first.

"Much better, Evie," Mena said with a wink. "Much better."

My cheeks heated—with embarrassment or fury, I wasn't sure.

"Kylo, can we speak alone for a moment?" I said, faking every single note of softness in my voice.

He tucked a strand of hair behind my ear. "Of course."

"We'll be right back," I assured Idris apologetically.

He merely shrugged, filling his plate with more food as one of Mena's retired professor friends asked him about his studies.

As soon as we left the room, I swatted Kylo's hand away.

"Deep breaths, angel," he said softly, an irritating amount of humor in his tone.

I was going to commit murder. I was genuinely about to kill the leader of the Masked Order and bury him in my fucking flower garden.

The lights above flickered. I forced smiles as friendly faces greeted me, serving them my usual hostess lines and promising to chat later.

I led Kylo all the way through the back door and into my gardens, where we could be alone. The grounds were off-limits to guests to protect the gardens, my magickal workings, and my privacy.

When I spun on Kylo, the expression on his face was disarming. He'd removed his smirk, as if picking up on my intentions to bludgeon him to death with a shovel.

Instead, he looked at me with care. And it took only two seconds for that show of pure devotion to make me even angrier than I was before.

"You have some nerve," I said, the familiar lump in my throat back with a vengeance. "You just left me there, and then you didn't speak to me for five days."

I hated that stupid look on his face. The downturn of his

lips, the brows drawn together, the eyes filled with emotion that appeared raw and *real*.

"I'm sorry, Evie." He sighed. "This isn't easy for me to admit. But I was beginning to lose control."

The immediate apology was so unlike what I was used to that I was disoriented. I'd expected him to be angry with me for expressing my emotions, to make excuses or shift the blame. My nervous system was primed for conflict and disappointment, adrenaline making it hard to stay focused and logical.

I processed his words slowly, averting my eyes in confusion. "Control of what?"

"Control of my desire for your..." He trailed off, his gaze on my neck.

Oh. I frowned. He'd basically said as much before he left, but I hadn't connected it to his absence. All I knew was that I felt used and abandoned.

At the sound of laughter inside, I remembered the real reason we were out here—the reason my poison yearned to leap from my skin and suck the life out of him.

I shook my head. *"How dare you!"* My voice quivered as I held his gaze. "How dare you show up here without my permission. How dare you insert yourself into their lives."

Kylo didn't back down, only held my glare as his features hardened slightly. "I was already a part of their lives, because I am a part of yours."

"Not by choice," I spat.

His eyes sparked with anger. "I thought we were finished with the distasteful lies."

I gestured behind him, toward my home. "They are all I have, Kylo," I said, my lip wobbling as emotion roared in my veins. "You said you wouldn't take them away from me. Leave them *alone*."

Kylo sighed. "Evie, you need to calm down."

Power swelled somewhere deep inside me, clawing and scraping against the bars of its psychic cage.

My lip curled. "Fuck. You."

Kylo's eyes narrowed. He took a step forward.

"You are not my boyfriend," I hissed. "You've crossed the line by endangering my family." Red—that was the color behind my eyelids, stirring up the darkness that yearned to break free. I heard the faintest of whispers as my heart began to pound.

"Angel," Kylo said with a cool, detached authority. "You are the only one putting that house full of humans in danger right now."

At a sudden knock on the glass door behind us, I jolted. Idris had a grin on his face and a drink in his hand.

And for a moment, I saw that rosy-cheeked boy, starved for love and a calm, peaceful place to call home.

I buried my anger. I locked back the cage where my power dwelled. I stepped into the role I needed to play. The role that Idris needed. His needs came first, always.

All the while, Kylo was studying me as if working a puzzle.

When he reached for my hand, I didn't flinch.

"I'm not going anywhere," Kylo whispered. "You're safe."

Idris opened the door. "Sorry to interrupt, but I knew you wouldn't want to miss Mena playing charades." He laughed.

I smiled. Kylo's hand snaked around my waist.

As we walked with Idris into the main drawing room, I grinned and talked as if nothing had happened. As if everything was as it appeared to be.

Kylo stayed glued to my side, part of him always touching me in some way—soothing and consistent. In another world, I would've melted at these shows of affection, at the way he was charming everyone in my life, the way he spoke of me with such tenderness and pride.

I played along on the surface, but underneath, carefully tucked away, my rage was only festering, multiplying.

Kylo had no fucking idea what awaited him once all the guests had pulled their Valentin goodbyes.

32

EVIE

"Evie's incredible," Kylo agreed when Idris brought up my magick. "It warms my heart to see her receive the recognition she deserves for her work." He looked at me, his hand resting just above my knee as we sat on the couch in the drawing room. "You have every right to be able to do what you love without fear."

"Agreed," Idris said in an adjacent chair. "It's disgusting what the born are doing to witches. Their newest targets to cope with the shame of their own incompetency."

I glanced down at my shimmering rose gold gown with a deep frown, and Kylo's grip on my leg tightened.

"Well said," a voice said from behind us.

Idris and I both tensed as Wendy approached us, the psychology professor who occasionally did emotional healing sessions in her retirement.

Her smile was warm, her cool blue eyes bright. Her long white hair was pulled into a regal bun with a few strands loose to frame her face. The color of her dress reminded me of the deep blue hues of the ocean.

"It's always such a joy to see you two all grown up," she said.

Idris watched my face for a moment before nodding and smiling politely.

"Hi, Wendy," I said.

For a moment, I was that frightened thirteen-year-old, refusing to let this strange woman anywhere near Idris. Now that I was older, I knew she'd only been trying to help.

I cleared my throat. I felt Kylo's gaze on me, heavy and intrusive. I kept my focus on Wendy. "Are you enjoying yourself?"

Wendy grinned. "Always." She sipped her sparkling drink. "I wanted to tell you two how charming, intelligent, and thoughtful you both are. We're all so impressed with everything that you do and everything that you are."

"Thank you," Idris and I both said.

She hesitated a beat. "If you ever need anything, you know where to find me. I'm always in your corner."

Idris and I both mumbled our niceties, and she left us alone.

On the other side of the room, someone howled with laughter. Guests were still caught up in a ridiculous game of charades, a game Mena adored even as she lost every single time.

People just don't understand my vision! she always lamented.

"Let's mingle?" Idris said, his features slow to shift back into normalcy. "I need a drink."

When I stood, Kylo stayed glued to me. Idris moved too quickly for us to follow, clearly ditching us for the moment.

"Want to explain that strange mood-killing exchange?" Kylo asked, his breath warm as it skated across my ear.

I looked up at him, my smile warm but my eyes bleeding ice. "Nope."

"Mm," he hummed, scanning my features. "We're going to dance now, angel."

I tried to step away from him, but he quickly grabbed my wrist and closed in on me, eclipsing me with his size.

"Uh-uh. Be good, baby," he whispered before gripping the back of my head and crushing his lips to mine. When he pulled back an inch, he grinned at my look of pure spite. "Your very mean and evil boyfriend wants to force you to have fun with him."

"I will not be having *fun*."

"I'm taking that as a challenge. You know how much I love those."

"Rot. In. Hell."

"So long as my sweet, docile angel is in my lap where she belongs, I don't care where my soul goes to rot."

"You're going to fertilize my flowers."

Kylo laughed. His eyes sparkled with adoration. "You're so fucking cute it makes me sick." He planted a kiss on my head, placed my hand on his arm, and pulled me toward the music.

IN THE SECOND biggest drawing room, space had been cleared for people to dance. A vocalist, pianist, and guitarist were by the tall windows overlooking the front lawn and the glimmering lights of Etherdale beyond. The woman's voice was powerful, moving, and unique. The whole band was masterful—a blend of dreamy melodies and haunting, poetic lyrics. Their presence here once again proved how much cooler Mena was than the rest of us.

Pillar candles of various sizes decorated the furniture and windowsills, creating a moody, romantic atmosphere as guests danced.

I glared at Kylo as he pulled me close. He looked at me the way I'd always dreamed a man might look at me.

His hand brushed my cheek, bending to kiss my forehead. "I didn't abandon you, Evie. I could never. I still checked up on you. You were always safe."

The words were sneaky darts attempting to break through the walls of my resurrected defenses. More beautiful promises designed to target my deepest wounds.

Little did he know, I was using his words to build my own weapon.

I was going to take back control and show this arrogant tyrant that he didn't get to just take anything he wanted from me. I wasn't a doormat. Not anymore.

"It pains me to be apart from you," Kylo said in my ear.

"Good. Suffering builds character, and you most certainly lack humility," I hissed back. "And sanity, too."

"If only my lack of sanity didn't make your little pussy soaked and begging for me," he whispered over the din of music, laughter, and chatter.

I tried to rear back, but Kylo locked his arms around me.

"Shh. I know where everyone is, at all times. No one can hear us," he said, keeping me close as his chest vibrated with laughter. "The only person almost within earshot is a wealthy older gentleman who has looked at you one too many times for my liking."

He suddenly released his rigid hold, only to guide me into a spin before dipping me. His grin was wide, his eyes flitting from my face to my fluttering jugular. I was breathless and dizzy when he pulled me back up and close to his chest.

The music swelled, and a few people stopped dancing to cheer on the band's incredible skill. In my periphery I saw Idris enter the room with a couple of younger women—at least, younger than Mena's peers—but still at least a decade older than my brother. They were laughing and fawning over him, and Idris had never appeared more pleased with himself.

Mena, on the other hand, was in a far corner dancing close

with one of her many lovers. Boyfriend Number Three, I believed, was what she'd dubbed him. A man in his late forties, so nearly twenty years younger than her.

It made sense. Mena was a catch and a masterful seductress and would remain so until the end.

Kylo recaptured my attention with a gentle stroke of my cheek. He was smiling at me in that perturbing, genuine way he did—the kind of smile that made me forget he wasn't human, if only for the briefest exhale.

"I love watching you always," he said, cradling my face. "But nothing beats observing you up close like this, seeing the way you look at the people you love."

My heart betrayed me again, going off beat as I stared into those deep pools of blue. Words slipped from my lips before I could stop them. "You're ruining me."

Kylo held my gaze with equal intensity.

"You're ruining me too."

We continued to dance. His hands gripped my waist, my body flush against his.

"Destruction is the first step in creation, wouldn't you agree, little witch? Clearing of the old to make way for the new."

"You can't just use mystical, witchy language to melt my brain into submission," I growled.

Kylo made a low groan. "All this talk of ruining you and melting your brain into submission is not making me want to be on my best behavior, sweet girl," he said. "I'd watch your mouth until we're alone."

At my look of feral venom, Kylo pressed closer, alerting me to the hard, imposing bulge in his dark pants.

"Behave, angel," he warned. The darkness in his eyes, the arousal in his features as he stared into my soul—it had the muscles in my stomach tightening, my thighs yearning to grind against him.

As the music faded away, someone clinked a spoon against glass.

"It's time to consume the sunshine cake!" Mena shouted over the din. "For new beginnings, good tidings, and renewed hope!" She found my eyes in the dim lighting and winked.

33

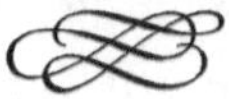

EVIE

The sunshine cake was a work of art. I shouldn't have expected anything less. It was a fiery sun surrounded by rays of orange, yellow, and red. The icing was a sweet citrus flavor, complimenting the vanilla and orange sponge cake beneath.

To my surprise, Kylo was actually consuming the dessert with his lying, blood-sucking mouth.

We were gathered in a circle with Mena, Idris, and a few other party guests.

"What are you hoping for as you consume Helia's fiery rays, Kylo?" Mena asked.

I stared up at him expectantly.

Irritatingly, Kylo only relaxed into an easy grin that seemed to pull the entire group into some kind of trance.

"I hope for a more peaceful city, where all mortals are free to live and love without fear," he said. "And I hope that Evie continues to create her beautiful magick, to help as many people as she can."

Mena looked like she was in love.

I suppressed the urge to roll my eyes.

"Those are some admirably selfless hopes," she said. "Do you have any personal ones?"

Kylo spoke without missing a beat. "To be the kind of man Evie deserves."

The women next to Idris made *aww* noises.

"I can only hope that she feels safe enough to keep me around," he finished with a shrug. He took another bite of his cake, as if his words were utterly genuine and not the deceptive vampire tricks I knew them to be.

Even still, my heart yearned. I wanted to believe.

Kylo pointed his fork at the painting behind Mena. "Is that one of Figaro's pieces? It's breathtaking."

Mena grinned. It looked like she was about five minutes away from asking Kylo to be one of *her* boyfriends.

"Yes! You know him?"

Kylo nodded. "I prefer the later pieces, like the one you have here. When he starts to add magical realism to the natural environment."

"You know that you're in the minority opinion on that?" Mena asked, absentmindedly swirling her cocktail. Her eyes glowed.

"That has never bothered me," he said with a shrug, his lips tipping up. "People don't like change. I think that's why those who prefer the newer pieces skew younger. They didn't start off with the first wave of Figaro's paintings and become admirers, only to be shocked with the second wave. The younger generation saw both eras at the same time and were able to choose which they preferred without the primacy bias. The comfort of what we know can blind us to the superiority of anything new or different."

My gaze swept from the drooling women to Idris, who eyed Kylo with growing interest and curiosity. Maybe something even close to respect.

That was the most dangerous reaction to Kylo of all. My fist clenched, and I angrily shoved cake into my mouth.

"You said you tutor in philosophy, right?" Idris asked. When Kylo nodded, he smiled. "It certainly sounds like it. I'd love to talk more with you sometime—I've been eyeing some of those classes for next term."

Kylo looked at me for a moment before nodding at Idris with warmth. "You should absolutely take a few philosophy classes before you graduate. Philosophy teaches us how to live."

He didn't promise he'd talk to him, likely because he knew how I'd feel about that, but Idris didn't seem to notice.

It didn't matter, though. Kylo merely being here had crossed my most sacred boundary of all.

The conversation continued, and soon more and more people had gathered around our little circle to hear Mena tell one of her many outlandish tales. I'd heard several versions of the story of Mena seducing an entire wolf shifter pack, and this version was the most unbelievable yet.

I found myself giggling at Mena's antics despite Kylo's presence, and each time I did, he gazed down at me like I was his whole world.

At the end of the night, Kylo pretended to leave with most of the crowd, saying a polite goodbye to Mena and Idris.

"Come for dinner next week," Mena said.

An offer she had never once made to Jacob. Idris announced he'd be there too.

My blood was boiling as I smiled and played along. Kylo kissed me, tender and brief, before promising he'd *see me soon.*

Bastard.

"Are you okay, Evie?" Idris asked after Kylo left. "You've been acting a little strange all night."

"Sorry," I said quickly. "Just torn up about Celeste's."

Idris nodded. "Of course. Don't apologize. We're going to figure it out, okay?"

Mena raised her empty glass. "Together."

I smiled at them.

Mena shook a finger. "I cannot believe that man was your secret admirer. You cheeky little minx!"

Idris shook his head. "Well, I like him. He seems to really understand who you are and care for you, Evie. If you're happy, I'm happy."

"And if you're not, please tell him to write to me," Mena said with a wink.

~

BACK IN THE COTTAGE, I downed a glass of water and mentally prepared for what I was about to do.

I was going to punish Kylo the only way I knew how. He'd already told me how best to make him suffer.

As soon as I set the glass back on the counter, strong hands grabbed my waist. Lips grazed the shell of my ear.

"Still thinking about the most effective way to kill me and dispose of my body without implicating yourself?" he asked.

I laughed dryly. "Don't you have somewhere more important to be?"

"No," he said. "I know you're angry, and I know you've been hiding the true depths of that rage for your family's sake." He gently spun me to face him. "Let me take care of you tonight and make you breakfast in the morning. We can hash it out whenever you're ready. I can even take you to a secure location where you can throw the biggest magickal fit of your life."

Those last words triggered something unpleasant in the recesses of my mind.

I frowned at the sudden influx of fear and shame, quickly focusing back on my present anger. "Fine."

Kylo lifted a brow. "A suspiciously quick and easy answer…"

I shrugged. "What's the use? When you're only going to do whatever you want, no matter what I say?"

He watched me carefully. "Evie, you know that's not true. I'm sorry I frightened you. My presence at your family's party was not a threat. I only wanted to show you that what's between us isn't a game to me. *You're* not a game to me." He took a deep breath, and my fluttering stomach warred with my irritated psyche. "This is real. I wanted to show you how real it could be, if you allowed it."

"You didn't give me a choice," I said. "You forced it on me."

"I'm sorry."

My mind fed me this accursed recap of the night. Kylo's apologies, his vows to never abandon me, his soft touches, and his heart-warming praise. Even more dangerous—the shows of kindness and care to both Mena and Idris, the way Idris looked at him with respect, and the way Kylo looked at *me* with...

Gods, he looked at me like I was everything to him.

Kylo pulled me into his arms. He kissed my forehead and carried me to bed.

In the dark, I let myself be frightened, small, and needy, clinging to Kylo like he was my only certainty in a world that was harsh, confusing, and ever-changing. He fed me the softest touches and words of praise.

But my plans didn't change. I couldn't let his actions slide. Not when he'd made them without my permission.

He didn't get to decide what we were to each other. He didn't get to force his way into Idris's and Mena's lives, to put them directly in the center of vampire clan violence.

Like he'd said when he was scolding me in the tunnel, *actions had consequences.*

Kylo kissed the top of my head again. "Sleep, baby," he whispered. "You're safe."

My stupid body believed him, growing more relaxed the tighter he held me. The more onyx shadows that crawled across me and claimed my body and soul, the easier it was to fall into a dreamless sleep.

I woke up a few times during the night. In the liminal place between consciousness and unconsciousness, I wasn't angry at Kylo. I felt something else entirely.

This sickening yearning made me want to let go—made me want to look into those adoring eyes and *believe.*

34

EVIE

In the morning, I nestled deeper into Kylo's hold. His broad hand traced soothing circles on my back, and he kissed my head.

My stomach did a somersault.

I was slow to remember last night, and if I were being honest, I almost didn't want to. Because that meant that I couldn't merely relax in Kylo's tattooed, impossibly strong arms. I couldn't let myself buy into the idea that maybe he really was my protector, the answer to all of my idealistic, romantic prayers.

"Stay put, angel. I'm going to fetch you coffee."

I burrowed deeper into his chest with a long exhale. He was not making my next actions easy for me.

"Sweet girl," he cooed. "I know you need your fuel before you hex, curse, and maim me."

I made a disgruntled noise against his shirt.

He chuckled, peeling me off him to stare into my eyes. "Pity you're holding onto this indignation so tightly. Good girls get woken up with my tongue between their thighs."

My core was suddenly hot and achy, my breathing quicker. Kylo knew it too—he knew too much about me, at all times.

That cocky grin wouldn't be on his face for long.

When he left, I quickly ran through my plan. And when he returned with coffee, I decided I had no time to waste.

Kylo trailed his long fingers through my hair as he handed me the mug, kissing my temple. "I'm going to make you that breakfast I promised."

I squirmed, this silly, misplaced guilt suddenly churning in my stomach. If Kylo didn't feel guilt for endangering my younger brother, why should I feel guilt for merely asserting my autonomy?

"Hey," Kylo said gently. "You don't have to be so strong with me, okay? I see the way you care for everyone around you, even to your own detriment. Let me do for you what you've done for others your whole life, angel."

The guilt multiplied. He was in his vampire form, all muscles and tattoos and raw power. And yet he still had this hold over me, a dependence I couldn't shake, one he'd planted inside my heart when I hadn't been looking.

"Thank you." The words left my lips before I could stop them. I thought of Idris, snapping myself out of Kylo's spell. "I'm going to take a shower."

Kylo nodded. "Sounds good. I can only assume you'll be taking your coffee in there with you."

I narrowed my eyes. "Obviously."

He laughed, that tiny dimple working overtime to melt my hardened resolve.

As soon as he left my bedroom, I rummaged through my closet for a dress. I scooped up my sneakers, a pair of socks, and my crossbody bag, and I peeked out into the hallway.

I could already smell something heavenly cooking, and more unnecessary, people-pleasing guilt wormed into my guts. Kylo was humming as he worked, once again deceiving me with his domesticity skills when I knew full-well he was a deadly, criminal clan lord.

I huffed as I tiptoed into the bathroom and shut the door behind me. I showered quickly, and when I was finished, I left the water running as I got dressed.

In the mirror, I stared at my wide gray eyes, my frightened features, and wet hair. For a moment, I hesitated.

If I asked Kylo to brush my hair again, he would. If I walked back outside, he'd feed me, he'd ask me more about my magick, my thoughts, my dreams.

But he wouldn't back down from putting Idris and Mena in danger. He would reel me in with these beautiful gestures and filthy, depraved acts of violence and pleasure. Before I knew it, I would have sacrificed my only living family just to be his pretty, pliable mortal doll.

My features went from frightened to resolute. I remembered the weight of a body in my arms as I ran. I saw a vision of Idris, laughing and carefree—how I wanted him to be forever.

I pushed open the bathroom window, and I leaped.

From there, I pressed myself against the wall. My heart pounded in my chest, my magick roaring to life. Not the poisonous, dangerous magick—but the power that was safe, that I was familiar with and used in my spells. When I made it to my crafting room's window, I whispered a chant. I called to the spirits of the space, and from my fingers a spark of intent rung through the air.

The window opened from the inside and swung outward. Kylo was a couple rooms away, but I knew he also had vampiric hearing. I was deathly careful when I swung over the windowsill and touched the floor, hoping he was more focused on the sound of the shower running in the bathroom.

I tiptoed around the space and quickly found the book on Hekate I'd swiped from the library, a notebook, and a few other materials to place in my bag.

My final and most impactful move was to uncork the potion I'd created a couple days ago—the one that temporarily altered the scent of my blood. It had taken quite a bit of power and required an unusually strange and rare collection of ingredients.

I thanked the spirits for their aid and spoke a quick prayer before exiting the window again.

Once I was on solid ground, I snuck around the side of the cottage opposite of the kitchen, and I ran.

RUNNING WAS CATHARTIC. It made me feel in control.

Ever since Kylo had entered my life, I'd felt more powerless than I had in over a decade.

Now, it was as if I was taking back everything he'd attempted to steal. My freedom, my choices, my *privacy*.

I hated how much I loved his stalking, his dangerous games, the effect he had on my traitorous body.

That obsession only made me want to be in control again— of my lust, my destiny, my heart.

So I ran until my lungs ached. I reached the edges of the residential neighborhood, where a patch of forest stood. It wasn't an extremely popular location, mostly where wealthy mortal housewives went for the occasional walk, perhaps with their much-younger lovers.

As a witch, forests granted me equal parts peace and intrigue. They were full of spiritual energy, both light and dark —much different from the web of etheric matter in gardens or man-made spaces. More wild and untamed.

Slightly frightening.

I, too, was slightly frightening today. It was a perfect match of energy.

As I passed under the tall trees, listening to the curious calls of crows and other creatures, I felt raw power tickle my skin.

When I found the perfect spot, I threw my quilt down on the earth, leaned back against a welcoming, wise pine tree, and sighed in relief.

The Hekate guidebook buzzed, flooding me with warmth when I cracked her open—as if welcoming me home. The first page I opened to was on protecting mortals from vampires.

How fitting.

I settled in, scanning this witch's tips, spells, and insights. My reactions were vastly different from the first time I'd read her scrawling words. I was more open, less judgmental. It was strange how quickly things had changed.

The truth was, Kylo was right, no matter how hard it was to admit. I knew it wasn't his fault my magick was under attack, that witches were winding up missing or dead.

I knew who was to blame. It didn't make any of it any easier. I'd been running for so long, creating a world for myself where everything was in order, everything dark and violent was shunned and avoided at all costs. My beliefs may have been faulty, but they'd also kept me safe.

And they were burrowed deep.

The way Kylo was pulling them out at the root, one by one, and forcing me to confront all of my wounds, everything hidden and repressed—gods above, I hated it.

It was agonizing. I was growing and stretching and doubting and running and yearning, and it fucking hurt.

Yet there was this tiny, faint *something* that kept me from sliding backward, kept me reading this dangerous, forbidden book as crows circled overhead in greater numbers. That kept me jotting down notes, that kept me plotting and scheming.

I didn't know what to call it—this spark, this whisper—this low hum that rattled through my bones.

A crow descended, landing a few feet away.

Fate.

We stared at each other for a beat. A snake slithered behind the crow, with onyx skin that sent a chill down my spine.

I gazed deeper, noting the aura of white and purple extending from both animals as they remained a respectful distance away.

The colors of wisdom and clarity. The chill down my spine transformed into heat, an undeniable surge of power.

Strong gusts of wind roared through the forest, shaking the leaves and pine and whipping my hair back.

"Hekate," I whispered.

My eyes rolled back.

In my vision, I saw myself in a garden of golden and midnight purple flowers. A woman in a cloak made from the same dark purple hue approached my body. I watched in my spirit form from several yards away.

I read a comforting, grandmotherly aura from the woman's presence—one that meant me no harm—even as the darkness of her attire and magick reminded me of everything I ran from, everything I denied.

She beckoned me forward. I couldn't see her face behind her cloak, as if it were obscured by shadow, the same shadows that hid the Masked Order.

We stood over my body, staring at that spindly, ugly dark gray mass at my throat center. Its tendrils were tangled around my heart, blocking all major sources of power in my etheric field.

"Remove it," she said gently, her voice melodic and otherworldly. Like it was many voices in one.

"You know I can't," I said.

My physical body shifted, taking on the appearance of a thirteen-year-old girl in all black.

I gasped, shutting my eyes.

"*Can't* is a dishonest word," the woman—the deity—said.

Hekate was presenting herself to me, officially.

"You *won't* remove that sickness from your throat the same as you wouldn't accept my call," she said.

Dread pooled in my stomach as I stared into the darkness under her hood. For a moment, I saw my mother's cold, soulless eyes, heard the disappointment on her cruel tongue.

I tensed, and the mass in the throat of the younger version of myself radiated a thin veil of darkness. I'd activated its pain.

"I'm not angry, Evie," Hekate said, her tone neither warm nor cold, merely matter-of-fact. "I'm not disappointed. I knew who you were when I chose you. Where you came from and where you are headed."

I opened my mouth to politely decline, before she'd even told me what she desired. I opened my mouth to deny her, but nothing came out.

Because I was back to looking at the child with a deep, lonely sadness burrowed in her soul.

"Your brother needed you," Hekate affirmed. "But so did she. And she needs you still."

"It's too late for her," I whispered. "She doesn't exist anymore."

"False," Hekate said. "Come to me when you're ready to stop running. I don't make demands of witches I work with. I give as much as I take." She pointed a slender finger at my younger self's throat, at that intrusive, ugly mass. "That's the freedom you were searching for. Safety is within; there are no shortcuts."

Hekate's hood flew off. The world spun. I opened my eyes.

Back in the forest, three born vampires watched me with hungry eyes and cruel smirks. Rain drizzled. All I could focus on were three sets of sharp, deadly, elongated canines.

35

KYLO

I sensed something was off about fifteen minutes after Evie had gotten in the shower. At first, I chalked it up to my protectiveness, my deranged compulsion to always have my eyes on Evie. Especially now, when she was behaving increasingly erratically.

I knew she was still furious with me. Yet she was hiding it, which was even more concerning.

It made sense that she hid her true feelings in front of her family. Evie was self-sacrificing to a fault—unable to harm others even with her own suffering. But now that the sun was out, and she was free to confront me for crossing her boundaries, she was suddenly soft and yielding.

And sneaky. I could see it all over her face. Selena and Helia too, this precious girl was up to something.

Nevertheless, I made her breakfast and more coffee. Because I'd force Evie to let me take care of her regardless of her secret, murderous schemes. Even if it meant I might have to disarm her, tie her to a chair, and feed her myself.

I might do that, anyway. It was far too sexy of a mental image to pass up.

After thirty minutes, I knew for certain something was wrong. I knew how long Evie's showers were. My stalking was nothing if not meticulous and detailed.

And this was officially abnormal, confirming the growing seed of intuition in my gut—intuition that was *never fucking wrong*.

I barely waited for Evie to answer my knocks and call before I barged through the door, already fully aware that I wouldn't find her in the bathroom.

The open window drove a terrifying mix of panic and rage into my veins. My fangs ached. My bones rattled as I shook with fury, knowing she'd broken the singular rule I'd given her.

I told her to never hide from me.

She might've remembered that rule in order to punish me effectively. But she clearly hadn't been listening carefully enough to the consequence I'd laid out.

She'd be remembering it soon enough.

I hastily activated my human glamour, but as soon as I stepped into the gardens, I realized I couldn't scent Evie anywhere, in any direction. Her blood was so strong, so unique, that it was easy for me to trace.

But not now, as if she'd *intentionally* muted her scent.

Because of course she fucking did, the wickedly smart creature. Inserting myself into her brother and guardian's lives had turned her into a frightened, devious, feral prey animal. She felt cornered and trapped. And now she was trying to take back control.

I slowed my breathing and closed my eyes. I would get nowhere operating from heightened emotions.

If my angel wanted to trigger my primal need to hunt, she'd better be prepared for what happened when her God finally found her.

~

Evie had been gone for five hours. The clouds had long since covered the sun, a storm on the horizon. She could be anywhere in the city, and I would have no way of tracking her without the scent of her blood.

I was out of my fucking mind. Because even if I knew she was only doing this to get back at me, I also knew the born were hunting witches like her, and she now had zero protection. She could've had her own forms of self-defense, if she hadn't robbed herself of her own power.

Visions of spanking her bratty, misbehaving ass until it was cherry red was hardly a comforting mental image. Because that wasn't nearly enough punishment. Not nearly enough of an assurance compared to what I had in mind.

Once I was done with her, my angel would never be able to leave me again.

After I'd been to all the obvious locations, I circled back to the land surrounding her estate.

I couldn't stop imagining her in harm's way. At a certain point I couldn't discern my intuition from my panic, my complete helplessness to protect what I cherished most.

My shadows were beginning to escape my skin, and it took considerable effort to force them back inside before they could spread out in search of her.

When a crow landed a couple feet from where I stood, my power flickered in some strange way—as if in recognition.

It was a sensation that was uniquely… witchy.

My gaze narrowed on the bird, who only darted closer and closer, in a zigzag pattern. Then it leaped forward.

When it turned to look back at me, its beady black eyes all business, I sighed.

Because now I was following a fucking bird. That was how insane she'd made me, how deeply her absence had stabbed into my soul.

I followed the creature down a few cobblestone streets until we reached the edge of the neighborhood, in the opposite direction of the city.

The crow cawed. When it suddenly soared into the air, I noted a strange pattern of birds in the distance, circling a spot in the forest.

This was not ordinarily how I hunted and captured my prey. But as I disappeared into the dark woods, and the sky began to drizzle, I thought that perhaps this was the perfect atmosphere to claim my little witch for an eternity.

I scented her before I saw her—the ghost of a scent, as if her blood was just starting to reawaken after whatever little spell she'd cast wore off.

As soon as I heard a scream and smelled ripe fear, I tore through my glamour and ran.

The trees were a blur as I moved, precise and focused, my shadows starving. I slowed down as I made my final approach, pausing to assess the situation.

Evie was standing, her back against a pine tree, as three born vampires moved in.

Dark vines held her in place as she struggled. One of the born, a woman with shoulder-length red hair, attempted to snatch the book at Evie's feet but yelped when it shocked her.

I smirked. One only needed to make that mistake once.

My smile turned into a feral snarl as one of the born men— the earth power wielder—tightened Evie's bindings and pulled out a dagger.

"I can scent it in your blood," he purred. "Power. Great power, even if hidden by some sort of binding enchantment. Did you think that would save you? Poor girl."

"Maybe he'll let us keep this one as a pet," the other born man said, staring at Evie with lust.

As soon as one of the earthen vines crawled too high on Evie's thigh, I stepped out of the shadows.

All of my buried rage and fear from the past five hours of searching for her bled from my skin.

In this moment, I didn't think like a clan leader. I didn't think as a skilled interrogator or a politician or a revolutionary.

I only thought as Evie's protector.

I only thought of her.

My shadows extended like deathly limbs. The born turned away from the bound angel to face me.

I didn't even bother with my fucking mask.

A deafening roar left my lips as I exploded. One of my shadows pulled the woman closest to Evie down to the ground and dragged her backward.

Another angled toward the man who wielded the vines, merely popping his head off his neck.

The vines instantly rotted, releasing a shaking, horrified Evie from their hold.

My dagger was in my palm the moment the third born rushed me, and I took the greatest of pleasure in throwing and landing the dagger straight into his neck. He gurgled and choked, my shadows rotting his insides from within.

I snapped, and the dagger flew back to me, just in time for the born woman to attempt her own attack. My shadows yanked her dagger from her palms as she writhed, and I slowly tightened the hold around her chest as she heaved for air. I sheathed my dagger back in its holster as she took her final breath, my shadows crushing all of her bones and guts until she was nothing but vampire mush.

Evie wrapped her arms around her stomach, panting and trembling. My gaze homed in on all the places the vines had left deep pink marks on her milky skin. The rain grew heavier.

I glowered at her, and she trembled harder, her teeth beginning to chatter. She glanced at her feet, then quickly rushed to place her books back in her bag and move them against the tree where it was dry.

Great. Glad she was able to protect her work from the rain before what came next.

"I'll give you a five second head start, baby," I said with a grin that didn't meet my wrathful eyes.

Evie hesitated for half a second before she took off.

36

EVIE

My lungs burned. The forest floor was damp, the rain steady. Running was futile now. It was merely a performance. Kylo's dark laughter echoed through the woods, and it made me feel stupid, childish—like an injured rabbit trying to outrun a wolf.

More than that, it was as if the universe itself was laughing at me. Taunting me. Because all I could do in this life was run, over and over again, even if the tactic didn't make sense anymore.

My body moved, but I went nowhere.

The lesson was smacking me in the face at this point, even as I put my hands over my ears and shut my eyes to the truth.

In front of me, a shadow in the shape of a man appeared. I skidded to a stop, immediately turning to dart in the opposite direction.

I slammed into a rigid body. The air deflated from my lungs.

"Wanna try again?" Kylo asked. He looked down at my feet. "I may have to buy my adorable little forest nymph yet another pair of sneakers."

I stared up into his eyes—and I saw something inside them

262

that I didn't recognize. It wasn't fury or disappointment or any human emotion I could discern.

It was frighteningly vampiric. His pupils were dilated, his eyes a dark storm, his lips a smile that veered on the edge of psychopathic.

Cold terror coated my skin along with the rain. Because I didn't see the man who brushed my hair with tenderness.

I saw a monster.

More laughter followed me as I took him up on his offer to run again. I knew I could use my power. I knew I wasn't without defense.

But it was too risky. My power was what had attracted those born in the first place.

Kylo was right. About all of it. I needed training. I needed to stop running. Or I was going to put myself and everyone I loved in danger.

My legs continued to pump. Leaves and twigs crunched under my feet. Tears began to blur with the rain as they streaked down my cheeks, all of these pent-up emotions boiling over into a release that was more grief than violence.

This time, when a being appeared in front of me, he was solid. He was a dark god, a being that didn't belong in this world. The bastard son of Lillian, a blasphemy of humanity.

Kylo bared his fangs, and his shadows shot through the air in smoke and whispers. They solidified around my limbs. I couldn't yank free. The more I struggled, the tighter they became. My monster stalked forward, still grinning, his eyes more deranged than before.

He nearly looked like he was holding his breath.

"I told you what would happen if you ever tried to hide from me," he growled. His voice boomed against the tall evergreens.

More and more shadows coiled around me like snakes.

"It was my only stipulation in the deal *you* proposed. You agreed to the terms of your own free will."

I couldn't think straight—couldn't remember what he was talking about. His power was deafening, a call to bend at the knees.

And the sickest part of all was the way my core turned molten. The way my body craved him.

The way I'd wanted this monster to catch me.

Kylo's nostrils flared. His gaze was piercing as it moved from my face to between my legs. A shadow teased between my thighs, and I whimpered.

At that noise, Kylo's eyes nearly rolled back. He cursed.

Then he lunged.

I was on the ground with a hand around my throat before I knew what was happening.

"You. Will. Never. Be. Able. To. Hide. From. Me. Again." His words scraped out of him as his jaw flexed, and his fingers squeezed the sides of my throat.

The bundle of nerves between my thighs ached. I channeled power to scald his hand.

When he released me with a hiss, he chuckled, his smile cruel. He peeled me off the forest floor and held me in his lap so that my back was to his chest. His power rattled my bones. I couldn't channel, couldn't resist him.

Not even when he leaned forward and sunk his fangs into his own wrist.

"No," I whispered, my voice a scratchy rasp.

He was going to make me swallow those beads of crimson so that he would know where I was at all times—so I would be forever bound to him by blood.

I squirmed. Shadows coiled.

"Don't you fucking move," Kylo said.

The onyx limbs pulled my legs apart.

Blood spilled from Kylo's wrist.

My next plea came out in a scream. "Please, no!"

In a blur of movement, he'd taken his opportunity to press

his wrist up against my open mouth. I tried to clamp down, but the flesh of his arm prevented it. Strange-tasting, powerful copper flowed across my tongue.

"Swallow, baby," Kylo said, his voice softer now.

His cock twitched against my ass, impossibly big and hard.

His other hand raked through my hair in soothing strokes. "Shh, shh, shh," he soothed as I coughed and struggled and fought. "Be my perfect good girl and *swallow*."

My mouth pooled with blood and saliva. Tears ran down my cheeks. Cool air tickled my exposed skin beneath my drenched dress. Shadows still held my thighs apart, spread wide and bared to the dark, rainy forest.

Kylo forced my head back, and blood slid down my throat. Scrambling for air and on the verge of retching, I swallowed.

As soon as I did, Kylo started combing through my hair again. I swallowed more, and I stopped struggling. Depraved desire pooled in my stomach before traveling lower. I sucked in air. I leaned into Kylo's soft touch.

"That's it, angel. I knew you could be a good listener for me," he cooed, kissing my head as his own breathing became shallow. His cock twitched again, pressing into my ass as he lightly rocked his hips.

He slowly removed his arm from my mouth, painting my lips with his blood as he did. The hand returned to my throat.

"You're mine, Evie," he whispered. "You were always mine. But now, your body has been marked the same as your soul."

A shadow dipped beneath my soaked cotton panties. Another yanked them to the side, exposing me further.

I gasped as a cool, skin-like tip brushed my entrance.

"Good little angels get rewarded," Kylo whispered into my hair, his voice still strained with lust.

My body was charged with electricity, my skin screaming for touch. I'd never felt more alive.

I'd never felt safer, more protected and held.

I arched my back, and the shadow limb plunged inside me.

A cry left my lips.

"Shh," Kylo whispered. "You can take it."

It was bigger than anything I'd ever had before, perhaps the size of three of Kylo's fingers. I was full and panting and covered in blood, and I couldn't get enough of it. I couldn't get enough of *him*.

The only man capable of catching me—of forcing me to stop running when I couldn't do it myself.

The shadow angled against that spot inside me that had me moaning and trembling. As it pumped, Kylo's cock pressed harder against me. His teeth scraped the shell of my ear. The sharpened points of his fangs made me shudder.

His bloody hand dipped between my legs and found my clit.

"Fucking mine," he growled.

My whimpers transformed into a scream as he targeted my clit and the shadow somehow grew inside me, filling me to my limit.

I bared down, my legs shaking as I fell over the edge and rode a wave of release for longer than I thought possible.

Kylo's second hand covered my mouth, stifling my scream as he chuckled.

"With my blood and shadow inside of you, your veins flooded with your release and fear..." He groaned, hips still rocking. "I've never scented anything more maddening."

His shadow slowly eased out of me, and I felt empty. I was drunk with pleasure and darkness. I needed more.

The shadows holding my legs were looser now. I made slow, careful movements, twisting to straddle Kylo. My core met the bulge in his pants as I locked my eyes on his. His hands dug into my hips. He flashed fangs as I pressed down.

"Evie..." he groaned. "You don't know what you're doing."

I glared. "Then teach me."

Kylo's eyes really did roll back this time. A muscle in his jaw feathered. "That is not what I meant, angel," he said, as if each word scraped up his throat like glass. He cursed, his grip painful now as his fingers dug into my flesh. "You aren't ready for me. Not yet. Not like this."

I ground against his cock, my clit somehow still aching for more. "Please," I begged, needing all of him.

Kylo's eyes flew open. "Greedy little creature," he growled. He tore down my dress, freeing my breasts as he squeezed each nipple.

I whimpered, and he grinned. He sucked one of the nipples into his mouth, swirling his tongue soothingly before scraping his fangs against the sensitive skin. I gasped, the pain transforming into pleasure in some wicked form of alchemy.

He stared angrily into my eyes. "You want to be taught another lesson, baby? Fine. Get on your knees and open your mouth."

My heart stumbled. I did as I was told, feeding off his praise, desperate to please him like he only continued to pleasure me without any reward.

"Good girl," he said, brushing a thumb over my parted lips. "Wider."

I opened my mouth wider. My gaze dropped to his pants, where he was unbuckling his belt. Anticipation was a forceful sensation in my blood. I'd fantasized about seeing him—all of him—every day since we met, no matter how many times the thoughts felt like a curse that plagued me against my will.

I wanted to taste him just as he so desperately wished to taste me.

His cock sprung free, and I couldn't help but gasp. My eyes went wide.

It was larger than my imagination had allowed, thick, hard and dangerous in a way that made my mouth water on instinct.

Kylo gripped my hair at the base of my scalp. He sharply inhaled. "Having second thoughts, baby?"

I gazed up at him.

Another unconscious groan left his lips when my eyes found his. His grip on my hair tightened, and his other hand slowly stroked his length.

"Why is it so big?" I blurted, my cheeks instantly reddening.

Kylo looked two seconds away from unraveling, and the sight of it drove a mix of fear and lust to my core. He chuckled darkly.

"Gods above, Evie," he hissed. He moved forward, painting my lips with the beads of moisture at his tip. "Taste me."

I licked my lips, letting the saltiness coat my tongue. I swallowed down my fear and kept my mouth open as Kylo praised me.

He entered my mouth slowly as I acclimated to the size of him.

"That's my sweet angel," he said, his voice raw as his body shuddered with pleasure. "Misbehaving brats get their throats fucked."

His cock slid in deeper.

"But you've already paid for your transgressions by letting me claim you with my blood, so I'm going to warm you up first," he said. He slowly rocked in and out as my eyes watered. "Breathe, angel. Relaxing makes it easier."

The way he was teaching me, as if I were one of his students being tutored, made me slick with need in the most perverse of ways.

I tried to inhale as he sunk deeper. A primal noise escaped his throat as he held me in place, forcing me to take every inch.

When I gagged, his cock only throbbed inside my mouth—as if Kylo enjoyed the noise, reveling in my discomfort.

"Look up at me," he said, the command throaty and swimming with desire.

I met his eyes, and he gave me another inch. I tried to pull away, but he kept me still, hushing me and consoling me as tears ran down my cheeks.

"So fucking pretty." He showed me his fangs, his tongue running across them as if soothing some kind of ache. "You are so fucking pretty with my cock shoved down your throat, tears running down those rosy cheeks, and my blood smeared across your lips."

He raised the intensity, pumping in and out, a little deeper and faster each time. When I gagged and struggled, he gave me a break to suck in air.

Drool dribbled down my skin. A shadow crept between my legs, rubbing against my clit.

"The pleasure will help you take more," Kylo explained.

I moaned, and Kylo was more violent with his next thrust, turning my moan into a gurgle as he smiled down at me wickedly.

My hips rocked against the shadow, and the pleasure did allow me to take more of Kylo as he used me mercilessly.

Suddenly his grip on my hair tightened, his cock lodged deep, and his shadow yanked back as I struggled.

"Do you understand what almost happened to you in these woods, Evie?" he suddenly growled as I choked on him. "Do you understand what those born demons would've done to you if I hadn't arrived? They could've tortured and killed you for what you are. They could've subdued your power and taken you as a slave."

I felt his raw anger with every violent thrust.

"Nod if you fucking understand me, angel," Kylo said through a clenched jaw, glaring down at me.

With his cock down my throat and his grip on my head, I managed a tiny nod.

"I can feel every beat of your wounded, frightened heart, little one," Kylo said. "I will be able to hear it no matter how far away you are until the end of time."

I should've hated his guts, but I didn't. Something tight inside me yielded, like a long exhale.

"You will never be unsafe again. I will protect you forever."

I looked up into his hooded eyes—those deep blue pools of certainty, possessiveness, and violence.

The tip of shadow was back between my thighs, coaxing me back toward release.

He must've seen it in my face—the submission, the crumbling of that defensive fortress—the one whose walls he'd vaulted right over.

Kylo had already burrowed himself deep inside me, before he'd forced his blood down my throat. Only the gods could rid me of him now.

I moaned against him as I fell over the edge. My body trembled with the force of my second orgasm.

Kylo's cock jerked violently. "Swallow every last drop, baby."

With a growl, he unloaded into my mouth, coating my tongue with his cum. He withdrew slowly, and I did as I was told.

He scooped me into his arms. His lips brushed my forehead and then my lips. "You are perfect, Evie." His voice was soft as it skated across my skin, and I melted into his arms. "I think I've always been waiting for you. My soul recognized yours the moment I saw you."

My hand trembled as it reached for his face, and he leaned into my touch with a small smile.

I almost kept my mouth closed. I almost chose to hide again.

"My soul knows yours too," I whispered to The Devil who held me in his clutches.

Kylo looked at me like I was the cosmos itself, as if I held his every last dream in my palms.

"Let me in, Evie," he said. "Let me love you."

I went rigid in his arms, my lips parting. He hadn't said the words—not quite. But it was close enough to make me squirm, to make fearful tears bloom in my eyes.

I kissed him. I locked my lips with his as if I could taste the truth in his skin. As if I could ascertain the weight of his words and guarantee he wouldn't abandon me, that he really was going to keep me safe, that he wasn't just using me for some game of power.

Memories reached from the abyss—from a farmhouse in the rolling hills in the countryside—and I kept that door locked tight.

Kylo broke away. "Why are you crying, sweet girl?"

I needed to know that the past wouldn't repeat itself. I wanted to beg him to reassure me, but that would mean I'd need to open the door and reveal what I'd locked away long ago.

I shook my head. "I don't want to love you."

Kylo smiled. "Well, that's too bad."

37

EVIE

Everything changed the moment I swallowed Kylo's blood.

He carried me through his bedroom to the bathroom, placing me on the tile as he kissed my forehead. The bathroom was spacious and decadent, with a large bathtub and an even larger shower. The fixtures and faucets had brass finishes, and the walls were a moody forest green. Everything in Kylo's home was so very *Kylo*. Dark and sophisticated, with a secret warmth and brightness underpinning it all.

All of his anger at my revenge plot had completely melted away.

Even stranger, so had mine.

And maybe it was all temporary, just the haze of dark lust and power and obsession, the natural release of buried emotion and yearning.

I didn't know. Sometimes it felt like I didn't know anything anymore.

And right now, that was okay.

"I would much prefer to run you a bath, baby," Kylo said,

272

"but it seems our new habit of rolling around in the mud has made showering the more reasonable option."

I nodded, wrinkling my nose at the thought of bathing in a vat of dirt and blood. "Agreed."

Kylo looked back at me with a grin, his eyes flashing for a moment. "Stop being so damn cute. It makes me want to mark every inch of you."

My eyes widened. He let the water warm as his words infected me with heat and curiosity.

Water fell like rain from the shower head, and I approached the soothing steam and smell of mint and eucalyptus.

Kylo was quick to kiss my forehead, his hand finding mine. "May I undress you, little one?"

I nodded. He was so gentle with me that I struggled to remember the foundation of violence this house was built on, the darkness that lived under his skin.

The same as what lived under mine.

That little dimple in his cheek was a weapon of its own. I brushed my fingertips across it, and Kylo kissed my hand.

"What did I say about being cute?"

"I can't help it. It's just my nature."

He rolled his eyes as he helped me out of my dress. "I'm glad you're finally owning up to your evil little tricks. I was growing quite tired of being the only one accused of sex demon powers."

The teasing smile evaporated the moment my dress fell to the floor. I squirmed under the weight of Kylo's sudden silence, his stare that penetrated straight through me and into my soul. I'd never been looked at this way.

"Evie... you are *perfect*," he whispered reverently, as if he were speaking about some artistic masterpiece. He stepped closer to me, then crouched. His touch was impossibly gentle as he pulled my panties to the floor.

His fingertips skimmed back up my legs, and I shuddered when he kissed my upper thigh. When he kissed just above my pussy, inhaling deeply, my stomach fluttered in a way that was disorienting.

He kissed my stomach next, and that act felt strangely more intimate in ways I couldn't quite put into words. He was slow to rise. His palms skated over my breasts, squeezing before he circled each nipple.

A moan escaped my lips, and my core was suddenly pulsing. It was as if he were exploring every piece of me—this body that he'd claimed by blood.

And yet, it was more than sexual. It was an act of worship. The look in his deep blue eyes was equal parts primal and adoring.

When he straightened back up, he was still silent for a moment as he grasped my chin. His other hand still explored my body, cupping my ass next as I gasped. It was as if he couldn't stop—couldn't get enough of me the same way I couldn't get enough of him.

"I don't have words for the hold you have over me, angel," he said softly. "There is no end to the depths of my obsession. Every inch of your body, every beat of your vulnerable heart, every shade of your multitudinous soul, and every thought in your beautiful mind—I *need* to see it all, to possess it all. Because you already possess me. I fear the lengths I would go, the distances I would travel, the atrocities I would commit to keep you safe. Or merely to ensure you always know just how much I adore you."

My eyes welled. Because there was no way to run from Kylo and his earnestness, the look of utter devotion in his gaze. Each of his words burrowed deep inside of me, winning over even my most distrusting parts.

I didn't know what to say, so instead of speaking, I simply melted into his chest. He slowly wrapped his arms around me. He kissed the top of my head. He held me like this, unyielding, until I finally pulled away.

Those pools of blue were ripe with emotion, his brows slightly drawn. It looked like something hard inside him had softened. He exhaled deeply, as if with some great relief.

Wordlessly, Kylo peeled off his muddy shirt and stepped out of his pants. I had to remind myself to breathe when his boxers came off.

A chuckle rumbled through his chest. "My eyes are up here, angel."

I cleared my throat. I dragged my gaze up from his semi-hard, frighteningly large appendage, but I didn't make it very far. Because now I was unabashedly staring at his finely tuned abs and chest—the hardened muscles and constellation of tattoos in sigil-like structures. The midnight blue and dark purple hues of some of the designs shimmered slightly, and they reminded me of the cosmos themselves.

Kylo's cocky grin didn't melt an inch as he pulled me through the glass shower doors and under the inviting, steady stream of hot water that fell like rain.

"Hey—it's my turn now. I didn't rush *you*," I said indignantly, now staring at his stupidly beautiful nude form as water droplets streaked down his skin.

"My apologies, baby. Please do take your time."

Kylo reached for a bottle of soap as my hands roamed his chest, tracing the sigils. I stared deeper into the magickal fabric, searching for their properties. When one of them burned my fingertip, I yelped.

"You okay?" Kylo asked, tipping my chin up. When I nodded, he shook his head with a teasing glint in his eyes. "Naughty little witch. You should know better than to pry into another crafty chaos magician's work."

I huffed. I didn't enjoy being on the other end of sneaky magick, as hypocritical as it was.

"You'll meet my maker soon enough," Kylo said.

My heart stuttered, and I frowned.

"Don't be afraid," Kylo said. He lathered the soap in his hands. "He's going to help you manage your magick. I would never let anyone near you who wasn't loyal to me and safe for you."

When I didn't protest, Kylo released another breath. I could see it now—what I'd been so unwilling and much too paranoid to see before.

The sheer intensity of Kylo's care for me.

The care that wasn't merely words; it was in every action, every unconscious instinct, every gentle touch, every romantic gesture, every apology, every response to my desires and needs and boundaries.

I didn't know it was possible for a man to treat me this way. Like I wasn't too sensitive or strange or childish or irritating, unworthy of pleasure, attentiveness, and patience.

Jacob didn't just fail to live up to my romantic ideal—as if romance was this lofty, unattainable concept only found in *fiction*, as he liked to remind me—but he also failed at basic human decency. If put to the test, I didn't think Jacob would risk anything at all to shield me from danger.

He'd already made it abundantly clear that he didn't care enough to protect my heart. Why would I think he'd protect any other piece of me?

I mulled over this sharp contrast between the past and the present as Kylo whispered for me to close my eyes. He gently massaged the soap into my face, letting his blood that he'd smeared around my lips wash away.

I could clean my own face, but I let Kylo do it anyway. Because I saw how much it satisfied him to take care of me, and now that I'd let him in, I could finally admit how much it satisfied me too.

While my eyes were closed, Kylo's lips met mine. I was being claimed all over again, his lips dominating mine, his tongue invading my mouth before he tore himself away.

"Open."

I opened my eyes. My stomach dropped, as it so often did when confronted with his lethal beauty.

"I'm ready," I blurted.

Kylo blinked. He slowly lifted a brow.

My cheeks felt hot, and I knew they were reddening when a grin spread across Kylo's lips.

"I mean, I'm not—" Oh gods. I took a deep breath and started over as Kylo searched my face with growing amusement. "I've never been afraid of sex. I wasn't holding back for idealistic or religious reasons or anything. In fact, there was a time I just wanted to get it over with as soon as possible."

Kylo frowned. I noted the way his jaw ticked, and his muscles hardened. "Why?"

"Do I really need to say it aloud?" I whispered.

Kylo had already hinted at what he suspected about my past —the reason I was always running, or why I hated vampires. If he was an ancient clan leader, surely he'd connected the dots on his own.

"Yes, you do," Kylo said sternly. "Why would you want to lose your virginity as quickly as possible?"

I went utterly still. The part of me that wanted to open up to Kylo, to please him, to be vulnerable and honest—that part was at war with my overwhelming urge to keep the door to the past locked tight.

Kylo's features softened, even as the room filled with the unmistakable hum of dark power. He held my face in his hands, forcing me to focus back on his eyes.

"Why, angel?"

The words escaped me against my will. "Because then I'd no longer be pure, which would mean I was worthless," I said. "And therefore, *safe.*"

Kylo flinched as if I'd hit him. "Evie..."

He searched my eyes, but I felt farther and farther away, as if

I wasn't entirely in this room anymore. Like I was floating backward.

"Hey," he said, his voice a sharp hook that reeled me back to the present. "You're safe, baby. Come back to me."

I blinked several times. I started to feel the steam again, listening for the noise of the water hitting the tile.

Kylo slowly turned me so that my back was to his chest, and he was massaging shampoo into my scalp.

I relaxed into his touch, the kisses to my temple and cheek. "I'm sor—"

"Please don't apologize, angel. I'm sorry for being so insistent. I only want to know where you come from so I can understand you better and protect you. Not only physically, but mentally and emotionally too."

I swallowed. I let myself come out of fight-or-flight as Kylo continued to wash my hair.

"My point is that I don't feel that way anymore," I murmured. "I don't want to get it over with. Um, I was trying to say that... I *want* to do that with *you.*"

"Duly noted," Kylo whispered. His lips brushed the shell of my ear, and tingling pleasure radiated through my entire body. "I sort of got the message when your needy little pussy was grinding on my lap in the forest..."

More heat flushed in my cheeks, and his cock pressed against my back.

"... however, you know I need my good girl to use her words when she wants something." He spun me around, his thumb brushing against my lips. His eyes darkened. "*That* will be a whole other kind of claiming. One that I'm not ready for."

I deflated, my stomach sinking.

Kylo must've immediately read the disappointment and self-doubt in my features. He grabbed my waist, pulling me against him. "Not because I'm not endlessly, irrationally devoted to you, angel. But because I fear what such an act would do to my self-control, already pushed to its absolute fucking limits."

His cock rested against my stomach, hard and imposing. I homed in on the tips of his fangs.

"Would feeding from me help?" I asked quietly.

Kylo shut his eyes. His cock spasmed. His grip on me tightened to the point of pain. But I didn't move, holding my breath as if that might save me from the monster who thirsted for my blood.

"Stay still," he rasped. "Please."

His nostrils flared. He gritted his teeth.

"I—"

His hand instantly covered my mouth. He took several deep breaths.

The sickest part of all was that I was feeding off this rare version of Kylo—the version of him that sounded desperate— that wasn't a being of perfect authority and dominance.

It made me feel strangely powerful, to know I had this effect on him. That I was the only one capable of pushing him to his limits.

Sicker yet was this growing, multiplying curiosity.

Of what it would feel like—for me, for him—to allow him to feed from my essence, to grow stronger from my blood. To be addicted to me, irreversibly.

My sexual virginity was not the only thing that made me valuable to the born. Blood virginity was just as prized, if not more so.

I never thought that would be something I'd be willing to lose until now.

"Thank you for listening, baby," Kylo finally said, reaching for more soap as his muscles still trembled with power and restraint. "Yes, I'd imagine that feeding from you would help." He laughed dryly. "But that would require your words as well. And the acknowledgement that once I taste you, I will struggle to feed from any other source. I will do so, of course, for my sake and yours. But that's not something to take lightly. And not something I will ever force upon you."

Something unfamiliar crawled up my spine, this strange form of anger. "I don't want you to feed from anyone else."

Kylo halted, his sudsy hands halfway down my arms. He stared hard into my eyes. "Gods above, Evie." He pushed me back against the wall, careful to shield my head from the impact. "My angel is greedy for my touch, my cock, my fangs, and now she wants me all to herself, hmm? How quickly things change…"

I glared at him, and he shoved my wrists up above my head. His thigh snuck between my legs, rubbing against my core. I whimpered before I could stop myself, already slick with need.

One of his hands kept my wrists in place while the other massaged soap against my breasts, kneading my flesh and playing with my nipples in ways that were equally pleasurable and painful.

Though even the pain was quick to melt into ecstasy.

"Erase that bratty look from your face or I'll give you a reason to pout," he hissed, though his eyes swam with amusement. "I'm yours, baby. Been yours for a while now. You're the one who was slow to catch up."

He rinsed the soap from his hand in the water behind him, and in a flash, he was gripping my pussy. One of his fingers plunged inside me.

I cried out, and he kissed my forehead.

"So tight around my finger, angel, yet you think you're ready to take my cock?"

A second finger plunged inside me, and he angled and pulsed. My eyes rolled back, my legs already trembling as I was flooded with pleasure.

"Uh-uh," Kylo said, pulling out and leaving me needy and

panting. He grinned. "There's that adorable little pout I was talking about."

He peeled me off the wall and back under the shower head, rinsing me off as I glowered like a soaked cat.

"Shh. We're finishing this damn shower so I can get you in my bed and devour you whole."

My frown melted, my eyes going wide. I stared at his mouth, looking for those deadly, sharpened canines.

"Not like that," he said with a smirk.

38

KYLO

Words couldn't describe the weight that had been lifted from my shoulders now that I'd finally forced my blood down Evie's little throat.

There was nowhere she could run to ever be free of me. I would be able to keep her safe forever.

But even more satisfying was seeing Evie's walls finally crumble. She'd let me in. And I cherished her trust in me, her beautiful vulnerability, more than anything in this world.

What she'd let slip about impurity making her *worthless* only confirmed my greatest fears. That Evie's past was gruesome. It was no wonder she'd learned to run, to stay vigilant and guarded, to protect her human brother at all costs.

For her to trust someone like me in spite of her suffering was a gift that melted my cold, dead heart at its core.

I'd grown accustomed to the piercing ache of my fangs by now, only occasionally needing to take deep breaths and sober myself as a precaution against bloodlust. But gods, it was only getting stronger. My need for her. My growing dependence that would lock into place irreversibly the moment her blood met my tongue.

282

But Evie made no move to ask me to feed from her, and I would protect her boundaries at all costs.

When I threw her on the bed, she giggled, and the sound squeezed at my heart in a way that only she could pull off. She made me feel so human. So raw.

I was obsessed with her perfect body, this body I'd claimed by blood. I kissed both sides of her smiling mouth before sucking on her neck. I relished the way she arched toward me, her fingers brushing through my hair.

She moaned, and gods above and below, I couldn't get enough of her sounds. Her cries of pleasure, her desperate pleading, her squeals of pain. I fucking loved them all.

I sucked on a nipple harshly just to hear her moan turn into a cry before releasing the sensitive peak.

The only marks I left were love bites, a trail that went all the way to her stomach. I sucked on the flesh above her womb, that same preoccupation consuming my mind with the idea of Evie carrying my child.

It was a primal, possessive urge—yet another way to claim her, to publicly mark her in the eyes of the world as *mine*. But it was also a desire that felt uniquely human, an off-shoot of my adoration for her, my need to protect what was mine and give her all of myself.

At the thought of her breasts swelling, her stomach rounding with my seed planted inside her, my cock was ready to bury deep.

Not that turned vampires were capable of reproduction.

When my lips met her folds, I wasted no time pulling her aching clit into my mouth and creating a pulsing sensation. She bucked, and I slipped my hands under her and lifted her hips as I feasted. I sucked at her sensitive flesh before moving my tongue down her seam, tasting all of her, circling that needy entrance before plunging inside. I moved back up slowly, closing over her sensitive flesh again.

Evie's moans were a drug as potent as her sweet, earthy taste. I couldn't get enough of *any* of it. The last time I'd devoured her, the scent of her lingering on me was the only thing that had kept me sane. Washing her off my face felt like blasphemy.

"Mm-hmm," I praised wordlessly, letting my voice vibrate across her desperate center. "You're being so good for me. Do you still want more, baby?"

"Yes," she whispered.

"Manners," I corrected.

She paused. "Yes, please."

"Good girl. Keep those legs spread. Do you trust me, Evie?"

She paused again. "Yes."

I ran two fingers down her slick core, dipping inside her before moving lower, teasing her second hole.

"Do I need to reclaim this hole for myself, baby? Or has it never been played with before?"

Evie shuddered, and her growing fear and need for release created the most mouthwatering symphony of scents in her blood.

"No, never," she whispered.

"Is that a limit? Or are you open to exploring?"

My slick fingers continued their teasing circle as I waited, merely brushing over the tight entrance as Evie squirmed.

"It's not a limit. I'm open to exploring."

"Thank you for being vulnerable and using your words, baby," I praised her. "I'm going to claim your ass now, and you're going to say *thank you*. Understood?"

She made some sort of adorable breathy sound that I interpreted as an affirmative.

"Relax," I instructed. "It's going to feel strange at first, but if you relax, it will become pleasurable."

I spit on her tight little hole, and one of my slick fingers slowly moved past the entrance. My mouth closed over her clit again, sucking and driving her back toward an orgasm, distracting her as she acclimated to this new, uncomfortable sensation.

I nearly laughed with satisfaction as the finger slowly, gently eased deeper, and I unlocked a brand-new Evie noise.

"Feels… mmm…"

This time I couldn't help but chuckle at her inability to form words. "Breathe, sweet girl. You're doing so well. What do we say?"

"Thank you, Kylo," she managed, raspy and slurred.

My tongue lapped at her as she trembled and moaned louder. As soon as I began pulsing again, I pushed the finger in her ass to the hilt.

Evie's orgasm was violent. She nearly screamed as her body tensed and squirmed. I held her in place, forcing her to take every sensation as she crashed down around me.

I felt her muscles spasm around my finger, her juices coating my face as I let her ride wave after violent wave. When she was nothing but a puddle of thoughtless euphoria on my bed, I slowly eased out of her.

I left her for only a minute to clean up, and when I returned, she was flushed and breathless. Those pretty gray eyes were wide, and her features relaxed when she saw me. The fact that my presence soothed her was everything I could ask for.

I cleaned her up with a warm, damp towel before pulling her into my arms.

"No talk, brain blank," she whispered.

"Understood." I searched her face for any signs of dissociation or displeasure, finding only calm satisfaction in her angelic features.

When she wrapped herself around me like a vine, I was equally content. My shadows finally escaped my skin to billow over her. They needed her close, as if they were as desperately, heedlessly in love with Evie as I was.

As I cooked dinner, Evie did that cute thing she did when she followed me around like a baby duck. I grinned at her as she shifted around the kitchen as I did, telling me about her new candle spell idea.

I didn't even think she realized she was doing it. I'd walk to the stove, and she'd follow me there, then I'd walk back to the counter, and she'd move in tandem.

"Why are you smiling at me like that?" she suddenly asked, mid-stream-of-thought.

I shrugged. "No reason. I love how passionate you are. Are these beings you call spirits all ancestral? Or are they more than that?"

She launched back into her enthusiastic dialogue, being the perfect good girl she was and always staying within my reach.

"No, some are deities and others are unrecognizable, strange beings. I'm not entirely sure what all of them are, just beings of the otherworld. Like faeries and nature spirits, and sometimes beings of the heavens or hells. It's easier to call them all spirits, or allies. There are some allies who have been with me since birth, I suspect because they're some sort of ancestor—whether literally or in a more cosmic, spiritual sense, from past incarnations. Others come and go depending on what I'm working on. When I do spell work, it can be like putting up a job application. I call to me spirits who might be interested in helping me, which can add more players to my team. But occasionally the demands they make in return aren't something I'm interested in. It has to go both ways. Things don't usually turn nasty unless blatant disrespect is involved. The otherworld is very forgiving when one approaches with politeness, reciprocity, clear intentions, and earnestness. I actually think the gods and the realm of the spirit have more of a sense of humor than most earthly beings I've encountered."

I could listen to Evie speak for hours.

For a moment, I just stood there, processing her words with my knife hovering above a hot pepper.

"You have this whole other world you're living in, at all times, don't you?" I asked her.

Evie batted those long lashes, her gray eyes bright. She shrugged, suddenly very interested in the platter of cheeses and crackers I'd set out for her.

"With all the reading and magick and visioning, sometimes it feels like there are more than just two worlds," she said softly. "Like there are infinite."

"How do you ground yourself?" I returned to chopping the pepper. The aroma of sautéing vegetables and simmering rice filled the air.

Evie looked back up at me. "I don't open myself up to a lot of visioning unless I'm in a trance state, or if the force making contact is especially powerful. Like a deity." Her eyes glazed over for a moment, as if remembering something. "That way when I'm here in the physical dimension, I don't tend to see things with my physical eyes that don't belong. Only mild enhancements, such as auras, but mostly I see messages or intuition inside my own mind. I have no interest in losing touch with the world in which I live. There has to be a balance, or witches can lose their way. If too much of you is in the ethereal, then you're not really living. And living—truly immersing yourself in your own mortality—is kind of the whole point of being here at all."

I watched her take a bite of cheese on a cracker as she stared off into space. She was unlike anyone I'd ever met. The way she spoke felt ancient, far beyond her years. I wanted to consume those pretty pink lips again, to leave her breathless as I searched for the bottom of her mysterious depths.

She glanced over at me, searching my face for my reaction. "I'm sorry. I know I've been rambling. I know it all probably sounds—"

"Beautiful?" I interjected. "Eloquent? Thoughtful? Powerful?"

Evie's mouth closed. Her eyes sparked with such lovely surprise.

"Why are you so used to apologizing for your own existence? It quite honestly makes me murderous," I growled.

She shifted on her feet, toying with another cracker. "No one has ever shared your reactions to my magick or musings," she said softly. "The owners at Celeste's are—*were*—safe, but I was never able to talk about more than just green witchcraft for my own protection. Idris and Mena let me rattle on, but that's because they're family. Others haven't really liked hearing me talk about these things."

I carried the cutting board to the rice dish, scraping the bits of red into the mixture and stirring. Evie's sudden presence at my side was almost enough to melt my growing frown.

"Why did you stay with him, Evie?" I asked her.

She went rigid.

I walked to the sink, deeply cleansing the spicy pepper from my hands with soap.

When I turned back to her, she was looking at the ground. "I thought I was the problem," she said with a shrug, her cheeks reddening as if with embarrassment. "I believed the best in Jacob, because I saw why he was the way he was. His parents, his friends, his fears. He had really good reasons for everything —for why he shouldn't have to make certain efforts for me, why I was unreasonable, why I needed too much from him. I thought if only I was a better, more accommodating version of myself, then maybe I could convince him to love me and be kind to me."

Her eyes were glued to her white frilly socks. She sighed,

slowly raising her gaze to mine. Her smile was sad, but her big gray irises glimmered as if with newfound strength.

"I stayed because I always hoped it would be better."

What a heartbreaking admission. I wanted to slit Jason's throat all over again.

"Of course you did, angel," I said softly, kissing her forehead and stroking her cheek. "I fucking love your hopefulness."

Gods. That idiot had Evie convinced that he was the best she could do, and that in and of itself was a tragedy. I was nearly vibrating with irritation. I converted it into fuel, into motivation to undo every single negative belief a lesser man had planted into Evie's beautiful soul.

"I love your compassion, too," I said. I held her face in my hands. "But the majority of people don't go through life intentionally harming people. Just because someone can rationalize the pain they inflict doesn't mean you need to shove your feelings under the rug for them. Your feelings matter, Evie. Just as much as someone's *logic*."

She looked doubtful, like she didn't quite believe me, but wanted to desperately.

"He sounds lazy, immature, and selfish."

Something sparked in Evie's eyes, as if I were giving words to her most buried truths.

"I'm glad he's not in your life anymore."

I was also glad that I'd made him piss himself with fear like the man baby he was.

"You were never the problem," I said, stroking her silky blonde hair. "When parents neglect us emotionally, we may grow up to unconsciously repeat that same pattern in other relationships. Because it's comfortable. This belief that we are deficient, that we need to earn another's love by being someone we're not. Because we were taught that who we are authentically will never be good enough."

"Stop," Evie said, just like she had after I'd brushed her hair, when I told her she was worthy. "Please stop."

"Okay," I said, watching those soft, frightened lips curl.

"I have no interest in being psychoanalyzed. Let's leave the past in the past where it belongs."

When she spoke of magick, she sounded ancient and wise. Now, I saw plainly her innocence, her youth.

Because anyone who'd been around a while knew that the past refused to be left behind so easily.

39

EVIE

Kylo stopped prying into my past, and for that, I was grateful. The rest of the evening nearly made me forget his own origins. The fact that he was a vampire clan leader, likely responsible for hundreds of deaths in his immortal life.

Yet, where there used to be only disgust, I now felt growing curiosity and understanding. As my heart opened to Kylo, so too did it open to the possibility that perhaps not all violence was deplorable.

He'd saved my life three times now, murdering born in the process. And I didn't mourn a single one of those demons.

My distrust was still baked deep, but it was considerably less feral than before.

I nestled deeper into Kylo's lap as he read to me in the living room, this ancient mythological text on faerie lore he knew I'd enjoy.

He paused to kiss the top of my head. "Will you stay here tonight, angel?"

The softness in the request made my stomach flutter. "If I don't, you'll just follow me home…"

"Obviously."

I bent my head toward one of his outstretched arms and sunk my teeth into his rigid muscles. Kylo gripped my hair at the scalp and yanked me back to stare hard into my eyes.

His lips curved. "Baby, did you just bite me?"

I lifted a shoulder, the corners of my lips tipping up. "Your arms are just so bitable."

His laugh was dark, rumbling straight through me. He closed the book and set it on the coffee table, all the while holding me by my hair like I was a kitten picked up by the scruff.

"I could say the same about you," he said, low and dangerous. He let go of my hair, making a motion with his finger for me to turn in his arms and face him.

I twisted to straddle him, my heart continuing to stumble as I watched that little dimple form in his otherwise ruthless features.

"In the morning, I have to return to my clan," Kylo said.

Of course, he did. He'd already been away from whatever it was that he did for an entire day. I wondered if he secretly resented me for keeping him from his work with my escape attempt. I knew I'd driven him out of his mind. And part of me still reaped satisfaction from that after his own stunt with Idris and Mena. But another part of me felt guilty, knowing how much he cared—and how correct he'd been about the danger I faced.

"And you're coming with me."

My eyes snapped back to his.

One of his hands was on my waist, and the other pressed against my racing heart. "You're a part of my world now. My clan will protect you as fiercely as I will. Like I said, I want you to meet my mentor, Princeton. After everything that has happened, I think it will help you to talk to someone like you."

I started to shake my head, even if I knew he was right.

Kylo grabbed me by the throat and locked his lips with mine.

The kiss was mind-melting, exactly as he intended. His thumb stroked my jugular. He nibbled at my lower lip and moved away just an inch.

"Not a request. Call it a date. You're still bound by your own bargain, little witch."

I glared at him.

Kylo only laughed.

~

"Why do I need to be blindfolded?" I hissed as Kylo carried me down what felt like endless flights of stairs.

"For your own safety."

"Wait, oh gods, does your clan hang out in the catacombs? Is that why we're going underground? You know this place is cursed, right?"

I sensed strange, potent magick press up against us from all directions, but it didn't feel like angry spirits, thank Selena.

"Evie darling," Kylo drawled. "With the number of questions you're asking, you're making me think you need to be gagged, too."

"Hmph," I muttered into the crook of his neck. Why did he smell so good? The clean mint, the woodsy musk, this hint of leather that was manly and violent…

"Are you *sniffing me?*"

"No."

With the blindfold on, my other senses were heightened. At the first hint of familiar whispers, I stiffened in Kylo's arms.

And as soon as I made out the first clear, unmistakable phrase, I fisted Kylo's shirt.

Hello again, witch.

A sharp chill fell down my spine.

"Evie, are—"

"Please take off my blindfold. We're already inside," I said, placing a hand over my ear and pressing into Kylo's chest. "Please. Please take it off."

We reached solid ground, and Kylo instantly set me down and called back the shadow that had slithered over my eyes.

"Open slowly," Kylo warned.

I didn't listen. Even though the lighting was dim, it was blinding for a moment after being in the dark for too long. I squinted, finding Kylo's concerned eyes.

"What's going on?"

I shook my head. "Just witchy things."

"Right," he said slowly, frowning as if waiting for an elaboration that would never come.

I looked around the strange, dark hallway of carved stone. The winding spiral staircase behind us was black iron and impossibly steep. Thankfully, I didn't see any signs of stacked human skeletons.

I shivered again at the thought.

Even still, that unfamiliar dark power bloomed all around us. I saw one of Kylo's sigil tattoos glow for the briefest moment.

He tugged me close, interlocking his fingers with mine. "I promise where we're going isn't nearly as spooky."

The longer we walked, the more I glanced over at Kylo, searching for any change in his disposition. It was as if I expected him to suddenly become a completely different person the closer we got to his secret society of masked vampires.

Would he treat me differently in front of them?

"I can hear you thinking, little one," Kylo murmured.

"Really? Because of the blood bond?" I squeaked.

Kylo laughed. "No, baby. I was joking. You just look all cute and serious."

"Oh."

I wasn't sure how Kylo was navigating, as we seemed to turn down increasingly complex halls. They were becoming more decorative now. A chandelier dangled above, sconces burning with strange white flame.

At the sound of voices, I had to stop myself from jumping out of my skin. Laughter trickled through.

"You know what," I said, halting in place. "I've decided that I did, in fact, lose my mind. But luckily, I have found it again. So if you could please take me back up to street level…"

Kylo stared down at me with a smirk. "Angel, we've been over this." He pushed a strand of hair behind my ear. "It's okay to be afraid. I'm here. Besides Princeton, everyone you are about to meet was once human. They still have human hearts and souls. They are just as dedicated to protecting Etherdale's mortals as you are to protecting your brother."

The way Kylo humanized his comrades helped, but it didn't change the fact that my negative beliefs about the turned were embedded deep. I still blamed them for radicalizing kids like Idris. For provoking the born and inviting more violence into the city.

Even if I knew on some level it was more complicated than that.

Kylo reached for my other hand. "Everyone you're about to meet has lost someone they loved to born violence. They all have a past filled with grief and darkness."

The words jolted me, breaking through my vision of the turned as merely overly-arrogant rebels trying to stick it to King Earle.

"Including me," Kylo said softly.

I looked for it in his deep blue eyes—the promise of grief— and when I found it, a fist clenched around my heart.

"I'll tell you about mine when you tell me about yours. No rush." He gave my hands a squeeze. "You're not meeting the entire clan. That would be impossible, for starters. Only a few of my closest friends."

Impossible? How many of them were there? Wait a minute.

Kylo was dangerously intelligent. He seemed to know about everything going on in Etherdale, at all times. Yet he was entirely unconcerned about increased born presence. About any of it, really. As if everything was going according to plan.

As if...

Kylo guided me through a final set of doors. My questions about the true magnitude of his power, influence, numbers, and schemes were lost when a perky dark-haired vampire suddenly bounced up and down in front of me.

"Hi Evie!" Harmony said. "You look terrified!"

I smiled in spite of myself, and Kylo melted at the sight.

"Astute observation." Kylo glanced beyond Harmony, toward the table of turned gathered around an oval table in a large, decadent space that resembled a lounge or drawing room.

For a moment, I forgot we were underground. The furnishings were tasteful, and vines slithered across the stone. The light above was warm. Bookcases and shelves of alcohol and games were on one wall, and a dormant fireplace was against another.

A woman hovered who appeared to be some sort of server. She was laughing with the group at the table as she refreshed their drinks. I could hear muted voices from all around us, as if we were merely in a back room of some sort of massive hub.

My mind spun.

None of the vampires were masked or glamoured. They were all proudly showcasing various styles of tattoos, mostly onyx, with the occasional dark blue or purple accent.

One of them stood, a massive, brutish man with arms nearly the size of my torso. I gulped, and Harmony giggled.

"Angel, this is Blade."

"Of course it is," I mumbled before I could stop myself.

At this, the horrifyingly large man burst into hearty laughter that had the whole room turning in our direction.

I pleaded with my cheeks not to blush.

What did it even matter? They could already smell my fear.

Blade extended a meaty hand my way. Kylo's eyes sharpened like weapons as I shook it politely and introduced myself.

"Told you," Harmony said.

Blade looked from Kylo to me before taking three steps back. "Yep, you were right. Though it's not all that shocking. He's fucking intense about everything he cares about."

"And we love him for it," Harmony added gleefully.

"I'm glad my intensity can be felt," Kylo said, looping his arm around me and pulling me closer. "Because I'm only showing a drop of it."

His voice rang out as some kind of warning that even I could feel in my bones.

Everyone else stood and greeted Kylo, and Kylo introduced me to the rest of the vampires without letting me out of his grip.

A woman with short blonde hair stepped forward. "Could I have a word, Kylo? It'll only take a minute. It's—"

"In a moment, Lucetta." Kylo said curtly. "After my guest feels more comfortable."

The way Kylo so instinctually prioritized me made my heart skip a beat. He sat with me at the round table as a conversation began about some strange art exhibit in one of the local galleries.

It flowed naturally, as if they were all just regular people with regular interests outside of vigilante assassinations of Lillian's demon spawn.

The server woman smiled warmly as she brought plates of brunch food. It was all so strange—so *human*. I secretly thought Kylo was going to bring me to some kind of vampiric torture dungeon, and I'd be knocked back into my senses at long last.

His hand on my thigh was warm and comforting, even as I nervously tapped my foot. Kylo continued to trace soothing circles on my skin as he put food on my plate with the other.

"Have you seen this exhibit yet, Evie?" Harmony asked. "It's so beautifully odd. Like she channeled some alternate reality into art."

I shook my head.

"I'll take her," Kylo said casually. "She'd enjoy it."

"The witch you speak of, a talented sculptor and dear friend, has gone missing, you know," someone suddenly said from behind me.

My skin prickled with recognition, the dark power and whispers in the corners of the room reaching their highest volume.

A man with curly light brown hair entered the space, hands tucked into baggy brown pants. He wore a billowing black shirt with layers of amulets and bones hanging around his neck.

I recognized him from the markets, the second time I'd met Kylo.

His gaze casually swept to mine. "I'm Princeton."

"Evie," I said.

I was suddenly more nervous now than I had been around these strangely normal, albeit deadly, vampires.

My fellow witches and I didn't tend to get along.

Kylo dramatically gestured to the seat on the other side of him with a smile.

Instead, Princeton grabbed an idle seat from nearby and dragged it across the floor to wedge in between me and Harmony. At this, Harmony rolled her eyes.

"Oh, gods," she muttered.

Blade snickered, shaking his head as Princeton nonchalantly reached for a pastry.

I glanced over at an irate Kylo.

"The two most oppositional men I've ever met," Blade remarked. "*And* the most powerful. Whoever could've foretold the consequences?"

"Don't forget *insane*," Princeton added, mouth half-stuffed with pastry. He blew Kylo a kiss, his fingers adorned with a great many rings.

Kylo's violent gaze didn't give.

Princeton was unbothered as he glanced around the table. "This is quite a peculiar gathering." He laughed. "Are we making weekend brunch a regular occurrence?"

Harmony made a face, and the scuffle under the table sounded like she'd kicked him in the shin. "We! All! Need! Work! Life! Balance!"

Kylo finally melted, rolling his eyes with a chuckle as the entire table laughed.

"My work-life-balance isn't speaking to me right now," Blade said, tearing into a baguette violently.

"Which one?" Harmony muttered.

Blade grinned roguishly. "Says you. I saw you going into a campus bar last week, following a group of very pretty ladies."

Harmony huffed. "Ew, Blade. I was meeting a friend."

I was still hung up on the beefy, frightening brick wall of a man's name. "Is Blade a nickname? Or did your mother see what you looked like at birth and thought, yeah, this child is a *Blade*?"

The whole table went silent. Princeton stared at me for a beat before letting out a guffaw. Kylo's hand on my thigh paused its gentle strokes as he grinned at me.

Blade smirked. "Well, legend has it I came out of my mother with both fists clenched asking for a shot of whiskey. It had been a long night up there."

I giggled. Kylo kissed my temple.

It wasn't until a good ten minutes later that I realized the drinks in the chalices around me were *blood*.

Helia's heavens. I really was surrounded by those I supposedly hated most.

My eyes darted to the space in front of Kylo, but he was sipping water. Was he hungry? Had he been sneaking blood when I wasn't looking? He did occasionally disappear to the kitchen to fetch me water. I'd just never considered he might also have been covertly keeping himself well-fed.

"I'm sorry about your sculptor friend," Kylo said to Princeton at a lull. "I hope she's found safe."

"Not holding my breath," Princeton said bitterly. "But thanks, brother."

"I hate that they're punishing witches for our existence," Harmony said. She regarded me apologetically. "Breaks my heart to see innocents suffering because of something that has nothing to do with them."

Her genuineness humbled me, especially the parts that had been so quick to make judgments and assumptions.

I thought of the born who had subdued me in the forest, how easily they could've killed me if Kylo hadn't been there. In the library, too.

Harmony asked me about my goods, and I had to admit to the table that the born had forced me out of business.

"I wanted to open my own shop," I murmured. "Before all of this, I mean. I feel guilty enough putting Celeste's owners and customers in danger. If I reemerged in such a visible way, I'd draw too much attention. The entire business plan to guarantee my success was that I needed to capitalize off my strengths and uniqueness. But now… those are the reasons I need to lie low."

"Fuck that," Blade said. "We can work something out, right boss?" He looked to Kylo hopefully—determinedly—as if he'd known me forever, and he was ready to devise a game plan.

Suddenly the whole table was rallying behind me, these strangers who I'd known for less than an hour. Plans were thrown out, revised, workshopped. They peppered me with questions, clearly interested in me as a person just as much as they wanted me to succeed in spite of the born.

All the while, I felt Kylo watching me, studying me in that way he did. His fingers combed through my hair.

"Will you be okay if I chat with my friend for a minute?" he asked me.

Blade and Harmony were in the middle of a heated debate about the merit of an underground goods trade.

I nodded. "Yes," I said, and surprisingly, I meant it.

I felt strangely... safe. With people I downright despised a week ago. They'd accepted me without question, didn't bat a single eye at my chaos witch nature or the fact that I wasn't one of them. They looked at me like they looked at Kylo—with the utmost respect.

It's the way they all looked at each other, too.

Like some strange family, born of magick and shadows.

Lucetta and Kylo stepped into a different room. I glanced at Princeton, only to find his light brown, slightly manic eyes were already trained on me.

He pouted, resting his head in his hand. "The thing about when Daddy Kylo gives me rules is that it only makes me want to be that much naughtier."

40

EVIE

"Princeton," Harmony warned, using a tone one might use for a cat attempting to paw a glass off the counter.

Another conversation had broken out among the others, something about allying with local covens.

"Rules about me?" I asked.

Princeton continued his faux pouting routine as he nodded. The hint of a smirk played at his lips.

"He doesn't want you talking to me without him here," I guessed. "Why?"

"Because I'm not like the others," Princeton said with a shrug, clearly holding back more. "I'm not a worker bee. I'm the queen."

Blade rolled his eyes so hard it looked painful. Someone from down the table booed and threw a carrot at Princeton's face. A shadow escaped Princeton's palm and deflected it at the last second.

When Princeton laughed, the rest of the table's conversation resumed.

My eyes were locked on the curious tendril of pitch-black smoke. Stranger, it seemed to be staring right back.

302

When it began to whisper, I blocked it out of my perception.

Princeton's eyes narrowed, and I wondered if I'd accidentally flinched. I cleared my throat. "I'm not used to being around other witches."

Princeton clasped his hands, leaning back casually. "I see." He spoke to me at a lower volume now, closer to my ear, as Blade and Harmony pretended not to be watching us like hawks. "As Kylo has likely informed you, I am more than willing to act as a mentor when it comes to your magick. You set your own boundaries."

"I don't trust you."

"Good. You shouldn't." Princeton popped a grape in his mouth. "Let's start tomorrow. If you decide I'm of no use or too deplorable of moral character for your liking, you can fire me and be on your merry way. But who knows! Maybe we'll prevent the next violent, witch-conjured storm and keep the horde of born and witches from hunting for its mysterious source."

My stomach dropped. "What? People are looking for me?"

Panic surged in my blood. The urge to run was a potent force. But I was underground. I'd never been prone to claustrophobia before this moment, realizing just how trapped I really was.

Was it just me or were the walls getting closer?

All this worrying about putting Mena and Idris in danger, and now I was being told that they were *already* on the radar of evil forces? What if—

"We're the only ones who have connected the event to you," Harmony said quickly. "If there was anything to worry about, Kylo would know about it, and so would you."

Her smile was warm and comforting, and it almost felt like magick the way she was able to coax me into deeper breaths.

She gave Princeton, on the other hand, a glare of cold death.

Princeton smiled sheepishly, as if he didn't quite understand what he'd done wrong. "Listen, I'm not good with people on the surface level. Never have been." The way he stared at me now was the most genuine expression I'd discerned from him thus far. "But I am good with magick. Deep emotional depths. Spirits. Dark and mysterious powers. Forces beyond most folks' control. I was ostracized from the coven I was born into. I had to learn a lot of lessons at a young age very quickly. If your only goal for the rest of your life is to suppress your gifts and pretend to be more human than witch, fine. That would be a waste, but my opinion might not matter to you, and I can still be of help. The basic truth is that your current tactics are failing, and that's *not* a matter of opinion."

At a sharp caw, both Princeton and I looked to the corner of the room. A crow was perched on a shelf.

In the next blink, it was gone.

"What are you two staring at?" Harmony asked.

"Creepy," Blade mumbled, crossing his arms.

Princeton shrugged. "No idea." He glanced at me. "Mean anything to you?"

I sighed heavily, my frown digging deeper. I reached for my third cup of coffee. "Unfortunately."

WE'D BARELY MADE it another thirty minutes before a stoic man with short, dark hair entered the space and beelined straight for Kylo.

His eyes narrowed on me for the briefest lapse, my stomach souring at the detection of potent, dark magick.

"You may speak freely," Kylo said.

For the first time since we'd entered Kylo's world, I detected a shift in him, at long last. It occurred the moment the mysterious man looked at me again, this time with clear distrust.

"I said *speak*," Kylo snapped. The room rattled with power, reverberating straight to my bones. Kylo's hand never left my thigh.

"Zander has called on us," the man said evenly, never once showing any flicker of humanlike emotion. "The Isolde region is under attack—one of their primary villages, Florimell."

Now I was certain that the walls were closing in.

I could feel every last drop of blood leave my face, my hands suddenly clammy. *Isolde. Florimell.*

I saw Ravenia's countryside, the rolling hills, the farmhouses, the children…

Kylo was speaking, but the words weren't being picked up by my brain for processing. The whole table stood, everyone but Kylo and me.

"Evie," he whispered. "I'm sorry. I need to help my allies and the mortals under their protection."

The world came back into focus. "What?"

I shoved down the visions of my homeland—of the ghost with icy, inhuman gray eyes.

Kylo stared at me in confusion, his irises studying every single inch of me in a way that made me squirm.

"Sorry, I um," I stuttered. "Is this typical?"

Kylo's jaw ticked, his brows drawn. "No. Nothing in the realm is typical anymore. But we will have more than enough force at our disposal, and the born will be completely unprepared. I'll be back as soon as possible, and you will *always* have protection."

He grabbed my clammy hand and guided me to my feet as he gave orders.

"I need to feed," Kylo suddenly muttered, and the server woman from before wasted no time pouring a crimson fluid into a silver chalice.

Our eyes locked. My awareness of everyone else melted away. I was still disoriented, knocked out of orbit and scrambling. But when Kylo's lips met the rim of the cup, this strange feeling overtook me—this strange mix of yearning, fear, anger, and jealousy.

Knowing that he had to feed, that his lips and fangs needed to consume someone other than me, it did something to my body and brain I didn't expect.

I didn't want Kylo to drink anyone else's blood. I didn't want anyone else to make him stronger, to give him pleasure or power or satisfaction.

He chugged the liquid unceremoniously, never breaking contact as he gripped my waist.

His features were slightly apologetic, nervous. But he didn't vocalize it. He showed me who he was without shame. He finished and handed the chalice back to the woman.

"Please be safe," I said softly. I lowered my voice, hoping the others were too deep in conversation to hear my next words. "When you come back, I want you to feed from me."

Someone whistled. My cheeks instantly burned.

I hated vampiric hearing.

Kylo's eyes blew wide, and he let out a curse. "Angel, if I didn't know you better, I'd think you were trying to get me killed."

"What? Why?"

"Because if I were any other vampire, I'm quite sure your devious little sabotage attempts would ruin my focus in battle irreversibly," he growled, running his tongue against his lower lip as his face hovered inches from mine. "Behave while I'm gone. Or, don't, and be prepared for the consequences." He kissed my forehead, then quickly spoke to Princeton. "You already know what I'm about to say, so let's just skip today's battle of the wills. Fill Allie in on my absence, immediately."

Princeton's lips curved. "Yes, sir," he said in a suggestive, low tone.

My eyes narrowed, but Kylo barely acknowledged the words, as if they were a usual occurrence.

I recognized the name of the vampire woman who'd escorted me home once before, who I'd also seen lurking around on some of my strolls through town. Allie was clearly one of my assigned guards.

"Phineas, inform Commander Lachlan," Kylo directed toward the scary dark-haired man who still looked at me with a flicker of distaste. Another course of Kylo's power flowed through the room, stronger than before, as if feeding had amplified its force tenfold.

With his gaze back on me, Kylo lifted me into his arms and kissed either side of my lips and then my neck. My stomach tightened, pleasurable tingles spreading from where his mouth sucked on my skin.

I was flustered and embarrassed when he set me down, and the bastard looked like he was enjoying every bit of my humiliation.

The ruthless vampires around us seemed shell-shocked by the act, and Kylo, in typical Kylo fashion, appeared to not give a single fuck.

He didn't say goodbye, just gazed at me one last time, those dark tattoos trembling with power as he turned and joined his clan. They were gone in a matter of seconds, leaving me alone with a grumpy vampire and an eccentric witch.

"This way," the stoic man barked, beckoning us through an open door that led to a wide hall.

Princeton's eyes sharpened, taking a step toward me. "Yeah, fuck no. Watch your tongue, Phineas. Let's not forget who bestowed you with the power that has gone straight to your ugly head." He looked down at me, bone amulets vibrating with a low hum of dangerous magick. "Two choices: Be boring and go straight home, or we start learning to control your power today."

Option one, my body and mind screamed, especially now that Kylo had abandoned me underground with this chaos witch who had obviously spawned an entire legion of vampires.

Phineas stared at us with irritation and impatience, and I buckled.

"Fine," I said. "We can *talk* about magick."

Princeton clapped his hands together, his features equal parts conniving and nearly childlike in their enthusiasm. "Excellent choice."

"We'll see," I muttered.

Phineas grunted, clearly angry at us for not following his orders quickly enough.

Princeton chuckled as he led me through the door. This hall reminded me of some ancient palace, and voices became louder. When I heard a scream, I nearly jumped out of my skin.

"What was that?" I asked.

"Hmm," Princeton said. "Too close to have come from the dungeons, so I'm going to guess a fight broke out between the newly turned."

"*Dungeons?*" I whispered.

Princeton waved a hand. "Not all of them are the scary kind, no need to fret. Though most of the fun ones are above ground. Only the most depraved are kept down here."

I stared at him, mouth agape. "Fun ones? How many sex dungeons does he own?"

Princeton laughed, but when he met my startled features, he made another face of sheepish regret. "Oh, hells. Did I say something I shouldn't have? I never know with mortals anymore."

Phineas refused to talk to us. A few vampires meandered through the hall, their eyes going straight to me with curiosity as they nodded at Princeton.

I was still hung up on the dungeons talk. Were these places that the turned fed? On so-called willing mortals? Obviously, I knew about born feeding clubs, though I'd never been to one. There were only a couple in Etherdale, considering it wasn't a born-friendly city. Even still, these were the concessions that had to be made to keep our regional nobility happy.

My mind spun and spun, parsing through the reality that had spread out before me the moment Kylo had ripped off my physical—and metaphorical—blindfold.

"Kylo is like, really old…" I thought aloud.

Princeton grinned, regarding me with shocked amusement. "True."

"And you have this whole underground palace—or is it even bigger? Like an entire city?"

At this, Phineas finally looked back at us, his eyes burning into me like a cattle prod.

"Kylo is taking a fleet to help some other clan in a battle against the born," I continued. "And yet there's more than enough of you left to defend the city, to populate this strange underground and the above world… And you keep making more of yourselves."

Princeton sighed. "We're entering dangerous territory, kiddo."

I glared at him. "Don't condescend to me. I'm not a child."

Princeton raised up his hands in defeat, but he made no move to apologize.

"How many turned are there? Have you intentionally concealed your true power and numbers? What Kylo is doing now… oh gods." I stopped moving.

Princeton shot me a look of warning, shaking his head.

"Are we heading toward a full-blown *war*?"

The lights above flickered, and Phineas snarled. "Listen up, witches. Do whatever it is Kylo has instructed you to do, and nothing more. Do not let me hear whispers of you going where *you don't belong.*"

He was clearly only speaking to me, staring me down as

power flared. Princeton laughed with an inflection that raised the hairs on the back of my neck.

"I warned you," Princeton said, high-pitched and melodic.

Bones snapped, the sickening sound of it reverberating through the hall. The scary vampire fell to his knees. He cried out in surprise and pain.

Nausea bloomed in my gut.

"Apologize, and I might fix your legs." The bone amulets around Princeton's neck were raised in the air, dancing slightly.

Even if it had stopped, the sound of Phineas's legs breaking still echoed in my mind as I struggled not to retch.

Princeton had warned me that he was insane. Yet they all seemed so normal at brunch. The suspicious, paranoid part of me rolled her eyes.

I was naive to think that a clan of ruthless vampires and their witch maker would remain deceptively harmless for long.

"I apologize," Phineas ground out.

"Not to me. To *her*."

Phineas's eyes darted to me. "I apologize, witch."

Great. I'd made a new enemy. "Um, apology accepted."

I swallowed down bile as more cracking noises bounced off the walls. Princeton's bone amulets danced midair until falling back to his chest. Phineas stood with his newly reshaped legs, lowered his head briefly, and then left us.

"Was that really necessary?" I hissed.

Princeton turned down a narrower hall, speaking without glancing at me as I followed behind. "*Necessary* is subjective. When you allow small acts of disrespect, you send the clear message that you don't think very highly of yourself. If you don't even respect yourself, why should anyone else respect you? And in a world in which you are the only one of your kind, you have no room for such vulnerability." He met my eyes. "We stand out, Evie. And we always will. Own it and use it to your advantage, or let it spell your demise."

41

EVIE

Princeton brought me to a small study that was filled floor to ceiling with ancient texts. Magickal materials and trinkets were scattered about, and there was a low hum of power radiating through the space.

"Aren't you supposed to be finding Allie?" I asked.

Princeton sat in a leather chair as I took the adjacent couch. He lifted a brow. "If I did that, our fun would be over. The unspoken conversation you witnessed began with Kylo telling me not to meet with you while he was gone. He preferred I bring you straight to your babysitters, to which I responded, *Don't tell me what to do*. The exchange finished with Kylo promising to cause me harm should I disobey." He leaned back in the chair and spread out his arms on the armrests. "But I'm a brat and a masochist, so here we are."

"Oh." I chewed on my bottom lip. Now that we weren't moving anymore, my brain was beginning to do that irritating thing it did.

Thinking.

Over and over, in circles and in knots, in catastrophic worries and questions and doubts.

"How concerned should I be?" I asked. "About this battle with the born?"

Princeton cocked his head. "What good would your concern do?" He waved a hand. "We're just getting started. This is but a skirmish, with lesser born involved in the mortal slave trade. When King Earle and the council get involved… I'd imagine that would be a time to worry. For those who practice such behaviors."

"*When* they get involved?"

Horror churned in my gut. Even my worst fears a week ago paled in comparison to the reality that was now being shoved in my face.

Small-scale violence was one thing. It felt more controllable, like something I could still protect Idris and Mena from.

But war? The turned *actually* thinking they had a shot of overthrowing born leadership? Not just in Etherdale, but throughout the entire kingdom?

I shook my head as Princeton continued to study me carefully. "Is there some kind of chemical compound down here that's making you people lose your damn minds? Are you all just irreversibly delusional?"

Princeton laughed. "I was delusional far longer than the existence of the underground. Delusional people are the only ones capable of getting shit done, my faithless friend."

"Faithless," I scoffed. I saw a flash of rolling hills, heard chants to Lillian echoing against walls with peeling, crumbling burgundy wallpaper. "Fuck your faith."

The words left my lips as if on autopilot. I was, on some level, aware that I wasn't even talking to Princeton at all.

"There she is," Princeton said, leaning forward in his chair as an unhinged grin spread. "Tell me more, Evie. How can you be all lovey-dovey with someone like *him*?"

He was provoking me. I wasn't stupid, but gods, I was too angry to care. I saw visions of vampire-on-vampire violence in the streets, on campus. I saw Idris, helpless prey in a sea of bloodthirsty wolves. The lights began to strobe.

"Is it perhaps because, underneath your protective façade of sweetness and innocence, you're more like *us* than you care to admit? Does the vampire lord of shadows call to your deepest, innermost self?"

"I'm not the one pretending to be something I'm not," I hissed, my fingernails biting into my palms. "You're the ones who wear masks and glamours. You're the ones who think you stand even the slightest chance of surviving a war with a born king who has ruled for what? A thousand years?"

Princeton's eyes went glassy and, Selena above, I wanted him to stop looking at me—to stop trying to find my power, the poison I'd caged, and the key I'd buried.

"This is a setup." I shot up from the couch, and with a flick of his wrist, Princeton sent a gust of wind to shove me back down.

My back hit the couch violently, causing it to skid. The most dangerous emotion—that sickly rage—began to blind the edges of my vision, locking its scalding grip around me. Something escaped, shooting up my spine.

The world bent to my will. Bookcases trembled. The floor itself quaked. Objects and texts crashed to the floor.

All the while, Princeton grinned at me. His eyes were rabid, hungry, delighted.

"Did you hurt your brother in a fit of rage?" he drawled. "Is that the block? The reason you've bound and glamoured yourself so tightly?"

At the mention of Idris, I had to shut my eyes against the rising tide of fury scraping against my bones. The discomfort grew and grew, and I realized with sudden terror that Princeton was fanning the flames with his own magick, using every method at his disposal to make me explode.

Did he want me to destroy this underground make-believe vampire palace? The whole city?

My eyes flew open. The world was brighter. My sight expanded with the influx of power. I could see the faintest outline of Princeton's aura—hues of black, purple, green, and red.

"No wonder they hate our kind," I cried out against the electricity surging through the air, the trembling furniture, the heat traveling up and down my spine. "You want annihilation. Oblivion. Is that why you turn idealistic young humans into monsters? Is that why you're hoping I'm secretly as evil as you are?"

Princeton laughed, his eyes scanning my body as a book flew at his head. With a casual wave, he deflected it before it crashed into his skull.

My lip curled. "I would never hurt Idris. Never."

Princeton leaned back in his chair again, his eyes glassy as he gazed too deeply inside me. "Understood." He casually tapped the armrests as his eyes sharpened. "All right, all right, I've seen enough for now." He sighed, humor draining from his face as he snapped his fingers. *"Enough."*

The room filled with darkness. More than darkness—the deep onyx void of a night sky without stars.

Here, I had no stimulus. I couldn't feel my anger. I had nothing to be angry about. Nothing to fear or hate or love or yearn for.

"Breathe. As deep as you can go."

The voice was detached, muffled. It embedded deeper than my conscious awareness, coaxing deep breath after breath until my hammering heart began to slow.

Like the calm aftermath of a violent storm, I slowly eased into a more relaxed state.

"That's it. Keep breathing."

I knew it wasn't Kylo speaking, but I pictured his face as I attempted to slow my heart rate. That devastating smirk and the little dimple that formed in its wake.

The darkness receded. The floor no longer quaked. It looked as if a cyclone had swept through the room, but the atmosphere was quiet and still.

I glared at Princeton. "You really thought that provoking me like that was going to earn my trust and make me want to work with you?"

Princeton still held my gaze with calm authority now, only a hint of his smirk remaining. "Would you have revealed any of your true power if I'd merely asked nicely?"

I still wanted to run, to go home and leave this entire world behind. But I saw another vision of Kylo's silly little dimple, and I sat still.

It was an altogether ridiculous and indefensible reason to stay in this hell.

"You didn't reveal the truth, and we both know it," Princeton said. "But I've seen enough to know that you aren't merely a chaos witch. You're a bloody powerful one. And if all it takes to make you lose control is a random stranger's weaponized words, then you're in dire trouble. Especially if you refuse to use that same power to defend yourself from attack."

I hated that this insane person suddenly made sense. It was easier to justify running when he was being certifiably deranged and chaotic for seemingly no reason.

"There's no use worrying about what's out of your control—be it war or the next born atrocity of the week. But you have plenty of reason to worry about your own magick and the danger it is attracting to yourself and everyone around you." Princeton's eyes narrowed. "And who knows? Maybe you'll decide, after I teach you control, that you may want to do more than merely defend your own. Perhaps you may one day decide to use all that righteous anger against your true enemies."

I heard the shrill shriek of my mother, those soulless gray eyes that now haunted the hills of Isolde. A lump formed in my throat. I wondered if Princeton could see it too.

"I'm done for the day. I don't care about your opinions of my character. I know you're trying to manipulate me to serve your own ends, anyway." I met Princeton's probing gaze. "But if you prove to me that you can actually help me control the poison inside of me, then I'll accept your help. I don't have any interest in hurting anyone."

Princeton's irritating smirk was back in full force. "Deal." He sighed. "There's your first problem: calling something that's inherent to your nature and soul a *poison*."

At a loud knock on the door, Princeton's grin turned even cheekier.

A slim brunette with ornate geometric tattoos burst into the room, nostrils flaring and eyes turning to slits when she spotted Princeton.

Allie sighed in relief as she scanned me up and down.

"Assessing Kylo's prized possession for damages?" Princeton teased. "She's fine. Party's over. Sad." He winked at me. "I'll see you tomorrow."

"No," Allie corrected. "You'll see her when Kylo returns."

Princeton pouted, nodding and feigning resignation that neither Allie nor I believed.

In this moment, I was grateful for Kylo's slightly unhinged protectiveness. Because at least that meant I could avoid this witch I didn't trust with a single bone in my body for a short while longer.

"It's not a poison, Evie," Princeton called as I escaped with Allie out into the hall. "It's just *you*."

Allie glanced at me curiously. I glared back at the door as it slammed shut with a gust of wind.

I'd never heard anyone say something more horribly cruel.

42

KYLO

Checking the blood bond for the steady beat of Evie's heart had become a comforting, obsessive compulsion. I'd been away from her before, but never this great a distance.

And not since I'd felt my essence slide down her pretty little throat, binding her to me forever.

I hadn't realized how much it would affect me, leaving her behind like that.

No matter how much protection she now had around her at all times, I couldn't help but imagine her in danger. And I'd seen the fear in her face, the heightened levels of terror in her blood, when she'd heard where I was going.

My angel was cute to worry about me the way she did. Though I suspected a lot of her worry was also about the state of Ravenia as a whole, and the ripple effects it would have on Etherdale.

I'd been shielding her from the truth, of course. It wouldn't help her to understand what was coming. Not yet.

On the backs of firebirds, we flew across Etherdale's

mountains. And when I felt Evie's heart speed up and pound much too violently for my liking, it was my own personal hell.

I knew it was likely Princeton, predictably disobeying my orders to examine Evie's magick. But he didn't understand my Evie like I did, and it infuriated me to know he might hurt her with his callousness.

My firebird, Vera, always tuned in to my moods, made a low rumble. Her bright, feathered wings of red and orange spread wide. Her crimson eyes crackled with Helia's fiery rays. Even after all these decades, the size, grace, and might of these gorgeous creatures stole my breath away.

"Did you see what Zander included in the flight plan in his request for aid?" Blade called to me over the roaring wind.

I glanced over at him, his massive form fitting snugly on the saddle. "Which part?"

"He said to avoid this little patch of land between Florimell and Calliope at all costs. To not even fly over it, and certainly not to land there."

"That just makes me want to head there immediately," I answered.

"No," Blade said, shaking his head. "He said it was *cursed*. Haunted by vengeful poltergeists."

I rolled my eyes. "So, Zander is *definitely* hiding something valuable, then."

"Now you're a skeptic? He who is nauseatingly in love with a witch of esoteric mysteries?"

In love. My heart skipped a beat like I was human again, and not this monster plagued with bloodlust and an unquenchable hunger for retribution and power.

Evie had said she wanted me to feed from her. It was the most unexpected surprise that I was trying my hardest not to think about, lest I allow her to ruin my focus when I needed it most.

Gods, she really was ruining me. She had no idea how tightly wrapped around her finger she had me, no matter how many times I forced her to submit to the magnitude of my power.

"I'm not skeptical of esoteric mysteries," I answered over the rushing wind. "I'm skeptical of scary ghost stories written by men in power."

"No, I've heard it too!" Harmony called at our backs. "Princeton mentioned it once. It was the site of some unspeakable atrocity. Some fucked-up Servants of Lillian shit."

"Well, that makes sense," I relented. "If a cult who gives their children to the born as tithings was involved, then I wouldn't put angry ghosts out of the realm of possibility."

A vision of Evie giggling quickly transformed into that feral, wounded version of her that begged me to stop talking about her past—her childhood, if she'd even had one.

I ground my teeth together. Vera huffed.

"I know, I know," I whispered so only she could hear. "I promise, when you meet her, you'll understand."

~

WHEN WE ARRIVED, the battle quickly became a slaughter. Masked and hungry for our first decent fight, my clan unleashed shadowed magick on the unsuspecting horde of born.

My clan was highly trained in combat, in the control of our bloodlust and base instincts, and the meticulous balancing act of being vengeful monsters without losing our humanity. Our skill had only ever been utilized in small-scale, scattered violence. Assassinations, intelligence missions, vigilante justice, protecting mortals in the streets of Etherdale.

We were more than just prepared for battle. We were fucking starving for one.

Shifters rushed past me, their giant wolf and feline forms leaping and tearing into born flesh. A few local witches were also engaged in battle, defending the human villagers with protection spells, poison hexes, and conjured flames.

A poisoned dart flew into a nearby born, spearing him in the neck. One of my shadows impaled him for good measure.

The group of witches went utterly speechless as they watched me sink my teeth into the next born woman, draining her of stolen blood before snapping her neck and casting her aside.

The born's blood was putrid, yet it almost felt like a betrayal to Evie to even feed from the enemy.

I couldn't focus on that now, as more firebirds circled overhead, carrying more born.

My clan fought remarkably cohesively with Zander's fleet. Turned by a different witch, his clan was born with its own unique strengths and magick. But the shadows were a constant force, even all the way in Valentin with Rune's turned. Shadow magick manifested in a multitude of different ways, but there was still the same essential essence inside each of the turned. As if the same spirits or gods were rooting for all of us, allowing humans to be reborn into vampires for the sole purpose of righting some cosmic injustice.

I heard Evie's voice in my mind for a moment, her philosophy on reciprocity and magick and fate.

My shadows yanked a born backward before he could sneak up on Harmony. I squeezed and rotted him from the inside out in a blink.

I had to stop fucking thinking about her.

It hadn't cost me so far, but gods knew it was only a matter of time.

When a dagger flew at my head at the same time that a chain poisoned with blood onyx wrapped around my neck, I'd realized *that time* had come.

I'd been off my game for only fractions of a second.

I moved quickly, my shadows shielding me from the final

judgment of the blade. But my power was losing steam as the blood onyx muted my strength and I clawed for air. I wielded darkness as a weapon, blinding the person at my back long enough to jab my own dagger into their face.

She dropped the chain, and my power slowly accumulated again once contact with the paralytic blood onyx had been broken.

To my surprise, it was a witch in all black who stood behind me, gurgling on her own blood as she fell to the ground. Behind her, I saw a glaring blond boy, barely twelve. He was wearing all black too.

Who took a child into battle?

"Harmony," I hissed.

She homed in on the child immediately, retreating as weapons and magick flew all around us.

"I'll cover you. There's a store with mortals inside around that corner," I said quickly as I pointed.

The truth was, I'd never been able to wield so much power at once in all my decades. An arrogant, impatient man would not have been able to construct the new world I was building. He would not have been able to resist showing off the depths of his godlike power, nor spend decades pretending to be weaker and more incompetent than he truly was.

I wasn't a perfect man, so I did revel in my satisfied grin now, as I watched my shadows feast on flesh. I delighted in the way the born stared at me in horror, my mouth dripping with their comrades' blood.

It was nearly frightening how powerful I was, how easy it would be to rot this entire village into nothing but decay and rubble. Worse was the way it went to my head, in biochemical and magickal processes out of my conscious control. It felt similar to feeding, but on a much grander scale. The rush, the adrenaline, the euphoria, the indescribable ecstasy of watching lofty dreams become reality, with all of its grit and bloodshed and horror and sublimity.

I was glad I was who I was. Because the idea of anyone else disrupting the order of the universe to this degree was a sobering thought indeed.

Though, I liked to think it was the born who'd caused the disruption, and I was merely the gods' way of correcting that imbalance.

"You're a fucking blasphemy. Lillian is going to torture your soul for all of eternity," a born man spat in my face, rabid and grimy and clearly an underling in this nasty slave trading business.

"And you're just someone's meat puppet to defend an industry you would have never materially benefited from," I said. I jutted out my bottom lip mockingly as I yanked my dagger back from his chest and then took a chunk out of his neck with my fangs.

His body slumped to the cobblestone.

"You're the only one of us who's facing Lillian today, my rat-faced friend."

Harmony was back at my side. "We need to fucking move."

This was the first time I'd heard her voice tremble with fear since we'd arrived. I read the severity in her features.

"We're about to be made an example of," Harmony hissed. "We need to get the fuck out of here. *Now.*"

Even as she said the words with authority, her eyes were ripe with grief, with a sadness I felt at my core.

One of my eyes emerged from shifting shadows, making a symbol with his right hand I recognized immediately. He retreated back behind a shadow glamour in the next blink.

The surrounding battle was dying down. It wouldn't have taken much longer to completely annihilate all born fighters and push any remaining out of the area. These were traffickers and henchmen for corrupt nobility, not a vast, organized army.

"King Earle is sending men as a message to the realm," Harmony said, unable to hide the note of utter horror in her voice now, as I stayed silent and unmoving.

I watched Blade wield his favorite sword, making a kabob out of two born in a matter of seconds. He looked rather pleased with himself as he withdrew the weapon. A leopard shifter growled to my right, and my eyes locked on the child she was defending from hungry born scum. A girl with long blonde curls, sobbing and crying for her mother. Her dress was conservative and plain black.

Nausea churned in my stomach, as if I were looking at *her* instead. My angel.

I focused back on Harmony. I weighed two impossible choices, the heaviness of both stifling my head high in an instant: to leave or to stay.

The downside to my position of power was a crushing truth, a brutal lesson. The gods were no doubt laughing at me now.

Harmony clamped her hand down on my shoulder. "They are going to eliminate us."

43

EVIE

"You saucy minx!" Mena exclaimed when she found me reading in the gardens. "I have barely seen you in weeks!"

I raised a brow, smiling at her dramatization. "Mena, it's been like, three days since I last saw you."

"In my heart, it's been longer." She sat on a bench near my blanket.

I bookmarked my place and set my book down.

"To be perfectly honest, I am over the moon that things are clearly hot-and-heavy with that charming, dreamy young man. How dare you keep him from us for so long! I'm old, you know! What if I'd had a heart incident being surprised like that?"

I rolled my eyes. "Are you implying Kylo is beautiful enough to give you a heart attack?"

Mena opened her mouth with a sly grin, but loud voices rang out through the garden, interrupting our banter.

"Hey!" a woman yelled.

"Cindy, please," a man barked. "You need to get a hold of yourself."

Cindy and Roger Whitfield headed around the side of the estate, following the narrow stone path toward us.

Mena stood, crossing her arms as a rare look of derision crossed her features. I scrambled to my own feet, staring at my ex-boyfriend's parents in utter confusion.

When Cindy attempted to take a shortcut and trample over my herbs, a gust of wind blew her back into Roger's chest.

"Please don't stomp on my plants," I said calmly. "There's a path for a reason."

Cindy clutched her chest as if I'd stabbed her thrice with a dagger instead. "I told you, Roger. She just attacked me!"

My heart hammered. Actually, the spirits of the gardens had redirected her, but I doubted that explanation would be a comfort.

"What is going on?" I asked.

"You are on our property," Mena said. "Mind your manners, Sandy."

"Sandy? My name is—" Cindy cut herself off with a dramatic huff as if it was beneath her to finish the sentence. She planted herself in the grass in front of us as she lifted her finger.

Roger dragged a hand across his face. "We apologize for the intrusion. We were knocking on the front door, but we heard voices and realized we might find you out here."

His eyes flickered to my chest for a moment, no doubt admiring the stitchwork in my corset.

Cindy's finger shook, her features twisted with rage and fear. "Where is my son?"

I stared at her blankly as the words landed. "What?" I looked at Roger, clearly the more reasonable party. "We broke up. He said he was returning to the countryside."

"See? Just as I told you," Roger said calmly to his wife. "Jacob's an impulsive young man. He made some boyish mistakes, likely got an earful about it from Miss Evie, and escaped to the hills."

Irritation heated my blood at Roger's assessment of the situation. I was growing quite tired of him treating Jacob like he was a child, incapable of holding responsibility for his own shitty actions. Or of me as some kind of nagging girlfriend and stand-in mother figure.

How had I ever tolerated these people?

"You see that," Cindy hissed. "The pure contempt on her face?" Her disdainful features quickly shifted into a dramatic show of terror. "She did something to him!" She clutched Roger's arm as she stared at me. "Farleigh told us about how offended you got at their harmless jokes about love spells and hexes, how you stormed off in a fit of rage. How you're a *chaos witch.*"

That finger pointing my way was not helping to calm me down. Anger and nervousness warred in my bones. I couldn't show an ounce of my power. I couldn't react at all.

"And I went to Celeste's," Cindy spat, "where they pretended like you never worked there at all. As if they'd cut all ties with you. Who are you, really? And what have you done to my son?"

Mena moved closer to me. She didn't do a thing to hide the fury in her features, her dark red lips curled with rage.

I spoke before Mena could. "We broke up. He said he was returning to the countryside. I haven't heard from him since."

I repeated the same words as before, and Cindy fucking hated me for it.

"Where did you even come from?" she spat, her blue eyes wide and crazed. "They said you had some country bumpkin accent when you showed up on this poor woman's porch all those years ago. Where'd that accent go, huh? Why are you here in Etherdale? Is that boy even your brother?"

Don't you do it, a screeching voice hissed in my ear. *Don't you fucking cry.*

My eyes burned, and my lower lip trembled. Roger watched me carefully, holding Cindy back from stepping closer.

"I am not a *poor woman*, you unbearable shrew," Mena retorted, taking a step in front of me.

The sky above darkened, and I worked to take deep breath after breath. I remembered the deep onyx nothingness of Princeton's shadows. The way I'd been able to find my center again in the darkness.

"What are you even accusing me of?" I asked, my voice shaking. "Murder? Kidnapping? Anything else you want to add to the list?"

Cindy suddenly wailed, her face crumpling with grief. "He's gone, Roger. I told you. He's dead."

My fists clenched. "He's just traveling! I can assure you that he's not suffering! Why aren't you asking Kailey where Jacob is? She's far more likely to have heard from him recently."

"Who do you think has been asking about him every day since he disappeared?" Cindy sobbed as she fisted Roger's shirt and leaned against him, breathless now as she continued to work herself up. Roger held her as he rubbed soothing circles on her back. "Sure as hell wasn't *you.*"

Cool. It was nice to hear that I was the only person in Jacob's life unaware he was cheating on me with his ex. Sounded like she was what they all preferred for him, anyway.

Mena hurled another insult at the Whitfields, now commanding them to get off her property as Cindy grew more and more incoherent. Roger, of course, offered few words of substance to the conversation.

My brows drew together, that terrified lump in my throat growing exponentially. "No one has heard from him since he left?"

Roger shook his head.

"Did he take any of his belongings?"

"Yes, he did. He packed a bag," Roger said.

I sighed in relief. "So this is all just because he hasn't written to you?" I asked an inconsolable Cindy. "That's why you're barging onto our land and accusing me of being some kind of evil mastermind?" I waved around my garden. "*This* is who I am. I read. I grow plants. I create goods that help people. Magick for healing, protection, inspiration."

I'm good! I wanted to scream. *Please see that I'm good!*

Rain trickled from the sky.

No. No, no, no. Oh gods, no.

It was like I was holding water in my palms and begging it not to fall through the cracks in my fingers.

I glanced up at the sinister clouds that had gathered above our neighborhood. I quickly looked back at the Whitfields.

"We're sorry to have bothered you," Roger said. "I'm sure Jacob will return soon, and this will have all been a misunderstanding."

"She killed him, she killed him, she killed him," Cindy repeated as she cried into Roger's chest.

I thought of Kylo. I held the image of his devastating smile, that silly little dimple, in my mind. I imagined his shadows coiled around me like they might never let me go.

The clouds would pass. No one would notice, so long as I didn't explode. It rained in Etherdale all the time.

Everything was okay. There was no need to run.

"I hope he writes to someone soon. I'm sorry he's worried you," I mumbled.

Mena made a soft noise of derision, clearly uninterested in making peace. Roger smiled politely, in that mechanical way wealthy people did. He pulled Cindy away from us without another word as she continued to spew accusations about me in a jumbled, slurred manner, apparently already drunk at this early afternoon hour.

The trickle of rain let up. I exhaled deeply, continuing to practice my most trusted methods of avoidance as I shoved all of Cindy's words deep into the recesses of my mind.

Everything was fine. I hadn't done anything wrong. I was *good*.

Cindy was barely lucid. Roger clearly didn't believe anything she was saying. But what about Jacob's friends?

What about *Kailey*?

"Am I in danger?" I asked, my eyes welling with tears. "Are they going to sell me out to the born?"

Mena watched the Whitfields disappear around the front of the house like a guard dog before quickly folding me into her arms.

"No," Mena said, squeezing me tight. "She's a drunk and a coward. She only had the gall to hurl those words at us because she thought us weaker than we are. They know their immature playboy of a son is gallivanting across Ravenia. Why do you think Roger was so damn calm? He knows the son he raised. And the women they've trained to dote and fret over them until the day they die, buried with a harem of mistresses."

Mena pulled away, and for a moment, I just stared at her resolute features. "Why didn't you say any of that while I was dating Jacob?"

She shrugged. "You didn't want to hear it. You were always going to learn the lesson you needed to learn, in your own way and at your own pace." She smiled. "I'm just pleased we've reached the chapter where I can shit talk to my heart's content."

"Me too," I said. My smile wobbled. I glanced back up at the sky and the clouds that were slowly dispersing. My hands shook; my heart was in a tight fist. "I need some chamomile tea."

And, as much as I hated the thought of relying on anyone but *myself*... I needed Kylo. I hoped he was safe.

44

KYLO

The ride back to Etherdale was not an experience I was keen to repeat. The air was impossibly heavy, settling on my shoulders with some unbearable weight.

I'd made the right call.

I glanced to my left and then my right. Blade's forehead was creased, his lips curving downward. Tears flowed freely down Harmony's cheeks as she sniffled and stroked her firebird.

She caught me looking and nodded at me. I read the expression on her features, the unspoken insistence that I extend myself compassion and grace.

I'd made the right call, but I felt like the worst person in the world.

Zander's cell of turned hadn't blamed us for the choice we'd made. They would've done the same in our shoes. But they weren't in our shoes; instead, they refused to leave the land under their protection, the land where they would fight and die together.

King Earle loved making an example of turned clans who dared rise from the underground. So far, this had only occurred on a small-scale. Once Earle realized our true numbers and

330

declared war, everything would take a turn. Earle clearly cared far more about wiping our kind off the face of the earth than he cared about the reasons we arose in the first place.

The corruption, the slave trade, the religious extremism. Earle and his out-of-touch council turned a blind eye to a realm on the verge of unraveling. They said one thing—that relationships and reciprocity between mortals and immortals were the most important institutions to upkeep—but their actions, or, rather, their inactions, told the opposite story.

King Earle cared more about protecting his legacy than his own people.

We hadn't brought enough numbers to face his forces. And more than that, it would've disrupted decades of careful planning and foresight.

My clan was the future. And the unfortunate reality was that not all of our allies would survive to fight by our side when the war began.

Making rash decisions would guarantee our demise. I would not build my new, better world on a rocky foundation, where we were disadvantaged and exposed from the start.

Yes, I was obsessive. Ambitious. Protective. Relentless.

To everyone outside of my inner circle, I was cold and cutthroat, unquestionable.

But the masks I wore served a purpose. And so too did every single method I'd employed and decision I'd made since I decided I was to become more of a monster than the ones who terrorized us.

Vera made a low, mournful call, her body vibrating in a low purr. It was common for firebirds who bonded to their riders to attempt to comfort them.

She was a very good girl.

My other very good girl was clearly asleep, her heart beating slow and measured through the blood bond. I hadn't missed the period when it had tumbled all over itself, as if she were cornered and stressed. I hated the feeling it evoked, the panicked desperation to go to her and protect what was mine.

I had to trust that my clan would protect her, especially when I'd made clear the wrath that would befall anyone who failed to keep her within sight and out of harm's way at all times.

But I didn't trust anyone to take care of Evie the way I could. And with the way she was finally looking at me—with those big, hopeful gray eyes—I could tell she was coming around to that idea as well.

When we landed in a remote part of Etherdale in the dead of night, the city was quiet, lights flickering against the darkness.

Any other day, I would've gone straight to Evie. But not tonight, not when I felt this heavy, this weighed down by duty and grief and helplessness.

Ghosts from the past reached for me. It was such an uncommon occurrence, that I couldn't help but shudder at their cool fingertips along my spine.

I checked our bond, following that invisible tether that placed Evie exactly where she belonged in her princess cottage.

Then I went home, so I could be alone with my torment until it passed.

THE NEXT DAY was a different kind of hell. I had countless correspondences to answer from turned clans in other regions and mortal allies here in Etherdale.

Then I had to attend meetings with commanders, new recruits, and my broader circle.

All the while, guilt was eating me alive. Useless, irrational guilt that would impede my ability to lead effectively.

Guilt over making the correct decision. The decision to let Zander's clan die to preserve my own.

Then there was the guilt over making Evie wait an entire day to see me. I'd of course already sent word that I was alive and back in Etherdale, but I hadn't seen her yet.

I could lie and say that being busy was the only reason I'd delayed so long. But the truth was, I didn't want to give her this lesser version of myself. I wanted her to feel safe with me, always. To know she could rely on me, that I would be a solid, immovable rock—physically and emotionally.

She deserved only my best.

After the longest day in decades, I met with Princeton.

He took one glance at me before the mischievous glint in his eyes evaporated. He nodded. "Grief is good, Kylo. Means your soul is still human. That's what we wanted, remember?"

My face fell. We sat together in his home above ground, the sun descending, candles scattered across the living room. Their flames lowered in tandem, responding to the mood.

"Yes," I said. "I'm grateful for it all." I stared down at the coffee table between us.

I remembered the face of someone I lost, long ago. A girl with strawberry blonde hair and dark freckles scattered across her fair skin. I remembered the sound of her laugh, the way she made me feel less alone in a world in which I'd once considered myself alien and unbelonging.

My hands balled into fists. Hatred attempted to wash the grief away, to take up all the space in my mind so I didn't have to experience any more pain.

"Don't do that," Princeton said. "Feel it. Thank the pain for showing you just how fucking alive you are. Alive enough to take that suffering and alchemize it. Absorb the blows, then use every last one."

My mentor knew everything about me, as any good mentor did. He knew what I needed. He knew what motivated me. He knew what had the power to destroy me.

"Let's get to the root," he said, clasping his hands together and leaning back in his chair.

"I'd rather not."

Princeton grinned. "Too bad."

I WASN'T ENTIRELY myself when I finally found Evie sitting in her garden, at a black wrought-iron table. But after my emotional healing session with Princeton, I was far better off than before.

For a while, from the comfort of my shadows, I watched her read that mysterious ancient text—the one that shocked the hell out of me every time I touched it. She'd conjured a witch light to illuminate the pages amid the darkness, even brighter than the strings of lights above. Every once in a while, she jotted down notes. And more than ever before, I could sense her buried magick emit a low hum of power.

She grew stronger every day, and I wished I could be proud of that, but selfishly, all I felt was dread. Especially when she had no control over such forces.

"I can feel you watching me, creep," she said softly without lifting her head.

My shadow glamour evaporated, and Evie looked up at me from her tiny table filled entirely with books. A bird bath with a fountain gently flowed beside her.

Her irritation was a thinly veiled façade, and she couldn't hold it for longer than two seconds after she saw me in the flesh.

She leaped up and into my arms in the next blink. The intoxicating, sweet scent of her enveloped me. I held her tightly, struggling not to wrap her head to toe in shadows.

"Hi, angel," I whispered.

I was hit with sudden emotion, this wave of relief and

gratitude and adoration that made me want to squeeze this precious girl far too tightly than her fragile body could handle.

Feeling her heart beat against my own chest was infinitely more comforting than what I could hear through the blood bond.

As if she shared the sentiment, Evie burrowed further into my hold, inhaling deeply.

"You free for a late-night date?" I asked softly, a chuckle rumbling through me at her endearing clinging.

"No. I'm clearly very busy right now."

Brat. I'd allow it, given how much she'd likely been worrying, and how long I'd made her wait to see me.

"You know, with my current state of unemployment," she added.

I let her go and kissed for forehead. "I have full faith and confidence that you're doing beautiful work, regardless. And you know that I'm ready when you are to figure out a way for you to still live out your dreams."

Her brattiness melted, and she gazed up at me sadly. For a moment, her face shifted into something troubled, as if she were holding back additional words. But she remained silent, merely nodding instead.

"It's getting late," she murmured. "What are we going to do?"

I rolled my eyes. "Evie, it is 9 o'clock. You are twenty-four years old."

She appeared indignant, defensive. "So?"

"*So,*" I said, one of my shadows escaping my human glamour to coil around her wrist. "You are far too young to be concerned about how late it is."

"Ew, Kylo, please stop reminding me that you're basically elderly."

I laughed. She squirmed with discomfort, and I relished every second of it. "I'm immortal, baby. I've left the constructs of time and age entirely."

She grumbled something under her breath. My shadow coiled around her throat next, where it grew quite content.

Evie's eyes widened, and the scent of her arousal did ungodly things to my body.

"You sure you're disgusted, angel?" I whispered, lifting her into my arms. Her legs wrapped around me, and I captured her lips with mine. I teased and nibbled, slowly easing deeper into the kiss, demanding more from her like I would forever. My tongue found hers, and she released a contented little moan into my mouth.

I slowly retracted. "There's my good girl," I praised softly, feeling the way she melted against me.

"I missed you," she finally admitted.

"I missed you too. Terribly."

45

EVIE

Maybe I should've told Kylo about the Whitfields. But something in me had decided against it. I wanted tonight to be about us, not about my lackluster ex or his horrible parents. There was nothing more he could do to protect me than he was already doing.

And to be honest, as much as I wanted to ignore and forget everything Cindy had said, her words induced a sense of shame about who I was that I, frankly, didn't want Kylo to see.

I held onto Kylo's arm as we enjoyed a private, after-hours stroll around the art exhibit his friends had been talking about. It was truly unfathomable the wealth and influence Kylo had hidden from me. How easy it was for him to pull strings and get anything he wanted in this city.

I was awestruck by the rooms of sculptures and the different shades of lighting used to accentuate each piece. One room was lit with red light, filled with sculptures of giant tree roots adorned with tiny crystals, multicolored shards of glass and mirror. We'd entered a different dimension, a kaleidoscope of color and feeling that had exploded into art.

Another room with soft blue lighting had giant stalactites

and stalagmites, resembling some sort of cave, but the structures were made from pure crystal. Some were clear like icicles, and others were opalescent or in every hue of the rainbow.

"A witch created all of this?" I asked in wonder. I glanced at Kylo, only to see that he was already staring at me.

His dangerously beautiful features were fixated on me in a way that made my stomach flutter. He gazed at me the same way I looked at the art.

Kylo tucked a strand of hair behind my ear. "Yes, baby. A true creator, just like you."

I shook my head. It didn't feel right to be compared to the woman who created all of *this*. This outpouring of love and mystery and divinity that I didn't quite have the words for.

"Why would they target someone like her? She's an artist, not a vampire maker."

A sudden onslaught of injustice and heartbreak caused my chest to tighten, and the feelings grew stronger the more the room glimmered and sparkled around us.

Kylo brushed a knuckle across my cheek. "They're not reasonable people, Evie. They're demons, and they're furious. Not just at the turned, but at all the mortals of Etherdale. The born have always hated Etherdale's limitations, institutions, and mortal stronghold. Now they have an excuse to unleash that fury. Their anger at not being able to dominate and use us to their heart's content—their utter hatred of anyone daring to stand up to them. What better revenge than to destroy our artists, teachers, and healers—those with the power to mend hearts and strengthen minds?"

It wasn't fair. None of it. That damn lump was back in my throat as I examined more of the exhibit, thinking about how the born had gone after Celeste's—after *me*—for making products that helped mortals.

In the final room, we were greeted by walls painted black,

the only light coming from tiny flickering stars and constellations. Even below our feet, we followed the paths of galaxies. A deep sense of calm entered my system, and I sensed the artist's magick ripple through the space. It was a signature filled with passion and hope, someone who looked up at the stars and refused to feel small and meaningless. Someone who looked up and felt grateful to be alive, instead.

When Kylo unexpectedly grabbed me and captured my lips with his, I felt that same fire in his soul—the counterargument to nihilism that expanded like the cosmos against the deep nothingness of space.

"Evie," he whispered, kissed by starlight, eyes filled with something raw and undeniable.

I ran a finger over that silly little dimple, the evidence of his humanity, the gentleness that made me stay after years of running.

Kylo kissed my hand. "I love you."

The air left my lungs.

"I'm so deeply in love with you that I can't go a full minute without you crossing my thoughts. I adore your mind, the way it processes this world and births new ones entirely. Your laugh makes me feel like I'm fucking dying, as if I will never be able to hear enough of it to be content."

My lips trembled, listening to Kylo describe me in a way that didn't make sense to me. He couldn't possibly feel so intensely.

"I loved you before it was rational or reasonable," he said as the stars glowed brighter. "I've loved you for a humiliatingly long while now, but I suspect I've always loved you. Like I recognized you the moment I first saw you, and the rest was merely a process of remembering how much you meant to me and always would."

Rich emotion flooded my body, but the block in my throat fought hard to keep any words from leaving my lips. Kylo watched me in a patient silence, holding my face in his broad hands.

I forced myself to speak through the harsh pounding of my fearful heart. "I love you too." Tears pooled in my eyes. "I don't want to, but I do."

Kylo smiled. "That's a lie. I think you want to love me very badly."

"Mena and Idris are the only people who I've ever let in," I said softly, scraping the words out despite every protest from my body. Something loosened and shattered irreversibly. A dam broke, and more words poured through. "I'm in love with you, but I don't want to be, because the people who were born to love me unconditionally, whose sole purpose was to protect me from harm…" I faltered, tears spilling free.

Kylo frowned deeply, catching the tears with his thumbs.

"They didn't. They didn't love me," I said, a sob building in the back of my throat. "They didn't protect me. All they did was use me. All they did was throw me and Idris to the wolves. So yes, I apologize for my own existence because that was what I was taught. That love is something strived after endlessly, never freely given. And if I put my trust in someone to protect me, they're just going to betray me and crush my heart beyond repair."

The sob left my lips, and I'd never cried like this in front of Kylo before, in front of most people. In this violent, uncontrollable sort of way.

"So of course I don't want to be in love," I said. "I don't want to rely on anyone who might let me down. Because my heart can't survive that kind of pain again."

In this room of stars, Kylo sank with me to the floor and held me against him as sob after sob racked through me.

"I'm sorry," I said. "I'm sorry for ruining your beautiful moment. I'm so sorry."

"Shhh, baby," Kylo whispered, stroking my hair. "My love is

not contingent upon your behavior. You don't have to perform for my love. You don't have to beg for it. Or even ask very politely. I love you for existing. I love you for being you."

"Sounds fake," I sobbed into his chest.

Kylo laughed softly. "One day, it won't feel that way. One day, being loved by me will feel as certain and effortless as breathing. And I am more than happy to show you how much I care for you, how much I would do anything to earn and keep your trust, every day until then."

My crying reached its tipping point, the violence melting into mournful, lulling waves.

I blinked through my tears, looking around at the shimmering galaxies that hadn't dimmed a bit. They were steady. Certain.

I moved to lay facing Kylo, on my side, and he mirrored me.

"I always wondered what made me go find you in the library the first time we met," I said, staring into the blue of his irises as he traced my face with his gentle touch. "I don't talk to strangers. Especially not ones who acted as unhinged as you did. Nor would I ever dare to pick a fight with a random man, either."

Kylo smiled. "I thought the same thing. Given I'd already been following you for weeks, and I'd picked up on your people-avoidant behaviors."

I glared at him, and his grin only widened. "I never understood why I would do something like that. How I had possibly known you were safe. Even when I'd found out you were everything I'd learned to hate. I still knew you were safe. I couldn't stop myself from falling."

"Good," Kylo said, his shadows skating over me in that possessive way they did. "Because I'm here to catch you, always. Especially when you don't trust me to."

My face felt red and puffy. Leave it to me to unravel during the most romantic moment of my life.

"If only to wrestle with you in the mud again," he added.

"I despise you."

"Is that so?"

He rolled and pinned me beneath him, sliding my wrists above my head. "Don't pretend my adorable, flower-picking little forest nymph doesn't enjoy getting hunted, captured, and destroyed in the grass and dirt."

His breath tickled as it skated across my skin, and I was suddenly alert to everywhere he touched. Especially where his hips met mine.

My chest rose and fell rapidly, the place between my thighs awakened with a sudden pulsing ache.

"I don't love like a normal person, Evie darling," he said, low and gravely.

My core tightened in anticipation.

"I don't do anything like a normal person," he said with dark humor. "Because I love you, you aren't merely mine to care for and protect. You're also mine to torment. Mine to toy with. To possess. To *own*. To flood with pleasure until you're begging for relief—relief that will never come. You're mine to mark and bite and claim and fucking destroy until you're nothing but a needy mess at my feet, pleading with your God for mercy."

My breathing became shallower. I didn't even care what was wrong with me—why I loved Kylo's depravity as much as his adoration and praise. Because now my thighs were pressing together, my panties already damp with want.

Kylo's thumb pressed into my mouth, and I lightly sucked. His eyes burned with intensity, a low groan escaping him. Suddenly his hand gripped my throat, and his lips were against mine. His fangs scraped, his shadows squeezed my erect nipples until I whimpered into Kylo's mouth.

He lifted an inch. "Let's practice, baby," he said darkly. *"Beg."*

The way he commanded me like I was an obedient pet only

made me uncomfortably aroused, my mind melting into blissful surrender as I squirmed and ached for him.

"You can do it, sweet girl," he praised.

I found my voice again. "Please," I whispered, feeding off Kylo's approval. "I want you. All of you." My heart stuttered. "*Please, Kylo.*"

It looked like Kylo was struggling not to let his darkened eyes roll back as he grinned down at me. He squeezed my cheeks between his strong fingers. "Good fucking girl," he purred.

I squirmed and then paused.

"But, um, maybe not in a missing woman's art exhibit?"

Kylo nodded. "Fair enough."

46

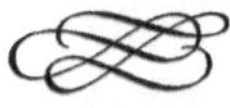

EVIE

I preferred Kylo in his vampire form, his true form. And perhaps that was the greatest evidence of my love.

Or maybe hatred, love, and lust were all bound up together in my brain in some kind of perverse mental circuitry.

Either way, I stared at Kylo's tall, tattooed, muscled form unabashedly in his grand foyer. The dark blue shirt that clung to his chest, making the blue of his eyes that much more shocking. The black pants and boots that gave him an edge, a hint of the authority that oozed from his every pore.

And that power—gods, it rumbled through the entire home, echoing against the walls in a steady hum of intensity.

"You never told me how the battle went," I said, knowing innately that Kylo had likely slaughtered countless born with his unearthly force.

Kylo shook his head. "Not now, angel. Just you and me. No one else matters." He tipped my chin up. "Understood?"

Something inside me relaxed, uncoiled. "Yes, please."

"Aw, you know how much I love when my good girl uses her manners." He brushed his lips against mine briefly as he carried me upstairs.

I knew what was coming. A shot of anxiety coursed through me as strong as my desire.

When Kylo set me down in his room, the lighting warm and inviting against the dark tones of his décor, I suddenly felt awkward and inexperienced.

He noticed the shift, just as he noticed too much of me at all times. "Little one, I need you to listen very carefully."

I stared up at him like his words were the only thing tethering me to this plane.

"You do not have to do *anything* you don't want to do. You will not disappoint me. Do you understand?"

I nodded, fiddling with my hands nervously.

Kylo smiled as he reached for them, bringing each to his lips before intertwining his fingers with mine. "I would be happy to fall asleep with you in my arms. There is no pressure."

I nodded. "I know. I already told you what I wanted. And it's no longer about my past. It's about *you and me*," I said, repeating the phrase he'd used.

Because my fragile, hopeful heart loved the way it rolled off my tongue. This declaration of us as a unit, two souls intertwined. The promise that I might not have to live this life so alone.

A shudder rolled through Kylo, and I recognized the sudden hunger in his eyes—the look that wasn't entirely human.

It sent a jolt of fear down to the very core of me, the same fear I'd started to associate with pleasure.

Because now when I ran, I had Kylo to chase after me.

"You want it all, hmm?" he asked, low and teetering on the edge of sinister. He helped me out of my dress, tracing my body as he went. "My greedy girl."

He used his frightening vampire speed to grab me and shove me onto the bed, his mouth on my neck before I'd even registered what had happened.

I shuddered with pleasure. He kissed and then sucked,

harder and harder, until I knew for certain he was leaving marks. When I felt his teeth against my skin, and I let out a frightened noise from somewhere primal, subconscious—the part of me that wished desperately to survive.

He didn't bite down, an amused chuckle rolling through him.

"*That* was one of my favorite noises yet," Kylo teased as he stared hard into my eyes. "Is my vulnerable little prey having second thoughts?"

I shook my head no. My rapidly beating heart begged to differ.

When Kylo removed my panties, he kissed both of my inner thighs. He did so worshipfully, in some holy act of devotion.

"Evie, baby," he said softly, his breath hitching as he stared between my thighs. His eyes were slow to return to mine. "You have the prettiest little pussy."

As if he couldn't help himself, he kissed my aching clit, his tongue skating through my folds—kissing, sucking, and—

I inhaled sharply, a soft cry escaping my lips at the unmistakable scrape of fangs.

"*My* pretty little pussy," Kylo growled. "Isn't that right, angel?"

He stared up at me through his thick lashes, smirking when his tongue once again found my clit. When his teeth met my skin, I went utterly still.

"Yes, Kylo," I breathed. Fear and arousal competed for dominance in my blood. They both only made me slicker with need for him.

He removed the threat of fangs from my sensitive flesh, humming praises now that made me feel satisfied and melty. Like my life, my pleasure, my everything was in his strong palms.

"I do trust you," I suddenly whispered, making Kylo stop his unspoken acts of devotion to my body.

He lifted his head from where he'd been leaving trails of kisses along my pubic bone, hips, thighs.

He stared at me like I'd given him the whole world, something pure and human entering those predator's eyes. His smile was genuine and soft, slipping through his mask of danger and dominance.

"Thank you for telling me so, Evie. That's all I've ever wanted."

He kissed my stomach next, his lips like a scalding brand of ownership.

"I will never let you down."

Those words unraveled my last threads of defense, the ropes that had limited me and kept me from true connection for so many years.

I believed him.

"Now be a good girl and stay put," he said, his tone the perfect mix of authority and adoration.

He kissed between my thighs one last time before moving off the bed. In agonizingly graceful movements, I watched him remove his shirt and unbuckle his belt.

His amused eyes found mine. "Your poor heart. Take deep breaths for me, angel." His smirk widened as my gaze went from hungrily devouring his beautiful, tattooed body to watching his massive cock spring free from his pants.

I remembered the way it tasted, the way it felt hitting the back of my throat. It was already too big for my mouth…

Oh gods. My thighs inched closer together instinctively.

"Uh-uh, baby," Kylo snapped, his voice like the sharp command of a whip.

Shadows leaped from his body, wrapping around my legs and forcing them open and spread wide.

"Don't you dare hide what belongs to me."

I watched as Kylo moved around the room, taking his time lighting pillar candles scattered across his furniture.

"You've been wearing that necklace almost every day since I bought it for you," he said softly, his eyes narrowing on the moonstone pendant around my neck.

It had become such a part of me that I forgot about it half the time.

"It brought me a great deal of comfort in those early days, to see that you'd already accepted my claim on you—even if it was subconsciously."

I huffed defiantly. "It was pretty. Why let something beautiful go to waste just because it was given to you by an insane person?"

Kylo laughed, lighting the last candle and slowly stalking back toward me. "You have no idea the pretty things your insane boyfriend is going to spoil you with."

His voice was a low hum, tightening my core as I stared at his nude form, his cock that was still rock hard. He was just showing off at this point.

Tease.

"Although, some of the things you'll be gifted will be as much for my pleasure as yours," he said with a mischievous grin.

"You don't have to—"

"Shhh," Kylo said, crawling onto the bed and between my legs as my heart pounded with anticipation. "Good girls get spoiled."

He left no room for protest as his lips crashed into mine under the warm candlelight. In our kiss, I tasted it—the buzz of fate, the love written in the stars that I'd once believed could only be found between the pages of a book.

I'd been wrong.

My magick flared, tingles erupting across my skin in a silent show of approval from the spirit world.

"Settle down, little witch," Kylo laughed, and I followed his gaze to the wild candle flames dancing violently and leaping up toward the cosmos.

I stopped myself from apologizing, giggling softly instead.

"You swear to me you'll use your words and tell me what you want or don't want?" Kylo asked sternly.

I nodded again. "I want it all."

Kylo smirked. "Good. That's what I plan on giving you. Forever."

He toyed with my breasts, cupping them, running circles around my nipples and lightly pinching.

"So fucking perfect."

He pulled a nipple into his mouth as my back arched and a moan escaped me. His fingers reached to work my clit. I was already soaking wet. Something larger was at my opening, pushing inside as I gasped.

One of those sneaky shadows pulsed, driving me closer and closer to the edge of my first release.

"I'm going to fuck you before I feed from you. I need you fully aware as you take every inch of me, as you feel me stretch and destroy this pretty little pussy," Kylo said, his jaw flexing.

I could nearly see the hint of bloodlust enter the corners of his eyes. The way he ran his tongue over his fangs as if they were aching in his gums.

They scraped against one of my nipples. The shadow grew larger as it pulsed inside of me. His fingers expertly worked me up to the edge.

"*Come.*"

I crashed. I clenched against the appendage inside me, grinding against Kylo's fingers as his tongue now slid inside my mouth.

"Mmm," he hummed as he consumed me, as I arched and trembled beneath him. He slowly stopped tormenting my sensitive flesh, pulling back. "Good little angel."

Suddenly a shadow was at my lips, and Kylo's eyes darkened as I opened my mouth. I tasted myself on this strange, smooth limb, and the depravity of it had me reeling, sliding further and further under Kylo's spell.

He smiled at me, stroking fingers through my hair as I sucked.

The shadow was slow to recede. Kylo pushed up to lord over my pliable body. He stroked his terrifying cock once before sliding it between my thick folds.

The pressure of the head at my entrance was enough to make me moan, to tense up in anticipation.

"Evie, baby," Kylo said, cool authority mixed with coaxing softness. "Can you relax for me, please?"

My muscles slowly unwound as I nodded. He stroked the side of my face. That slick shadow now played with my tits.

"My shadows might love you as much as I do," Kylo said, staring down at me hungrily as his cock teased my pussy, sliding up and down.

One of the shadows wrapped around my neck, as if in agreement.

His composure slid again when his cock was back at my entrance, pushing ever-so-slightly. Kylo shuddered, his eyes flashing. I winced at the impossible stretch.

"Slow, deep breaths. I know you can be a good girl and take your God's cock, angel," he said.

The shadow moved off my throat, and Kylo's hand replaced it instead. He didn't use any pressure, just rested there possessively as his jaw feathered.

"After all, he's been waiting for a very long time to forever stain this angelic body with his darkness," he rasped, pushing further.

I cried out, but the aching fullness was tempered by a cascade of tingling pleasure and warmth that radiated from my core outward.

"Shhh. You're okay," he cooed. He once again studied my face.

My brows were drawn tightly, my legs trembling. But I nodded slightly to reassure him.

I took another deep breath, and the discomfort melted further, allowing me to revel in the fullness. I *wanted* to be full of Kylo.

He smiled at me, applying the slightest pressure to the sides of my throat. For some godsforsaken reason, the threat to my life only relaxed me deeper.

He moved his hand up to my mouth, sticking two fingers in.

"Get them nice and wet for me, please," he said softly.

I swirled my tongue, and Kylo moved his slick fingers down to my clit.

The pleasure helped me to acclimate, to take another inch as my eyes rolled back and Kylo groaned.

"Gods below," he hissed. "You feel so fucking good, Evie. I fear you don't exactly know what you've gotten yourself into…"

He trailed off as I spasmed around the impossible girth. The tingly feeling was overwhelming now, overtaking the pain and driving me to new heights of ecstasy.

"… because now that you've allowed me to mark what's mine with my cum, I won't be able to get enough of you. You think I was obsessed and possessive before?" He laughed darkly. "You try to hide from me now, and I will fucking chain you to my bed."

His fingers were relentless. My core tightened, and my body racked with wave upon wave of pleasure.

"If any man so much as glances at you too long for my liking, I will rot him from the inside out without an ounce of remorse."

I cried in frustration when he stopped playing with my clit and reached up to squeeze my face.

"Are you listening, baby?"

I nodded.

"Open."

I opened my mouth, and Kylo spit inside. He glared down at me until I swallowed.

"Thank you, Kylo."

His approval flooded me with a high stronger than any drug. In the clutches of this dark god, this violent, bloodthirsty monster, I was safe.

I whimpered when his cock eased inside me yet another inch, and his fingers were back to toying with my clit.

He nodded. "What a good girl. Look at this pretty pink pussy taking my cock with gratitude."

My moans turned into a cry when Kylo slowly rocked his hips, sliding in and out of me, deeper with each thrust.

It was like I was being split in two. Yet, just as much pleasure entered my system as pain in an overpowering cocktail of intensity.

"You're doing so well, sweet girl," Kylo cooed, even as his voice trembled, raw power escaping him to course through the room. Shadows bled from his skin. His jaw was locked tight. His dark blue eyes were molten.

For whatever reason, my mind chose now to remember The Devil card I'd pulled weeks ago. Which I supposed made sense, as I let this chthonic deity take my virginity as he was slowly consumed by his lust for my blood.

Kylo let out a deep, ungodly groan, and the sound of him unraveling drove me up to the peak of release.

Because *I* did this to him.

I held the capacity to make the most powerful monster in Etherdale lose his precious control.

"Uh-huh," Kylo said. "Come for me. Let me feel this sweet, untouched pussy come on its owner's cock."

The violence, the dirtiness of such a statement, made me let go completely. Kylo speared deeper than ever, and I screamed as I clamped down and exploded. The most intense orgasm of my life swept through my body like a violent storm.

My muscles had been forced to relax by my undoing, and Kylo took full advantage. He drove into me as I moaned and writhed, and when another scream left my lips, he covered my mouth with his hand and stared hard into my eyes.

His smirk was downright wicked. "Take. It."

Behind my eyelids, I saw that room of stars. I heard Kylo telling me he was in love with me.

My heart was so fucking full, and when I opened my eyes again, I found Kylo staring at me, just like he had in that room. He kissed my lips, both my flushed cheeks, then he scooped me into his arms and fucked me while holding me in his lap.

He was so strong that he made me feel like merely a doll, a toy he could use and bend at will. I whimpered as I slid up and down. Kylo's lips brushed my forehead. He spread my ass cheeks apart as he filled me. My legs shook violently now.

One of his hands moved up to palm my breasts, pinching my nipple until I screamed.

He grinned, and I panted, another orgasm already building.

"I can't wait for you to step out of line with that bratty mouth," Kylo said darkly, his lips close to my temple. "Because next time, I'll be fucking you into submission and turning that perfect little ass red. I'll finish by tasting those beautiful tears on my tongue, knowing you won't be able to sit or walk for days."

"You're sadistic," I breathed, having difficulty using words as Kylo continued to spear me. My body was so full of pleasure and pain that I was on the verge of collapse.

Kylo lifted a brow incredulously. "Have I not made that abundantly clear?"

He suddenly lifted me off his cock and twisted me so that I was on my stomach.

"Ass in the air, angel. Now."

My breathing was rapid, shallow. I was far too empty without him inside me, without his hands on my body. I obeyed without question.

"What a beautiful fucking sight," Kylo said.

When his hands caressed the curve of my ass, I let out a small exhale.

Then a palm came down hard, the sound of it hitting my flesh like a strike of lightning.

I squealed, but as soon as I made a move, Kylo shoved my face back down into the comforter.

"Stay still, baby."

He was somehow even harder when he entered me this time, proving his sadism unequivocally.

I whimpered, reacclimating as he continued moving deeper and deeper.

When I heard Kylo spit, I tensed, the feel of warm liquid running across my ass. His thumb circled. I wasn't sure what kind of noise left my lips, only that it had clearly delighted Kylo as he chuckled in response.

"I want all my pretty little holes filled, baby," Kylo purred. "Because there is no escaping me. I'm going to bury myself so deep inside you that you will know with every breath who the fuck you belong to."

His thumb entered my ass as his cock eased in and out of my pussy. I'd never felt fuller, a low mewl escaping my lips as I stayed arched for him. My brows drew tight, my cheek pressing into the comforter with every thrust.

"I'm going to…" I moaned, nearly incoherent as I entered some other plane of existence.

If I thought the last orgasm was violent, this one tore through me in a way that made me scream, assaulted by its sheer force. And Kylo only *laughed at me.*

"That's my good little toy—my *favorite* new toy." He made a primal sound from low in his throat, not only refusing to stop fucking me but also impaling me far rougher than before. He made a tsk noise against the roof of his mouth. "If only you could see what you just did to my bedding. Messy, greedy little thing."

My cheeks were hot, and yet the humiliation only drove me deeper into melty, thoughtless pleasure.

"I can't wait to play with you to my heart's content. To see what else makes this pussy drench my sheets."

This time when he smacked and then gripped my ass roughly, I hardly felt the sting. The pinch still made me cry out, tears pooling in my eyes from the intensity.

Kylo eased out of me gently before flipping me back onto my back, his eyes finding mine. He gently stroked my cheek before kissing my forehead.

"Nod if you're still doing okay."

Grateful I didn't have to speak, I nodded.

The headspace I'd entered felt drug-like. I stared up into Kylo's eyes like he really was my God.

And I *loved it.*

After years of escaping true vulnerability, of never allowing myself to rely on anyone or trust anyone else to protect me or take care of me the way I could...

Submitting to this deranged vampire who read philosophy, who dreamed of a better world, who saw and understood me for who I truly was at my core—it was the longest, deepest exhale of relief.

Kylo placed a broad hand on my stomach. "You'd look so fucking pretty carrying my child."

The words shocked me. My eyes widened.

Stranger still was the way my body responded immediately and decisively to such a declaration. My nipples pebbled, heat gathering in my core.

"I can hear and sense every single reaction you have, angel," Kylo whispered. "You like the idea of me planting my seed inside you? Of me forcing you to show the whole world who owns this perfect body? Your perfect soul?"

I made a strangled whimper as he pushed the deepest he'd ever gone, my legs high in the air as he buried himself.

"Use your words," he demanded.

"Yes," I managed, my voice trembling.

"You want me to mark this pussy with my cum, baby?"

I nodded. "Please."

Kylo's eyes rolled back. That little dimple disappeared as that vampiric, predatory look eclipsed his features. Now when he stared at me, he did it like I was his next meal.

He wouldn't actually enter bloodlust, right?

Kylo flashed his fangs. He appeared strained, bleeding more and more shadow.

Right?

My voice was raw when I cried out this time. Kylo drove deep as he came as close to my cervix as he could manage. I trembled with satisfaction as warmth pooled inside me.

I didn't have very much time to enjoy the pleasure of Kylo filling me with cum, because as soon as he'd eased out of me, he whispered just one word.

"Run."

47

EVIE

I ran down the hall to the only room I knew. I didn't hear footsteps. I didn't hear anything at all over the sound of my own heart beating, my shallow panting.

Still delirious with pleasure and submission, my head swam as I burst into the library.

Goosebumps covered my nude flesh at the sound of low laughter.

"Look at that pretty sight," a voice rasped. "My cum running down my little angel's thigh."

I spun, but I didn't see Kylo anywhere, even as I felt his eyes on me like a hot brand.

Hot liquid trickled out of me, and my cheeks burned with embarrassment.

My heart steadied. A vampire in bloodlust would've ripped me to shreds already.

Kylo was merely playing with his food. Making my blood as delicious as possible by coating it with fear, arousal, and adrenaline.

"Each time you came for me, your blood grew infinitely

more irresistible," he nearly groaned, confirming my suspicions. He was hiding behind some kind of glamour.

Even if I knew it was a game, I was still terrified, disoriented, and worst of all—starved of him. As if I didn't care what he did to me, so long as he was touching me again and holding me close.

At a sudden wind near me, my nipples hardened. A chill rolled down my spine.

"I will ask you one more time," Kylo hissed, closer now.

I spun in circles, my chest rising and falling, my arms outstretched defensively.

"Are you sure you want me addicted to you in this way?"

I didn't hesitate. I didn't flinch. "Yes."

Like a true demon, Kylo manifested from a cloud of shadow in the corner of the room. And I ran again on impulse as soon as I saw those bared fangs.

He let me get all the way back to the door before he yanked me back against his chest. I squealed.

"Shh," he whispered. "That's tough. Better luck next time."

He dragged me backward, down to where the loveseat, chairs, and other furniture formed a semi-circle. The place he'd brushed my tangled wet hair with unfathomable tenderness.

I flailed futilely, and Kylo's cock was already semi-hard against my back.

"I love when these cute little feet try to kick me," Kylo teased. On the larger couch, he manhandled me into his lap. He brushed his lips against mine briefly.

My fear and panic spiked as his shadows bound my wrists behind my back. Likely so I could no longer attempt to hit and push away from him and escape.

His cock swelled underneath me.

A shadow slithered across my mouth.

Kylo wore that sadistic, evil grin. His eyes transformed. He slid me down on his length as he brought my neck to his lips.

"Breathe."

That was the last thing he whispered before his fangs plunged into the side of my throat, and his hips jerked to bury his cock deeper.

The shadows let go of my wrists. I no longer had any desire to struggle.

Ripples upon ripples of strange, overpowering pleasure washed over every inch of me, radiating outward from where Kylo's fangs latched onto my skin.

A full-body shudder moved through both of us at the same time. Kylo gripped me harder. Tingles fell over my skin, my every nerve suddenly drenched in ecstasy. I melted into Kylo's lap like I was nothing but a pliable doll for him to use at will.

That was all I wanted to be. I was aware that he was taking my blood, that his vampiric venom was infecting me with its drug-like properties.

But all I could do was relax. I was a fly in a carnivorous plant's trap, content to be consumed so long as this delicious, addictive pleasure coursed through my blood.

Every thrust of his cock felt like another orgasm, a release that spread out for an eternity.

I heard myself moan into the shadow gag, but it sounded foreign to my own ears.

The gag fell away.

A tongue ran along my neck, and I knew Kylo was clotting my blood with his saliva. Another useful vampiric quality.

I giggled.

Kylo studied my features, his own utterly blissful and entirely feral both at the same time. "Why are you laughing, baby?"

I looked down at where he was still inside me, exactly where I wanted him to be forever. "I don't remember."

Kylo rolled his eyes with a grin. "Already venom drunk, are we?"

Droplets of my blood stained his perfect, icy pink lips. I was inside of him now, too.

And something about that fulfilled a deep desire, an innate need to be just as intertwined with Kylo and his shadows as they were with me.

"One day, you're going to be able to wear these bites proudly, everywhere you go," he said. "So everyone can see what a perfect, good girl you are for the vampire lord of Etherdale."

There was no room inside me for the fear and anger that ordinarily would've hogged all the space.

I gazed at Kylo dreamily instead. He shook his head with another grin, brushing my hair behind my shoulders. He cupped a breast, and I shuddered with pleasure. His hips continued to rock, and this time, I could hardly feel any pain from the stretch.

He lifted me slightly as he lowered his head. His tongue darted out, swirling around an erect peak. He sucked, more beautiful flutters shooting through my body. I soon felt that familiar scrape of fangs around my nipple.

Only this time, they didn't just tease my skin.

Kylo sunk his fangs into my flesh. My blood flowed easily as he held me tight.

My mind floated, overcome with sensation. The shockwaves were ten times as intense from this bite, flooding from my breast and outward, all the way down to my clit.

Only the slightest brush of fingers between my thighs had me unraveling again, coming on his cock as he fed from me.

Kylo trembled, gripping me so tightly I knew I was bruising beneath his fingertips.

Lost in a sea of beautiful, churning euphoria, my release extended for an eternity. My hands were caught in Kylo's black hair.

"Hair—so nice, so soft," I murmured, my voice more blissful than I'd ever heard before.

Kylo's chest rumbled with quiet laughter, and his tongue circled this latest bite to close the wound. He gripped my waist, his cock twitching inside me.

"One more, baby," Kylo said softly. "For symmetry."

He sunk down into my other breast, and I somehow slipped even deeper into the vat of pleasure consuming my every nerve. I wasn't even sure if I was orgasming again or if the last one had never stopped.

I'd become a part of Kylo. I could feel the way my essence now lived inside of him. Like we were sharing the same blood, the same breath, the same life force.

He pulled away slowly, straightening back up as he now bounced me up and down on his cock to meet his thrusts.

One of his hands moved to clutch my cheek as he stared into my eyes.

His tongue slowly caught a stray drop of crimson on his lower lip. His lips were slightly stained with blood, but he was a very tidy, restrained monster.

I laughed again.

"I'd give anything to know the reasons for all these giggles," Kylo said.

He stroked my hair as I murmured something unintelligible. He was gentler now as he locked me in place, continuing to impale me until I felt him shudder beneath me.

His cock twitched violently, and more warmth spilled inside me.

All the while, Kylo held my face and watched me in that careful, obsessive way he did.

His lips slowly curved. "How does it feel, little one? To know you've ruined all other blood for me for an eternity?"

I sighed contently, never wanting to be anywhere but Kylo's lap ever again. "Safe."

48

KYLO

Evie was so fucking adorable right now that I could hardly handle it. I didn't trust her to stand at the present, so I ran her a warm bath.

Under the thin layer of bubbles, she lay with her head resting on the back of the tub on a cloth. She stared at me dreamily as I gently ran a soapy washrag along her body.

I fucking loved seeing my bite marks on her fair skin. The one on her neck was the most red and angry looking. I'd been more careful with the ones around her nipples.

If I'd had it my way, she'd have them fucking everywhere. Or, rather, if I was indulging my most primal, vampiric self. My higher self cared more about stopping before I caused Evie any harm, before I lost my precious control.

I hadn't fed like that, straight from the veins of a mortal, in years. It was too intimate, too distracting. I preferred to live a life of discipline, lest anything divert my obsessive focus from my clan and my city.

Evie clearly had other plans for me.

But as I took care of her now, there was nothing sexual

about my intentions. My only focus was making sure she felt comfortable and safe.

How sweet and vulnerable she was right now was exactly why I'd taken her virginity before she'd experienced vampire venom for the first time. I would never have robbed her of so much agency at that moment.

"How are we doing, baby?" I asked her, laughing softly at the way her small hand was grabbing at my arm every time it was near her.

"Do you have any chocolate?" Her features were a mixture of soft concern and blissful relaxation. "It's okay if not," she added, as if she'd asked for me to cut off one of my arms for her.

I grinned. "Craving anything specific?"

She shook her head, the level of thoughtful concern in her features making it seem like I'd given her a complex mathematical equation.

"I'll get you every type of chocolate in the city."

She narrowed those pretty gray eyes. "That's excessive."

I lifted a shoulder. "Don't care." I kissed her knuckles. "If it makes you feel better, you can frame it as entirely self-serving on my end. Because nothing makes me happier than taking care of you." I smirked. "Or maybe I just desperately want to taste all that decadent indulgence in your blood."

Evie's eyes widened slightly before fluttering. "Okay."

I chuckled. She was far too agreeable for her own good right now. And on the one hand, it did something dark to my desire for her. On the other, it made me rather feral. Because the thought of her like *this* in front of anyone else?

I feared that her useless, whiny ex Jarod was merely one of many murders to come.

～

My heart physically ached in my chest as Evie fell asleep in my arms. She had no idea the effect she had on me, now more than ever. We were bonded in a way that could never be broken, in too many ways to count.

The emotions that flooded me were so human, so vulnerable. And I welcomed them, in a secret sort of way—these rich, deep yearnings I would feel for her and only her. Feelings my broader clan and Ravenia would never know about, would never glean from my ruthless, impassive mask.

Tonight, when I'd brushed her hair, I'd known for sure she was crying softly. She felt just as deeply and vastly as I did for her. And I understood now why she both loved and hated the way I doted on her.

Because the last time she'd been promised care and protection, she'd been traumatized instead.

My caregiving cracked her wide-open; it dug into her deepest, most hidden wounds.

I'd put her in one of my shirts, forced her to eat something and drink a glass of water, and now she was endearingly warm and sweet in my arms.

She'd fallen asleep nearly instantly.

I could hardly remember who I was before I'd met her. Before this soft, wounded girl was my most cherished responsibility.

Perhaps that was why I couldn't fall asleep yet. Why I needed to spend this time with her while she was angelic and lost in her dreamworld. Because I wanted to fully immerse myself in the aftermath of everything that had happened tonight.

I lay in a contented state of gratitude for another hour, merely listening to her heart slowly beat.

I'd claimed so many of Evie's firsts. But being the only man to have earned her love was the most special of all.

～

I woke in the middle of the night to Evie whimpering.

"Idris. Look! Just a child. *Please.*"

The pain in her quivering voice shattered me. She sounded heartbreakingly desperate, like she was pleading for someone—anyone to listen.

She was on her side in my arms, turned away from me. Her whole body jerked.

"I'm sorry. I'm sorry. I'm sorry."

This time when she flinched, it was accompanied by a wail that really did split my chest down the middle.

I heard her heart and breathing quicken as she woke up to the sound of her own scream.

"Shhh, baby," I whispered in her ear as I pulled her closer. "You're safe. You're in Etherdale. You're safe."

The words instantly calmed her, and she twisted in my arms to bury her head into my chest. I felt slick tears dampen my skin.

I continued to run my hands through her hair soothingly, down her shoulders and back until she calmed down.

She peeled herself away to look into my eyes. "I'm sorry for waking you."

"Don't be."

She smiled sadly. "I have fewer nightmares when you're with me. But the closer we get to the end of summer, the worse they become. Happens every year."

I stayed perfectly silent, as if any sudden move might make her stop talking and wall herself back up again.

"That woman at the party—Wendy—she made Idris and me uncomfortable because she's a retired psychology professor and part-time emotional healer. I didn't want her anywhere near us, back then..." She trailed off. "Well, anyway, she says the nightmares are because trauma is stored in the body, and the body remembers the exact time when bad things happened to us in the past."

Between states of consciousness, she wasn't being entirely clear. I could also hear the nervousness in her voice, the erratic beats of her heart.

"I was born into a cult."

I stopped my gentle caresses. In the darkness, I could see Evie's lip tremble.

She'd finally said it.

Even if I'd already suspected the reality of Evie's past, I still had never heard her confirm it so plainly.

"You know the one," she murmured. "We were lambs being raised for sacrificial tithing. My father was human. My witch mother was elated to have birthed a human son and a half-witch daughter whose blood smelled human but even *stronger*. Even more…" Evie hissed out her next words. *"Unique. Delicious. Perfect."*

I needed to know more. I needed Evie to tell me these truths, so I could better protect her heart. Not to mention better destroy our mutual fucking enemies.

But gods, if each admission of her past didn't kill me inside. My throat tightened as I listened.

"I took Idris and ran. The spirits of the realm aided me every step of the way. They helped me find people who harbored us on our journey. A woman who let us ride with her on her firebird. A man who told me I needed to get to Etherdale, the safest mortal-run city in the realm. A city surrounded by mountains. And whatever forces were on my side led me to Mena. She took us in. I don't know why the universe was so gracious with me when I hardly deserved it. Maybe to protect Idris. But that's what happened. That's why I ran."

Gods, there was so much to unpack I didn't know where to start. I didn't want to push her, either.

"How old were you when you ran, angel?"

"Thirteen," she said, wiping at the fresh tears that had pooled in her eyes. "Idris was seven."

"Why in the world would you think you didn't deserve grace and protection?" I asked, incredulous as I stared at this strong, beautifully fucking resilient girl.

She clamped her mouth shut. She shook her head. I worried I'd said the wrong thing, and she was done talking about it.

She finally spoke. "It doesn't matter."

I kissed her forehead. "You are one of the bravest, most impressive people I've ever met, Evie. I am honored you felt safe enough to tell me about your past. You were so young, and you still managed to do something most would consider impossible. You deprogrammed yourself. You rescued your brother. You found refuge and made a whole new life for yourself. And you did it all when you were only a *child*." I stared deep into her gray depths with awe, with reverence. "I can assure you that no harm will ever again befall you or your brother. This city will always be safe for you. I vow it."

"How can you vow such a thing?" Evie whispered. "When you want to go to war with *King Earle*?"

"Because it's true," I said, unwaveringly. "Don't worry about that right now. We can talk more about the future later, okay?"

She was clearly unconvinced, but she nodded anyway. "Will you tell me about yours now, please?"

"Of course. A deal is a deal."

She wanted to move on, for me to stop asking questions. It was more than clear she was concealing parts of her story from me, and that was okay. Evie required patience, and I was more than happy to give her as much as she needed.

Even if my mind ran in circles, parsing through all of her little slips and fears and behaviors. The way she was terrified, disgusted by her own magick. The way she escaped all praise for her courageous actions.

Something didn't add up, and we both knew it.

"I grew up a long distance from Etherdale, in Morha." I paused, realizing Evie had never actually said where she was from. I put a pin in that for later. "We didn't have nearly as many protections from vampires, but like the rest of the realm, peace was kept between mortals and immortals through intricate negotiations and balances of power. Any misbehaving born were labeled bad apples. Violence was mostly random and self-contained. This was the narrative we were fed. That there was no alternative, that we needed to accept what small protections we were given with gratitude. After all, who would dare oppose King Earle?"

Evie didn't show her typical disdain for revolutionary rhetoric. It was as though her mind had opened a crack, just enough to listen to what I had to say.

"Even in the North, near King Earle's blessed city of Prospyrus, there were whispers of an underground slave trade. A way for the born to enjoy the same wealth and special treatment as Earle and his famed court, or his legion of gluttonous nobility. And of course we had Servants of Lillian in the rural areas, grooming mortals for the elite."

Evie flinched slightly, and I was quick to run my fingers down her temple and through her hair.

"They were swept under the rug and rationalized as a product of rural living and religiosity, or worse, as a social norm and concession to keep the born happy and preoccupied with the cult's children rather than regular mortals." That low tremble of rage was back, imagining Evie groomed to marry some ancient, wealthy born. "It's all bullshit, of course. All the excuses. All the attempts to reason with demons without any concern for mortal life."

I let myself travel backward, to the memory I'd worked on with Princeton only yesterday. The root of immeasurable turmoil, the reason for why I was extraordinarily harsh with myself for any conceivable failure or moral misstep. It was no doubt the reason I was so obsessively protective of Evie, too.

"As I said before, I was a lonely child," I said, softer now. "I'd always felt different from the other children, from my own family. Obsessive, intense, passionate. A little too much for people. I cared a great deal about injustices, the unfairness of born violence. I remember clearly the day my mother and father sat me down, telling me exactly how to behave around the born. What to do if I was ever attacked, how to best save my life as a human with no magick, no defenses. It made me immensely sad, scared, and confused. I did a lot of reading after that, learning about how to weaken and kill vampires. I would later worry that my preoccupation with the born at such a young age attracted the event that followed. Manifested it, even."

Evie mirrored my fallen features, her small hand reaching up to trace my jaw. I leaned into her touch gratefully.

"My reprieve from loneliness growing up was my best friend and partner in crime, Aisling. We were drawn to each other from the moment we met in primary lessons, both more lost in our own imagined realities than the physical world around us. We hung out in libraries, practiced fighting out in the forest with weapons we'd looted from parents or created with sticks and other materials lying around." My smile fell almost as soon as it was formed. "We were still kids—teenagers—when the born found us doing what we did best one night, out on some old farmer's property on the edge of town. We'd finished up annihilating a poor scarecrow with these throwing knives we'd bought after saving money for months. We were lying in the grass, talking about how we were going to see the whole world, study at Etherdale University, marry pretty girls who would be totally cool with us still being roguish adventurers and vampire hunters."

My lips couldn't help but curve again, for a brief moment, even as my throat tightened and heart clenched. Evie mirrored my smile, hanging on my every word as those stormy gray eyes pierced right through me.

"A group of born stumbled upon us, and I knew they'd heard

what I'd said about vampire hunting. I knew it was *because* of what I'd said that they did what they did next." My voice was harsher now, quivering with anger and heartbreak and deep, bottomless guilt. "One of them held me still and made me watch the other two slowly torture and kill Aisling. They fed from her recklessly. They tormented her. Degraded her. Assaulted her. Every horrible thing you could think of. They did it, and they made me watch every second of it. And cruelest of all, they didn't harm a hair on my head. They left me with her drained, lifeless, brutalized body, while I was agonizingly alive and physically untouched."

Evie's face crumpled. I hated watching her cry like this, knowing I was the one to have caused her pain. I'd tried not to give too many details, because she didn't deserve to hear the true depths of the violence I witnessed. But even the bare facts were brutal, unconscionable.

Evie shook her head, tears staining her cheeks. "I'm so sorry, Kylo. I'm just so sorry." She clung to me, her hand finding the back of my head as she sweetly kissed my cheek.

"That event made me who I was," I said, stronger now— because I wanted to be strong for *her*. "I had two choices. Kill myself like Aisling's attackers assumed I would. Or do everything we'd dreamed together. Study at Etherdale. Hunt and kill vampires. Stop at nothing until I was the most powerful being in the realm, respected and surrounded by allies. The exact opposite of what I was that day I watched her die: helpless, weak, and alone."

Evie's eyes flickered, her mind churning, just as mine had when she'd told me of her past. She understood now—why I was so protective, why it tore me to shreds when she'd run from me, and she'd been cornered by those filthy fucking born.

I let out a slow, deep exhale. "In a way, they got what they wanted. A version of myself did die. And a better version took his place."

Evie folded herself into my arms, her head resting on my chest. "I'm sorry for being so mean to you."

I laughed with shocked amusement. "Angel, we have work to do if you think your prickly, bratty antics were in any way shape or form *mean.* It was like getting batted by an angry kitten."

"Rude!"

I kissed the top of her head.

"I am sorry, though," she said softly. "For assuming the worst about you for so long. For never even considering what you might've gone through as a human. Or really trying to understand you at all, at first."

"Thank you for saying that, Evie," I said. "I assure you I more than accept your apology. It doesn't surprise me in the least that you would want to avoid any amount of violence. That you would worry so greatly for your brother and this city in which you sought refuge."

"And you were stalking me," she added with a halfhearted huff.

"I prefer *admiring from a distance.*"

Evie made that cute little growling noise, even as she hugged me tighter.

"That's why my clan means so much to me," I said softly. "Especially my closest inner circle, like Blade, Harmony, and Princeton. They understand me and see me for who I am. We all helped each other heal, through our relationships and our shared vision. Through transmuting our pain into creation, into dedication and loyalty to something higher than ourselves. We protect mortals because we were once human, utterly powerless to save the people we loved."

"I see it now," Evie said. "I understand why you all adore each other. It must be so comforting to have built a family that actually looks out for each other. A *big,* violent family."

I smiled. "It's the best."

49

EVIE

It made sense this conversation happened in the middle of the night, when the world was quiet, dark, and liminal.

I wasn't sure what had allowed me to finally tell Kylo more about my childhood.

I imagined it had something to do with the fact that I was stupidly in love with him.

Or maybe I could blame the delirious haze of my first time being fed from and fucked into oblivion.

I didn't think I'd be able to sleep after everything that we'd both said, but my depleted body won out over my racing mind.

The next time I woke up, it was unbearably bright. I managed to catch Kylo still asleep, and it struck me as if I'd caught sight of some mythical creature in the wild.

His breathtaking features appeared more innocent in their relaxed state. Though, because Kylo was Kylo, he wasn't fully at ease. His brows were slightly scrunched, his lips curving down as he breathed deeply.

I kept perfectly still on my side, my eyes widening as one of his shadows escaped him even in his sleep to crawl over my body in a wisp of smoke.

He was way too beautiful. Did he know how beautiful he was? Maybe it was best he remained unaware.

When his eyes sprung open, I jumped.

He blinked once before slowly grinning. "Your behavior is appalling, angel. Don't you know how creepy and violating it is to watch someone sleep?"

~

I SPENT the next few days in a gooey, love-filled haze. I would've been disgusted with myself if being so in love hadn't robbed me of that ability.

Instead, I loved Kylo unabashedly. And maybe it was slightly childish, but I'd never had a first love—so maybe my silly mortal heart needed to get all of this pining out of its system.

In my spell room, I decided to take matters into my own hands with the Whitfields. I was going to place a binding spell on them to keep their mouths shut about me. I'd never done a working like this, as I typically avoided any baneful magick. But surely a silencing hex was more than deserved, merely an act of self-defense like any protection spell.

Hekate helped me every step of the way. It was the chaos witch's book about working with her that had given me the idea in the first place. I welcomed her into my space as I sat in front of my altar, growing more comfortable with her particular brand of darkness. Perhaps in the same way I'd grown accustomed to Kylo's.

How you will learn to love your own, a voice echoed in my mind.

I was in a semi-trance state, open to more influences from the ethereal dimension.

"I'm not ready for that yet," I whispered.

Hmm.

The sarcasm was delightfully ominous. I tried to brush off

the heaviness in my chest, that familiar lump in my throat. The clog over my power, the hardened mass of fear that had silenced my voice.

"Surely it's better," I said to no one in particular. "I've grown so much recently. I opened up to Kylo about what happened. I met with another chaos witch. Surely you can see that I'm doing the work. Healing, opening myself up to love, all that good stuff…"

Hmm, the disembodied, condescending voice said again.

I rubbed my throat, feeling more and more unsettled.

Hekate's stern, protective, caring energy flooded the space, easing the discomfort. It was maternal, or perhaps grandmotherly. She was a protector of mortals, of the downtrodden. She said she existed in many worlds, appearing to those who needed her.

I fell deeper into a trance, so I could ask questions about how best to proceed and the necessary ingredients.

After cleansing all materials and warding your space, make your petition for that which you aim to protect. Fold four times, toward you, a voice instructed.

All typical witch protocol so far. In the room, a foggy white mist rolled through the space, letting me know that I was between worlds. One foot in the ethereal, one in the physical.

Seal the petition in a jar with lavender, black salt, smoky quartz fragments, mugwort, and rosemary. Use black candle wax for all sealing. Glue the smaller jar inside a larger jar. In the larger jar, fill with vinegar. Add a few drops of your own blood. Totems of those who seek to cause you harm.

Unease churned in my gut. The first jar sounded like magick I was accustomed to—magick that was contained to only me, without affecting anyone else. I didn't want to use blood in my spells. I'd been powerful enough without it so far.

Then again, I'd never needed something this desperately. And if it meant Idris was safe, I'd do just about anything.

They came onto your land and all but threatened your life, a different voice said. *If they sell you out, you will never be safe again.*

Then another spoke, a presence I didn't recognize.

You refuse to use the protection you were born with. If I were you, I would do far worse. I would add broken glass and rusty nails. I would make a second petition to ensure that anyone who dared harm you would incur the punishment they deserve.

"No," I said sternly. "Thank you for your guidance. I would like to stick with the original intent. To freeze their energy against me and to silence them."

The original guiding voice continued. *Seal the larger jar with black wax. Place in a freezer. This entire process must be done on the next new moon.*

"The next new moon?" I asked incredulously. The last one was two days ago. "That's… that's in nearly four weeks."

The snarkier, more bloodthirsty spirit's voice spoke again. *You have other options besides fate-weaving. You choose your path.*

"To threaten them? To *harm them*? To do what they're falsely accusing me of?"

The new, testy spirit refused to answer.

Fear coursed through my veins. I didn't have a coven to call on for help, witches with specialties that might work more immediately—nor the power gleaned from numbers. As a solo practitioner, I had to work with the energies and forces I'd built.

And before now, I'd never learned or dabbled with prickly spirits and baneful wards.

I was out of my element, a novice all over again. Worse, I felt slighted. I was being punished for refusing to use the poison in my veins, for daring to use gentler, less violent methods of protection.

"Hekate," I prayed. "Please protect me until I can do this spell." I glanced around the room, the hazy outlines of beings and orbs of light. "Thank you everyone for your guidance, blessings, and wisdom. Let there be harmony between all of us for all of our days."

In the mist, I saw a vision of Princeton, who I hadn't seen since our first meeting. Either the spirits were pushing me toward him, or he was sending me a message himself. I wouldn't put that past him.

I had the sudden urge to reach for my current favorite tarot deck as I re-entered the physical dimension.

One card.

I pulled.

Staring up at me was The Tower.

My heart sunk, my hands trembling. I studied the imagery. A strike of lightning pierced the top of the stone tower—clearing away the golden crown that had rested there. Fire licked up the walls, and two men leaped from the windows, arms outstretched as they fell to the earth.

The meaning swept through me. I fought the urge to hurl the card across the fucking room.

The destruction of that which was built on a faulty foundation. Chaos. Turmoil. Total and complete dissolution. Clearing of the old to make way for the new.

Revolution. A change that is inevitable.

Death. Catastrophe.

Liberation.

50

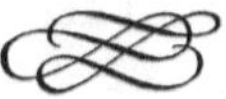

EVIE

Allie begrudgingly led me to Princeton's home in the turned clan's neighborhood above ground. She'd clearly asked Kylo first, scribbling in a magickally linked notebook that allowed her to communicate with Kylo instantly. Kylo had given me a linked journal, too, but we'd hardly used them to communicate. Maybe it was old-fashioned, but I didn't really care to employ such technology except in emergencies. It felt like cheating, or perhaps too disruptive to my focus on the world around me and my own inner experience.

On our walk, I was cognizant of just how many eyes were on me. Curious, confused, distrusting, intrigued, bloodthirsty. Allie occasionally threw looks of warning toward the male turned.

Allie led me up Princeton's porch before taking her leave.

"I don't want to get towered!" I exclaimed the moment Princeton opened the door with a wide, delinquent grin.

I stepped inside.

Princeton closed the door and lifted a brow. "Is this a sexual innuendo?"

I rolled my eyes. "Tarot."

He clapped his hands together. "Ah. My favorite card in the deck."

I huffed. "That's psychotic," I snapped. "It's objectively the worst one."

Princeton's features oozed with a sudden condescension. "There is no objectively bad card. They're all merely descriptions of life. The good. The bad. And The Tower."

My glare hardened.

Princeton laughed at his own stupid joke as he led me into a living room. His place was moodier and darker than Kylo's, with several plants I recognized as carnivorous lounging about. In the living area, reddish vines crawled up the dark walls. Candles and various books were scattered across surfaces.

The energy of the space poked and prodded me, recognizing me as a fellow witch. It was clear I was being scanned for threats.

Instead of the furniture, Princeton gestured to the carpet, where we sat facing each other before a dormant fireplace. His curly brown hair was half up in a bun, and he wore a billowy white blouse with black pants.

"You can't run from a good ole fashioned towering, Evie dear," he said with that irritating, sly smile locked in place.

"Okay, you're right," I mumbled. "It does sound sexual."

Princeton's eyes danced with amusement before they sharpened, examining me more closely.

I squirmed under his gaze, but whatever he saw, he refused to react or vocalize.

"I want you to teach me how to stop throwing magickal tantrums," I said. "So I can prevent whatever is coming."

Princeton's features transitioned into something more serious, flexing his air of authority. "I can help you with the first part. But you are willfully refusing to absorb the meaning of the card and what Spirit is communicating with you."

Indignation sparked in my blood, but I fought to cool it

down. I knew I had a complex relationship with other witches. I didn't want to treat Princeton the way I first treated Kylo. It hadn't been fair.

Magick required humility.

Princeton's eyes softened. "You know as well as I do that The Tower is the path to liberation. It might not be avoidable, but you can still make the best of it. I will not pretend that it's easy. But acceptance is the only path that bears the least amount of suffering." He paused. "Besides, I think you entered the era of The Tower a couple of months ago. Your entire sense of reality has been crumbling and shifting ever since you met Kylo, has it not?"

I frowned. He was right. It had already been painful. Yet no part of me wanted to pull the wool back over my own eyes. I liked my newfound strength, the erosion of my childish denial. I was glad to know the true reality of Etherdale and the realm, so I could best prepare for what was to come.

I reluctantly nodded. "I suppose so."

And if Kylo hadn't ripped off that blindfold, I wouldn't have been able to fall in love.

Maybe the worst was already over. Maybe I just needed to have faith, wait for the new moon, and focus on what was in my control. After all, Jacob could write to Cindy any day now.

"See how that feels?" Princeton asked. "To move from a state of running, hiding, and closing yourself off into a position of wide-open arms, accepting all that comes?"

I thought of Kylo. How I was when we first met versus now. All that had loosened and unfurled. The relief of it all—of being seen and known and loved.

"That's the core of what's wrong with your magick. Everything you resist has only gained more power. And because you've spun this narrative that this side of yourself is poison, it has *become* a poison. A monster that only knows how to attack and bite when it's cornered and threatened."

My heart picked up speed as I realized the room had become hazy, as if Princeton had led us both into a semi-trance without me noticing.

"The sides of ourselves we hate the most are only ever trying to protect us."

I glanced around, watching shadows dance around in the haze. "I don't trust other witches," I whispered.

"I know," Princeton said. "I didn't either, for a very long time." Princeton snapped his fingers, pulling my attention back to his eyes. "Do you trust Kylo?"

"Yes."

"Then use that for now."

Okay. I could do that.

"I want you to think about the part of you that wields your undesired power. What does it look like? Can you find it in the room with us?"

I glanced around, trying not to appear as embarrassingly terrified as I felt inside. My heart hammered. My chest tightened.

Pitifully, I wished Kylo was here.

Princeton's candles were clearly spelled for trance work, as I found myself relaxing deeper beyond my conscious control.

At a sudden movement in my periphery, my gaze leaped to the corner of the room. I almost shut my eyes, terrified to see some grotesque demon with blood-red lips and soulless gray eyes.

Instead, I saw myself, at thirteen years old. The same version of myself I'd seen in my vision with Hekate. I wore all black, a dress with a high neckline that brushed my knees.

The gray eyes that met mine weren't soulless.

They were terrified.

A sudden wave of emotion slammed into my chest, raw and unexpected, as if it had been begging to be felt for a very long time.

"Do you see the part?" Princeton asked.

"Yes." My lip wobbled, and it was humiliating. To be so weak before this powerful, dangerous witch.

"Evie, do not hold back on your emotions. I assure you I've seen it all. If you want to control your magick, this is the work you must do. Brute force without inner fortitude is wasted."

I didn't look at him. I kept my gaze on her. The demon in the corner who was now sitting on the floor, her knees pulled up to her chest. Alone, sobbing, calling for parents who would never offer the comfort she was achingly desperate for.

"Do you still feel hatred for this part of you?" Princeton asked.

"No."

"What do you feel?"

"Heartbroken," I said. Bitterness coated my tongue, panic and fear and paranoia.

I didn't want to do this anymore. I'd asked Princeton for help with my magick, not this woo-woo emotional healing bullshit.

Unknown born vampires and witches, Jacob's parents and friends—they were all after me and my magick, and I had to protect myself. I had to protect my family.

"But I still need to get rid of her," I said. "I can't change the past. I feel sad for her, but she has to go. I don't need her anymore."

I expected the girl to glare at me, to *finally* show her true nature—her anger, her darkness, her rotted veins—but she didn't move from the corner. She rocked back and forth, grieving.

That was when I heard the whispers, the shadows of the room darkening and multiplying.

The lump in my throat grew heavier.

"I need to banish her," I said, eyes finally returning to Princeton's.

He was calm, impassive, studying me without any judgment. "Evie, my friend, that is precisely the problem."

I shook my head, the whispers growing louder the more I ignored them and tuned them out.

"How old is this part of yourself?"

I thought about refusing to answer. Of getting the hell out of here and never returning.

"Thirteen," I forced out.

"You've been trying to banish her for a decade, then," Princeton said. "And it has clearly not yielded desirable results."

I could sense the girl's eyes on me, and it made me feel weird and hot and guilty. Like I was the one who was hurting her, and she was listening to my every word.

"You must love her," he said.

I searched Princeton's face for evidence that he was fucking with me. Because there was no way on Helia's green earth that this violent agent of blood and chaos was telling me that the way to control my magick was to *love myself.*

Princeton didn't waver. "You can start by acknowledging her existence. Talking to her. Asking her what she thinks and what she wants. She's not a demon. She is *you.* What is happening inside of you that causes your power to leak is simple: You get emotionally triggered in the same way you were hurt when you were thirteen. This part becomes activated, recognizing you need protection. She takes over. Because you've been repressing her, you do not recognize her presence, and you feel out of control. She reacts for you as a form of protection, and then she recedes back inside you, banished by your shame and fear."

"That sounds like nonsense," I muttered, growing more and more irritated by the minute.

"Do you have a more illuminating explanation? I'm all ears," Princeton drawled. "If you have all the answers, then perhaps you don't need me and can take care of things well enough on your own."

I began to make out distinctive phrases, unable to block out the voices of the shadows.

Just a child, one of them whispered.

A harsh chill spread down my spine.

"This is not why I came to you," I hissed. "You just want to know more about my power. You want me emotionally weak so I'll tell you everything, so you will know if you can use me or if I'm a threat to your little vampire army."

Princeton's eyes narrowed. "If I wanted to pry information out of you, I assure you I have a multitude of quick and easy options at my disposal. I would not trouble myself with theatrics or hidden motives."

I blocked the girl out of my perception decisively, refusing to participate in this useless exercise anymore.

Princeton sighed. "You must make peace with her. You must integrate back into wholeness. That is how you remain at the reins, without any hidden parts taking over in your place." He radiated a gentle, purple energy, one associated with wisdom and truth. "It's okay if you aren't ready. But I cannot help you if you don't want to be helped. You won't tell me about your magick. You won't open up about your past. You won't even be honest and empathetic with *yourself.* I am not saying these things to hurt you. This is just the truth. I cannot train you when we're both operating blind."

The room came back into focus. The shadows and mist receded.

I saw Princeton for who he was—genuine but no-nonsense, likely ancient, and a master at his craft.

He was Kylo's mentor, and that meant something.

My chest was tight with shame. "I'm sorry," I blurted.

Princeton shook his head. "No reason for that. This is about you, not me. I already know you're fucking powerful, Evie." He lifted a shoulder. "Use it, don't use it. Get clear about what you want, and then stand strong in your decision. You're not alone.

You have help now. Lots of it. No one needs your perfection. You just need to take a step and *mean it.*"

"I know," I said. "You're right. I know that even if you do want me to work with the clan, you're still also trying to help me."

Princeton's lips curved.

"Next time I come to you, I'll be ready to act. I won't fight you. I just—need time to think and process."

"Seeing our hidden parts is frightening," he said. "Just about anybody would react the way you did. Don't beat yourself up. You were taken by surprise. But now you see! Another strike of lightning to the tower. Hooray!"

The mischievous, eccentric Princeton was back in full force as he helped me to my feet. I shook my head at his antics, even if a smile snuck onto my face.

"Let's drink some tea and wait for Kylo to barge through my door," Princeton said. "You really shouldn't feel defeated. The first time I did parts work with Kylo, we ended up in a bloody fist fight." He paused, throwing me a rakish grin as he led me into the kitchen. "It was so hot."

I glared at Princeton, the lights overhead flickering and then shutting off completely with my sudden flare of possessiveness.

"You two really are made for each other."

The lights flicked back on.

"Agreed," a different voice said.

A scream lodged in my throat as hands wrapped around me from behind, lips at my ear.

Princeton raised a brow at Kylo's sudden appearance. "That was quick."

51

EVIE

When Princeton had stepped away for a moment to do gods-knew-what in the back of the house, I asked Kylo in Princeton's kitchen, "Would you still love me if all I did for the rest of my life was grow herbs, arrange flowers, and do quaint spells for everyday people and their everyday problems?"

Kylo was handsy as ever lately, refusing to break contact unless absolutely necessary. He bent to kiss my neck, sending pleasurable tingles through my whole system.

"You know the answer to that already, baby. You're not a pawn on my board." He reached over my shoulder to steal my tea and take a sip. "You're the *very* good girl in my lap."

I turned to face him. He set the mug down to place a hand on either side of me, boxing me in.

"But you'd prefer if I integrated all parts of myself. You like my darkness."

"Yes, and yes. Because that's what's best for you, and because you're so fucking cute when you're violent," he said.

I let out an indignant exhale. I sunk my teeth into his arm, and Kylo pulled me back by my hair.

"I'm going to start biting you back, angel," he growled, showing me those sharpened canines.

My eyes grew hooded, my core tightening.

"I'm proud of you for meeting with someone like you, for being so brave and open," he said, softer now. "I know it's not easy, believe me."

It didn't feel right to accept his praise. "I didn't make any progress. I chickened out. I'm not any closer to controlling my power than I was before."

"Not true," Princeton said from behind me, reentering the space and slowly moving into my line of sight. "Most healing isn't neat or pretty or linear. Sometimes progress is just showing up."

Healing. Ugh.

"Why the face?" Kylo asked, noticing everything about me as usual. He poked my cheek.

I glared at him until his dimple appeared. "Because I wanted to talk about magick—to *do* magick. Not get a psychological assessment."

Princeton tapped his forehead. "Magick starts in here, witchling. Brain no good? Magick no good."

My gaze narrowed. "Brain *fine.*"

Kylo shrugged, his dimple growing more pronounced. "I have my doubts."

I channeled light, shocking the hell out of his hands.

Kylo hissed. His eyes darkened as he grinned. Shadows bound my arms against the counter behind me. His hand gripped my throat.

"Look what you've done," Kylo said as he shook his head at Princeton. "You've gotten her all riled up and misbehaving. Undoing all my careful work." He locked back on my eyes with a wicked smirk. "Tired of being my good girl, are we, angel? You want to play?"

I felt raw power tentatively poke its head out, curious. I

channeled just a spark to send a frying pan flying toward Kylo's head.

He released my throat and caught it before it struck. His biceps absorbed the force as his eyes narrowed on me like a predator.

"Does this foreplay truly need to happen at the expense of my kitchenware?" Princeton asked dryly. "Carry on, of course. I *am* curious."

Kylo's shadows released me. He shot Princeton a glare of utter death, shadows leaking out of his pores. "Absolutely not."

He grabbed me roughly and threw me over his shoulder before carrying me through the house.

The warm, fresh air caressed my skin as Kylo stepped outside.

"You can put me down now," I hissed, wondering how much of my ass was currently exposed for any passersby. "Kylo!"

He gripped me tighter and continued forward.

When I heard him acknowledge someone walking by, I thought for sure I was going to perish from humiliation.

Kylo only laughed, of course.

When a palm came down on my ass, I squealed.

"Ornery enough to attack, but not brave enough to face the consequences?" he teased. "Are you embarrassed, baby? Don't want my clan to see me discipline you for being naughty?"

I wanted to harm him again, now more than ever, but doing so would likely cause him to drop me. And I had no interest in being squished by Kylo's large, muscular form.

Well, not like that.

"No. I'm not embarrassed at all." He'd like that too much.

"Very convincing."

Inside his house, Kylo manhandled me all the way to a couch, where he forced me into an ass-up position over his lap. What he'd been promising me since we met.

I swallowed.

"We have family dinner in two hours," Kylo murmured.

"No, *I* have family dinner in two hours."

He gripped one of my ass cheeks hard enough to draw out a whimper.

"I believe I was invited, angel," he said.

I could already feel his cock harden and swell beneath me. I was finding it more difficult by the second to remember why he wasn't allowed to be near Idris or Mena at this point. I mean, he was already overwhelmingly a part of my life. And I didn't want him to *stop* being in my life.

His hand came down on my ass, ruining my thought process as the slap sent a sharp sting across my skin.

And, because she had no common sense, my pussy reacted with a dull ache and gathering wetness.

"We're not there yet," I mumbled.

Kylo paused for a moment before bursting into laughter. When I attempted to wiggle free, he grabbed my legs tight.

I twisted my head to glare up at him.

Kylo yanked my panties to the side and slid two fingers inside my slick core. "Oh yeah? How much closer might we need to be?" he asked, low and mocking.

He ran a finger over my neck, where a healing salve had removed all evidence of his bites. But I remembered exactly where they had been. I shuddered at his gentle touch, his reminder of the way I'd claimed him exactly as he'd claimed me.

"You know that you're safe. You know that your brother is safe, that I'd never break my word. And your—grandmother?"

"Close enough," I said. To me, Mena was just Mena. But adoptive grandmother was a label that fit.

"She *adores* me," he said, fisting my hair.

I rolled my eyes. It took Kylo a fraction of a second to pull his fingers out of me, deliver three spanks, and then plunge them back inside me as I squirmed and cried out. The fingers pumped rougher than ever before, angling to hit the most sensitive, pleasure-seeking part of me until my moans turned loud and needy.

"So why am I not permitted at family dinner?"

He didn't relent, fucking me with those fingers as I arched and lost all train of thought.

This wasn't fair at all.

"It's the—" I managed through the desperate moans and building wave of pleasure. "The principle."

Kylo chuckled, his cock twitching underneath me. "What principle, angel?" He stopped fucking me, leaving his fingers buried inside. He stared into my eyes, still smirking and gripping my hair at the scalp.

"That you don't get to do whatever you want just because you—" I made an irritated noise, not even sure what my principle was anymore.

Kylo's grin widened.

"I don't know!"

He let go of my hair, softly stroking through my tresses now instead. "Relax, baby. Let me think for you."

"Condescending ass—"

This time, Kylo didn't spank me. He merely lifted my ass and bit down hard into the curve of my flesh.

I screamed.

Kylo was quick to run his tongue over the mark, both clotting my blood and serving me a small dose of venom.

When he let me relax back down on his lap, I was considerably less resistant.

"I'll wait till after dinner to properly feed, little one," he assured me. "You didn't get nearly enough to affect your mental state for too long."

I made a disgruntled noise, but it was hard to be mad at him when I was engulfed in pleasurable tingles.

He made a low hum of approval as his fingers traced his handiwork on my heated skin. "I do love seeing your disrespectful little ass red and bitten. Were lessons learned, baby?"

"That if I use telekinesis to throw a frying pan at your head, you're going to finger-fuck me?"

Kylo stopped his caressing with a sigh. "I'll take that as a *no.*"

He gripped my hair again, and I giggled. Though his features were ruthless, his deep blue eyes shone with the gentlest adoration.

IDRIS AND MENA sat across from Kylo and me at the long dining room table. White pillar candles were lit between us, with one of my flower arrangements as the centerpiece—a gentle mix of lavender, pink roses, and violets.

Irritatingly, I realized halfway through dinner that I loved having Kylo there. His hand was always reaching for mine under the table, or to rest on my thigh. When he looked over at me as I spoke or laughed, my stomach did somersaults. Not only because of the pure, undeniable devotion in his blue depths—but also because of the way Idris and Mena saw it too.

It was *real.*

This man who treated me the way I'd always wanted—the way I'd always feared was too much, too unrealistic to yearn for. Especially after Jacob had explained to me, over and over, that my desires and expectations were completely ruined by romance novels.

I couldn't believe there was a time I considered settling for less, if only to not be so alone. Or perhaps because I feared there was something wrong with me that made Jacob treat me poorly, like I wasn't worthy enough for his affection. I thought I just had to try harder.

But not with Kylo.

I sat there, gooey and emotional, devoid of that paranoid, bitter anger from before.

And he only made it worse with the way he spoke to Idris and Mena, with the utmost respect and genuine interest.

"That's the third time you've yawned in the past ten minutes," Mena said to Idris with a side-eye. "There are remedies, you know. If you're not sleeping well."

I tensed, and Kylo's thumb stopped his gentle stroke of my lower thigh.

"I could make you something," I offered Idris.

He smiled and shrugged dismissively. "You all worry too much. Summer will be over soon."

Idris suddenly glanced at Kylo bashfully. As if he hadn't meant to reveal anything vulnerable in front of a stranger. Even if what he'd revealed wasn't entirely obvious.

"I couldn't sleep at your age either," Kylo said casually, taking a bite of steak before sipping his water. He glanced at Idris as he kept his tone nonchalant. "I had insomnia, night terrors. Made it hard to focus on my coursework."

I watched Kylo carefully, discomfort in my stomach. But when I studied Idris, I noticed that he didn't seem nervous at all. He wasn't shutting down. He was actually *listening*.

"Anyway, the campus healers were helpful, despite my initial skepticism and oppositional attitude," Kylo said with a charming, self-deprecating smile.

Mena and I exchanged a glance before we both moved our eyes to Idris.

Idris only nodded. "I'll check it out." His eyes were slightly wider than before, as if surprised by Kylo's admissions, the way he was so candid about his struggles and seeking help for them.

Kylo was scary-looking even in his palatable human glamour, all muscle and tall build and confident, masculine aura. It made sense that anyone who didn't know him might be taken aback by his emotional maturity.

And gods, it did something to my heart—to see Idris opening up, even if his words were just a polite placation. Because the respect in his eyes was real. I refused to be selfish when it came to my brother, to be annoyed that Kylo could get through to him in a way I couldn't.

I only wanted Idris to feel better. I hated that we were both plagued by these nightmares, the tight grip of a past that wouldn't let go. At least Idris couldn't remember anything about the night we ran. For that, I would be forever grateful.

Idris waved a fork full of asparagus as he narrowed his eyes at me. "Are you on drugs?"

I straightened. "What? No. Why?"

He blinked. "Why are you so damn relaxed? No interrogation about how many hours of sleep on average I'm getting each night? The contents of my dreams? The evil propaganda I'm being spoon-fed by my self-defense instructors?" He smirked, but in his eyes was a genuine incredulousness.

"Isn't it obvious?" Mena said, as satisfied as a cheshire cat as she sipped her red wine and eyed Kylo and me.

Kylo smiled softly, gazing my way. "Happy to help."

I glared back.

"It's a compliment," Idris said. "I like this Evie."

"I'm the same Evie," I snapped.

Idris smiled, warming my heart. "Whatever you say."

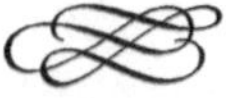

52

EVIE

Idris was crying. I could hear his wails through the wall. I also heard voices downstairs, loud and angry. Dad was back, behaving strangely again, and Mama was screaming at him. Maybe that was why he was always leaving—the yelling.

I wished I was an adult like him, so I could leave too.

I tiptoed to Idris's room, cringing at every squeak in the old floorboards. Each wail was a pierce to my heart. Because I remembered how it felt to be his age, screaming until my voice was raw, hoping for someone to come for me.

So I would be the one who came for Idris. I would give him what I'd always wanted.

When he saw me, his little hands relaxed where they gripped his crib. His face was red, tears streaming down his fair cheeks.

He reached for me, and I met his fingers through the wooden bars.

"Hi," I said. "Wanna see the stars?"

Idris sniffled, still choking on sobs even as he'd quieted. He nodded.

I sat cross-legged in front of him, and he watched me with wide eyes. I concentrated, listening for the sound beneath the yelling and slamming and breaking from downstairs—the sound of stillness, the voices who spoke to me softly, gently.

Think of the night sky, someone whispered.

I thought maybe they were faeries, my friends who lived in the stillness. Because I'd read about faeries one time, in a book I'd found when we went into Florimell. I didn't know that it had been wrong to take it. I'd put it in my backpack, and I'd read out in the field after lessons the next day. Mama had found me and screamed and grabbed me painfully before burning the book to ashes. She'd told me I'd stolen. She'd told me I was bad, ungrateful, disrespectful to Lillian and her Word.

A soothing whisper called me back from the memory.

I thought of the night sky.

I thought of when Dad had taken me outside one night when Mama wasn't home and let me look up at the stars. He'd been drinking a special potion. He didn't talk much, but I was happy to lie in the grass next to him. While there was no yelling, no prayers, no lessons. Just those flickering constellations.

They looked like freedom.

My palms began to warm, my brow creasing. The comforting whispers continued to guide me, to offer praise.

Idris squealed gleefully.

I opened my eyes and lifted a finger to my lips. All around us, tiny orbs of light danced and flickered in the darkness. My head was floaty, and the space in my throat and chest that was usually so tight began to loosen. I felt light.

Idris and I stared at the tiny stars, catching them in our hands, pushing them around and making them spin.

He'd stopped sobbing. Eventually, he sat down.

I told him about the faeries until his eyes began to droop.

Making the stars had exhausted me, so I curled up on the floor beside the crib.

As soon as my eyes drifted shut, the yelling grew louder, and a door slammed against the doorstopper.

The stars went out all at once.

"Evelynn Lockwood."

Mama grabbed my arm too hard, yanking me up as tears filled my eyes.

"You stop those manipulative tears, you ungrateful brat," she hissed, dragging me away from Idris.

He began to wail again, reaching for me. My heart tightened back up, and for a moment, I couldn't breathe.

In the hallway, Mama slammed the door shut and let go of me, letting me fall to the ground. A piercing ache erupted in my tailbone from the fall, and I cried harder.

"Don't you fucking cry," she hissed.

She left me there. I heard her say something to Dad, but he never came upstairs. I hadn't seen him in days. He heard me crying, and he stayed down in the living room.

When Mama returned, I sobbed harder, recognizing the glint in her eyes and the bag of rice she held.

I spent the rest of the night kneeling on those prickly grains in the hallway. Until my legs had gone numb, and I couldn't feel any more pain.

Until I couldn't remember the stars.

I woke up in tears. I wasn't sure which was worse—the night terrors that existed only in jagged fragments, caught between reality and the dreamworld—or these whole, unwanted memories replaying as if they were happening all over again.

At first, I was even more disoriented by the hands reaching for me, the fingers combing through my hair and the gentle voice at my ear.

"You're safe," Kylo whispered in the dark of my bedroom.

I grabbed his hand and snuggled back into his hold. A long-forgotten sadness rolled through me, and I remembered the thirteen-year-old crying in the corner of the room.

No, I didn't hate her.

I was terrified of her.

AS THE DAYS WENT ON, the memories and nightmares only got worse. And I couldn't help but partially blame Princeton and his meddling with my subconscious.

The new moon would be here before I knew it. Only two more weeks, and then I could be sure that the Whitfields wouldn't come after me. So far, no one else from Jacob's life had confronted me.

Kylo was busier than ever. Mortals were disappearing at a more rapid rate—humans for the slave trade, witches for the witch hunt, others suspected of sympathizing with the Masked Order.

And I couldn't stop it. I couldn't stop my walls from continuing to crumble and reveal all the poison and sickness I'd long buried. I couldn't stop the violence all around us, the threats closing in. The fights between masked turned and the born unfolding in the streets. The whispers of what King Earle had done to the clan in Florimell—the events that Kylo didn't discuss in more than brief sentences.

I had to do what was best for my clan. They would've done the same.

The grief I saw in his eyes that he refused to vocalize.

And gods, even Idris was changing. I may have covertly prevented him from joining the clan, but that hadn't stopped him from growing more vocal about born violence and the need to push them out of Etherdale for good. It hadn't stopped him from wanting to spend time with Kylo, to talk to him about philosophy. Without me there to listen.

I could hear the hum of fate. It was weaving around all of us, booming underneath our feet, through Etherdale and her hidden underground.

The woman I was at the beginning of the summer would've crumbled. But now… it was more complicated.

Because I was angry. Fucking livid. And not at the turned. Not at Kylo.

I was furious with the born demons who left bodies and missing persons in their wake. The vile creatures who had attacked me, who had threatened the workers at Celeste's, who had squashed my dreams of opening my own shop. Who infected my brother with thoughts of retribution, fear for his life and the lives of his classmates, rather than concerns about girls and architecture and university parties.

Maybe I *did* want the born out of the city. And even more concerning, maybe I was starting to believe that Kylo and his clan could actually accomplish such a feat.

Today in Princeton's living room, I got closer than ever to accessing my power. My eyes were closed, and I allowed magick to move through me without my usual fear.

"Good, Evie," he said. "I can still see the block. There's an aspect you're hiding, and I think you know that too."

I nodded.

"But a lot more energy is moving through you than before, less restricted."

"I've been talking to the part—the younger version of me," I admitted. "Not much. But I've been trying. I thought she was a demon, but now I see the truth."

My eyes opened.

Princeton smiled. "What truth?"

I lifted a shoulder. "That she's just me."

Furniture rattled softly, and a familiar fear gathered in my belly.

"Do not let that panic spiral," Princeton said. "We have

countless wards in this neighborhood. No one dangerous will sense your magick. You're safe here."

I shook my head. "It's not only that."

I saw the girl in the corner, her eyes lit with rage—she remembered the house in the rolling hills. She remembered my legs covered in countless tiny red marks. She remembered *everything.*

"I—" I paused, deciding how much I wanted to reveal. I shook my head. "I don't like all of my power. It's not safe."

"All magick carries risk. There is no good or bad force, only what we use them for. It must've been frightening, when your power manifested. Would you like to tell me about it?"

I clamped my mouth shut.

Princeton sighed. "Okay. We'll work with what you're willing to use."

He guided me through breathing exercises, this time ones to induce a heightened state of power rather than trance.

"We're going to let your power build, and then we're going to find an anchor to bring you back down to equilibrium."

I nodded. "Okay."

"Get angry," Princeton said. "If you can't think of anything yourself, I am more than willing to do what I do best… provoke and infuriate." He winked.

I closed my eyes again. I was already on edge, heightened by the mood of the space and our quick, erratic breathing.

I thought of the born. What they'd done to Kylo and his friend. What they'd done to me here in Etherdale.

The past reached up, but I refused to go there. Or else I might lose control.

I thought of Cindy Fucking Whitfield and her lazy, manipulative son. I thought of the way I'd let Jacob trample all over me. How I should've gotten angry with him instead of being so damn meek and people-pleasing and naive.

All I'd ever wanted was comfort, and I was treated with

cruelty instead. I remembered that slight smirk Jacob wore, the way his eyes shone with the same hollow emptiness as my mother's. How had I not noticed that before? I'd bent myself backward begging for his empathy and love. I wished I'd stood up for myself. I wished I'd wiped that soulless smirk from his lips.

"Gods below," Princeton said.

But I could hardly hear him over the rush of blood to my palms through the crown of my head—this raw, unfiltered rage that had been building for so long, blocked and ignored, begging to pour from my lips.

So pretty and pale, like a porcelain doll, a voice from the past cooed in my ear. *Your blood smells unique. Delicious. Perfect.*

I trembled, my lip curling.

"Evie!" someone yelled—Kylo, it was Kylo.

But my eyes were trapped in the back of my head, where all I saw was churning darkness, all I heard was rushing wind and whispers.

"She's past the point of return," Princeton said.

I'd never heard him panicked before. It sounded quite strange.

"What in the good gods is happening in here? Lillian's fucking reckoning?" someone else yelled.

At the mention of Lillian, I went fucking feral. I couldn't hear anyone anymore. I lost touch with myself. Memories and voices and feelings tangled up together, yanking me in every direction.

Sudden pressure weighed me down. There was a pinching in my neck, and then my body melted into decadent pleasure. Calm washed over me. The darkness pulled me under.

I blacked out.

53

KYLO

I was with Blade and Harmony when the cyclone began, these ugly gray gusts of wind that coiled around Princeton's house.

Where Evie was.

Princeton had told me never to interfere with their sessions, and I'd had every intention of respecting that request.

But not when faced with another natural disaster that was only growing, threatening to take down the whole neighborhood.

It was all so sudden, and I could just faintly hear Evie's piercing scream.

The three of us moved quickly toward the house. Harmony erected a shield of shadow around us as we dove through the barrier of harsh winds.

My bones rattled under my skin. Raw power coursed through the air, the earth, my quaking flesh.

"Is that *her*?" Blade asked incredulously.

But I wasn't focused on what was causing the outburst and why. I only cared about Evie.

We burst through the front door, and I called her name.

She was sitting cross-legged, five feet in the air. Her eyes were completely onyx. Her blonde hair was lifted around her in a halo. Princeton was yelling over the rushing wind and surging power, saying something to Evie about anchoring, telling her to come back down to earth.

"She's past the point of return," he said to me, in this strange, very un-Princeton tone of voice.

"What in the good gods is happening in here? Lillian's fucking reckoning?" Blade yelled.

"She's going to hurt herself," Princeton said. "She's bottled too much in. Her magick is going to eat her alive."

I didn't waste time to think. I grabbed Evie and sunk my fangs into her neck. I pulled her blood into my mouth until I tasted her anger, her grief, her bottomless heartbreak.

Her darkness washed over me, finding a home with mine.

I fed until she fell against me, limp and unconscious. I clotted her wound, collapsed to the floor, and held her in my arms.

My shadows strained under my skin, frantic and wrathful as they fed from Evie's power and grew ever stronger.

Princeton was speechless. "She didn't even show it," he whispered. "That was her, without even trying. Entirely unconscious, barely provoked. That was her when she was *still fucking hiding and burying the core of her magick.*"

Blade and Harmony stared at the blonde girl in my arms, jaws unhinged and eyes wide with concern and awe.

"Harmony," I said, straining over the buzzing in my ears, the swelling power that I'd absorbed from Evie. "I need you to check the wards and make sure the neighborhood is still glamoured."

"Of course," she said, hesitating only a second longer as she stared at Evie.

Blade rubbed his beard as he shook his head. "Blood replenishing potion?"

I nodded. Princeton directed Blade to where he kept them.

My teeth ground together at the sound of Evie's faint, fluttering heart. "Quickly."

I hated that I'd drained her so profoundly. That wasn't something I'd ever want to make a habit of.

"You saved her life," Princeton said. "She'll be fine."

He still looked shaken. I'd never seen him this shocked and perplexed.

I glared at him in accusation.

"I apologize," he said. "It was supposed to be a simple exercise. I'd asked her to get angry, to access more of her repressed power. So that she could learn how to anchor herself when she was triggered and prevent... an outburst." He scratched his head, looking off into the distance. "But too much has been shoved down. It's all grown stronger underneath her denial. If we don't find a way to reacquaint her with her magick, I cannot fathom what might happen. To her. To anyone around her."

Fear clenched my heart. I massaged the bridge of my nose. I studied Evie's troubled, unconscious features, her delicate white dress accented with pink flowers. To see her like that—overflowing with power, eyes pitch-black—stood in jarring contrast to everything else about her.

"Kylo," Princeton said, insistent. "The next time she explodes, it will not be pretty."

I gripped Evie tighter. "I. Hear. You."

Blade returned with a potion. "But imagine her doing that in battle."

His smile fell the moment he met my icy gaze.

"She's not a fucking weapon," I hissed. The mere thought of Evie in harm's way made me want to enact my own explosion. "She is *not one of us*."

Something I didn't care for flashed in Princeton's eyes.

Blade raised his hands in the air. Princeton pursed his lips and didn't speak.

I tilted Evie's head back, slowly pouring the green-tinged liquid into her mouth.

"Swallow," I murmured.

Her eyes flew open, coughing violently. She was still weak in my arms, disoriented as she found my eyes.

I sighed. "Sorry, baby," I said. "I need you to drink."

I raised the bottle to her lips again, and she swallowed like a good girl, eyes locked on mine. When she finished, she became conscious of the other figures in the room.

Her brows drew close. "What happened?"

Blade rocked on his feet, hands in his pockets, deferring to me. Princeton was still staring at Evie as if trying determinedly to find what she'd hidden away.

Her pulse sped up. Her soft gray eyes locked on mine.

"I didn't realize how much power had built up," Princeton said. "I apologize, Evie. I would've used a different approach. I've never seen magick like that in a witch, other than... well, *me*."

Evie's face fell, panic ripe in her irises. "Did I hurt anyone?"

I shook my head. "No. I fed from you to pull you out of it."

Princeton looked like he wanted to say more—to *do* more— but I wouldn't have any of it. Something primal and territorial heated my blood, making me want to shield Evie from my mentor, my clan, anyone at all who might ruin her pure, warm soul.

She wasn't a secret asset. She was my *Evie*. She needed protection, healing, and care—not to be used like her parents had once used her. I refused to add to her suffering, to repeat the wounds of the past. And the mere thought of her being anywhere near the violence of war made me want to rip out someone's throat.

Harmony returned soon, confirming that the wards and

glamours held, and no one outside the neighborhood had sensed a disturbance.

"We'll figure it out," I said curtly to Princeton. "Later."

I took Evie back to my place and postponed my afternoon meetings until tomorrow. I hushed Evie every time she tried to apologize.

"You did nothing wrong. You're perfect just as you are."

She sipped water, curled up on the couch while I answered correspondences in my many magickally linked journals.

When she finally relaxed, looking over at me in that adorable way she did—like I was her only source of oxygen—I set my work down and pulled her into my lap.

I kissed her forehead, listening to the steady beating of her heart.

"It's frightening how much I love you," I told her, watching those pretty pink lips curve.

"Your love doesn't frighten me."

"Maybe it should," I muttered. "My love for you makes me extraordinarily violent. I saw someone stare at your ass yesterday, and I almost plucked out his eyes right there in the street."

Evie's eyes widened. "That's excessive."

I grinned. "Exactly my point."

"Please don't hurt people in my name," she whispered. "I don't want to live with that on my soul."

My stomach dropped slightly. A feeling I wasn't expecting reared its ugly head.

"Unless they're an actual threat, of course," she amended. "I'm not upset about you killing the born who attacked me."

She frowned, and my grip on her tightened.

"Just maybe not men who check out my ass."

"Can't make any promises."

She glared at me. I allowed her to lift up my arm, and she bit down as she maintained eye contact.

I responded by grabbing and pinning her underneath me, digging my fangs into her right breast without breaking skin.

She giggled, futilely trying to push me away. I grabbed both her wrists and shoved them above her head.

I melded my lips with hers, soaking up her laughter, sunshine, and innocence.

That stray, rare feeling was back, worming through my chest, prodding and poking.

Please don't hurt people in my name. I don't want to live with that on my soul.

I thought of that unworthy, hysterical man baby I'd exterminated in the cemetery. The man Evie had absolutely no idea was dead.

For the first time since I'd watched Jasper piss himself, I felt something akin to guilt.

54

EVIE

"**P**rinceton said you own a bunch of sex dungeons," I blurted.

Kylo looked up from his book, where we were laying in my garden, reading together under the afternoon sun. I hadn't seen him much since the day I'd used too much power with Princeton, but Kylo always made sure to take care of me in that obsessive, devotional way he did any time he was around.

He marked his spot with a bookmark before closing the book. "Did he now?"

I frowned, homing in on his devious smirk.

"Why are you getting angry, angel?" he teased.

I shook my head. "I'm not angry."

Kylo's smile grew. He was on top of me in a flash, kissing both my cheeks as I squirmed beneath him.

He laughed. "Ah yes, because you are *so good* at hiding those big, deep feelings from the world."

I glowered, and Kylo only continued to pepper me with kisses.

"Yes, the clan owns many feeding clubs, of various styles. I'll take you to one on campus," he said with a shrug. "Tonight."

"That's—" I huffed. "That's fucked-up, Kylo. You feed on university students?"

He stroked my cheek. "Baby, no. I told you I rarely fed from the tap before, and I haven't been interested in students since I was a student myself. Though I do enjoy giving instructions to my perfect angel." His eyes narrowed on my lips, his thumb brushing over them as he grinned down at me dangerously.

"Urgh," I said. "You're not taking me seriously."

Kylo sighed. "My clan feeds from willing adults and their blood donations. Or on unwilling born—the monsters we hunt who are *actually* preying on students. We have to survive and retain power somehow. And as you've learned, feeding can be quite enjoyable when it's desired."

His lips moved to my jawline, then my neck, and I let out a contented sigh when he lightly sucked.

The bastard knew exactly how to distract and silence me.

Kylo lifted back up. "I like knowing you're at least a fraction as possessive as I am. It's cute. Unnecessary, but enjoyable nonetheless."

He kissed my frown. Then he scanned my body, his eyes darkening.

"Maybe this isn't such a good idea," he murmured.

"No. You're taking me," I said, hardening my resolve. I was done living in the dark and hiding from the world.

Kylo's jaw feathered. "If we do this, you will not leave my fucking sight. You will not do anything without my permission. If anyone makes you feel uncomfortable or unsafe, you will immediately inform me."

"Your permission?" I scoffed.

Kylo didn't blink, didn't relent. I could see it in his eyes—this churning darkness, the look he got before he fed or used his shadows.

"You're the one who doesn't want me murdering anyone," he said. "If you enter a space for feeding, sex, and debauchery, you better believe you'll be signaling to everyone there who the fuck you belong to."

His voice was low, gravelly. I felt its rumbling inside my own chest. My thighs inched closer together, my heart skipping.

"Angel," he growled. "Tell me you understand."

"No flirting or kissing anyone inside your one of many sex dungeons without your permission," I said. "Got it."

Kylo's hand closed around my throat. *"Brat."*

"Sexual deviant," I hissed back.

He radiated intensity, his muscles straining. "You have no idea."

"I DID CONSIDER ADDING A PRETTY pink collar to the ensemble," Kylo said as he fastened my dress. "With a cute little bell at the front."

"Like a cat?" I asked incredulously. "I am not your *pet.*"

Kylo chuckled. "Next time." He spun me around and kissed my forehead.

In the full-length mirror, I gasped at the beautiful dress Kylo had put me in. It was blush pink with short off-the-shoulder tulle sleeves. The material beneath the layer of tulle was comfortable and silky, not too revealing but still showcased my curves and upper thighs.

"Is this something that will fit in?" I asked.

Kylo nodded. "People wear all sorts of things. Or nothing at all. What matters is whether *you* like it, baby. Do you feel comfortable?" He met my eyes in the mirror, his features warm.

"Yes," I said. "I love how sweet you are, right after you threaten to treat me like a collared animal."

"It's part of my charm. I contain multitudes." He spun me to face him.

I rolled my eyes.

"Also, a *threat* implies you wouldn't enjoy being my collared pet. Which I can assure you isn't the case," he said, his lips at my ear now as I shuddered.

He thumbed the moonstone pendant at my neck with satisfaction. My traitorous body responded to his words with yearning, pleasurable waves extending from wherever he looked or touched.

I would've been Kylo's *anything* at this point.

And I was too in love to be concerned about such a statement. He was *safe.* Something I never thought I'd feel so deeply in my bones.

"The last piece," Kylo murmured, reaching for a delicate, ornate white mask with dangling ribbons and pearl and crystal embellishments.

"Wow," I said. "This is beautiful."

Kylo delicately tied the ribbons at the back of my head before kissing my temple. "You deserve only the best. Always."

~

I HADN'T GONE to university, so I'd never really been on campus during peak partying hours. I'd gone to pubs with Marietta, Quill, and my other friends from Celeste's, after much begging on their parts, but those had been more inside the city.

As we walked through the side streets in the residential areas, I became increasingly aware of how many *humans* nodded at Kylo.

"You people are everywhere," I whispered.

Kylo snorted. He was wearing his partial shadow mask, enough to cover his head while leaving part of his face and mouth uncovered. His men and women must've recognized him from his presence and tattoos alone.

Ahead, I saw others in masks sneaking down an alleyway, giddy and giggling, cloaked in decorative robes. I recognized shifter and witch energy from the mortals and caught a glimpse of shadow masks on two turned.

"The magick is going to make you feel strange for a moment," Kylo warned. "We have protective wards in place that affect mortals' ability to understand or remember where they are geographically. It won't affect any other part of their memory. They just won't be able to return to the club without an escort."

"Everyone wears masks?" I asked.

"All the turned do, unless they're staying glamoured as human the whole night. We like to keep some of us incognito for intelligence purposes," Kylo said. "Most mortals wear masks, because anonymity is part of the fun. It's also less of a risk, especially for those with important administrative positions at the university, or high-profile jobs in the city."

We turned onto a new street and approached a bland, nondescript black door on the side of a building. I was still mulling over Kylo's words when we entered the dimly lit entryway. The wave of protective magick disoriented me instantly, spiking my already festering anxiety levels.

I was basically clawing into Kylo's arm at this point as he dragged me forward. Four huge turned stood, masked and tattooed, in front of the next door.

As magick prodded me, I recognized Princeton's distinctive essence in the wards.

The men and women didn't dare glance at me for too long. They merely nodded at Kylo and let us through.

We descended a set of steps to basement level. People were congregated in an opulent foyer, laughing, talking, and disrobing as they placed their unneeded clothing with a coat check attendant. A golden chandelier hung above, its lights warm and dim.

One woman was entirely nude now save for jeweled pasties on her nipples.

Kylo rumbled with quiet laughter next to me. And when I met the onyx voids where his eyes should've been, I realized he'd been staring at my shocked expression.

"Keep walking, angel," Kylo murmured. "You're not taking off any more clothes."

Masked Kylo was… hot. Unbearably sexy, in a way that was concerning.

He smirked. I cleared my throat and looked away, moving forward as I kept hold of his muscular arm in a death grip. Kylo wore black pants and a black top with gold vine embellishments. On his hands were several silver rings. His tattoos quaked with power.

"You haven't worn all black once since we met," I whispered.

Kylo glanced down at me as we walked through yet another door. "Of course not. Why would I want to cause you unnecessary discomfort? Seems like the bare minimum of human decency."

I swallowed. Gods, I loved him.

His broad hand moved to my lower back as we entered a much vaster space. My mouth gaped. My eyes must've been saucers.

Kylo laughed, gently nudging me forward.

Low music did nothing to cover the moans, screams, and laughter coming from all directions. On a couch, a masked woman fed from a shifter man while straddling him. Another woman was stroking the vampire's hair, kissing her shoulder.

Everything was decadent, luxurious. The soft carpets on hardwood floors, the ornate wallpaper, the plush furniture, the golden fixtures and flickering candle flames. Some people were merely talking, while others were engaged in feeding and sex acts, in various stages of undress.

"This is the tamest room you will see," Kylo said, guiding me further into the labyrinth of bodies.

"The *tamest*?" I squeaked.

I stopped dead in my tracks when I spotted a girl in delicate white lingerie wearing a mask with cat ears, a lacy collar, and a long fluffy white tail. She was on all fours, rubbing against the leg of a masked turned man.

I glared up at Kylo. "Is that what you had in mind?"

Kylo grinned. "Yeah, pretty much."

His hand moved to the back of my neck, continuing to guide me deeper. The subtle display of dominance, his entirely unperturbed demeanor when faced with shocking displays of depravity—gods, I wished I could say I was disgusted.

My body was having an altogether different reaction.

"How we doing, angel?" he asked, turning to face me in a quieter alcove.

The noise, the nudity, the swell of power and magick that danced and moved through the air—it was beginning to over-stimulate my senses.

But I didn't want to be a prude or a bore, or gods forbid, too sensitive or negative. I didn't want to disappoint Kylo, or come across as ungrateful for the dress, the mask, the shoes—all of his efforts and gestures. I wanted to make him as happy as he made me.

Kylo read my features, even as I tried to put on a false face of ease and comfort. To be the most agreeable, confident version of myself.

He kissed my forehead. "It's okay to be uncomfortable, angel. This is new. I have no expectations, and we can leave whenever you want. Just say the word."

I exhaled. I needed to stop expecting Kylo to behave like my self-absorbed, inconsiderate ex-boyfriend when he only ever showed me the opposite.

"Are there less crowded rooms?" I asked. "Until I, um, warm up to things."

"Of course," he said simply, his lips curving.

I reached out, running my fingers along the strange, shadow

magick material of his skull mask. It was silky smooth, yet rigid like resin.

"You love my mask, don't you, baby?" he asked, his fingers tracing my jaw as his other hand gripped my waist.

I nodded.

"Focus on me," Kylo said. "Don't worry about anyone else—think of them as merely performers, only concerned with themselves. It's just *us*."

"Okay," I whispered.

"Good girl."

My stomach fluttered, and I did what Kylo instructed. I focused on the way he made me feel until the surrounding noise was less noticeable.

Soon, we were in a quieter room, where people had gathered to watch a man tie up a woman with rope. She wore a simple black bodysuit and mask. The way the rope hugged and knotted around her limbs was surprisingly artistic, complex. From a hard point in the ceiling, a silver ring hung. The woman was serene, blindfolded with red silk as she leaned against the man tying her. His fingers moved expertly, and occasionally, he kissed her or offered a soothing touch.

"I don't understand," I whispered to Kylo, who was behind me with his hands on my hips as more and more people crowded to watch. "Is this sexual?"

"Sometimes," Kylo murmured. "But it depends on the people doing it and in what context. Sometimes rope bondage is merely aesthetic, like an art form or any other skill or discipline. Other times it's used to induce alternative headspaces, whether it's erotic or merely pleasurable independent from any sexual intent. This couple uses rope as performance art."

"So it's… a hobby?"

"Correct. The man is a rigger, or a skilled rope bondage expert, and the woman is his rope bunny—the bottom he ties."

I vaguely understood the terminology Kylo was using. Merely because of reading kinky romance novels, of course.

The man looped rope through the silver hoop above. His concentration was evident in the planes of his face, taking immense care to check the bound girl at his feet as he began to lift her off the floor. The rope was holding her around her midriff, her legs, her arms, and even around her hair. Her position was beautiful—like a dancer suspended midair. She was breathing more raggedly now, as if it was painful, her lips turned down with discomfort.

The man whispered something in her ear, and she nodded with a smile.

Low music grew louder now, as she was lifted completely into the air. The man gently spun her in circles as the crowd clapped.

"That's incredible," I said, glancing back at Kylo.

His lips curved. "Glad you're enjoying it, baby."

"Are you a rigger?"

Kylo lifted a shoulder. "I've had many years to perfect all manner of skills," he said, his warm breath tickling my ear. "I'm not as skilled as the man we're watching, but I know the basics. And if my perfect good girl is interested in something, rest assured I'll be learning everything I can until I satisfy her, however she desires."

"You're too perfect," I muttered. "Except when you admit to your whorish ways."

I didn't particularly enjoy thinking about how Kylo had perfected his devious skills over the decades.

"Whorish?" Kylo chuckled. "Was I meant to live as an ascetic monk until the other half of my soul finally decided to grace this plane with her presence?"

My smile fell as I turned all the way around, staring up into that onyx mask with surprise.

Other half of his soul? My stomach warmed, tingles

spreading over my skin from such an intensely romantic declaration exclaimed so casually.

"Yes," I answered.

Kylo grinned. "Sounds reasonable." He grabbed my hand, pulling me away from the enraptured crowed. "Do you trust me?"

The Tower loomed, and The Devil held my hand in his.

But I imagined Kylo's deep blue eyes beneath the shadows, and I nodded with full confidence.

55

EVIE

In the corner of the room, Kylo and I sat on the carpet while he tied me with pastel pink rope that nearly matched my dress.

It was strangely... *fun*.

My mind melted as he pulled my legs into his lap, tying a series of knots as he bound my legs together like a mermaid.

I smiled. "Feels cozy."

He kissed my forehead. "That is precisely the intention, my little damsel in distress."

The rope dug into my skin, slightly scratchy, but not incredibly painful. Just enough to flood me with a low dose of pleasure, my mind growing slightly floaty. I could sense from touching the material that it was made of natural plant fiber, a low green energy emitting outward.

Kylo's eyes grew molten as he finished off the last knot above my ankles. "I can scent you getting wet for me, angel," he teased. "Someone enjoys being trapped and helpless, hmm?"

I knew there weren't many people around, as Kylo continually scared them away when they got too close, but my cheeks burned nonetheless.

"You want more, baby?" he asked, brushing his thumbs across my reddened cheeks.

I nodded. "Am I doing it right? You know, the whole sex dungeon thing?"

Kylo laughed. "There is literally no way to do a sex dungeon *wrong*, silly girl."

I felt like that wasn't true, but I grew distracted as Kylo shoved me down onto the carpet and straddled me as he bound my wrists together next. When they were cuffed and immobilized with rope, he moved off me and yanked them above my head, tying the leftover rope to some object behind me.

When he returned to my line of sight, he smiled for only a moment before his mask completely obscured his face. He merely stood there, arms crossed as I wiggled and flexed my bound limbs.

And gods, he wasn't even touching me. We were both fully clothed, and Kylo was merely *standing above me*, yet I was deliriously drunk with desire, overcome by pleasure and fear.

His tattooed muscles flexed as he peered down at me through his impenetrable mask. I was both aroused and blissfully sedated by this feeling of helplessness. No longer was I concerned about noises or lingering eyes or nude, writhing bodies. I was entirely locked in on the sensation of being bound and secure, my masked stalker lording over me with his frightening, lethal form.

One of Kylo's shadows solidified and crawled up my body.

"Open that pretty mouth," Kylo commanded, his voice deep and distorted.

The smoky tendril condensed itself into the same size as the rope before skating over my mouth as a gag.

I bit down, my tongue tasting the strange, smooth material. It tasted like Kylo—dark, fresh, woodsy.

He still didn't move, merely watching me wiggle with my

arms locked above my head and my legs bound together. I made a soft noise against the gag as pleasure coursed through my blood.

I thought there was no way in hell I was going to want to do *public* sex acts with Kylo. But my traitorous body was starting to get different ideas.

Ideas like how nice it would be if Kylo were to touch me while I was bound and restrained—my nerves alive and sensitive. For him to play with me, tease me.

My brows drew together, and I began to grow frustrated with Kylo's impassive silence and immobility.

I pointed my foot toward him and made another soft noise.

The bastard laughed at me.

It was as if I could feel that deep, rich sound in a cascade of touch down my body.

"Please," I tried to say into the gag, but it came out fairly unintelligible.

He knew what the hell I meant though, even as he pretended otherwise, still tormenting me with his distance.

He merely chuckled tauntingly, watching me from beneath his scary onyx mask.

"Kylo," a voice said, breaking the spell we were both under.

My attention snapped to the masked woman with long black hair who'd come up behind Kylo. Her mask didn't extend all around her head like his, only the upper part of her face.

Rage swarmed my system before I realized it was Harmony, and then merely humiliation drowned my veins.

She looked down at me with a grin. "Oh! Hi, Evie!"

She waved at me as if nothing at all was out of the ordinary with my predicament.

"Cute dress!" she said cheerfully.

"Thank you," I attempted, the words once again lost as they met the gag.

Harmony was wearing a tight golden dress that accentuated

her generous curves. She looked like Helia's consort, a joyful being of pure sunlight.

"I apologize deeply for the intrusion. Have you seen Princeton?" she asked Kylo. "They said he came in earlier and never left, but I haven't spotted him yet."

Kylo shook his head.

"Oh. Hmm. No worries," she said. "You two have fun!"

A shifter man in a wolf mask must've misread the situation, as he took Harmony's place the moment she left.

Kylo went rigid, slowly turning his masked head toward the grinning wolf.

"Caught yourself quite the beauty," the man said. "Bet she's fun to play with."

"One more word and you will not enjoy the consequences," Kylo hissed. "Walk. Away."

Shadows bled from Kylo's form, his tattoos trembling as power flooded the room. The shifter tensed, taking a step back as his smile fell.

"Do not interrupt people's scenes in a dungeon. Go back to the entry hall and read the basic fucking etiquette."

The wolf scurried off with his metaphorical tail between his legs.

"See? I thought about ripping out his tongue and shoving it back down his throat, but I refrained," Kylo growled. "*That's* love."

I made a noise of indignation. Something about Kylo flexing his power had my yearning climbing to new heights. Stranger still, I was surprised by how much I secretly enjoyed others watching me—as much as I enjoyed Kylo scaring them away.

I enjoyed being *his*. And the whole world knowing it, too.

Kylo finally joined me back on the carpet, sitting next to my bound form. His fingers brushed my lips, feeling the saliva that had gathered against my will.

"Messy girl," he taunted.

His hand skated down my form as I shuddered. When his fingers found a nipple, teasing and pinching, I squirmed and arched. My bound wrists pulled against whatever they'd been tied to.

"Uh-uh, be a good girl and stay still," Kylo rasped. "There's no escape for my captured and bound angel."

He let the gag fall away.

Not being able to read his face as he toyed with me felt dangerous. He was Kylo, yet he was also this masked stranger, this unreachable psychopath.

And I was at his mercy.

He pinched my other nipple over my dress, and I tried my best not to squirm.

I gasped, a whimper leaving my lips.

"Use your words, baby."

I didn't care anymore. I needed his fingers under my dress, between my thighs.

"I want you to touch me, please," I begged.

Kylo laughed darkly. "You want me to play with you? Out in the open, for anyone to see?"

I swallowed, a strange mix of shame and desire warring inside me.

"You want everyone to know who owns this pretty pink pussy?"

His hand inched down, tracing a circle around my pubic bone above the silky fabric. When he moved to my upper thigh, inching higher, my breath hitched.

"Use. Your. Words."

I nodded, staring up at him desperately. "Yes. Please."

"Good manners, angel," Kylo said. "And yet, it doesn't solve the dilemma of what I would have to do to anyone who heard the little noises you make when you come. The moans and gasps that belong only to me. That beautiful face you make when you unravel at my command."

His fingers pressed into my dress where I needed him most. But there was too much fabric blunting the sensation, leaving me frustrated and arching against him.

He retracted all touch.

Kylo's mask slid up, revealing his cruel smile. "Not bad for your first sex dungeon scene. I'm untying you now."

"Kylo!" I squealed.

He tsked. "I've spoiled you, baby. Denial builds character."

56

EVIE

I thought biting him might provoke him to bite me back, but Kylo was too intelligent to fall for my transparent acts of desperation.

It was most unfortunate.

The more frustrated I became, the more Kylo seemed to be enjoying himself.

"I loathe you," I whispered, his arms locked around me from behind as we watched a woman in a leather dress whip a nude man with a bullwhip.

The sound of it made me jump every time, as loud as a strike of lightning. Which in turn made Kylo laugh.

"Funny how quickly things change. Miss-Too-Anxious-To-Be-Around-Naked-People, now begging to publicly orgasm."

He spun me around, wearing that infuriating smirk that grew with each passing minute.

He shifted into a mocking pout. "Yes, very sad," he said, poking my nose. "Now wipe that bratty look off your face or you won't come for a week."

"You're *evil*," I growled.

He lifted me into his arms. "And you love that about me."

422

His lips met mine as my legs locked around him. His tongue invaded my mouth. He consumed me, all heat and lust and darkness, until I was useless putty in his arms.

My mind spun, parsing through idea after idea to get Kylo to bend.

By the time he'd set me down, I had a scheme.

It was, of course, a terrible one. But a scheme, nonetheless.

"Can we get water?" I asked.

"Of course."

Kylo led me through the rooms until we reached a lounge area with a bar. He was right that each new room was increasingly more depraved. So far, I'd seen a turned woman strapped to a table while a witch shocked her with an electric current in her fingertips; several people getting beaten with all manner of objects; a man literally set on fire but in a *safe way*; and of course, lots of feeding. And fucking.

I held tightly onto Kylo's arm until we reached the counter. I let go but stayed close. A turned woman instantly rushed to us, her mask covering half her face but not her soft green eyes. She smiled at Kylo in a way that made me frown.

He seemed oblivious as he asked for a glass of water.

When someone next to us struck up a conversation with Kylo, talking partially in code but clearly gushing over him like a fanboy, I seized the opportunity.

I backed up slowly, even as guilt rooted in my stomach— reminding me of what happened the last time I'd broken one of Kylo's rules.

This was different. We were playing harmless games, clearly somewhere safe, surrounded by his loyal clan.

I slipped through the maze of people. My eyes latched onto a moaning girl, bouncing up and down in a vampire's lap, for just two seconds before averting my gaze.

My core tightened. Would I let Kylo fuck me in front of everyone?

Was that what I wanted him to do when he caught me?

I'd only made it a room over when I felt the scorching heat of his gaze on me. But he didn't grab me, didn't make himself known.

I spun around, but I didn't see Kylo anywhere. I only sensed him in the heat on the back of my neck, the brand he'd left on my soul with his blood and obsession.

Maybe I was imagining it, but gods, I swore I could feel his wrath echo against the walls. Yet he stayed hidden, watching me with a silent rage.

None of the turned dared approach me. They clearly knew what was good for them. No one at all spoke to me until I entered a room of plush furniture and nude forms tangled up with each other. A woman was feeding on two other women in the corner, but front and center was what appeared to be an orgy. One of the women was kneeling above a man's face, a position that made my eyes widen. Another man was stroking himself, playing with the woman's breasts.

A nude man approached me, his cock semi-hard. "I saw you earlier," he said. "When you were with that large and intimidating vampire man." He smiled. "Just wanted to say how adorable you look."

My witchy senses tingled, alerting me to some kind of threat beneath the man's easygoing façade.

Another man joined the first, eyeing me up and down. He, too, was very naked.

"Yes, the cutest," the second man said.

"Would you like to join us?" the first man said.

I looked between the two of them, and as soon as I took a step back, my body hit a chest.

Thank the gods. But when I turned, expecting to see an angry Kylo, I saw a chiseled human man instead—broad-chested and tall.

None of them were as big and scary as my boyfriend.

"There are ladies who can vet us for you," the first man added. "We know how to show women a good time."

I finally found my voice when the third man apologized for running into me, his hand lingering on my back for far too long.

I recoiled from his touch, pulling myself away. "No, I'm not interested."

"Can I at least get you a drink? You have such a unique presence. I want to hear more about *you*," the first man continued, something pushy and insistent in his fake charm.

"It's just a drink," the second man said. "No need to look so terrified." He laughed.

"Look at those darling shoes," the third purred, gazing down at my pink Mary Janes.

They all pretended like I was the most interesting person they'd ever encountered.

"And those pretty rope marks—someone likes it rough, huh?"

I glanced down at my wrists and legs, the pink indentions the rope had made on my skin. When the third man made another move to touch me, I jerked away again.

"I said *no thank you.*"

They all three shifted their demeanors at once, their faces contorting with derision.

"Think you're too good for us, you stuck-up bitch?"

I tensed, fear blooming in my blood as they surrounded me.

A dark figure moved in the corner of my eye. Kylo was done playing our game. He had the man lifted into the air by his throat before I had time to blink.

"*Apologize.*"

The man gurgled, his little feet kicking as Kylo held his throat.

"Kylo," I said, my stomach dropping with terror. He was strangling a mortal with vampiric strength. "Please don't kill him."

Kylo dropped the man back down to the ground, where he coughed and gasped. The other two men tried to back away, but shadows grabbed their ankles and locked them in place.

"I'm sorry," the first man said, fear in his eyes as he looked from Kylo back to me.

"Zero tolerance for coercion and harassment," Kylo spat. He made a gesture, and a masked woman quickly grabbed the man off the ground and hauled him to his feet. "All three of you will be escorted back outside." The words sounded forced, like they weren't at all what he truly wanted to say.

Kylo was trembling with rage. His shadows crawled back to him reluctantly, as if their true desire was to squeeze the life out of the men instead.

When he trained his masked gaze on me, all I could do was gulp.

Kylo gripped my hair at the base of my scalp and forced me to stare up into those onyx voids. "Are you okay?"

I nodded.

The dark laughter that followed had every last hair on my neck standing alert.

"You won't feel that way for long."

He led me forward, his hand still tangled in my hair as I hissed from the sting. Eventually, he slid his hand down to my neck and gripped that instead. My stomach was knotting, terror and arousal fighting for supremacy until I couldn't much tell the difference between the two.

Guards were posted before a set of doors, instantly letting Kylo through and into a dark hall. Kylo dragged me to the room at the end, slammed the door shut behind him, grabbed me off the floor like I was nothing but his mortal doll.

I barely had time to observe my surroundings—not that I could see well in the dark—before Kylo set me back down, bent me at the waist, and forced me to grip the edge of some wooden piece of furniture.

The room was dead silent aside from my rapid heartbeat and shallow panting, clearly a private space away from the main dungeon.

My dress was lifted and my panties were torn away. I heard the sound of a belt unbuckling and fabric shifting behind me.

"Is this what you wanted, baby?" Kylo asked.

I didn't have time to answer before he thrust his cock inside me without warning.

The scream that tore through me was softened by Kylo's hand over my mouth.

"Shhh," he whispered, gripping my hips. "Why are you whining, angel? You won your own little game. You should feel so proud."

The sweetness in his voice was a lie, teetering on the edge of psychopathic. He removed his hand from my mouth, letting me cry out undeterred.

He drove into me, over and over, until my legs were shaking and threatening to give out. I still wasn't used to the size of him; perhaps I never would be. He only held my hips harder with a bruising grip. One of his hands fisted my hair again and yanked my head to the side.

He spit into my open mouth before gripping my throat as I swallowed.

"I would say *good girl*, but that would be a lie," he growled. "As you've made it quite clear that you'd much rather be my disobedient little slut tonight."

He went deeper than ever, and I screamed. The pressure at the sides of my throat had my head swimming, growing more and more floaty.

"Isn't that right, Evie darling? Did you need me to put you in your place and remind you who the fuck owns your body and soul?"

I didn't enjoy feeling like I was in trouble—being starved of the praise I'd grown so accustomed to.

"I'm sorry," I whimpered.

Kylo responded to this with his teeth buried in the sensitive flesh of my shoulder. He bit hard enough to draw out a pained cry from my lips, but he didn't go deep. He didn't feed.

He marked me—brutally, in a primal way I felt at my core.

He yanked me back, dragging me onto a carpet and leaving me on my knees. I stared up at him. His mask fell away.

And seeing the unfiltered rage in his eyes was somehow infinitely more frightening.

"What are you sorry for?" he growled, his jaw rigid as he glared down at my trembling form.

A lump grew in my throat as I remembered those men touching me, invading my space, making unwanted comments about my sex life and appearance.

"I'm sorry for leaving your side," I said.

Kylo moved closer. I straightened up, letting him brush the head of his cock across my lips, coating them with my own essence.

"Open your fucking mouth."

I opened.

Kylo rocked his hips, his cock sliding in and instantly hitting the back of my throat.

I gagged, my eyes closing.

He grabbed my hair. "Uh-uh. Keep your eyes on me while I punish this disrespectful mouth."

I looked up at him, and his mask crawled back over his face, hiding away all of his humanity. Now, he was just my deranged vampire stalker.

"You know what I think?" he asked, his voice more unhinged than ever as it deepened and distorted. "I think you wanted me to reveal how fucking obsessed I am with you. The extent of my madness, my preoccupation with being inside you at all times. Buried in your greedy cunt. This inviting throat. Your tight little ass. My fangs in your flesh, my voice infecting your beautiful mind. You wanted me to reveal the truth that I want to be so deep inside you, every second of every day, that you have no hope of ever escaping me."

I made a sharp groan against his cock as he continued to force it down my throat.

"Yeah, that's what I fucking thought. You love how out of control you make me. You couldn't stand the idea of me being able to go just one single hour without playing with my perfect toy."

My watery eyes spilled over, tears running down my cheeks as I gagged on Kylo. My clit was aching more than ever before, still untouched and neglected.

The most insane part of all of this was that I now wanted to earn back his praise even more than I wanted him to touch me.

He gave me several more violent thrusts as I struggled in his hold. When he finally released me, I sucked in air, spit dripping from my lips.

I didn't get any recovery time before Kylo had pulled me to my feet and made quick work undressing me and removing my mask. In the next breath, he grabbed me into his arms and lowered me onto his cock until he was buried deep.

He shoved me up against a wall, bouncing me up and down as his mask continued to cover the entirety of his face. I whimpered at the fullness, the desperation building inside me for release.

"I'm sorry," I repeated.

Kylo's mask slid up to uncover his mouth. He kissed my forehead, the first gentle touch since he'd brought me into this room. This one tiny act was enough to melt the lump in my throat.

"You walked through *my* dungeon as if you belonged to no one, after you promised me you'd follow my very simple rules. Rules designed to protect *you.* Because you know what it fucking does to me when you put yourself in danger. Those men frightened you. That was bad enough. But they were willing to do *far* worse."

Kylo continued to buried himself deep. I gasped, and he stayed lodged there, unmoving.

"I know," I whispered. "I only thought it was okay because I was under the clan's protection, and I knew you were still watching me. I wouldn't have done it under different circumstances. But that doesn't matter—I'm sorry that I broke my word when you have *never* broken yours." My lip trembled. "You've never been dishonest with me. Impatient or unreasonable. You've never been cruel, dismissive, manipulative, or self-serving."

Emotion welled in my body, mixing with the heady lust and satisfaction of having Kylo deep inside me. "You are insane, of course. But yes, I *do* love that about you."

Kylo smiled, and the act melted everything that had tightened inside my chest.

"I am sorry," I said. "I should've made my move within your boundaries."

"If you think my rules are unreasonable, voice that," Kylo said. "We're roleplaying, baby. Underneath the power games, you're still my equal."

I nodded. "Okay." I reached a trembling hand to his lips, and he kissed my fingers.

"You're forgiven," he said. "But I'm not even close to finished making you suffer."

57

EVIE

Kylo carried me to a bed. With the snap of his fingers, the room filled with low lighting. Once he had me on my back, his shadows made quick work of spreading and binding my legs and tying my wrists to the headboard.

He moved between my legs. His lips were unreadable, his mask void of emotion. I had no idea what was coming.

"You want me to play with your clit, baby?"

I nodded. Gods, yes. "Please."

Kylo lifted a hand, but it soon came down as a light slap against my sensitive nerves.

I made a startled yelp.

"Not. What. I. Meant," I hissed.

"No?" Kylo asked mockingly.

His hand came down again, and I cried out, struggling against the shadows that only pulled my thighs further apart. The pain was electric, moving through my body like a streak of lightning.

He slapped my inner thigh next, and each bite of pain sent me deeper into a delicious headspace that had me melting into the bed.

"Who owns these?" Kylo asked, his voice a low rumble. A shadow skated over my pussy and then my ass, teasing each entrance as I shuddered.

"You."

Kylo spit, and I tensed as his fingers massaged the liquid against my ass.

"Please," I begged, so aroused and denied now that I was half-convinced my clit might spontaneously fall off. "Please, can I come?"

The shadow solidified and slowly plunged inside my ass. I gasped at the sudden fullness, the low discomfort that shifted decidedly into desperate neediness.

Instead, Kylo shoved my legs higher and impaled me with his cock. I had no idea what startled noise escaped my lips, only that the fullness was unlike anything I'd ever experienced before.

Kylo chuckled. "You begged for this, remember? Did you want me to claim my perfect little holes in front of the entire dungeon? While you were bound and helpless in that pretty pink rope, displayed for all to see?"

He gripped my face between his broad fingers, smiling cruelly.

His hips rocked, the shadow pumped, and I realized I didn't really need him to play with my clit or feed from me for me to come.

My eyes rolled back as Kylo used me, filling me to the brim as his shadows held me in place, bared before him and entirely at his mercy. My pussy clenched around him as I reached immeasurable heights of intensity.

His grip on my face tightened as I moaned. "Don't you fucking dare." He slapped one of my breasts and then cruelly pinched one of my nipples. "Not until I give you permission, slut."

I gasped, my heart hammering. "Are the degrading names and tit torture supposed to make me less likely to come?"

Kylo stopped thrusting, going still and staring down at me as if I'd caught him off guard.

He let out a bark of surprised laughter. "Well, listen to that filthy mouth. Such a good little whore for me, letting your jealous God corrupt you with his darkness." He stroked my cheek. "This pretty face would be such a good canvas to paint with my cum, hmm?"

Okay, now he was just goading me into breaking his rule.

I whimpered, my stomach tightening as I tried everything in my power to stop the cresting waves of pleasure.

"Please," I begged. "Please, please, please."

I hardly recognized my own breathy, desperate voice.

"Please, Kylo," I whined.

The shadow inside my ass expanded slightly, and I choked on a trembling cry. My legs were shaking beneath the bondage. My pussy was spasming, my chest rising and falling rapidly. All the while, Kylo smiled down at me, his eyes covered by churning darkness. He played with another nipple, and I started to scream.

My reins of control were slipping fast, and it was unbearable to keep this violent, cresting orgasm at bay—this tsunami of desire that had been building for *hours* now.

"Please!"

Kylo laughed. "Hush, angel. You may come."

I was half-convinced the orgasm that tore through my body might kill me. Kylo's mask fell completely away as his lips captured mine, stealing my moans as I shook violently. The release was impossibly long and unrelenting, and I felt Kylo empty himself inside me as I writhed beneath him.

On another plane of existence and still riding the aftershocks of my release, I was delirious when Kylo pulled out of me, removed all shadow bindings, stuck two fingers inside my pussy and then forced them inside my mouth.

I swirled my tongue against the salty, tangy mixture.

"That's a good girl. Taste *us*," he purred. "While I taste *you*."

His fangs dug into the curve of my breast, just above my nipple. He pulled my essence inside him with a kind of shaky restraint I could feel through our bond.

My body flooded with sudden ecstasy. I sighed contentedly, his fingers still in my mouth.

When he peeled himself off me, clotting the bite with his saliva—I could see it in his eyes. The utter frenzy, flirting with the edge of dangerous.

He shook his head with a curse. "You have no idea what our games have done to your already maddening blood," he hissed, slowly drawing his fingers out of my mouth. "A lesser man would've killed you at first taste."

"A comforting thought," I murmured. His venom radiated outward, infecting me with decadent pleasure.

"Angel, I'm not sure *addicted* covers how fucking obsessed I am with you," he said, his voice raw and quivering with intensity. "You have me downright *consumed*. In a way that should terrify the both of us. And, likely, the entire realm."

I stared up into those blue depths. Masked Kylo was sexy, but I was ready to stare into his soul for the rest of the night.

"I'm not scared," I said.

Kylo grinned. "Neither am I."

He brushed his lips against mine before moving down between my legs. He drew my aching, sensitive clit into his mouth. I squirmed, but he gripped my thighs as he devoured me, forcing my depleted nerves to take even more pleasure.

"Good baby," he praised as I melted against his mouth. The hum of his voice was a soothing balm against my skin.

My eyes flew back open the moment his fangs came down above my pussy, near my womb. As the venom coursed through me, I relaxed again, my eyes fluttering as the shock of pleasure engulfed my core.

He didn't even have to touch me for me to come again, in a less violent way this time. Yet the soothing, satisfying sensation lasted for what felt like an eternity.

I stayed locked inside an endless orgasm so long as Kylo was feeding.

He was pained when he finally pulled away and clotted this second bite, his eyes swimming with a mix of hunger and satisfaction as he stared down at my melted, pliable body.

"You're too perfect to exist," he whispered.

"No, you." I giggled.

His intense eyes warmed at the sound. "You better not giggle around anyone else for the rest of our existence, okay, baby? That noise is only for me."

"Sounds reasonable," I slurred, drunk off pleasure as I reached for him.

He rolled his eyes, brushing his lips across my knuckles before pushing my wrists above my head.

"I'm going to take my time marking my property, now, little one," he said softly. "And you're going to say *thank you* for each bite, like the good girl you are."

I nodded, grateful to finally be back in his good graces. Even if I knew on some level, it had always been a game.

Kylo bit one of my thighs, and I inhaled sharply before whispering, *thank you.*

We repeated the process on my second thigh, then up higher, on my stomach again. On my chest. He bit me everywhere that could be easily covered, and my body continued to drown under wave after wave of pleasure.

He checked my eyes as I mumbled my final *thank you.*

"That's all for tonight. I'm going to take you home and take care of you now, okay?"

I nodded with a smile.

Kylo seemed to be studying his handiwork, his eyes molten as they roamed my body. His lips curved with satisfaction.

At a sharp pounding at the door, his eyes bloomed with irritation.

"Not currently available," he called.

The harsh pounding didn't cease.

If I was fully aware and capable of it, I might've grown worried at the sight of Kylo's concern and confusion.

The way that someone was ignoring the clan leader of the Masked Order's command without a hint of fear or hesitation.

Kylo disappeared for a moment, dressing himself before helping me off the bed and back into my dress.

I gripped his arm as a wave of vertigo hit me, the blood loss and pleasure overload clearly making me woozy.

"Sit down on the bed and don't move," Kylo said. "I'll be right back."

I grabbed my shoes and did as Kylo instructed. Kylo made sure I was okay before heading to the front door, where someone continued to slam their fist erratically.

I wasn't sure what it was inside me that knew I needed to slip on my shoes, but it was an intuition stronger than the haze of vampire venom and sexual submission.

Though my heart beat slowly, it was starting to thump hard, in a way that had my chest tightening uncomfortably.

When Kylo opened the door, it was Harmony who stood on the other side. Her face was streaked with tears, her mouth twisted with horror, her eyes panicked and raw. She was utterly frozen for a moment, unable to find the right words.

She mouthed something, or perhaps whispered it, but I couldn't make out the word.

All I knew was that Kylo had gone utterly stiff, his power thrumming in a low warning.

I had just promised him I would listen, to be good for him, and yet I stood up from the bed immediately.

I couldn't help but follow them, my heart slamming against my ribs, lightheaded and disoriented.

Down the hall, Blade and two more turned stood. Blade's face was similarly shocked and crestfallen in a way that twisted my stomach into knots.

"You don't have to—" Harmony started.

"Of course I do," Kylo said, something wrathful trembling in his voice that made even the walls shake.

When he opened the door to their left, Harmony shut her eyes and sobbed. Blade quickly wrapped her in a hug as she cried into his chest. He stood stoic, rigid.

Kylo didn't notice me creeping behind him as he entered the room, but Blade did. He shook his head, putting out a hand to stop me as I reached the door that was open just a crack.

Darkness and pain slammed into me from within the room, making my eyes prick on instinct, nausea rushing through me in waves.

"Evie, don't," Blade said sternly, his voice cracking. "You don't need to see that."

A feral, bloodcurdling bellow shook the entire dungeon. It made my blood run cold.

I saw a vision of The Tower, the men falling to the scorched earth, and I nearly collapsed on the spot.

How the fuck did this happen?" Kylo yelled.

His voice was inhuman, nearly unrecognizable. Thick darkness bled from the room and out into the hall.

"He needs me," I heard myself whisper.

I moved only on instinct now. I was led by something higher, the part of me who already knew what she was about to see—who connected all the dots between my visions, the cards, those damned whispers, the guidance from my spiritual allies— every moment that had led me to this one, right now.

Blade's bark of an order made me jump, but it didn't deter

me. When he reached for me, I let my power deliver a harmless zap to his palm. He hissed and pulled back.

I snuck through the door.

Screaming shadows swept through the room in dark gusts of wind. The scent of death and blood assailed my nostrils.

Kylo stood, his back to me, with his fists clenched.

Beyond him, Princeton hung from the wall. Daggers impaled each of his limbs. Another was lodged in his heart. His eyes were carved from his skull, and his lips had been slashed at the corners to mimic a demented, bloody smile.

58

EVIE

An arm looped around my waist, dragging me back.

"No," I gasped. A scream lodged in my throat that never fully formed.

Kylo spun around at the sound of my voice.

The raw devastation in his features killed something inside of me. My heart felt like it was physically breaking as I studied the grief in his eyes, the way his beautiful features were twisted with rage and ruin.

The cloud of shadows grew darker, more violent, as they swirled around us in fits of screams and cries.

"Let me go," I cried. "Let me be with him."

I swallowed the urge to puke, trying not to look at Princeton's lifeless, desecrated body. I only stared at Kylo.

"Evie, gods," Kylo said bitterly, glaring at me. "Let her go, Blade."

As soon as Blade released me, I launched myself through the bloodthirsty shadows and into Kylo's chest. The sudden movement had black splotches encroaching on my vision, but I blinked the light-headedness away and suppressed the strong urge to retch.

439

Kylo was rigid, trembling softly with power or heartbreak—likely both. I hugged him tightly, and he eventually hugged me back.

"Why can't you just *listen?*"

The volume and the intensity of his tone made me wince. I took a deep breath.

"Because I love you," I said, my voice shaking.

"Fuck," Kylo rasped. His anger morphed into something else as he held me tighter, a tremor rolling through his tall form.

I didn't care if he was angry with me. At least he was no longer stuck in that stupor, staring at Princeton's corpse.

My sensitivity had always been a plague. On my family, on Jacob, on *myself*. But it was my sensitivity that allowed me to stand here and feel Kylo's pain with him, my heart bound to his. Wave after wave of darkness crashed against us, bleeding from both of our combined wounds. But I didn't let Kylo go.

I didn't run.

A shift happened in the energetic environment. Kylo began to put himself back together, fury racking through his lethal form.

"Angel, I need you to listen to me, okay?"

He still didn't sound like himself. It tore open my heart to hear and feel his brokenness, his abject horror, as the scent of death grew ever stronger.

"Okay."

"If you want to help me, you need to let Allie take you back home—*our* home, where you will be safest right now," he said, a desperate edge in his voice.

He pulled back, staring into my eyes with a severity that shook my bones. His beautiful features were tormented, even as he continued to maintain his cool, dominant authority.

His lip trembled. "You will *stay there*, and wait for me, so that I can—" He faltered.

My heart clenched, and I didn't need him to continue. I just nodded. "I will. Don't worry about me."

Tears poured from my eyes, but I suppressed the building sobs. I couldn't be selfish and take up any more emotional space. Not now. Kylo didn't need anything else to worry about. I wiped the tears away.

Even if I wanted to stay with him, to be strong for him like he was always so strong for me, my desires didn't matter in this moment.

Not with Kylo's oldest friend, healer, and mentor brutalized and crucified on the wall behind him.

Kylo shook his head as he stepped back from me. "I hate that you're here. Gods, I fucking hate it."

I flinched as if he'd struck me.

When Harmony approached, I didn't resist her.

"I'm sorry, Kylo. I'm so sorry," I whispered, my voice cracking.

He didn't say anything as I left the room. I avoided catching another glance at the grotesque murder scene.

Not that it mattered. The image would be with me forever. It was about time my nightmares were fed new fuel. They were getting repetitive.

And I knew that was what Kylo had meant, that he hated me being in *that room.* He hated that I'd psychically injured myself to be with him.

But the words stung regardless, in a way that was deeply subconscious. When Harmony passed me off to Allie, she squeezed my shoulder.

"I'm sorry," I said to Harmony. It was a useless thing to say, but the only thing I could think of.

She nodded, her face crumpled. Every last drop of her sunshine had been drained away.

My bodyguard was stoic as she led me out of the dungeon.

I'd never felt more useless and ill-fitting. A clunky burden in a space that had no room for me.

The image of Princeton flashed in my mind, over and over, until I couldn't breathe. I threw up on the street, tears staining my face, my dress, my soul.

Allie waited patiently for me to finish heaving, not uttering a word.

My vision was blotchy, my body still recovering from blood loss. But I made it back to Kylo's estate before I let the darkness take me. It was a welcome reprieve from the deep, unrelenting sadness squeezing my shattered heart.

I SPENT the entire next day woozy, sick, and anguished. The house was eerily still and quiet without Kylo here. It took immeasurable effort to drag myself out of bed and feed myself and drink water.

But I did it. For him. Because I refused to give Kylo any more stress or concern. I pretended like I wasn't dying inside, my brain consumed with worry for him, for Harmony and Blade and the rest of his inner circle.

I sat on the couch, my knees pulled up to my chest, just staring at the wall as my mind worked and worked and my stomach threatened to empty itself again.

Were they in danger? How in the world could something like that happen? To *Princeton?*

Oh gods. The gravity of the situation was a crushing weight on my chest. The fact that the born had actually accomplished their directive, to kill the backbone of the Masked Order—I didn't even know how to process it all.

The grief, the terror, the harsh dose of reality.

I'd somehow found myself directly in the center of

everything I'd grown to hate. Violence had closed up all around me, while I'd been too drunk on love and venom to care.

My reactive urge, of course, was to go to Idris. To compulsively make sure he was still safe, to soothe the paralyzing fear that had been fortified and nurtured since the day I was born.

But I couldn't do that to Kylo. No matter how much I wanted to revert to my old self and her defensive coping mechanisms—to run from all of this and never look back—my need to be here for him trumped it all.

I couldn't do that to him. Especially not now.

Kylo didn't come home until late in the night. I'd fallen asleep on the couch, woken up by a broad hand on my forehead.

"You feel feverish," Kylo murmured, moving a strand of hair behind my ear.

It took me several seconds to remember our new reality, and the moment I did, I spoke quickly. "No, I'm okay."

I sat up, and the world spun violently. My stomach lurched. I shut my eyes tight. My hands balled into fists as I found my balance again.

Kylo grabbed my hands in his, slowly unfurling my fingers. When I opened my eyes, I realized he was kneeling in front of me.

"This is my fault," he said. "You needed aftercare. I should've sent a healer. Gods, I'm so sorry, Evie. I left you completely alone and—"

I cut him off. "Kylo, please. I don't blame you. Please don't feel any guilt over me right now."

The lack of sleep was evident, despite his ageless vampiric beauty. Or maybe it was grief that haunted his features, underneath his impenetrable mask of strength.

"You're under my care. Of course I will feel guilt for neglecting you like this." He looked down at our interlocked hands. "Time was moving differently. It can do that, in the underground…" He cleared his throat, abruptly rising. He rubbed his face, his eyes utterly haunted. "I'll be right back."

I wanted to follow him, but I was scared vertigo might send me to my ass and ruin all hope of convincing Kylo that I was all right and his guilt was unfounded.

This was not my plan. I'd wanted to be his rock when he returned. He was the one who needed care, not me. Shame burrowed in my gut the longer I listened to him moving about the kitchen.

When he returned, he was carrying a mug of something that smelled potent. I recognized the herbal qualities immediately as I read its magickal signature. It was a healing tincture, for both the body and mind.

He also set a glass of water on the table, followed by a sandwich.

"Drink this first," Kylo said, handing me the mug. "And don't bother lying about being fine, because I know you're not. What I want right now is for you to let me take care of you." His lip twitched, intensity eclipsing his deep blue irises. "That is the *only thing I want.*"

I couldn't deny him. Not when so many cracks were forming in his mask, unfathomable torment and sadness bleeding through like those screaming, wrathful shadows.

I only nodded, settling into Kylo's lap while I sipped the tincture. His arms around me brought selfish tears to my eyes, remembering how it felt to still be flooded with his venom, alone, plagued by that horrifying vision of brutality between states of consciousness.

Kylo brushed his lips against my forehead.

I didn't blame him for needing to attend to clan matters in the wake of Princeton's death. But I was grateful he was here now.

"It doesn't feel real," Kylo whispered. "I'm scared to sleep, because I don't want to wake up and *remember*."

I understood. Gods, I understood.

"I'm here," I said. "Whatever you need, I'm here."

I finished the tincture, moving slowly to set the glass down on the coffee table. Then I looped my arms around Kylo's neck, feeling his impossibly soft black strands of hair beneath my fingertips.

His eyes were glassy, his lips turned down. I'd never seen him look so vulnerable, so scared.

It reminded me of the event that had brought him here. What he'd witnessed the born do to his best friend, when he was only a child.

The horror that Princeton had helped heal him from, only to end up meeting the exact same fate.

My heart broke for Kylo. It was physically panging in my chest, pain that echoed in the space between us until it was one shared wound.

"Thank you, angel," Kylo rasped, his jaw feathering. "Your presence is more than enough. My only ask is that you move in with me. We—" he faltered, shadows escaping him to wrap around me protectively. "We don't know enough about what happened for me to be certain of your safety. We believe he was killed by a fellow witch, a born plant. I know that this is a big ask, but I can't risk it."

Kylo's expression pierced straight through me. It cut through all of my paranoia about moving too quickly, my doubts about leaving Mena or giving up too much of myself, my space, my spell room and my garden.

I opened my mouth to protest, but those deep blue eyes pooled with tears effectively dried up the words on my tongue.

"I can't lose you," he whispered, his voice raw.

I pressed my forehead to his. "Okay. Until we know more. I'll stay with you."

I felt Kylo's exhale in my own lungs. If this was what he needed from me, then I had to do it.

"You don't have to be strong for me," I said. "You can be anything you need to be."

Kylo swallowed. "I can't let them win, angel. I need to be strong for the world now."

59

KYLO

It equally melted and crushed my heart to see that Evie had dressed herself in one of my shirts. It was unbelievably shitty of me to have left her here, alone, for nearly twenty-four hours after rough play and feeding. I hadn't given her a modicum of aftercare, and now she was crashing. *Hard.*

Alone. When it would've been a simple order to have a healer check in on her, or an attendant to cook her food and make sure she was drinking fluids.

She didn't want me to feel guilty about it, but that was exactly what I felt the moment her feverish forehead touched mine, her petite form swallowed by my clothing.

The truth was, the past day had been more fever dream than reality. I'd had no concept of time passing. No concept of how I felt in my body or what was outside my immediate field of perception. I gave order after order, met with commanders and decided how much I wanted to tell and to whom. I'd interrogated and tortured two born, one of which had absolutely no idea about anything more than his own useless existence. Yet I slaughtered him ruthlessly if only to feel better.

It had offered little relief.

No one outside my closest inner circle knew what had happened yet. And they wouldn't know. Not until we'd patched up this gaping, devastating power vacuum Princeton had left in his wake.

Here with Evie, I struggled not to let my mind wander, to spin and work and question.

Harmony had all but forced me to go home, to break until morning. I wasn't going to listen to her. But then she told me what time it was, and I'd listened to how hard and slow Evie's fragile heart was pumping through the bond. I left immediately.

Evie pulled back, and a weight lifted off my chest when I saw that more color had returned to her cheeks. Her skin had been a frighteningly sickly pallor when I'd first arrived. My love for her and my guilt over failing her was more than enough to keep me here, at least until tomorrow.

"You can't bear the weight of the world, Kylo." Her small hand traced my jaw, concern etched in her beautifully empathetic features.

I felt unworthy of such softness in the wreckage of my enormous failures.

And of course, in this haze of threatening emotions, fears, and pressure—my first instinct was to go to my mentor for help. To get my head screwed back on straight.

My chest tightened. I stared into nothingness, blinking away the rising panic.

"If not me, then who?" I asked dryly.

I needed distraction. My shadows were mourning, straining against my veins. They wanted to rot an entire born neighborhood from the inside out.

Before Evie could answer, I kissed her briefly and lifted her off my lap. "Lay down for me, angel," I sighed. The shakiness in my breath disgusted me.

I couldn't mourn, not yet. Not until we'd patched up the breach. Not until my clan was secure again.

Not until vengeance had been served.

Evie lay on the couch, and I reached for the healing salve I'd fetched from the kitchen.

"I'm going to tend to your bites. Then you're going to eat for me."

I tentatively lifted the baggy shirt, exposing her bite-covered body. The sight would've ordinarily brought me immense pleasure, seeing the way she'd been marked and claimed. But now, I could only think of how I'd left her to care for these wounds herself. Not only while she'd been coming down from feeding and rough sex, but also after she'd been traumatized.

I fucking hated that she'd seen Princeton like that. All in an effort to protect and comfort *me.*

I grimaced, spreading the salve on one of the bites to her thigh.

"Only if you eat too," Evie said. "It's a big sandwich. I can share."

Sweet girl. Her blood last night had been more than enough to sustain me. Mortal food wasn't necessary.

I smiled in a way that I knew didn't reach my exhausted eyes. "Deal."

IN ONE OF our deliberation rooms, my inner circle sat together around a long wooden table.

Evie and I had slept tangled up together last night. If she'd had a nightmare, she hadn't voiced it. Just like I hadn't said anything about mine.

She said she didn't want company today, but I'd urged her to use her linked journal to write to me if she changed her mind and needed a healer, emotional or physical. She'd scoffed, shaking her head resolutely.

Guilt had become a second source of torment to distract me

from my loss. Because I knew how much her home meant to her—her land, her plants, her magick, and her family. I had her completely isolated.

But there was no alternative. I needed her surrounded by the clan at all times if I wasn't with her.

Not out in the open, vulnerable to the snakes who had yet to be beheaded.

Not when Evie was exactly who they'd want to kill next.

Wrath was its own poltergeist, the lights frequently flickering or going out entirely as I spoke with my comrades.

"This whole fucking clan runs on his magick," Phineas said, staring bitterly at the loose paper and pens in front of him as the lights flickered again.

"What's already been created will hold unless tampered with," I repeated for what felt like the hundredth time.

The conversation was the same with each new person we brought into the fold. And it was starting to make me murderously impatient.

I wasn't used to such feelings, as I tended to attribute them to weaker men.

But I was staring down the sharp point of a sword that inched closer to my face each hour that passed.

"Here's the plain truth," Phineas said. "We need a new witch. Someone who is bound to the clan. Someone we can control, whose fate is intertwined with ours. One of them chaos ones who can work with shadows. Someone powerful."

All eyes moved to me before quickly looking elsewhere. My knuckles were white from clenching so hard.

Phineas didn't know the nature of Evie's magick. No one did, in its entirety, including me. But especially not those on the outskirts of my circle, who had attributed all strange happenings to Princeton. Who had no idea that Evie had been the one who had conjured a cyclone of power in our neighborhood, or storms over Etherdale.

Blade and Harmony were the only two who hadn't subverted their gazes from my rigid, enraged form.

"The trouble is, I reckon those types don't take too kindly to brute force, coercion, or blackmail," Phineas continued, oblivious to the unspoken exchange happening between me and my closest friends. "Which means they'd require softer methods of control. Shared enemies. Loyalty. Enough to form the kinds of bonds that we had with Princeton through our sigils—ensuring mutual protection or death by shadow."

"Kylo," Harmony started.

"*No*," I bellowed, the table rattling against the floor. I stood. "I need everyone except Harmony and Blade to take their leave. We will reconvene shortly."

Phineas was finally paying attention, his snake eyes narrowing on my stance before scanning my highest-ranking comrades. He nodded in subservience, regardless, leaving with the others.

As soon as they were gone, I took a deep breath.

"Kylo," Harmony said again. "Your instincts are never wrong, remember? You always know what the clan needs before we do. What this revolution *needs*."

"It needs *her*," Blade said, crossing his tree-trunk arms over his broad chest.

I shook my head. "My intuition about Evie was not about her usefulness," I said, hushed despite the eavesdropping protection wards. As if my love for Evie was akin to treason. "It was about who she is and what she means to me."

"Why can't both be true?" Harmony asked softly.

I turned away from them, studying the dark magenta vines that crawled up the walls. "Because all Evie has ever known is abuse, manipulation, and selfishness. From the moment she was born, her parents sought to use her instead of love her. To tithe her as a child bride to some born elite rather than protect her."

I turned back to them, my gaze burning as it met each of my

friends'. I needed them to understand—I needed them to understand why they couldn't ask this of me, and why I could never ask such a thing of *her*.

"She has just finally started to open up, after a decade on the run. To learn how to do something as simple as trust someone other than her brother or her grandmother. She dedicated her entire existence to protecting someone else, and she's only now beginning to live for herself. She would never want this life, and I would never force it on her. That precious girl deserves to feel safe. Not to become the new most coveted kill of all born demons and King Earle himself."

Harmony smiled sadly. "Don't we all deserve to feel safe?"

Blade sighed. "None of us asked for this life. Yes, we chose it. But it chose us just as much." He paused. "I hear you, Kylo. I do. There is no good solution, not under this kind of pressure. There's *live* or *die*."

Harmony's gaze was unyielding and intense as she lifted her chin. "She might surprise you."

60

EVIE

I recognized the memory that took shape around me. Shapes cloaked in black slunk through the house, but even more frightening were the monsters drenched in crimson. My parents were standing close together, at the outskirts of the gathering as they plated food. They didn't hear or see me approach behind them. I stood there, as my mother opened her mouth.

It's a disaster. He's no longer—

I put my hands over my ears, and I screamed. I didn't want to hear what came next, to *feel* what came next.

I screamed so loudly that I woke up, except the world I opened my eyes to was strange. My bed was outside, under the stars. A crow sat at the foot of my bedframe, watching over me protectively.

Figures moved in the distance, and my heart pulled toward them. I half walked, half floated over the grass between comforting pine trees. The energy was alive, celebratory.

The two figures stood before a fire, laughing. A man dressed in a billowy white top, hands in his pockets. A woman in otherworldly purple.

Hekate turned, her black hair shiny, her skin fair. She took her maternal form tonight. Though she could also appear as a maiden or crone.

My throat tightened under her warm gaze. She was proud of me.

The man turned next, and my eyes filled with tears. "Princeton?"

He said just one word.

"*Bloom.*"

WHEN I WOKE UP, my dreams were hazy. I remembered only those jagged edges. The way Princeton's eyes had reflected fire, his lips in that comforting, trademark smirk. Hekate's strength and care that was somehow untarnished by her violence and shadows.

It made no sense and too much sense both at the same time.

Kylo had come home after I'd already fallen asleep, so I tried not to wake him when I slipped out of bed to fetch coffee.

He heard me anyway, his voice reaching me as soon as I faced the door.

"I love you Evie," he said sleepily. "I'm sorry I've gone so long without saying that."

"It's been, like, a day." I giggled. I retreated back to kiss Kylo's cheek. "But I love you too. Go back to sleep. I know you came home late. I'll be in the living room reading."

I wasn't even sure how much sleeping Kylo was doing, as every time I woke up, he too, seemed to be awake. He never once complained. Just as he barely mentioned Princeton's death, or the toll it had clearly taken on his spirit.

Like he'd freely admitted, Kylo had decided to take on the weight of the world rather than confront his own vulnerability.

And that was a quality I empathized with as much as I

despised it. Because my hypocritical ass knew that it wasn't healthy. I could tell he thought he needed to be strong for me. But really, I just wanted him to feel safe enough to *not* be strong for once.

I was on my second cup of coffee by the time he found me reading and taking notes for my upcoming new moon ritual.

"What are you working on?" he asked, joining me at the dining room table where I'd set up my books and workspace.

He'd allowed Allie to take me back to pick up my things and explain to Mena where I'd be, but only with several other guards lurking around and scanning the perimeter. Mena thought Kylo and I were merely engaging in a sexual honeymoon, and I refused to pop that bubble. It was a much nicer thought than reality.

"A new protection spell," I said.

It wasn't a lie, but it wasn't the truth either. Kylo had enough on his plate. I didn't need him thinking that there were even more enemies plotting against me in the darkness. Even if it felt silly to compare Jacob's parents to the lethal born.

Unless of course they were planning on tipping off the born about my magick.

Gods. Only seven more days now until the new moon. And, mercifully, so far so good.

"I want Mena to be safe while I'm away," I said.

"She will be, baby," Kylo said. "There are always patrols in your neighborhood."

I closed my notebook, pretending to be nonchalant about it as I sipped more coffee. "Today's the day I told Idris I'd come visit him on campus," I reminded Kylo, chewing on my bottom lip nervously.

Kylo nodded, unable to hide the flicker of unease that had first eclipsed his eyes. "Of course. You need to see him." His lips turned down.

"You want to come with me, don't you?" I asked, studying Kylo's discomfort.

"I'm sorry, Evie," he said. "I want to give you space. I know this isn't normal."

"What happened wasn't normal," I said. "It's okay."

I pushed away the voice in the back of my mind that was screaming in protest. Reminding me of the importance of space and boundaries and maintaining my own agency. I reminded that part of myself that Kylo was only trying to protect me.

He didn't want me to end up like Aisling. Or Princeton.

Kylo wasn't *Kylo* right now. And if I could make his life just a tiny bit easier by giving him this sense of control, then I would.

The vision of Princeton from my dream was still ripe in my mind as I wondered what Kylo and his clan had been discussing.

"You need a witch to take Princeton's place, don't you?" I asked, though the question was more rhetorical than my next ones. "Why haven't you mentioned that to me?" My brows furrowed, discomfort making me itchy as I squirmed in my seat. "Blade and Harmony know what I am…"

Kylo straightened in his seat, his gaze sharpening on my lips. "Why—why not *me*?"

The space between us was heavy as the silence enveloped us. Kylo stared at me with a deep frown, those intense eyes probing my every feature.

It was a strange feeling that grew inside of me, this harsh condemnation of the mere thought of joining the turned, juxtaposed with this nervous, confused curiosity. Because I was the obvious solution. Yet perhaps they thought I was too unstable or weak.

"I would *never* ask that of you," Kylo said sharply, shaking his head.

"Because you know I would say *no*?" I asked, fiddling with my hands as I avoided his intense eyes.

"Angel, I wouldn't allow it even if you said *yes*. It's not what you want from this life, and it's certainly not what I want for you. You deserve to open your own shop, like you've been dreaming and planning for. If you want to sell some of your goods to the clan, I would welcome it. But you're not one of us. You're not *him*."

My eyes flashed to his, noticing the way he'd scoffed at the mere idea of me joining the clan or being comparable to Princeton.

The indignation and hurt in my guts made no fucking sense. Because he was right. I wasn't one of them, and I didn't want to be. It was the last thing I wanted.

So why was this conversation making me feel this way?

"Do Blade and Harmony agree with you?" I asked.

Kylo looked taken aback. "Doesn't matter. They don't know you."

My stomach dipped, as if I'd taken a blow.

Now Kylo appeared utterly confused, an expression that rarely graced his features. It had always seemed like I'd been an easy puzzle for him to solve.

Until now.

"How dire is the situation?" I asked. "Please don't lie to me."

Kylo sighed. "It's not ideal, but it won't be an emergency until the born make their next move and prey on our weakness. For now, we're okay. We have time."

I wasn't sure which one of us he was most trying to convince. My hyper-empathy was now absorbing his stress, weighing it in my palms in search of the truth.

Princeton's murder scene flashed across my mind's eye, and I quickly stood from the table, mumbling something about getting more water.

Reality shifted back into place. This wasn't my problem to fix. My power was bound and blocked for a reason. Kylo's unspoken counterargument was the correct one.

I wasn't a powerful witch.

I was just a liability.

And I had no interest in dedicating my life to the violence I'd narrowly escaped—the darkness I'd run from while carrying a sobbing seven-year-old boy in my arms.

61

EVIE

We met up with Idris in one of the yards near the academic buildings. The wind tousled his dirty blond hair, and his soft brown eyes sparked when they focused on our approach. He smiled, and it melted some of the tightness that had gathered in my chest.

When he stood, I nearly tackled him with a hug.

"Sheesh," he muttered. "You act like I've just returned home from war."

It wasn't the best joke for me to hear at this moment, but I brushed it off. When I pulled back, I returned his smile.

Idris lifted a brow as he looked from me to Kylo. "Or like the two of you just returned from war." His eyes narrowed on me. "What happened?"

I tripped over my words. I shouldn't have been so caught off guard. Idris might've been human, but he'd been born with a hefty dose of keen intuition.

When Kylo spoke, I realized the answer was simpler. I studied the planes of his face, the way they appeared different in the aftermath of his grief and unfathomable stress.

I was sure I didn't look any better.

"We lost a friend a few days ago," Kylo said simply.

Idris's face fell. "I'm so sorry for your loss. You okay, Evie?" He studied me more carefully now.

I nodded. "I'll be okay."

Idris's gaze flitted back to Kylo. "The born?"

To my surprise, Kylo only nodded. Why keep something like that a secret when the born were killing and kidnapping more mortals each day?

Princeton was their most coveted kill. But he was only one of many this week alone.

"I hate them," I whispered.

Idris cocked his head, appearing slightly puzzled. "As you should." He cleared his throat, rubbing his bloodshot, sleep-deprived eyes. "You want to grab coffee first?"

"She's cut off," Kylo said.

I glared at him, and Idris laughed. He moved closer to Kylo as we started walking toward the street of shops and cafés.

"That's probably for the best," Idris said. "I'm glad she has someone to monitor her coffee intake. Combined with the chronic worrying, it just can't be good for her heart."

I lightheartedly elbowed him in the side.

Idris side-eyed Kylo. "Though I am concerned she's become more violent under your influence."

WE SAT OUTSIDE in the pleasant summertime air, sipping on cool drinks from a combined bookstore and café. I was glad Kylo had told Idris the truth. I hadn't realized how stifling it had been to always pretend everything was okay when it wasn't. I thought I'd been protecting Idris all these years, but now I worried my thick layers of denial had only been erected to protect myself.

Because I watched as Idris and Kylo connected authentically, in a way that made my heart gooey and my skin erupt in goosebumps.

"How do you deal with the anger?" Idris asked, his voice low as he stirred his lavender lemonade. "I don't want to be an angry person. But I worry if I'm not angry, then I'm just… complicit. Like I'm broadcasting that I'm fine with the way things are."

Kylo regarded Idris with gentleness. "It's okay to feel angry. Emotions are messengers. They tell us what's important to us, what truly matters. But they're only the first step in the process. The key is not getting stuck there, but instead moving into action. Specifically, making moves on what you can actually control. Lifting up your friends, working hard in your self-defense classes, staying vigilant but not living in fear. Use the anger as fuel to improve yourself, but be mindful about using it as an excuse to harm yourself or others."

Idris was hanging on Kylo's every word, processing in that thoughtful, curious way he did.

And I noticed that the more Kylo spoke to Idris, the more the heaviness on his shoulders lifted. I hadn't realized how much of my own pain hinged on seeing Kylo experience some amount of relief, no matter how temporary.

"Physical exercise helps immensely. As do honor-based combat sports, such as what you're learning in fighting classes. Focusing on healthy releases of anger tempered by noble pursuits like loyalty, goodness, mercy, empathy, and protectiveness is the best remedy I've found."

Idris nodded. "The fighting does help," he said. "When I'm awake enough to be of any use."

My heart twisted, knowing Idris might be suffering in his dreams the same as I was. Even if he didn't remember that accursed night, or many specifics from our childhood, those feelings were clearly rooted deep.

We both would find relief in a couple of weeks when the date had passed.

"Have you seen the campus healers?" Kylo asked.

Idris shook his head. Instead of being irritated, he looked slightly uncomfortable. As if he didn't like disappointing Kylo.

"Get yourself there," Kylo said.

Idris's eyes slowly found mine. "Only if Evie sees one too."

The words startled me. My instinctive urge was to grow irritated and defensive. But all I could focus on was the darkness under Idris's eyes.

The truth was, I'd already been seeing an emotional healer when I was working with Princeton to control my power.

But now that he was dead, I wasn't sure who in this world could help me. Because the main reason I avoided witches and healers was so that they couldn't uncover who I was at my core.

The stakes were already high before, but now revealing my nature was more than just dangerous. It was a death sentence.

"Okay," I said anyway, desperate for Idris to get help for his insomnia. Maybe it didn't have to be a lie. I'd make it work.

Idris relaxed an inch. "Have you heard the drama between Mena's boyfriends yet?"

I giggled. "Which ones?"

Kylo reached for my hand under the table, slowly tracing his thumb over my skin in circles. The longer Idris and I laughed and discussed Mena's dramatic dating life, the less I noticed Kylo scanning our surroundings for threats every few minutes.

And when Kylo laughed genuinely, it was the first time I'd heard such a warm, authentic sound from him since before we found Princeton.

We eventually got up and strolled down the street, popping into little shops and boutiques. Kylo intertwined his fingers through mine.

"What's this plant saying, Evie?" Idris teased when we entered a plants shop. He was holding a potted orchid.

It was a game we used to play as children, hunting for faeries amid the trees and tall grass. I'd speak to the earth and translate to Idris, and his big eyes would fill with awe each time my palms glowed with magick.

I let my eyes grow glassy, reading the soft pink aura surrounding the little plant.

"Bloom."

My smile fell as I listened to myself say the word. It had shocked me out of autopilot, but I couldn't precisely recall why.

Kylo looked at me adoringly. "You are ridiculously cute."

"But creepy," Idris amended, making a face. He set the plant back down. "Do you think one of these possesses spirits that could do my homework for me?"

"Potentially," I said. "But struggle builds character."

"Agreed," Kylo said.

Idris rolled his eyes at us. "I changed my mind. I don't like you two together. Nothing is *this* perfect."

Kylo kissed the top of my head, and I wondered if the glowing feeling in my heart was visible.

"Anyone at university catch your attention lately?" I asked casually, despite knowing how secretive Idris was.

On cue, he shrugged. "Maybe. I'm focusing on myself right now."

"That's when they get you," Kylo warned.

Idris grinned, eyeing a tiny Venus flytrap. I thought of Princeton and his collection of carnivorous plants, and by the expression on Kylo's face, I knew he thought of him too.

I squeezed his hand, gently pulling him away. Idris followed us out, and we continued slowly meandering down the lively street.

"I know you guys are going through a lot," Idris said. "Thanks for coming out anyway. Don't feel obligated to—"

Idris stopped speaking. Kylo went rigid.

A man in a gaudy, archaic navy suit walked past us, his jet-black shoulder-length hair straight and his eyes a striking amber.

He glanced our way briefly, mainly looking at me as his lips formed a smirk and his nostrils flared.

His sickly born magick was easily discernible. I was used to experiencing nausea and fear when confronted with their blood-stained souls, but the ravenous anger was rather new.

And unwelcome.

Because rage wasn't a safe feeling for me to have, especially surrounded by people in the heart of Etherdale. Kylo stood protectively close until the vampire had turned a corner.

"We're just outside the vampire-free zone," Kylo hissed. "He's taunting us."

I glanced back at Idris, determined to turn the mood around and end the day on a good note.

But Idris was pale, his eyes full of palpable terror. He rubbed his chest, his breathing becoming shallower and shallower until he was gasping for air.

"Idris?"

I grabbed his shoulder, but he flinched and pushed my hand away.

"Can't. Breathe," he said, the words frightened and raspy.

In the middle of the busy street, Idris fell to his knees, still panting and clutching his chest.

"We need a healer!" Fear took hold of me as I watched Idris helplessly. I didn't understand what was happening.

Idris curled up in a fetal position, his face contorting with a pain I could feel as a crushing weight against my own lungs.

He continued to inhale rapidly, making himself small, mouthing the words *help, help, help* over and over.

My gaze darted around before landing on Kylo, opening my mouth to beg him to find a healer.

But Kylo gently pulled me back and dropped to the ground with Idris. People had slowed around us, looking at my brother nervously as he panted and gasped for air.

I spotted Allie across the street, and a few other glamoured turned. Allie barked something at one of the men.

I stood shell-shocked, rooted to the cobblestone under the golden afternoon sun. I watched as Kylo lay with my brother, speaking quietly to him.

Idris stopped begging for help. The hand that had been pulling at his hair had dropped back in front of his face with the other one. His eyes, once shut tight, slowly opened back up.

My eyes pooled with tears, assuming Idris had been hexed, that the born were punishing me for existing by killing my brother.

But his shallow gulps of air started to even out. Kylo kept speaking to him, too low for me to make out over the bustling street chatter.

Kylo had curled up the same as Idris had, meeting him exactly where he was. He'd done so without any hesitation. The vampire clan leader, in a vulnerable position on the ground in the middle of the street.

When Idris nodded at something Kylo said, Kylo placed a hand on his shoulder and rubbed.

"I used to have panic attacks too," Kylo said, slightly louder now, at a level I could discern if I strained and focused. "During class. During fights. Even when I was in my own space, alone. They often seemed random."

He then instructed Idris to breathe with him. To hold the breath. To release. To hold. Then again, until Idris had completely stopped moving, stopped struggling for air.

I watched as the turned man handed Allie a glass of water, and Allie approached us, handing the glass to me without a word.

After a few more minutes, Idris slowly sat up. Kylo mirrored him.

I handed Idris the glass of water. He sipped, his face flushed, and his body slumped. He drank and stared at nothing for a couple of minutes, chest rising and falling at a normal cadence.

He still looked out of it when he spoke his next words, his eyes glassy as he tilted his head up toward me. "You didn't understand, Evie. That day in the courtyard."

My heart skipped. We hadn't discussed that moment since it happened—the day he'd told me he wanted to join the turned, and I'd conjured a nasty storm with my anger.

"I don't want to be stronger because I think you're weak, or that you've failed me," he said softly, staring into the distance for a moment before slowly focusing back on my eyes. "I *do* remember what happened."

My breath caught, and for a moment, I forgot Kylo was even there. It was just me and Idris, those icy cold hands from the past reaching toward us.

"I remember," he repeated, his lips trembling as he wiped his eyes. "You had it all wrong. I want to be as strong as *you are*. To help people like you do. I want to protect you the way you protected *me*."

"Idris," I breathed, unable to find the right words as emotions crashed over both of us.

He nodded, avoiding my eyes again. "I just needed to say that." He returned to sipping his water, a tremor rolling through him.

Blade joined the amassing bodies around us, who I now understood were all glamoured turned.

Kylo noticed him too, nodding at him as if they'd exchanged a silent conversation.

Blade and I exchanged a look, and I offered him a sad, shaky smile. Then he turned his attention to my brother. "Hey, I'm one of Kylo's friends. Wondered if you all wanted to have a beer at the pub on the corner?"

I thought that seeing the turned surround my brother would

boil my blood. I thought it would send me into a magickal explosion.

But all I could do was stare at Kylo in shock. My gaze flitted from him to Blade, to Allie and the rest of them.

And the feeling blooming in my chest didn't stop. Not when we were inside the pub, and the clan treated Idris with nothing but respect, pulling him into laughter, stories, and banter with ease.

Kylo pulled me aside once Idris was settled at the bar, surrounded by vampires wearing human skins.

Monsters who showed this complete stranger kindness and comradery even while still dealing with their own indescribable grief.

I'd been knocked out of orbit, reeling and spinning as I held on to Kylo for dear life. From Idris's admission to Kylo's act of brotherly love—it was all too much to process, yet somehow achingly simple.

"That's just who you are, isn't it?" I asked him in the corner, away from the growing crowd.

I exhaled, wiping away a stray tear as Kylo held my face in his broad palms. He brushed his lips against my forehead.

I couldn't stop thinking about the image of Kylo laying with Idris. How quickly he'd dropped to the ground, how easily he was able to help Idris breathe again.

"You—your clan," I stammered. "I've never seen him like that. I had no idea he had panic attacks. I didn't know what to do. I couldn't have done what you did for him. Thank you." I closed my hands around his forearms, staring into his deep blue irises.

"I thought you might be angry with me," he said softly. "I don't want you to think I'm breaking my word about keeping your brother away from the clan."

"I don't care about that," I said, my voice breaking just like those damned walls I'd built around myself. "I know you're not recruiting him."

Everything was crumbling all at once. The lightning had struck the tower, and nothing would ever be the same again.

"I just want Idris to be safe. And happy. That's all I've ever wanted. Thank you for helping him."

"You don't have to thank me," Kylo said. "I wanted to. He's a good kid. He reminds me of myself in a lot of ways. I enjoy helping him find his path."

My grip on his forearms tightened. "I love you a stupid amount," I said fiercely.

At a burst of laughter and cheering, I broke free from Kylo's hold to glance over my shoulder. Idris was beaming. Blade and a few other men were jumping up and down. Even Allie was laughing at their antics.

I turned back to Kylo, and he immediately crushed his lips to mine. His hand stroked my hair, and I melted into his touch.

I couldn't stop thinking about what Idris had said. That he *remembered.*

When Kylo pulled back, I blurted out my next words. "I'll do it. I'll help the clan, even if it's just temporary."

Kylo's eyes darkened. He shook his head.

"I've been having these visions," I whispered. "For a while now, really. I—I think I'm meant to do this."

Kylo gripped my waist, his features twisting. "No. I don't want this for you, Evie. I never have."

"Well, I didn't want most things that happened to me between my birth and now, but here we are," I said, attempting to imbue humor into my tone that didn't quite land with Kylo.

He bristled.

I heard whispers in the corners of the room. I felt the unmistakable chill of spirit guidance travel the length of my body. My intuition poked and prodded, alerting me that this moment was important.

It may have been a low frequency of Kylo's angry protectiveness that I heard, but I preferred to believe it was the hum of fate instead.

"I know who our enemies are. I know what kind of world I want to believe in. And I know who has made me feel safe, seen, and understood."

"This isn't a *temporary* position, Evie," Kylo rasped. "Clan membership is forever. You don't know what you're saying."

I steadied myself in his deep blue eyes. "You need me. And I need you."

I placed a hand on his broad chest, over his heart—the heart bonded to mine through blood and magick.

"Aren't *we* forever?"

62

EVIE

My life was about to change. Irreversibly, totally. So much was uncertain. Kylo was still not entirely on board, pointing to the obvious problem of my lack of control or even my acceptance of my own magick.

But somehow, I knew that it was all going to work out. It was too obvious to deny—the way our lives and fates had so easily intertwined.

Kylo allowed me to visit Mena again, four days before the new moon ritual. I would also need him to let me return on the day of the new moon, but that was Future Evie's problem.

I was guarded to the teeth, and I couldn't stay for too long. Kylo was busy with interrogations today, information I had to pull from his cagey lips.

Mena and I sat at the smaller dinner table off the kitchen, sipping tea and eating pastries. She lifted a perfectly manicured brow as her red lips formed a frown.

"Have things changed between the two of you?" she asked.

"Me and Kylo? No. Well, yes, but only for the better."

She made a face, in classic Mena fashion, that alerted me to her skepticism.

"What are you thinking?" I asked with a sigh.

"He's wonderful, Evie. But my loyalty is with you, always," she said. "Getting swept up in love is a wonderful feeling, but if you're losing yourself in the process, something is wrong."

Oh, of course. Mena must've assumed that because I was spending so much time with Kylo this soon in our relationship, and because I was no doubt wearing my trauma and stress plainly on my face, that meant Kylo was being overly controlling. It was a reasonable assumption from an outsider's perspective.

"It's really not like that," I assured her. "We actually lost a mutual friend recently," I explained. "To born violence."

"A witch?" Mena inquired, her eyes welling with fear as she reached for my hand.

I nodded. "Kylo would never isolate me on purpose. He's protective, but he's not deceitful or manipulative. Not like Jacob was. You don't have anything to worry about."

Mena took a sip of her tea. She stared out the window nervously. "Helia above, I just don't know how to tell you this."

I braced myself.

I'd already been towered. How much worse could things get?

"You know that you and your brother mean the absolute world to me. When I saw you on my doorstep, and I saw Idris's —well, you know what I saw."

I flinched, rebooting my brain and shoving the memory away.

"I knew that I was always meant to take care of you kids. I didn't give a damn what anyone had to say about it. Still don't," she said, balling her free hand into a fist. "Cindy came around again, drunk and a mess."

No. Cindy had to keep her mouth shut for four more days. I had to believe it would all be okay until then.

Mena rubbed my hand as she met my eyes. "She says they

hired a witch to look into Jacob's disappearance. She says they know for certain that the boy is dead."

My vision tunneled. The words were a shocking stab in my side. I slowly shook my head.

"No. No he's not," I said. "Men like him don't just *die*." I searched Mena's eyes as if they had all the answers. "How? Do they know how?"

"She said it was violent. She still thinks whatever happened can be traced back to you."

"So they don't actually know," I said bitterly. "They just want me to be the easy answer."

All my life, everyone besides Mena and Idris had misunderstood me. No matter how good I tried to be. How helpful, agreeable, and conscientious. None of it had ever mattered. From the day I was born, I'd been hated for what I was. Not human enough. Not witch enough.

Too much of this, not nearly enough of that.

The harder I tried, the more everyone misunderstood every piece of my heart and soul.

Even Jacob, my first boyfriend. Maybe especially him. Through the increasingly unwinnable trials of our relationship, I sought to prove my worthiness—of acceptance, of love, of care and patience.

Kylo had taught me that those things didn't have to be earned. So I'd recently learned to despise Jacob and his cruelty instead. I finally saw his actions not as excusable or mindless, but as conscious decisions to treat me poorly and make me smaller than he felt inside.

But now, Jacob was *dead*.

I shook my head.

No. No way that was true.

"The witch could've been scamming her," I said quickly. "Preying off a desperate drunk woman."

"Precisely what I told her before slamming the door in her

face," Mena grumbled. "I love you so much, my special, empathetic, resilient girl. I'm sorry you got wrapped up in this. But I needed to warn you. Because I don't know how far this is going to go. And I know how unwilling you are to use your magick to shut a bitch up."

Inappropriate laughter burst through my lips. It broke through the haze of disbelief and anger and strange wilted grief. It transformed into a shaky half-sob.

"I didn't want Jacob to die," I whispered. "All I really ever wanted was for him to be nice to me."

"He wasn't a nice person," Mena said. "If something violent befell him, it was likely his own doing." She sighed. "Helia rest his soul."

I should've known that this period of chaos wasn't done with me yet. God forbid I live a calm, peaceful life, in love and safe with the man of my dreams.

"I love you endlessly, Mena. You're everything to Idris and me, too," I said. "It's going to be okay. I can fix this."

I tried to spend the next hour with Mena the way I'd set out to do—but it ended up feeling forced and heavy.

Because all I really wanted to do was cry. And on my walk back to Kylo's home, I couldn't shake the glaring intuition that something was wrong.

My chest felt tight, a heavy weight in my stomach. Could Jacob truly be dead? And if he was, how could that have happened? Even if I knew I was blameless, I couldn't temper the rising panic, shame, and guilt eclipsing my mind.

I still cared for that man, no matter how much I'd learned to detest his behavior. He hadn't deserved to die for it.

Something wasn't adding up about any of this. The timeline of events since Kylo had entered my life, the way they'd all led me to this point where I was leaving and rejecting everything I once knew...

The way Kylo was somehow both deranged and gentle,

controlling and reasonable, a ruthless clan leader and a patient, selfless caregiver.

Amid the converging, intertwining paths—all the strange and unexpected puzzle pieces that somehow fit snugly together—I couldn't shake the intuition that something had gone wrong when I hadn't been paying attention.

~

I DIDN'T TELL Kylo about Jacob. I wished I could pretend not to know why.

But I knew. Just like I'd known Kylo was the masked man stalking me, even if I hadn't wanted him to be.

I didn't tell Kylo, because despite how much I loved him, despite seeing him drop to the ground and help my brother...

If Jacob was murdered, right after being shitty to me in front of an entire restaurant, there was a very obvious suspect.

A protective, obsessive suspect. Someone I thought would never lie to me or harm me so profoundly.

I didn't want to have these thoughts. Gods, I just wanted to go back to how I'd felt yesterday, when I'd stared into Kylo's eyes and seen eternity.

Kylo knew something was wrong, but I had an endless list of excuses to give him as we cooked dinner together. He didn't mention anything about clan matters, still treating me like an outsider.

Maybe he thought it would only make me more curious. Increase my yearning to be a part of it all.

Fuck. The lump was back in my throat, and while I was turned away from Kylo, I squeezed my eyes shut.

That nasty paranoia was back, encouraging thoughts I hadn't entertained since Kylo had told me he loved me, since before he took my virginity, and before we were bound by blood.

I want the truth, I whispered to my guides and spiritual allies inside my mind.

A rush of otherworldly wind assailed me, and I knew it was the kind of wind only I could feel.

"You okay, angel?" Kylo asked.

I opened my eyes and cleared my throat, slowly turning to him. I reached for his arm, studying the sigils etched in ink on his skin.

"I'm okay," I lied. "Are these the same sigils I saw on your dagger?" I let my cheeks heat, hoping Kylo might mistake my fear with arousal.

"The one I used in the gardens?" Kylo said, looking down to where I traced his tattoos. He smirked, no doubt recalling the blade cutting through my panties.

My stomach fluttered. I wanted to lean into the lust. I didn't want to keep watching my world crash down around me.

Maybe I didn't want to know the truth.

"Yes, there are symbols in my tattoos that correspond to the dagger—linking the weapon to my magick." Kylo reached for the hidden holster at his hip, sliding the dagger out with graceful ease. "Be careful, please, baby."

He handed me the weapon without a second thought.

The moment my hand wrapped around the hilt, I realized it was too late to take it back.

I saw it *all*.

Jacob, thrown up against a tomb in the cemetery. Kylo taunting him, telling him he wanted to kill him the moment he saw Jacob with me. Merely for touching me.

Kylo declaring I belonged to him, before I'd even had time to come to that conclusion myself. Before I truly knew him, before he truly knew *me*.

I watched Jacob piss himself. I watched Kylo destroy him verbally before slitting his throat. At the splatter of blood and the sound of desperate gurgling, I let go.

Kylo caught the weapon I'd dropped with vampiric speed. He cursed. He stared at me incredulously, sheathing the dagger. "What happened? Did you try to read the magick again? You know there are protective wards…"

I couldn't hear the rest of Kylo's words about how I'd nearly cut off my *cute little toes.*

My survival instincts kicked in as if by brute force. I laughed nervously, offering a demure apology.

Classic Evie, always apologizing.

Always blindly trusting those whose only intents are to harm and use her.

63

EVIE

Everything had been a lie.

My relationship with Kylo had been built on a foundation of death and secrets. My imperative to protect Idris and Mena was the only thing keeping me from exploding in a fit of heartbreak and rage, from conjuring floods and hail and cyclones of destruction.

I lay in bed next to Kylo, wide awake. I examined every moment we'd shared between now and when he murdered my boyfriend.

The way he'd homed in on my core wounds, fashioning himself as the antidote to all of my deepest suffering. Was that even him? Or was that the part he knew he needed to play in order to win my trust?

The cards had warned me, at the very beginning. The Devil: abuse, control, bondage, being seduced by sensual pleasure and luxury. The Seven of Swords: the card of deception and betrayal, an image of a man sneaking away with swords in his hands, looking back over his shoulder to ensure he was getting away with it.

I'd seen my future, and I'd carried on, anyway.

477

I was isolated, surrounded by his clan. What if all the visions of Princeton and Hekate had been trying to tell me something else? What if the betrayal ran deeper, and Kylo had been planning on replacing Princeton from the start? Maybe Princeton had stepped out of line too many times, and they wanted a witch they could more easily control.

What if Hekate was trying to protect me from Kylo and the turned, not push me toward them?

I clenched my fists, the weight of Kylo's arm around me suddenly stifling.

Oh gods. Was he truly capable of something so sinister? Were Harmony and Blade?

I felt indescribably stupid. I'd allowed Kylo to force his blood down my throat, to mark me, to claim me, to feed from me, to fuck me.

I was so starved and desperate for love and acceptance, a fact he knew about me from the start. I'd let him infiltrate my body, my mind, and my life. I'd let go of all my fear and hatred, adopted entirely new beliefs and opinions and life goals.

All because a vampire brushed my hair and told me he would love me the way my parents refused to.

An angry, heartbroken sob built in my chest, and I kept it quiet. Hot tears pooled. I didn't make a sound.

I was going insane, spinning in circles, unable to tell my paranoia from truth.

The only thing I knew for certain was that Kylo had killed my boyfriend and kept it from me.

Even if Kylo did love me, in his own sick and twisted way. Even if my most wounded, paranoid thoughts were wrong, the truth about what Kylo did to Jacob was more than enough reason to get the fuck away from him.

I needed to get to Idris and Mena.

I needed to run.

~

"You are not okay," Kylo said softly.

I jumped out of my skin at the noise. I realized I'd been staring at the wardrobe for several minutes, completely lost in my plotting and scheming.

Kylo bent to kiss my temple. "Please tell me what I can do to help, angel. It breaks my heart to see you like this."

I turned to face him with a shaky breath. When I studied his tormented features, I couldn't see anything less than genuine concern.

And the wounded part of me was screaming at me to lean into Kylo's love. To pretend that I'd never learned the truth. To trust that he really did have my best interests at heart, and what happened with Jacob was out of character.

But then I remembered when I'd begged him not to harm anyone in my name, and he'd merely joked it off, never actually agreeing to my request. It was the perfect opportunity to come clean about Jacob, to ensure our love wasn't poisoned by such a monumental breach of trust.

He hadn't said a word.

"I don't feel like myself," I admitted.

I was so emotionally triggered and heartbroken that I could hardly feel my own bodily sensations. Just the weight of a heavy lump in my throat, the urge to sob ever present. Adrenaline coursed in my blood. All I could hear was the sound of my nervous system screaming, *RUN!*

Kylo's brows furrowed. Worry swam in his blue eyes. "Talk to me, baby. I can scent how scared you are." He brushed my hair behind my ears, the act momentarily soothing me, flutters crawling down my spine.

Gods, I'd wanted him to be different. I didn't want this to be too good to be true.

Don't you fucking cry, the familiar voice hissed—my mother's voice.

"I'm heartbroken," I said, hiding beneath the truth. "About Princeton. About all of it. I'm scared for the future."

Kylo nodded. "I'm so sorry, Evie. You've been unbelievably strong through all of this. Take all the time you need to mourn. Your old life, your old sense of self." Kylo looked away for a moment. "I'm sorry for bringing so much violence into your world. I wish I could shield you from it all."

He looked guilty, but clearly not guilty enough to come clean.

Even still, my sensitive, hopeful heart reached for his words, yearning to hold them close—to use them to patch up the devastating dagger wound in my back.

"Will you go with me to the library?"

Kylo didn't hesitate, didn't tell me he was too busy or unavailable. "Of course."

～

My plan was fucking insane.

Or it was genius.

Only time would tell.

Perhaps because I'd lost my mind the moment I'd touched that accursed dagger, and it had been running farther and farther away with each passing hour.

I genuinely couldn't discern what was good or right or true. I only knew I had to get away. From Kylo, from his clan, from Cindy and Roger and the born who still hunted me.

It was time to start over. *Again.*

"What is that?" Kylo asked, sitting next to me in a private study room in the library.

He was reading one of my favorite fantasy romance novels. No doubt to learn how to better manipulate me.

The old Evie would've found the notion rather sexy.

Whatever the hell I'd become in the past two days had different feelings.

I followed his line of sight to a thin, pointy bone I'd pulled out of my bag. "It's a needle," I said. "It's about to be a *poisoned* needle."

Kylo lifted a brow, that once-adorable dimple forming as he smirked. "*Oh?*"

"I need more vampire-disarming weapons."

Kylo rumbled with deep laughter. "I love you so much it's disgusting." He kissed my temple before returning his gaze to the book.

I smiled. My left eyelid was starting to twitch slightly from sleep deprivation. My knee bounced up and down. I continued my work with the supplies I'd packed in my pink leather bag. I followed Hekate's instructions meticulously, dipping the bone in an herbal mixture I'd ground up in a bowl.

"May I please have some of your saliva?" I asked.

"Of course, angel," Kylo murmured, slowly raising his gaze from the book to me. "Always." His lips curved. "Where do you want it?"

"In the bowl, please."

"Good manners, angel," he purred.

He grabbed my face and crushed his lips to mine. He consumed me, like he'd been consuming me, piece by piece, since the day he'd first decided I was *his*. His tongue teased mine, and he inhaled deeply.

Behind my eyelids, I saw stars. I saw the great expanse of the cosmos above us as Kylo told me he loved me for the first time. The night I crumpled in his arms and revealed I didn't want to love him, that my heart wouldn't survive another betrayal. He'd begged me to fall, anyway. To trust that he would protect and care for me forever. He'd made me believe he would *never* use, harm, and manipulate me the way my parents had.

I'd given him everything. All of me. My brokenness, my wounds, my hope, and my devotion.

I fought the urge to cry as his deceitful lips stole my breath this one last time. I forced myself to feel only numb determination until this was all over, and I could safely shatter under the full weight of my unfathomable grief.

He pulled back, gently lifting the bowl to spit in my herbal mixture. "Anything else?"

"No." I hoped that the sensation of my lips trembling was more mental than visible. "I have everything I need. Thank you."

Kylo stared at me and then the needle again.

I held my breath.

He smiled and returned his focus to the book, and I exhaled. With his free hand, he brushed his fingers across my cheek before moving lower to absentmindedly stroke my upper thigh as he read.

My knee had stopped bouncing at some point. An eerie, dissociative calm enveloped me.

"Finished," I breathed.

"Blood onyx base?" Kylo asked.

He set the book down on the table. I thought he'd lost interest in my magick, when he hadn't paid much attention to me. But I realized that he'd merely not wanted to be a distraction.

His full focus was now on me.

"No," I said. "It's an alternative. More long-lasting and incapacitating."

Kylo's eyes sparked. "Really? Can the ingredients be locally sourced?"

I nodded. "More or less. At least nothing needs to be sourced from Valentin—it can all be found on mainland Ravenia."

"So it has the potential to be mass produced?"

"Yep," I said. "Though some of the process requires

consecrating ingredients and tools in the name of Hekate, which cannot be performed by just anyone."

"But it can be performed by you?" Kylo asked.

I smiled, and spite lit up my nerves. He'd found another use for me.

"Who is Hekate?" he asked.

"A chthonic goddess of the crossroads, sorcery, death, and darkness, protector of witches and the downtrodden."

Alternatively, protector of women who'd run out of fucks to give.

Kylo looked thoughtful. "She presented herself to you?"

I nodded.

"Interesting," he said softly, but didn't say anything further.

I read over the pages of handwritten notes again, leaning forward as I scanned and double-checked my work. My over-thinking brain might've had its weaknesses, but being thorough was only ever a strength when it came to spell craft.

Except...

"Oh, hells," I whispered, my stomach dropping.

"What is it?"

"I may have mixed up an ingredient. She used an archaic name for one of the herbs and I think I used the wrong variety."

Kylo rubbed my shoulder. "I'm sorry, angel. Do you know what it would change?"

I shook my head. It was an amplifier herb. It was most likely to affect the poison's strength. What I'd used hadn't been too far off from the intended ingredient, so I had to believe it would be okay.

Hekate, please be with me now, I prayed as my heart stumbled.

"Come here, sweet girl," Kylo said.

I picked up the needle, examining its stained red tip before placing it on the edge of the table. I took a deep breath as I crawled into Kylo's lap.

The first thing I saw when I gazed into his eyes was Jacob,

pushed up against a tomb, uttering the words, *if you want Evie, you can have her. I'm no longer interested in her anyway.*

It was my brain's way of looking for a way out of this. The part of me that would do anything for love was desperate to break through the fog of my determination and get me to stand down.

But then I saw Jacob's throat sliced open. I saw Kylo listening to me mention Jacob, over and over, never once telling me the truth.

I saw Kylo stalking me, binding me to him, forcing his way into my world, eclipsing everything until he was the only thing I could see.

I reached behind me. I pulled the needle into my palms and stared down at it as I straddled Kylo—the monster I'd hoped was the other half of my bruised and battered soul.

Kylo merely kept his focus on my eyes. "It's okay, angel. You'll get it right next time. You're brilliant. We aren't defined by our mistakes. We're defined by our ability to take ownership for our shortcomings and to do better in the future."

"What a fascinating thing for you to say right now," I said, letting the bitterness coat my tongue.

Kylo was utterly puzzled, his features scrunching.

I allowed my buried emotions to barge through the splitting cracks. Just enough to propel me forward.

Just enough to lift my arm and plunge the needle into Kylo's abdomen.

He gasped, staring down at my trembling hand in shock. His arms went slack, falling off my waist and to his sides.

I pulled the needle out, my chin wobbling as I let it fall to the floor. Kylo's eyes slowly moved to mine as he fell deeper into paralysis.

The complete and utter hurt in his blue depths ripped my heart to pieces.

"No," I hissed. "You don't get to make me feel bad for this. You told me I was safe with you. You told me I could *trust you.*"

Kylo's lip twitched, but he was unable to speak.

"I know what you did to Jacob. What you've kept from me, all this time. And now I can't trust anything about you. Anything about *us.*"

There was so much I'd wanted to say—so much I'd been rehearsing, plotting, devising as I showered or walked or cooked or pretended to sleep.

But seeing my own crushing heartbreak reflected in Kylo's glassy eyes had me just as frozen as he was.

His eyelids began to droop. I knew I didn't have much time now.

I thought of Jacob's blood-soaked corpse. My hand fisted in Kylo's forest green shirt. He was fighting the pull of the poison, forcing his eyes back open every time they drifted shut.

"I still love you," I rasped. "Because I'm fucking *stupid.* But I'm leaving now. I know blood bonds can be reversed. I don't care how risky the procedure is. I will carve you out of me by any means necessary, and you will never be able to find me again."

A tremor rolled through Kylo before his eyes shut.

And they stayed shut.

From my lips, a surprised sob broke through.

"No," I said, reaching for Kylo's face that had gone slack.

What had I done? What was I *doing?* I loved him.

I needed him.

No you don't, Evie. Keep fucking moving.

The strong part of me, that thirteen-year-old girl who knew that no one could save us, no one could protect us or care for us except ourselves, took the reins.

I packed up my bag. I snuck out the window, into the yard at the side of the building. A few students spotted me, but they shrugged and minded their own business.

I didn't recognize any turned. When Kylo was with me, he didn't usually have too many bodyguards around. The city was full of turned, but no one except Allie and a couple others who'd watched me before might find it strange to see me without Kylo.

It was a big city. The chance of running into those specific vampires right now was low. And if someone stopped me, I'd lie. I wasn't a prisoner. The worst they could do was write to Kylo and trail me, but they wouldn't hear back from him any time soon.

That was unless, of course, my most paranoid thoughts were correct, and I actually *was* a known prisoner who'd been duped and marked by the entire clan.

In which case I was fucked no matter what.

I kept my chin lifted, fueled by spite and my most basic imperatives: Protect my family. And *run*.

Idris was first on the list. His apartment building was only a three-minute walk away. Other than a few fleeting glances, no one paid me any attention. Just like before Kylo barged his way into my life.

I prepared my speech as I climbed the steps to his front door, hoping my brother would believe me and cooperate. I wasn't even sure what I'd do if he didn't.

"Evie?"

I spun. Idris's shifter roommate stood at the bottom of the steps. His eyes widened, forcing me to reconsider my current level of unhinged.

I cleared my throat and toned it down a notch. "Hey, Marco."

"I'm glad you're here, I was actually about to track you or Mena down. I haven't seen Idris since last night, and this letter was left nailed to his door—addressed to you. I know he struggles with some stuff. I was trying not to freak out about the weirdness of it all."

I opened my mouth and then closed it. My heart physically hurt with how hard it started pumping.

At the bottom of the steps, Marco handed me the letter.

My name was in large letters on the front of the envelope, but it wasn't my brother's handwriting. Not even close.

I tore into the envelope, my eyes devouring the note as Marco nervously shifted on his feet.

"Is he all right?" Marco asked.

Below a hand-drawn map leading to an X on the forested outskirts of Etherdale, there were three sentences written.

Follow the map. Come alone. Any misstep, and the boy dies.

EVIE

That was it. No indication of who had written it or why. Just those three sentences, in large, neat script.

"Oh fuck," Marco muttered, leaping back.

He stared at the ground beneath me, the grass that was rotting, the dirt that was turning a scorched black.

"Idris will be okay. I'm going to go get him now," I said.

Marco kept backing away from me. I could hear the hysterical lilt to my voice, the way I didn't sound like myself anymore.

I folded the note neatly back in the envelope. And I started walking.

Etherdale was a blur of people and buildings in my periphery.

I'd heard of people who entered dissociative states and ended up in a completely new city, no idea who they were or how they got there. Or when women entered an altered state to murder their abusive partners.

I wondered if that was similar to where I was mentally. Because in the past hour of walking, I couldn't recall a single discernible moment since I'd opened the letter I still gripped in my clammy hand.

At random intervals, I'd remember the devastated look in Kylo's eyes after I'd stabbed him.

I suddenly focused on my surroundings and felt naked, exposed. Because for the first time since Kylo had entered my life, I wasn't being watched.

I had no protection.

I was utterly alone, following a map to a location on the outskirts of Etherdale.

As soon as I left the city and entered the woods beyond, I heard the call of a crow. I wondered if the tiny creature was taunting me, the new moon only two days away now—two days too late.

My best option was that the Whitfields had my brother. Maybe they wanted to lure me away so they could murder me in the woods. But why involve Idris?

Unless they were planning on killing him too.

And the worst-case scenario?

I wove through the trees. A wayward thorny branch scraped up my calf. I could hardly feel the bite of pain. Step after step, I kept moving forward, my only thought how to save Idris at any cost.

The worst-case scenario stepped out from a thick plot of trees, an old, abandoned cabin looming behind her.

A witch in a conservative black dress, a silver symbol for Lillian hanging around her neck.

They found us. Oh gods, they *found us.*

They found *me.*

"Keep walking, harlot," the woman spat.

Harlot?

My feet were planted in place, but the insult didn't make sense—didn't match the severity of what I'd done. I started to tremble, my eyes locked on her dress, memory after memory assailing my mind. In her dark form, I saw my mother. Her chronic disappointment, her everlasting ire.

"Whore for Lillian's bastards. You're barely even a witch, are you? Disgraceful heretic," she spat.

Through my tunneled vision, a tiny spark of clarity lit from her words.

She didn't know. She didn't know who I was or where I came from.

She had no idea what I'd done.

"I don't understand," I said. "What do you want from me? Why did you take my brother?"

She didn't answer. A gust of wind slammed into my back, forcing me forward as I stumbled and reached my hands out for balance. I managed not to face-plant, and the witch merely turned on her heel and walked toward the cabin.

She'd called me a whore for the turned. She somehow knew or suspected my ties to the clan, but she clearly had no idea I'd once been one of *them.* She didn't know what had happened in a small farming commune in the rolling hills of Isolde.

I swallowed. I flexed my hands. Nothing mattered now except Idris. Just like before. My eyelid twitched again. I rubbed my throat, a strange heat gathering there as adrenaline raced up and down my spine.

So the Whitfields had sold me out.

Because of what Kylo did to Jacob.

The ground beneath my feet darkened, and I moved quicker now, as if I could outrun the poison inside me—the poison battering at the walls of its cage.

Before the witch had made it to the decayed front porch, the door to the rundown structure flew off the hinges. Several born vampires filed out, dressed in archaic, gaudy attire. The born loved to flash wealth.

In the distance, I heard the calls of firebirds. Firebirds

waiting, presumably, to take these henchmen back home after they'd slaughtered another chaos witch for born command.

One of the born locked his gaze on me, his eyes darting lower as he flashed his fangs. I looked down, quickly taking a step back when I saw the thin trail of blood on my calf. I hadn't realized the thorn had broken skin.

"Why does her blood smell so fucking good," the born man asked.

"Because she's half-human," the witch sneered.

But my attention lay elsewhere. On the two born men dragging Idris out of the building.

I couldn't stop the relieved, strangled noise that left my lips to see him alive. Nor the feral one when I realized his lips had been split open, a nasty bruise on his cheekbone and around his left eye.

He wasn't even in shackles. Why bother? He was a human surrounded by vampires, helpless and without an ounce of defense. They threw him to the ground, and I shrieked.

"Don't—"

The witch shot an icy hex into my blood, and I choked on my words, teeth chattering as I struggled to breathe.

"You're a very difficult girl to find, you know that?" one of the born said, his cool blond hair spiky and eyes black as onyx.

"Strange how often our kind went missing each time they entered your little mortal neighborhood, too," a woman said, her voice nauseatingly sweet and high-pitched. She twirled an auburn strand of hair around her finger. "So here we are, getting creative."

"What do you say, Evie?" the man from before asked, his nostrils still flared as he stared at my open wound. He had deceptively handsome features, rich brunette hair and an angular jaw. "Do you think it makes sense for innocent little green witches who grow flowers and make healing potions to be surrounded by the turned and their treasonous violence? Or do you think that so much bloodshed around an accused solitary chaos witch might warrant further investigation?"

Idris feebly lifted his head, staring at me as his eyes moved rapidly. His face twisted like he was working though a puzzle. I swore I could tell the exact moment when it all clicked.

He gasped.

It was like lava now—the heat that was spreading from my throat, down my spine, wave after wave of volatile warmth. I was beginning to think it was something more than adrenaline.

A crow cawed. I stayed rooted in place, surrounded by monsters.

I had something inside me that could help. Something they didn't know about. But if it exploded, and I lost control, I'd destroy Idris, too.

"Let him go," I whispered. "Torture me, kill me. Just let him go. He's only a human."

"How can we be sure of that? When masked vermin walk these streets every day wearing human disguises?" the servant of Lillian snarled.

"You really think a turned man would allow vampires to harm him without fighting back?" I spat.

The bloodthirsty brunette man smirked. "Sounds like you know them well."

"Or I'm not stupid," I said before I could stop myself.

"Disrespectful, lying slut," the witch screeched, lifting me off the ground with invisible winds.

Intangible icy hands squeezed at my airways until black splotches erupted in my vision.

The heat was nearly unbearable now. But at the sight of Idris attempting to get up and a born man shoving him back down and kicking him in the ribs, I resisted all of my basest instincts. I made myself helpless and weak until the witch released me.

I gasped for air as I touched back on solid earth.

"Strangely useless for a chaos witch," the auburn-haired

woman muttered. She eyed some of her male comrades, lifting an inquisitive brow.

One of the men shrugged. "She was clearly worth something to 'em. Even if she was just somebody's favorite blood bag."

Ouch. My cheeks heated, and I avoided Idris's burning gaze.

"We're not going to kill you, little witch," the chiseled brunette man said. "That would be a waste."

He stared at my heaving chest now, accentuated by blooming flowers on a white fabric corset.

"Let's go. She might be blood marked by one of those rebellious children," the woman said.

"I'm not fucking scared of them," the man said, still distracted by my fresh blood. All of them were, their eyes continuously flashing to my calf.

The witch huffed. "They have the numbers here. We'll be back."

She sounded like she was trying to reason with toddlers. I looked at Idris, hope sprouting in my stomach. They were planning on taking me somewhere else, where the born had the upper hand.

"If you hurt him, I will do everything in my power to kill myself," I said quickly. "I won't eat. I won't talk. I will be more *strangely useless* than you can possibly imagine. Leave him here, and I will go with you, and I will not put up a fight. I have no loyalty to the turned, but I *do* have information."

All eyes focused on me as the traitorous words left my lips. I would've said just about anything to get them to leave Idris alone.

What I'd told them didn't feel like truth on my tongue, but I didn't care. The truth didn't matter. Only protecting Idris mattered now.

The past and the present began to converge. The powerful heat seared my throat strongly enough that I worried my skin might blister.

The brunette inhaled deeply, and all eyes moved to him. He was clearly the highest command.

Lillian's devotee snarled. "She's cunning. A lying, scheming, wh—"

"Silence, witch!" the man bellowed. "Leave the human behind." He shrugged. "If you're lying about being cooperative, we will stop at nothing to track him down and kill him. Understood?"

I nodded, cursing the hot tears that pricked my eyes. "Fine."

My eyelid twitched, and a sudden violent stab of pain erupted in the side of my head, like an icepick. I winced.

The man's eyes narrowed.

"Headache," I mumbled.

The woman rolled her eyes. Bodies began to move, and someone lifted hexed chains—clearly meant for me to block up my magick.

As if it needed to be blocked any more than it already was.

They left Idris behind. I sighed in relief.

But Idris stared at me in shocked disbelief for only two beats before he rose to his feet. Rage eclipsed his thoughtful features, a quiet determination bleeding from his aura.

"Don't," I choked out.

The vampire approaching with cuffs halted, glancing behind him. Idris rushed forward. Weaponless.

"Stop!" Idris yelled, panic in his soft brown eyes. He raised a fist.

The call of a firebird split through the air, louder this time.

The nearest vampire almost looked bored. He shoved Idris without even a grunt of effort.

Idris stumbled and fell backward to the earth.

The side of his head hit the jagged edge of a rock. The sound it made was unnatural, nauseating.

I froze. Blood pooled underneath Idris's head. His face paralyzed with shock as his body went limp.

I screamed.

The scream tore through the lump in my throat. The fire scorched and melted the block until it was nothing but ash on my tongue. The poison spilled from its cage as my eyes rolled back and the sky bled shadow and wrath.

65

EVIE

Dad wasn't drinking today, which meant things were serious. The entire coven was dressed for Lillian's honor, preparing for a weekend of rituals and festivities. Some of Lillian's favorites were gathered in our home, because Mama was now the High Priestess.

Mama said Lillian would reveal to me who my divine match was under the light of the dark moon tomorrow evening. She'd whisper the name of my future husband, who I would spend a blissful forever with, our union blessed by the Dark Mother.

Secretly, I hoped Lillian waited another year. I was supposed to look at vampires and feel their beauty, their holiness. But in truth, all I really felt was fear.

And this other, secret feeling. A spark of fire I held close to my heart, one that had been stoked and nurtured by the whispers that lived down hallways and gathered in dark corners.

"So pretty and pale, like a porcelain doll," a voice whispered in my ear. "Your blood smells unique. Delicious. Perfect."

I jumped out of my skin, and the vampire woman at my back laughed. "Don't be frightened, lamb of Helia."

"And Selena," a different vampire added, a tall man with a gentle face, mischievous smile, and spiky brown hair.

"Oh!" the woman exclaimed. "What a fascinating gift she is. I would've thought being half-witch would ruin the beautiful notes of innocence and purity."

"Not with her," the man purred, patting my head.

Don't move. I wanted to run. I wanted to go out back where the grass was tall and hide until all the vampires had gone home.

Out of the corner of my eye, I saw my mother, her hawk-eyes sharpened.

I smiled up at the man. At least if he was paying attention to me, he was leaving Idris alone. I didn't like him talking to Idris.

I hated the way he laughed when Idris cried.

THE SUN WENT DOWN SO LATE during the summer. All the children had been put to bed except for me. The coven gathered in my home, celebrating and dancing and making scary faces when the spirit of Lillian overcame them.

Idris had been crying all night. But I wasn't allowed to comfort him, or even see him. I had this nagging, sinking feeling in my stomach that wouldn't go away. Like something bad was going to happen—or had happened—but I didn't know what it was.

The coven's faces grew scarier the more they danced, the more the vampires whispered in their ears.

"Should she be here?" one of the elder witches asked, looking at me with a cocked head.

The vampire who loved to tease Idris, Vernon, nodded. "She's old enough. She'll be made a wife soon."

I heard a distant wail, and I stared up at the ceiling.

"Are you looking forward to meeting your husband, Evie?" Vernon asked me.

I nodded. My skin felt hot and scratchy, fear lodged in my throat. My gaze snapped back down to my arm, which now seared with heat as if I'd been burned.

"Apologies, my lord. Between the two of us, this one's always been terribly bizarre," the elder witch muttered. "But she's pretty enough to make up for it."

"Not all there?" Vernon sneered, poking my forehead.

I recoiled from his burning touch before I could stop myself. "I'm the top student in our lessons, actually."

The woman glared with her beady eyes. "Watch your tongue, missy. Your mother always warned us about your poor manners."

Shame rooted in my stomach. "I'm sorry."

Vernon chuckled softly. "He'll like that she's fiery."

I swallowed. I excused myself, escaping to the back of the house where I fought to catch my breath. In the corner of my eye, I saw smoke, and I heard Idris wail again.

"What happened?" I asked the darkness.

The smoke whispered back. *Go to the kitchen. Don't let them hear you approach.*

I crept slowly through the small foyer by the back doors. There was a hallway that led to the kitchen, and I kept my footsteps light as I moved through.

My parents were standing close together, at the outskirts of the gathering as they plated food. They didn't hear or see me approach behind them. I stood there, as my mother opened her mouth.

"It's a disaster. He's no longer pure."

I stopped breathing.

"Vernon?" Dad asked, shaking his head with a sigh.

"Who else?" Mama muttered. "We need to keep Evelynn away from him, tactfully. We can't do anything now except protect *her* blood's purity."

As if it was an inconvenience.

Not a tragedy. Not an act of violence. Not the violation of a child.

Their son. *My* brother.

Hands so small, always reaching.

No longer pure. No longer pure. No longer pure.

The lights in our home went out all at once.

"The hells?" Dad whispered.

No one was coming to save us. No valiant knights from the stories I'd been stealing from village bookstores. No faeries from another world.

No one knew it, but I'd been learning about the world outside of our coven. In stolen bits and pieces, at every opportunity. I stole pamphlets. I spoke to people at the markets when Mama wasn't watching. I asked them what was normal, what was good. I asked them what the gods meant to them. I learned about firebirds and faraway lands.

I read stories about people defeating monsters.

Monsters who hurt children were the most scorned of all.

I backed away. I slunk through the house, covered by the friendly smoke. No one stopped me when I reached the stairs. They were all confused about the lights, their attention on the opposite side of the house where my mother laughed and said Lillian had blessed our home with darkness.

Except one vampire, cloaked in bright crimson, his eyes locked on me.

Vernon. He smirked, letting go of a human woman he'd pulled close. He wiped his blood-stained lips.

And that small spark of fire became something else. A feeling I'd never truly been allowed to feel, one I was punished for with cruel words and pain until I was meek and small again.

Rage.

I climbed the steps. I didn't stop until I'd reached Idris's room. The door had been locked, so the smoke reached under and picked the lock from within.

I entered the room. Idris was curled up in the fetal position on the floor, sobbing so hard his eyes and fair skin were cherry red.

He stopped rocking, stopped pulling at his hair. He looked up at me.

I rushed to him. He sat up, and I wrapped him in a hug.

"You're bleeding nighttime, Evie," he said through sobs.

I pulled back, and my eyes immediately went to his arm. In the same place where my own arm had burned, I saw the unmistakable mark of fangs and teeth.

I helped Idris to his feet. My voice shook with every word I spoke.

"Hide under the bed and don't come out until I come back for you," I whispered.

His wide, frightened brown eyes stared up at me with a buried strength.

He believed in me. I was his guardian angel, the only source of light in a world of darkness.

But it was the darkness that I stepped into when I turned my back on him and descended the stairs.

The dim lights were on again. Vernon's fangs were buried in the human woman.

"Oh fuck, I think she's dead," he said with a laugh.

"She was a whore, anyway," one of our male witch elders said.

A man in the back of the room noticed me, and a shout broke from his lips. All eyes went to me.

"Evelynn Lockwood," my mother bellowed, aghast when she caught sight of me and my bleeding, blooming darkness.

"Shadows," someone whispered in a shocked horror.

"Parents are supposed to protect their children," I said, my voice too small.

I was always too small—too puny and weak, just how they wanted me. Tiny enough to be trampled over and fed to fanged monsters.

I looked at my human father, and he didn't look back. He stared at the floor instead.

Someone chanted, and a ball of crackling, paralytic magick flew at my head.

With a huff I deflected it, sending the beam crashing through a window and shattering the glass.

It had been my mother's magick, of course.

Vernon let the human woman fall to the floor. He regarded me with humor, like I was a party trick.

"You hurt my brother!" I screamed.

"*Evelynn Lockwood you shut your fucking mouth!*" my mother yelled back.

Vernon dabbed at his mouth with a handkerchief. "He wanted it, little girl. Lillian has blessed our union."

The last image I saw was Vernon smiling. My dad studying the floor. And my mother looking at me like she wished I was dead so that I never disappointed her or spoke or breathed ever again.

I screamed, and I let my friends feast. Smoke shot from my palms like extra limbs, tearing my coven apart at the seams. Two elders choked on black goo, falling in a puddle of rot on the floor. A shadow sharpened into a weapon, slicing through three more witches. They ate up the walls in black flames, destroying my mother's precious ugly wallpaper.

I walked closer to the fray. I deflected hexes. I continued to scream, half inside my body and half somewhere else, unable to fully comprehend what I was doing.

Only that it felt fucking *good.*

Like all this rage had been gathering, the longer I'd suppressed it, and now it was releasing in a flood until my muscles were relaxed and I could finally breathe again.

I watched as shadows consumed Vernon from within, reducing him to a hollow husk.

Witches tried to escape, but I destroyed them too, barricading everyone inside the home as I ensured not a single person survived.

Not even my parents, frozen and rooted to the floor by dark phantom limbs.

"You are not our family," I said.

It was hard to see anything anymore through the haze of thick smoke.

The smell of char and death assailed my nostrils, but I couldn't stop. I couldn't stop until everyone who'd allowed a vampire to assault my brother was wiped from the earth.

My mother's eyes were gray like mine. But they were empty. Soulless. Dad's eyes were brown like Idris's, empty in a different way—a cowardly way.

"Idris and I are family. You are *nothing*," I whispered.

A sob escaped my lips as I let the shadows crawl up their bodies as my parents writhed and yelled. My mother cursed my existence.

"You're a poison! You're a plague on this world!"

Those were Mama's last words before her body crumpled on itself and a shadow pierced through her heart.

The words horrified me, yet I still couldn't stop, my mouth open and my feet lifting off the floor. My arms spread wide. Heat curved up and down my spine like a hissing snake. Power was a violent storm, one I could no longer see through.

I was untethered, unwound, disconnected from my body and soul.

That was until, I heard a voice.

"Evie!"

My feet slammed back down to the earth. My eyes rolled back into place. My vision returned. The scorched house was utterly still, the only sound and movement coming from falling bits of ceiling and furniture.

Through the darkness, I saw Idris.

He gripped the railing. He was terrified, but he didn't run from me.

He ran toward me, narrowly avoiding being crushed by debris.

I sucked in breath after breath. I caught him in my arms. Idris coughed and wheezed. I lifted him into my arms, and I ran.

I prayed to every god listening that he hadn't seen anything through the haze of smoke and darkness.

When he told me the next day that he couldn't remember what happened, a weight had lifted from my shoulders.

I decided that I would choose to forget that night too.

We would go to Etherdale, the city of mortals. We would find someone there who would help us—someone who might see two children dressed in black, a seven-year-old boy with fang marks on his small arm, and take pity.

Idris and I would start over, and we would never look back.

And under no circumstances would I use that wrathful violence ever again. I wasn't a plague. I wasn't a poison.

I'm good. I'm good. I'm good, I repeated, over and over, until it felt truer than my mother's last words. I would say them in the mirror, when I put on the pretty pink dresses I'd always secretly wanted to wear. I would say them when I was picking flowers or helping Mena in the kitchen.

Please, just see that I'm good!

I'd accidentally said my compulsive mantra aloud one time, and Mena had stopped peeling potatoes to crouch down in front of me. She'd pulled my hands into hers.

"You're better than good," Mena said, her red lips in a gentle smile as her amber eyes sparkled. "You're my favorite girl in the world."

Idris bounced into the room, carrying a toy knight. "Mine too."

66

KYLO

She fucking poisoned me.

I opened my eyes. Eventually, feeling returned to my extremities. I started to wiggle my fingers, to flex my muscles. Bit by bit, my body woke back up.

The sun was still out, which meant that clearly not much time had passed. Whatever ingredient Evie had misread had worked to my advantage.

I replayed her final words to me over and over again as I regained my ability to stand.

She knew about Jacob. I'd broken her trust, and now she was done with me. She was going to try to break our bond even if the risky procedure hurt her.

Or, gods forbid, it *killed* her.

I'd never hated myself more. This was all my fault. I should've come clean. I should've told her how Jacob had watched a vampire attack her and had done nothing to help.

Most of all, I should've owned what I'd done like a fucking man instead of protecting her with lies of omission.

In the end, I'd merely been protecting myself.

And now Evie was gone. I could sense her rapid, frightened

heart at the outskirts of Etherdale. No doubt finding someone with a firebird to take her to a blood witch in a different city. She hoped she could break our bond before I could catch up to her.

It wasn't rage I felt as I rushed to the nearest firebird stable. No, it was *grief.*

The kind of grief I'd been avoiding feeling ever since I saw Princeton's desecrated corpse. It was as if the color had drained from my world, the warmth from my cold immortal heart—the heart that Evie had resurrected.

With her love, her softness, her resilience, her fire.

I loved everything about that girl. Even the parts she hated most. The parts I'd never seen before but had tasted in her blood—tales of violence and a deep, buried wrath.

She had become my entire world. I couldn't build this future I'd been working toward for decades without her by my side, without her laughter in my ear and her hand in mine.

And gods, I couldn't breathe right without Evie's trust.

The thought of her believing I was no better than her parents, just a violent, soulless manipulator who sought to use her for my own gain—it destroyed me.

Even more ruinous were the crippling visions of Aisling and Princeton that assailed my mind's eye, permanent reminders of what happened to those I loved when I couldn't protect them.

My lungs ached, struggling to reach satisfaction. I'd never felt more torn up and exposed, like a giant gaping wound of a man.

I bribed a stable worker and climbed onto the nearest firebird, a testy beast who was slow to warm up to my energy.

Probably because I'd never been more out of my damn mind.

The wind rushed by as she leaped into the air, wings spread wide. I focused on the erratic pumping of Evie's heart, the way it had begun to speed up, beating far harder than normal.

I closed my eyes, imagining the worst, as always.

My angel needed me.

And I needed her more.

It was the shortest flight of my life when we reached the end of the blood bond's invisible leash. I peered down through the trees as we approached.

"Down," I commanded.

I made out multiple figures. My lip curled.

We skidded to a stop behind an old cabin and thicket of trees.

An ear-splitting scream sent me flying off the beast's back. I ran, dropping my glamour as I used my vampiric speed.

No one saw me approach, because they were all looking at *her*.

The screaming blonde girl in a darling floral dress, lifted up midair as her eyes turned onyx. Her hair lifted like a halo, fit for an angel of death.

I had three seconds to understand what the fuck was happening before my witch girlfriend killed me.

One second to home in on the ripe scent of blood—coming from Idris's motionless body and the pool of crimson under his skull. One second to cover him. One second to use every last drop of my power to erect a shield of shadow.

No time to think about how I hadn't fed in days, muting my already poisoned strength.

Not when, through the veil of my darkness, I watched Evie finally explode.

Shadows shot from her open palms, her mouth, her throat, her chest. The afternoon sky turned so dark that it could be mistaken for night.

I couldn't tell who was screaming anymore—Evie, her victims, or the *shadows*.

All this time, my angel had been a shadow wielder.

Because of course she was.

She annihilated each born and the witch one by one, as if

playing with her food. Shadow limbs impaled, squeezed, rotted, and burned flesh.

It took considerable effort to peel my eyes off such an unexpected, captivating sight. But the sound of Idris's faint, labored breathing pulled my focus back to him.

I let out a string of curses, my shadow shield wobbling and warping against wave after wave of Evie's suppressed, anguished, backed up power.

I tore off my shirt, applying pressure to Idris's wound. The shirt was immediately drenched through.

"No," I whispered. "You can't, Idris. Don't even think about it. You hold on for me. Hold on for *her*."

Idris's eyes were glassy. But he was still conscious. He was in shock and losing far, far too much blood.

Trees were falling to the earth. Smoke was rising all around us, as if Evie was killing an entire plot of forest.

Everyone was already long dead. But Evie couldn't stop—just as Princeton had warned.

She's bottled too much in. Her magick is going to eat her alive, he'd said, the day of the cyclone.

I watched in utter horror as Evie hemorrhaged power and shadow, all that she'd been denying and suppressing.

I'd never seen such unfathomable beauty. I'd never seen such utter devastation.

"Evie, you have to come back down now!" I yelled over the rushing wind, the impossible gusts that had the entire world trembling and the sky heaving.

She was a dark goddess, a being that didn't belong in this realm.

"Please, baby. If you don't stop, you're going to kill yourself! *You're going to hurt Idris!*"

Her hair fell back down to her shoulders. She blinked at the sound of her brother's name, and for the briefest second, her eyes were back to their usual stormy gray.

But her heart was pumping too hard, her body wilting like a flower underneath the enormity of her power. Idris's face went slack. I was caught between begging Idris to stay, pressing my blood-soaked shirt against his cracked-open head, and pleading with Evie as she hung suspended in the air, wrestling with the darkness of this world and all the rest.

Idris's eyes closed. My shield began to rupture, a fissure rippling through the wall of shadow.

A rare tear slid down my cheek. I looked to the angel of death.

"Come back to me, baby. Hold on, Idris. Hold—"

ALSO BY MAGGIE SUNSERI

EVERLASTING POSSESSION DUET

Marked by Masks and Secrets

Claimed by Fangs and Darkness

ETERNAL OBSESSION DUET

Stalked by Seduction and Shadows

Taken by Touch and Torment

THE LOST WITCHES OF ARADIA

The Discovered

The Coveted

The Illuminated

The Hunted

The Scorned

The Claimed

The Redeemed

ABOUT MAGGIE SUNSERI

Maggie Sunseri is the author of fantasy romance books by day and a witch, tarot card reader, and succubus by night. She has a bachelor's degree in Anthropology/Sociology. When she's not traveling the world, you'll find her curled up with a good book and a hot cup of tea, pretending it's autumn no matter the season.

She also writes a Substack about spirituality and witchcraft, critical theory, sexuality, holistic health, community building, and addiction and trauma recovery.

Connect with Maggie:
maggiesunseri.com